DEATH IN SHETLAND WATERS

By Marsali Taylor

Death in Shetland Waters

DEATH IN SHETLAND WATERS

Marsali Taylor

Allison & Busby Limited
12 Fitzroy Mews
London W1T 6DW
allisonandbusby.com

First published in Great Britain by Allison & Busby in 2017.

A CIP catalogue record for this book is available from
the British Library.

First Edition

ISBN 978-0-7490-2202-0

Typeset in 11/16 pt Adobe Garamond Pro by
Allison & Busby Ltd.

The paper used for this Allison & Busby publication
has been produced from trees that have been legally sourced
from well-managed and credibly certified forests.

Printed and bound by
CPI Group (UK) Ltd, Croydon, CR0 4YY

To Captain Sture and all the real crew of the sail-training ship Sørlandet, and to our beautiful ship: long may she grace the seas, and give such pleasure

THE CREW OF SØRLANDET

Captain Gunnar

Henrik	Mike	Johanna
Chief Steward	First Officer	Chief Engineer

Agnetha, First Mate	Nils, Second Mate	Cass, Third Mate
Red watch	White watch	Blue watch

Each watch has a watch leader and two able seamen (ABs)
For Cass's watch, these are: Erik, Watch Leader
Mona and Petter, ABs

Each watch has between fifteen and twenty-five trainees. In Cass's watch, they are: Aage, Anna, Ben, Dimitris, Ellen, Gabriel, Ismail, Jan-Ole, Johan, Ludwig, Maria, Naseem, Nine, Nora, Olav, Samir and Sindre.

Other officers:
Sadie, Medical Officer
Rolf, Bosun
Jenn, Liaison Officer
Lars, 2nd Engineer
James, Steward
Elmer, Cook
Laila and Ruth, Galley Girls

This is far too many suspects for even the most lively crime novel, so just to make things simpler for us all, I can tell you now that none of the trainees committed any murders on board.

LANDFALL, KRISTIANSAND

Monday 6th April

I stood on the dock beside the ochre tollbooth, Cat's basket in one hand, my kitbag in the other, and admired the world's oldest full-rigged ship. The morning sun shone on *Sørlandet*'s swan-white sides, and glinted off the double gold scroll at her prow; her three masts rose tall above the grey slate roofs and squared turrets of the *fin-de-siècle* tenements. The spider's web ratlines and delicate tracery of rigging were clear against the blue sky.

I still hardly believed my luck. There were fewer than a hundred and fifty of these large traditional sailing ships left in the world, and posts aboard were scrambled for, yet here I was, third mate of *Sørlandet* of Kristiansand, joining my ship. I lifted the 'Crew only' sign on the gangplank and went aboard.

It was a strange feeling to be back. Half of me was going, *Oh, wow, home!* as I looked around the scrubbed decks. *Sørlandet* had been my ship. I'd joined her when I was seventeen as a trainee for the summer, with money saved from winter waitressing, and

9

returned for two summers more, until I was competent enough to volunteer as an able seaman. My feet knew every inch of those ladders and ropes up in the air; my hands could feel the shape of her wheel. Until I'd got my own *Khalida*, she was the nearest thing to permanency in my roving life.

The other half of me was frozen with terror. After three years of living alone on *Khalida*, I was about to be cheek by jowl with twenty-plus unknown people . . .

Then a tall woman stepped out from behind the white engine house. She was dressed in paint-stained overalls, with a smear of white on her tanned cheek. Her fair hair clustered round her head in untidy curls, like a Renaissance angel; the sea's colour was reflected in her eyes. She held out her hand, then remembered the paint, withdrew it, and smiled instead. 'Hey, you must be Cass. I'm Agnetha, first mate. Welcome back aboard.' She waved her paint-stained hands. 'Here, I'll show you your cabin, so you can make yourself at home.' She called over her shoulder. 'Erik!' Her gaze dropped to my hands. 'Oh, you're the one bringing a cat.'

I nodded. 'Can I let him out?'

'For sure.'

I opened the basket and Cat stretched up, looked round, then jumped out. He was a beauty, my Cat, getting on for nine months old. He had a thick, smoke-grey coat faintly striped with silver, immaculately white paws and a great plume of a tail. He was used to making himself at home on strange ships. He paused to sniff Agnetha's outstretched hand, then headed off to explore, sniffing round the deck, eyeing up the aft corridor with wary interest and prodding a paw into the scuppers.

'He's a beauty,' Agnetha said. 'What's his name?'

'Just Cat.'

A lanky, brown-haired Norwegian came out from behind

the engine house, paint pot in hand. '*Hei*, Cass. Erik, your watch leader. You're looking for a berth for your boat, yes?'

I nodded.

'You sailed over?' Agnetha asked. 'From Britain?'

'Technically. Shetland.'

'Ah, Shetland!' They nodded to each other. 'You're practically Norwegian, then,' Agnetha added.

'Our house is two miles round the corner, at Eidbukta,' Erik said, 'and we have a pontoon in front of it. You're welcome to berth her there.'

My heart filled with relief. 'This is amazing. I really appreciate it. I'll pay you rent, of course.'

'Oh, we can work that out. If you like, I can give you a hand to take her round once we're off duty.'

Agnetha picked up a rag and wiped her hands down. 'Right. I'll show you your cabin, and you can get settled, then later, Erik and I can help you move your boat before you need to take out a mortgage for the marina fees.'

Just like that, I was in. Agnetha and I finished painting the midship deckhouse together while Cat explored round the deck, then settled himself on the mahogany berth in my cabin for his mid-morning snooze. We discovered we'd been on several of the same ships, and knew the same people. She and Erik helped me move my *Khalida* round to his house that evening, and we shared a huge pot of spicy stew with his wife, Micaela, and their two children, before Erik ran Agnetha, Cat and I back to the ship.

I went out with the crowd the next night, prepared to nurse an extortionately priced pint in a corner, and found Johanna, the chief engineer, making me the centre of attention: 'Was it really you who skippered the longship for that film with Favelle? Tell us about it!'

Jonas, Agnetha's watch leader, had worked at Roskilde, so he'd handled Viking replicas too. We compared experiences, splashed out on another pint each and then rose to head back to the ship. Rolf, the bosun, flung an arm around Agnetha's shoulders as we came out into the cool air. 'Let's start with an easy one.'

'You need to learn Rolf's songs,' Agnetha said, laughing, and launched straight in, in the middle of the street. *'What shall we do with a drunken sailor . . .'*

In those first days, Agnetha, Johanna and I became mates. We were the highest-ranking women aboard, and we recognised in each other a burning passion for the sea. Johanna was a rare woman in the mechanics' world, and Agnetha was determined to be the first female captain of a tall ship. We shared cooking until the galley girls came aboard, went shopping for the official navy cargo breeks, and sat together on the second platform of the mast, legs dangling, swapping confidences as we looked out over Kristiansand. I tried to explain my tug between my lover, Gavin, and the sea, particularly as our beautiful ship was about to become an academy. From the end of August, we'd be heading for America to take on a shipment of older teenagers who would combine studying for their exams with life aboard. The ship's crew was rejoicing at this financial security – tall ships gobbled money – but I'd be on the other side of the world for two years, and my heart went cold at the thought. Gavin and I had just found each other. We'd arranged to meet in two weeks, in the fjords, then again in Belfast at the end of June. I dreaded that our tentative love would stretch to breaking point across the Atlantic.

'If it's right, you'll manage,' Agnetha said. 'What's for you won't pass you by, my granny would have said.' Her fair skin flushed. She looked away from me, out into the darkening sky. 'I have someone, but it's all complicated. Don't let's worry about it! Now, what was that new song of Rolf's . . . ?'

ONE BELL

Casting off: Kristiansand

CHAPTER ONE

Thursday 25th June

At this hour, Kristiansand's old fish market was quiet, with the water reflecting the curved bridge leading across to the cafe and mirroring the wooden houses and dark red fish market. The ochre fishwife statue gleamed in the sun; the windows around her were closed, with no lights showing behind. The only sound was a sparrow cheeping as it checked out crumbs left by yesterday's tourists. Cat's plumed tail twitched gently; he began to creep forward, but his striped grey was too light against the tarred wood, and the sparrow grabbed its crumb and flew off before he was in pouncing range.

I was sitting on the middle row of decking steps to the water, the wood warm under me, idly watching an Aquador motorboat nosing its way into the dock. It was just after eight, and there was a whole-crew muster at nine, to brace us for our next wave of trainees swarming aboard in a whirl of kitbags and excited chatter. Right now the *Sørlandet* was ringing with the sound of iron hitting copper as Rolf hammered new beading on the upper serving hatch in the main cabin area, and stuffy with the smell of paint as Agnetha followed him with the best cream emulsion. It had made me feel slightly sick, so I'd grabbed Cat's lead, clipped it onto his harness and headed out into the peace of the Fiskbrabaren basin.

The motorboat paused by the steps to let off a dark, thick-set man, then purred away to the right, towards the concert hall. I called Cat away from his contemplation of the sparrows and followed it, through the dark passageway and out into the sunshine again, where curves of light rippled from the water onto the curved wooden overhang of the concert hall.

It was a beautiful morning, the herald of a perfect summer's day. Feather-white cumulus drifted in the summer-blue sky. Kristiansand's west bay lay in a curve of low hills, dark green with trees, the red roof of one of the larger hotels shining out against them and the light catching the long white span of bridge that crossed the fjord. Below it, the sea danced blue in the soft northerly wind. I paused for a moment to look out towards the open water. We'd have a good passage out into the North Sea, and, if the forecast was accurate, going up the coast first should let us get the sails up.

I turned away without looking and bumped straight into the man who'd come from the motorboat, my face ramming into his tobacco-smelling dark cloth jacket. There was one of those moments where we both moved the wrong way, and I found myself blocking his path. Suddenly I was conscious of the chill under this dark passageway, and how there was nobody else in sight. Cat felt like a target on his lead; I scooped him up, away from the dark workman's boots.

'*Unnskyld*,' I apologised, and got a grunt in return as he pushed past me. I stared after him, taken aback by the discourtesy. Not

Norwegian; Eastern bloc, I'd have said, Russian, maybe, with those flared nostrils and bull head. He had the shoulders of a man you wouldn't want to tackle on a dark night, and a convict haircut. There was a tattoo on his hand. *An ugly customer*, I thought, and wondered what he was doing lurking around the pristine tourist tables of the Fiskbrabaren.

He'd taken the brightness from the day. Cat miaowed indignantly and wriggled in my arms. I set him down and we went the long way back to the ship, with Cat scampering on the grass and leaping over the small herd of Shetland pony statues by the marina. Once he'd had a good run I put his lead back on and we walked sedately to the dock, where I unbuckled his harness. He trotted ahead of me up the gangplank, tail held high. I needn't have worried about how he'd take to life on a tall ship; he'd made himself at home as if he'd been born aboard. When it was cold and wet outside, he stayed in my cabin, or charged about the long below-decks tunnels running the length of the ship. On bonny days, he would strut across the main deck, pausing to let himself be admired by trainees. Now, since we were in port, he went straight up the stairs to the aft deck, where he could sit on a bench in the sun and survey everything that was going on below him. This, his pose said, was his ship, which made him the highest-ranking cat in the dock.

I wasn't finding it so easy. Of course it was amazing to be back aboard, to be part of a tall ship again. I enjoyed the company of my fellow sailors, the life that was absorbed in the needs of the ship. My heart soared at being at sea again. It was just that I hadn't reckoned on the difference between being an able-seaman volunteer and being third mate (navigation). My image in my cabin mirror filled me with pride and disbelief: this tidy ship's officer in the navy shirt with two gold chevrons on the shoulder, her dark curly hair tucked into a French plait. Only my eyes, blue in my tanned face, and the scar that bisected my right cheek, were my own. The rest belonged to the persona I had taken on: Cass Lynch, officer of the *Sørlandet*. Cass Lynch, officer, didn't climb masts, stand lookout or haul on ropes; she stayed aloof on the aft deck and told the helmsman what course to steer. She ate at the captain's table, cut off from the sounds of laughter that echoed from the other ranks' mess at the end of the corridor . . .

'Cass!' A voice broke into my reverie. I stifled a sigh and turned to face Nils, the second mate, my immediate superior and the only person on board I had difficulty liking.

Nils Karlsson was Swedish, and a stickler. He was in his mid thirties and had trained at the Royal Swedish Naval College. His light hair was still Navy-short, and he had toffee-brown eyes, a nose which jutted downwards like a heron's beak and a downturned mouth. I wasn't sure whether the disapproval was personal, or just that he worked on the principle of the office boy kicking the cat. Mercifully he was in charge of the white watch, so I only saw him at handover times, when he'd tell me our new course with unnecessary emphasis and point out the bits of my navigation that he'd reworked in the log. Naturally the ship's projected course had to be changed to allow for the difference between where you'd hoped to be and where you'd actually got to, but he'd change the compass heading by one degree, when you'd be lucky if the most competent trainee could steer within three degrees either way . . . I pre-gritted my teeth and turned to face him. '*Hei*, Nils.'

'The gangplank has been left unguarded,' he said. 'It's your watch, no?'

Well, no, actually, we were all just mucking in to get the ship ready, and official watches wouldn't start until after we set sail, but it wasn't worth arguing with Nils about. 'Yes,' I agreed.

Besides, we were all laid-back about the gangplank when in our home port. Erik had been on guard when I left, but I wasn't going to drop him in it.

'Was it guarded when you left the ship?'

'Yes,' I said. 'I'll have a word with the member of my team who was on guard.'

We glared at each other for five seconds. He had that schoolteacher's trick of staring at a spot just past my left ear, but I knew he was getting the full impact of my unspoken, *And I'm not going to tell you who.*

I unhooked the 'Crew only' chain on the gangplank and came on board. Nils had just stalked off when Erik hurried up, taking long strides over the wooden deck. He was dressed for duty in cargo breeks and a navy jumper. The breeze had tousled his light brown hair. 'Hey, Cass. Sorry to get you into trouble with our Nils. I got called away.' He grinned round at the deserted dock. 'If we find fifty refugee stowaways in the sail locker, you can blame me.' His tone was slightly rough, as if something was worrying him, and his chest rose and fell quickly.

I gave a dismissive wave. 'Why on earth would anyone who'd made it to Norway want to go to Britain?'

He laughed at that, but there was a forced note in his voice which made me uneasy. I'd need to keep an eye on him, maybe have a chat later if he still seemed ill at ease. In some ways I felt I knew him quite well, because of mooring *Khalida* at his pontoon, but that physical closeness meant that I tried to keep more of a distance between us, so that he and Micaela didn't feel I was living in their pockets. I hoped all was well at home.

I put my peg back in the hole marked with my name – the ship's system to see at a glance who was aboard – then headed to my cabin.

The officers lived along the corridor that led backwards through the last third of the ship, under the aft deck. It was like a country house, with a shining wooden floor, white v-lining and framed black-and-white photographs of *Sørlandet*. The captain's rooms and the chief engineer's were first – the two people you might need to rouse in an emergency – then the sick bay. My cabin was next, then the chief officer's, then Agnetha's with her door closed. I paused outside it, wondering if I should knock and check she hadn't slept in, but a closed door generally meant 'no entry unless in an emergency'. As I paused beside it, I heard the murmur of voices. *Complicated*, she'd said. I backtracked into my own cabin, dropped Cat's harness on the bed, checked my hair was tidy and my shoulder seams straight, and headed out to the main deck.

Even at its most relaxed, our ship's world was hierarchical, with the captain at the head of the pyramid. Below him were Johanna, for the engines, Henrik, the chief steward, and Mike, the cheerful and energetic chief officer. Below Mike were the three sailing teams, one for each of the ship's four-hour watches. They were headed by the first, second and third mates – Agnetha, Nils and I – each commanding a watch leader and two able seamen. Roughly level with the first mate were Sadie, the medical officer, Jenn, the liaison officer, who organised the trainees, and Rolf, the bosun, the singer, a lively, uncomplicated Trondheimer that I'd taken to straight away.

For this voyage I was mate in charge of the blue watch, on duty from eight to twelve. Mona and Petter, my two ABs, were already lined up for the muster. I'd just joined them when the captain came out around the midships deckhouse with one of the local police officers, Sergeant Hansen. I knew him because he was a cat-lover, and very helpful about what forms and injections Cat

20

needed to prevent him from being impounded as we travelled from place to place.

Captain Gunnar had one of those faces that was designed for a captain's table on a thirties luxury liner, with alert eyes under bushy eyebrows, a straight nose and a neatly trimmed white moustache and beard. He'd been the officer of my watch on my first time aboard, fitting in qualifications and voyages between teaching, and he'd risen in rank each time I was back. The beard had appeared at first officer stage, the silver hair at chief officer. He was retiring this year – Henrik was already planning his farewell party – and I couldn't imagine the ship without him. His demeanour was always grave, but today there was an extra frown between his brows, as if there was something to worry about. Sergeant Hansen was equally serious, the bearer of a storm warning.

Five to nine. Erik slid out from the aft corridor and into his place beside me, and Agnetha followed him, her fair skin white in the morning sunshine. Rolf came after them, with Nils on his heels and Mike following. Captain Gunnar gave Mike a quick glance from under his brows, and his mouth tightened. Punctuality, in his view, was next to godliness. Mike flushed, and slipped into his place beside the captain. Full house.

Captain Gunnar gave a last look around, then cleared his throat. 'Good morning, everyone. Sergeant Hansen has asked us to be especially vigilant today as the ship prepares to leave for Belfast.' He made a courteous gesture, indicating that Sergeant Hansen should explain.

The officer reddened, and stepped forward. 'We've had word through contacts that a person known to the police is in Kristiansand, believed to be making his way to the UK. We'd ask you to take the utmost care that he doesn't come aboard *Sørlandet*. I know how busy you are, dealing with trainees today, but we'd suggest extra precautions guarding the gangplank, allowing nobody unauthorised aboard, and checking people on and off the ship.' I felt Nils glance at me. Sergeant Hansen spread his hands. 'It's all very vague, I know. He's far more likely to try the obvious routes, but we didn't wish to overlook anything. Thank you.'

He made a stiff little bow, and left, leaving us all looking at each other apprehensively. *Known to the police* . . . That shadow I'd felt down in the Fiskbrabaren clouded my mind again. Then Captain Gunnar began to talk about the business of the day, and the arrangements for squeezing in our seventy trainees, the full complement. Many of them belonged to a large group of teenagers funded through the social work department. 'They'll have two group leaders with them, and be spread over three watches. You won't be able to stop them smoking, but make sure they only do it on the benches on each side of the engine house.' We all nodded; we knew the dangers of fire aboard. 'You are also to keep a vigilant eye out for drugs, though all these young people should be "clean".'

He assigned gangplank duty to the watch leaders, then dismissed us to our tasks. I'd worked up the navigation for leaving Kristiansand the night before, so I busied myself securing the smokers' benches with rope. I'd just done the port side when Johanna came up her ladder, bringing a warm blast of diesel-scented air with her. Her face was blanched. She stumbled to the bench and dropped onto it, moaning in pain, arms wrapped around her stomach. I leapt to her. 'Sadie,' she managed through chattering teeth.

I ran for the ship's medical officer. One look at Johanna had Sadie on the phone, talking appendix, and then we had to wait, helpless, watching her fight off waves of pain while the seagulls circled above us and the cars passed uncaring below. It felt like an hour before the yellow and green ambulance came racing down the highway and along Vestre Strandgate, siren screaming, and spun round to the quay. The paramedics jumped out, unhinged their stretcher and carried it up the gangplank. One minute more, and Johanna was strapped on. They trundled her down the gangplank and into the back of the ambulance, the paramedics moving smooth as clockwork. Sadie grabbed her jacket and ran after them. The siren restarted, the lights flashed, and Johanna was on her way to safety, leaving us standing at the rail, watching her go.

'She's in the right place,' Agnetha said. 'They can operate.'

I nodded. My throat felt tight. *An unlucky voyage . . .*

Captain Gunnar touched my shoulder. 'Cass, we will need a chief engineer until Belfast. Lars is not experienced enough to take over. Do you think your young friend with the rat could drop everything and come with us?'

He meant my friend Anders: engineer, Warhammer nerd and owner of Rat, who went everywhere with him. The minute he'd heard I'd got my tall ship at last, Anders had signed up for a trainee berth on one of our weekend shakedown trips, and had naturally gravitated to the engine compartment. By the end of the weekend, he and Johanna's conversation had become unintelligible to the rest of us, but they seemed to be talking about a serious joint engine dismemberment the next time he was available. I had hopes for that relationship . . .

I pulled my phone out, found his number and called it.

He answered straight away. 'Cass? I thought you'd be heading for the high seas.'

'We're trying to,' I assured him. 'Anders, Johanna's just had to be rushed to hospital with appendicitis.' His breath drew in with a creak like a moan of pain. 'Don't worry, she's going to be fine.' I crossed my fingers as I said it. 'Is there any chance you could join us for this trip? Seven days, Kristiansand to Belfast.'

'I would like to, very much,' he said. I could see him standing there in the workshop at his father's boatyard, in his green boiler suit, his fair head shining against the oily wood walls, looking around, thinking of what had to be done in the next week. The phone crackled as he moved to look at the wall calendar. '*Dagslys*, then *Maria Klara*. Listen, give me fifteen minutes. I'll need to talk to my father. Next week's a busy one, so I'm not sure if they can manage without me.'

I looked across at Captain Gunnar. 'Shall I give him your number, sir, so that he can call you back?'

The captain held out his hand for my phone. 'Thank you, Cass.'

I moved away until they'd finished. Captain Gunnar gave me the phone back, and I went round to secure the starboard bench, lashing it with cord to the iron struts by the deckhouse and wishing Johanna luck with all my strength. I was just winding the tail of the cord away when my mobile buzzed. *All set arriving plane mid morning see you aboard keep me posted about Johanna. A.*

My next task was to sort out the man-overboard boat, ready for leaving the dock. A couple of the trainees that had arrived last night were standing beside it at the rails, looking out over the sunny harbour. One was Ellen, a tiny Norwegian lady with china-blue eyes and straight white hair bobbed to frame her face. She was seventy-one this year, she'd told me last night, and had decided that now was the time to do all the things she'd ever wanted to. One of them was going on a tall ship, so here she was, excited as any teenager. The other was a little, fussy man called Olav, who I'd already marked out as the ship's gossip – there was always one. Beside them was someone who must have come aboard this morning, a dark man who was oddly familiar. I stopped for a moment, looking at him. Maybe it was just that he reminded me of my dad, the dark hair with the slight curl in it, the broad shoulders and long, straight back – then he turned, and smiled, and spoke in a voice as Irish as my dad's. 'Well, now, if it's not my little cousin. How are you doing, Cassie, after all these years?'

He was laughing at me, his eyes as blue as a Siamese cat's in his lean face. I knew him now: Sean, son of my Auntie Mary, Dad's younger big sister. We'd always spent Christmas in Dublin with Granny Bridget and Da Patrick, among a huge family gathering, and Sean and his twin, Seamus, had been the closest to me in age, the only ones that still counted as youngsters. They'd led me into quite a bit of trouble over the years.

'Well, well!' I replied. 'Sean Lynch, what are you doing here?'

'Oh, going home, young Cassie.' He gave me a long look, down and up again. 'Aren't you the clever one, all dressed up in your uniform. Are you the captain of this ship, now? I'd better mind me Ps and Qs, so I had.'

'Third mate,' I said. 'But what on earth are you doing here? I didn't see you on the trainee list.'

'Oh, I had business in Norway, and a holiday after it, and yesterday I heard about this ship that would take me right back to Ireland, so I thought I'd give it a try. I went down to the office and signed on this very morning. You won't make me work too hard, now, will you?'

'You'll have to join in the work of the ship, with everyone else,' I said. Sean had always had difficulty settling down to the task in hand, whether it was the mountain of dishes to be washed or trying to slip me into a pub for an underage pint. Seamus would work out a system, and Sean would be too impatient to follow it. Still, maybe he'd learnt discipline as he'd got older. 'What are you working at now?'

'Oh, a bit of this and that. Marketing, mostly.' It was vague enough to cover a multitude of sins, as Auntie Mary used to say about his explanations for a broken window. He grinned again, the charm turned up to full voltage. 'You know me, Cassie, never one to settle to a routine piece of work.'

When Sean turned the charm on was the time to watch him, but I didn't see any mischief he could get up to on board, and having him standing here, family, stirring all those memories of Christmas, gave me a warm feeling inside. I tucked my arm into his and squeezed it. 'It's good to see you.' I turned to Ellen and smiled. 'This is my cousin Sean, Ellen. I wasn't expecting him aboard.'

'I see that.' She smiled at him, getting his measure straight off, as if she had sons of her own. 'You'll have to behave, young man, with your cousin in charge. None of this Irish blarney.'

'You'll need to give me all the family news,' I said.

'Oh, they're all well enough. I've managed to escape the noose meself, but Seamus has a little girl, and another one on the way, and our Declan, now, he has five, all boys.'

Declan was only six years older than me. 'Five boys!'

'That he has, and a rumbustious tribe they are too, always up to mischief.'

'Particularly when you're visiting.'

He gave me a sideways grin. 'Now, Cassie, we always led you out of trouble again once we'd led you into it. Or Uncle Dermot would have had the hide off us.'

'It was me who talked us out of that row with the buskers.'

Sean waved a hand. 'All in the past, Cassie, my love.' He turned to face me, assessing. 'And what about you? Are you married now, or do you still have a lonely washing, as Da Patrick used to say, God rest his soul?'

I waved my hand vaguely. My relationship with Gavin was too new to share, even with family. 'Still the lonely washing with no man's shirt in it.'

'No truth in the rumour about a detective inspector in Scotland, then.'

Families. Dad gossiping, of course. 'I'm not doing his washing yet,' I retorted. He nodded, but still with that measuring look, as if he was working something out. He glanced aft over my shoulder, as if he was looking around for something, then shrugged the mood off. 'Now, what work do you want to set me to?'

'We'll be giving you an orientation tour once all the youngsters come aboard. For now, just settle yourself in.'

He nodded. 'I'll get me bag unpacked, like a good boy, and help out once you've got yourselves organised. I'm sleeping on one of the couches in the little cubbyhole at the end, fine and handy for slipping up the steps for a fly fag in the night.'

'The aft steps are crew only,' I told him austerely, and left him to it.

It was a moment before I went back to the man-overboard boat. There was an uneasy feeling down my spine. Sean had booked his passage aboard as late as this morning . . .

Known to the police. He'd been a wild teenager, with the potential to get mixed up in the wrong crowd, but I didn't want to believe one of my family had turned out as the sort of person the police warned you against.

I shook the thought away, and got back to work.

CHAPTER TWO

By noon the dock was thick with trainees, each one a little island surrounded by family and baggage. A group of boys laughed and joked together at the foot of the gangplank, eyeing up the masts with reasonably convincing bravado. Looking round I could see our ship was going to be a community of all the nations on this voyage: two African boys and three girls; five boys from the Middle East; a bonny blonde whose face said Danish; three lively Greek boys with a quiet, dark girl listening to them; two sporty-looking Norwegian sisters; and a pair of boys, one very tall, with enough likeness between them to suggest they were brothers. Standing aloof was a girl with a hat like a British woman police officer's tilted down over her brow, and a brightly coloured Bob Marley jacket. She was looking at the ship with a sulky expression, tilting her mouth downwards; the face I'd seen in the mirror in my teenage years in France. A knot of adults stood slightly apart from the sea of teenagers, kitbags at their feet.

Past them, in front of the ochre toll house, the chief officer,

Mike, was being seen off by his wife, Klaudina. I didn't know him very well yet, because he had a house here in Kristiansand, so didn't stay on board while *Sørlandet* was in port. He was from Cork, and in his early forties. He was tall and dark, that handsomely rugged look like Pierce Brosnan in his James Bond days, and infectiously enthusiastic over everything that went on aboard – I found him great to work under, and he went down a treat with the trainees. His wife was blonde and Swedish, with a pointed nose that reminded me of someone – cartoons of Mrs Thatcher, perhaps. She looked up at the ship and made a little face, then waved him away from her: *Off you go to your other woman!* her gesture said, with a hint of sharpness, as if she resented the hold the sea had over him.

I turned back to work. Jenn, our lively Canadian liaison officer, had set up a table amidships, just in front of the mainmast, ready to give out berth numbers, and file passports in the secure box. Mike went forward and welcomed the trainees in English first, then in his Swedish-accented Norwegian. He unhooked the 'Crew only' chain. The first of the Greek boys hefted his bag on his shoulder and stepped up the gangplank, to start the hour of chaos that followed the arrival of a new bunch of trainees.

I joined Erik and my two ABs in a line at the foot of the double stairs which led down to the banjer, the big saloon where the trainees lived. It was surprisingly light given that the windows were a row of portholes. The woodwork was cream, with the settee berths upholstered in a soothing oatmeal colour. The stairs divided the two sides of the space, and under them were rows of lockers. There were tables along each outer side, close enough to use the berths as seats for eating, and square seamen's chests as seats on the inner side. Each roof beam had hammock hooks screwed into it. The trainees were placed in watches, so that those not on watch wouldn't be bumped and bothered by those rising. My blue watch was on the starboard side, white was on port, and red took up my cousin Sean's 'little cubbyhole' and the end rows on both sides.

The first of the teenagers down the steps introduced himself straight away: 'Johan.' He was in his early twenties, a tall, slim boy with a cockscomb of fair hair above his brow and beautifully moulded cheekbones. If his confidence masked nervousness, it didn't show. 'I spent a year aboard *Sørlandet* two years ago. I can help here, if you wish.'

Someone who knew the ship that well would be a real asset on the watch. I set him to showing the trainees where their lockers were, and greeted and smiled as the banjer filled and filled. At sea, of course, there would always be a third of the trainees on watch. For now there were people everywhere, hauling out jumpers, jeans and oilskins, and stuffing them into their lockers. Already there were tablets and mobile phones trailing cords from the tabletops to the sockets in the wall. Among it all, Ellen sat quietly on her berth and knitted, pointing out a hammock number every so often, and learning the names of all the young people who would be surrounding her for the next week. Olav watched them all, his little eyes darting from one to the other, making connections between them. The noise was appalling: teenagers shrieking at each other, yelling with laughter and banging the doors of their lockers and the lids of the chests.

The adults came on last. The first for my blue watch was a man who gave the impression of being a fisherman, broad-shouldered and strong enough to haul the yards round unaided. My hand was lost in his. 'Jan Ole,' he rumbled. 'I do not go aloft.'

'You don't have to,' I assured him. 'You'll be worth your weight in gold on deck.'

He laughed at that. 'You are talking a lot of gold.' His eyes went to the hammock hooks. He reached out to give one an experimental tug, nodded in satisfaction, and headed for his locker.

'Aage,' the grey-haired man behind him said. 'I too do not climb masts.'

'Plenty else to do aboard,' I said. We'd need to see how many of my youngsters were climbers, but at least we'd have a good deck team.

I left Mona to do the hammock demo. Up on deck, Jen was tidying away the passports into her box. The UK customs would want everyone on board in a neat, alphabetical line, and this way we'd just line ourselves up, then Jenn would come along and dole out the passports. She lifted her head as I came up. 'Fantastic news of Johanna. It was her appendix, and they operated straight away. She'll be fine.'

I took the other end of her green tablecloth and helped her fold it. 'Oh, that's great! How long will they keep her in?'

'Only a couple of days. I spoke to her father, and she's going home to Oslo to convalesce. He said he'd see how she was after a week, so she'll maybe join us in Belfast.' Jenn dropped the cloth into her bag and we began unclicking the table legs.

A screech of brakes on the dock called our attention downwards. Only a taxi stopped like that, and a taxi it was indeed, with Anders' fair head beside the driver. He jumped out and began retrieving his kitbag and an armful of scarlet oilskins from the boot, along with Rat's cage. I hurried down the gangplank. 'That was quick.'

'I was lucky with the flights.' He gave me a hug, and Rat took the opportunity to slip from Anders' shoulder to mine. He was a large beast, not much smaller than Cat, with patches of glossy black on an immaculate white coat, long transparent toes and an agile, curving tail. He whiffled in my ear by way of greeting, and curled round my neck like a live stole.

'Cat will be pleased to see you,' I told him.

I took the oilskins and Anders hefted his kitbag. He wasn't tall, but compactly built, with strong shoulders. His hair was silver-gilt fair, his eyes the blue of a summer fjord, and he had a neat seaman's beard like an Elizabethan explorer. Looking at him, remembering living aboard my *Khalida* together, and feeling that sense of *my mate*, I tucked my arm into his. 'I'm glad you could make it.'

'My father is not completely happy, but I reminded him that Johanna and I were talking of giving the engine an overhaul, and it would look good on the yard's CV. What is the news of her?'

'Good.' I repeated what Jenn had told me. 'You don't need to join the watch introduction, so you would have time to nip up to the hospital. If you do, can you get her flowers from all of us?'

'They don't allow flowers in hospitals these days.'

Oh, he'd checked, had he? My hopes of a romance rose. 'Just dump your stuff in my cabin for the moment – I'm not sure where Captain Gunnar wants to put you.' Cat looked up as we entered, then rose, seeing Rat; Rat swarmed down my front and leapt for the bed, and there was thirty seconds of mutual whisker sniffing, then Rat leapt for the back of the berth and Cat followed him. I drew the curtain on the scampering noises and occasional soft thud of the Cat/Rat version of don't-touch-the-floor, and took Anders along to Captain Gunnar's quarters. 'See you later. We have the induction session.'

Not that I was allowed to join in, of course. The trainees were all called together from their exploration of the ship, and lined up in watches by the watch leader and ABs for each team, with a bit of shuffling about to get them in two straight lines and not leaning on the conveniently placed ship's rail, while we officers stood in a row in front of the mainmast, shoulders back, hands behind our backs. Once we'd got lines we could live with, Rolf took a photo of each watch and Jenn handed out the rota sheets. Only then did Captain Gunnar come out to greet them formally, imposing in his gold-braided jacket (I'd never seen him in sailing overalls) and leaning slightly on the polished walking stick that I suspected was more affectation than need.

As well as Olav and Ellen, my watch included the two brothers I'd noticed, the sporty Norwegian sisters, the blonde Danish girl (who looked miserably unsure of herself in this strange set-up), the quiet Greek girl and one of the Greek boys, masking his nervousness under constant movement and an echoing catchphrase of 'All right, all right, all *right!*' One of the African boys didn't seem to speak English, for when I looked around for who was persistently talking over the crew instructions, it turned out to be a tall, red-headed boy translating into Norwegian for him. He had the white skin of a true ginger; I hoped he'd brought sun lotion. We had three of the Middle Eastern boys, one dark and alert, the second already being heart-warmingly deferential to Ellen, who was standing squarely between them in her scarlet jacket and white knitted hat, and the third leaning back sullenly on the rail with his back-to-front baseball cap pulled down on his brow.

I cast a quick look down the names on the list Jenn had just given me and the photo Rolf had just pressed into my hand, still warm from the printer, and scribbled the names as Erik went through them. Olav, at the front, watching everything that was going on. The brothers were Ludwig and Ben, the sporty sisters Anna and Nora, and the blonde girl Nine. Maria and Dimitris. Ismail, and the Norwegian boy translating for him was Sindre. Samir, Naseem with Ellen, and Gabriel hiding under his cap. We also had Johan, already eyeing up the masts, and the massive fisherman Jan-Ole and his friend Aage. It was the makings of a good team.

We always did rig training before setting sail. Petter gave them a lecture on safety aloft (it boiled down to 'Hold on, and don't mess about'), and then everyone who wanted to go up the rigging was asked to hang by the arms from the bars above the main deck. Dimitris went first, and had no difficulty raising himself up from deck level; he obviously worked out on wall bars in a gym. Johan, after him, made it look easy. The Norwegian sisters bounced up like basketball players, swung, crooked their arms and made a controlled descent. Maria followed them; Nine shook her head and backed away. Olav looked up, then shook his head, and joined Aage, Jan-Ole and Ellen at the rail. The tall brother, Ludwig, could reach the bar without needing to jump; his younger image tried, and made a face. Sindre shook his head too, and Gabriel; Samir pulled himself up easily and went grinning to start fitting his harness. Naseem and Ismail lifted, swung, and joined Samir. Nine climbers was good, plus the three crew members; a fair number for working the sails. Petter and Mona made sure the climbing harnesses were fitted and secure, then Erik began to climb up the main mast, slowly, while the ABs helped the trainees safely onto the ratlines below him.

It was sensible to be afraid. *Sørlandet*'s ratlines, those segments of spider's web running diagonally up the mast, were more solid than many, with wire uprights braced apart by wooden footplates, but you were still climbing eleven metres up above the wooden deck just to reach the first platform. Erik led, and the first four followed him, climbing steadily up the swaying wires.

Dimitris was first to reach the platform. There was a triumphant grin on his face as he hooked an elbow around the ratline leading up to the second platform, and looked round at the air world of a tall ship: the heavy, horizontal spars, the tied canvas, the tracery of ropes and the wide sky behind. 'All right, all right, all *right!*'

Samir followed him, then Naseem, then Anna, scrambling up like a monkey, turning her size into an advantage by wedging her feet and hands into tiny spaces. Erik let them savour their triumph for a moment, then watched them cross the platform and descend on the dock side of the ship. His words floated down: 'Remember, you're not safe till both feet are on deck.'

Petter and Johan took the second group: Ludwig, Ismail, Nora and Maria. At the last moment Ben put on a harness and followed them. Having seen the others climb up there had given them confidence: they went up, slowly, steadily, dark figures against the blue sky, across the platform and down the other side. That was enough for one day; the harnesses clunked back into their nylon mesh laundry basket, and the whole watch headed forrard to begin their deck inspection: the foredeck and lookout area, the under-deck showers and heads, the bosun's stairs, the washing line for wet towels. In half an hour they'd made it back to me and were clumping up the aft steps to inspect the nav shack, the deckhouse where the navigation instruments were kept. Behind it were the metre-wide ship's wheel and the 'captain's coffin', the polished wood case which covered the steering mechanism. Then they headed below to the banjer, where Jenn explained mealtimes, gave them the lecture about not leaving their stuff lying about, showed them the lost property cupboard where they'd find it when they did, and released them to relax.

That all took until four o'clock. Three o'clock in Scotland. Gavin might be having his tea break. I felt tired, tired . . . I went across the gangplank, along to the peace of the grass in front of one of the posh hotels, and called him.

I was in luck. He answered at the second ring. I could imagine him at his desk or perhaps standing out by the river, taking a breather from the office, russet head tilted towards the phone, a curve to his mouth and warmth in his grey eyes as if I was there with him. 'Coffee break?'

'Nearly,' he said. 'I'll just get away from my desk.' I heard a door squeak open and close again, then the wind on the phone. 'How's it going? Do you have your trainees?'

'Millions of them. The ship is disappearing under a wash of teenage testosterone.'

'What watch are you on this time?'

'Blue.' It was the most difficult one for phoning each other; when I got up at 6.30, it was only 5.30 in Scotland, and then he was working all afternoon while I was free. As a recently appointed DI to the mobile serious crimes squad of Police Scotland, his life was busier than it had been in Inverness. 'I'll phone while there's still a signal.'

'Yes, please. So, any extra excitement?'

There was no reason why I should feel awkward about telling him; Anders and I were just mates. 'We've got Anders aboard, as chief engineer.' I explained about Johanna, then went on, in a more natural tone, 'And my cousin Sean's aboard too – gave me the shock of my life to see him. He's my dad's sister's son, one of twins, two years older than me. We all used to stay with Granny Bridget in Dublin for Christmas, and the trouble the pair of them led me into!'

'That sounds like what your Granny said.' I could hear the amusement in his voice. 'You'd be able to match them, even as a teenager.'

'Different league,' I said briskly. 'My only ever cigarette . . . my first pint of Guinness . . .'

'Shocking. Are you all set to sail?'

'17.00.' He felt so remote, with the trainees aboard and the sea road beckoning. I made an effort. 'What's the news at home?'

'Oh, quiet, except that there's another litter of kittens in the byre, all striped. Mother was threatening them with drowning, but I talked her out of it. You can never have too many cats around a farm. Kenny's at his wits' end over when to cut the hay, with this constant rain, and the grass has grown so fast that Luchag, you remember, the dun pony you rode, has had to be put on a tether to stop her getting too fat for the stalking.'

It was a different world, his farm at the end of a remote loch, steep and wooded like a Norwegian fjord, with waterfalls threading the hills. His brother Kenny was the full-time farmer. Gavin had a flat in Inverness, two hours' drive away, and he went home every free weekend. I tried to imagine myself turning hay or tending a litter of half-wild striped kittens, with a baby on my hip and a toddler at my heels. Maybe sometime . . .

'Poor Luchag. She won't like that.' The one thing I did know about horses was that they believed they were permanently starving. 'How about your suspected people smugglers?'

He went cagey, as if he was worried someone might be hacking in. 'Developments. It's nasty. I'll tell you the whole story when I see you.' He paused for a moment, then said, 'You don't sound as happy as you should with your ship ready to sail.'

I made a face at the hotel's immaculate lawns. 'It's nothing. Just one of those stupid feelings. A cloud hanging over me.' The wind spread the Norwegian flag at *Sørlandet*'s mizzen mast and the long banner at the top of the mainmast. I could feel her calling. 'I have to go. I just wanted to say hello before we cast off. I'll phone later. Would you still be awake at eleven, when I come off watch?'

'I will be.' He was laughing at me now. 'Go on, my Cass, get back to your ship, before she leaves without you.' *Go back to your other woman*, Mike's wife had gestured. But there was no resentment in Gavin's voice. 'You've only got an hour, and I'd guess a full hundred metres to walk, at most.'

I admitted it. 'Half a street.'

'My phone may go straight to voicemail. If it does, don't wait up for me to call back.'

That sounded like a stake-out on some damp piece of coast. 'I won't.' *Won't be able to*, I could have added, *after a watch at sea*. 'Good luck with it.'

'*Tapadh leat.*' Thanks. '*Beannachd leat, mo chridhe.*'

'Speak tae dee later.' *Beannachd leat* meant goodbye, a blessing on you, but I hadn't yet dared to ask the meaning of the soft phrase that came after it. Sometime, when we were alone, in bed . . .

I put the phone away, and walked straight into Micaela, Erik's wife, and their two children, there to see Daddy off.

Micaela was South American, and beautiful, with huge dark eyes in an oval face and a ripple of shining hair that she usually pinned up. Loose, it reached to below her waist. Their pre-children photos showed her as slim and lithe as a swimming fish, but two children and a love of cooking had thickened her slender arms, plumped out her cheeks and turned her life, it seemed, into a perpetual fight against becoming *fat*. Only fat-free items were permitted in her fridge, and she'd try one diet after another, being meat-free one week, then drinking only juiced vegetables the next. Erik remonstrated with her about it, and she just shook her head at him and went on to the next one.

'It's anxiety,' he'd told me, one night on a quiet watch, where the trainees were dozing on the benches, and the ship was forging steadily on across the water. 'She came from a repressive regime over there. She still expects a sudden knock on the door, and armed men bursting in. I don't know what I can do about it.' He'd looked anxious himself, talking about it, as if he was beginning to share her nightmare. 'Nothing, I suppose. My great-grandmother, she was here during the war. She never spoke about it, but I had always to call out who I was as I went into the house.'

Today, the skin around Micaela's mouth was drawn tight as she tucked her arm inside Erik's. 'I have brought you a cake, a *verdens beste*.' 'World's best' was a buttery cake layered with meringue, sliced almonds and cream, and scattered with berries. Micaela made it beautifully. My stomach paid attention; I reminded it that the cake was destined for the other ranks' mess. 'Here, remember now to put it in the fridge. What else? Oh, yes.' She fished out a bulging paper bag. 'Some rolls, with *brunost*.'

Brunost was sweet brown cheese. It was a credit to Erik's metabolism that he'd kept that tall, rangy Norwegian build.

'I helped make the cake, Papa,' his daughter Elena told him. She was just six, and would be heading for school in the autumn. She hadn't gone to nursery, for Micaela insisted on keeping her babies with her, but she was quick and bright, and thanks to Micaela she already knew all the basics like numbers, colours and her alphabet in both Norwegian and English. The four-year-old boy, Alexander, clung to Erik's leg. 'I put the cheese on the rolls, Papa.'

Erik put his arm round Micaela. 'I'll be glad of these at ten o'clock tonight.' I came forward to have Micaela wish me a good voyage and touch me with her cherished medallion of the Virgin of Sorrows, then I went back up to the aft deck and left them to say goodbye.

I was just relaxing on the bench beside the captain's coffin when Mona came to me and plumped herself down. 'I think we have rats in the sail locker. Can I see if Cat wants to go down, or would a rat be too dangerous for him to tackle?'

My thoughts went straight to Rat. 'Did you see it? Because Anders has come aboard. My friend who was on one of the weekend trips, remember, with his pet rat. Rat and Cat may well be charging round the ship together.'

Mona shook her head. 'I didn't see it. I just heard something moving in the sail locker as I put the suitcases away. I called, thinking it might be Cat gone down there while the trap was open, but he didn't come.'

'He might not have.' As the hatch was generally kept closed, he would have been reluctant to be thrown out by authority before he'd sniffed round every corner.

'I could feel I was being watched.' She shuddered. 'Petter said I was talking nonsense, but maybe we need a trap, so long as we made sure Cat didn't get caught in it.'

'Let's just check on him first,' I suggested. I led the way down the aft steps and to my cabin. There was a knot of fur on my berth, Cat's grey curled round Rat's black and white, with one striped paw round Rat's plush middle. Two heads lifted as we came in, both sets of whiskers radiating suspicious innocence. They could have been there half an hour or just two minutes. 'I'll go and check it out.'

The sail locker was forrard, at the bottom of the steep stairs leading down to the carpenter's workshop and two crew cabins, Erik and Petter on one side and the ABs from the red watch on the other. Mona had left the floor hatch open, so Cat and Rat could easily have scampered out again while we'd been talking.

I clattered down the ladder. It was a trapezoid space, framed by broad shelves that were filled with white canvas, a spare for every one of the ship's twenty-two sails. Half a dozen suitcases had been squeezed on top of the lowest shelf. Down here, the noises of the ship filtered away to a stuffy wood-smelling silence.

Of course, any sensible rat would have made itself scarce by now, which had been my intention. I paused in the middle of the room and waited. Nothing; but there was an alertness to the nothing that made me uneasy. I waited, counting up to a hundred in my head and feeling eyes on me all the time, yet there was still silence, not a rustle of canvas nor creak of wood to betray the presence of anything else in the locker with me. I tried to remember what was behind the shelves of canvas. Forrard, there was the well where the anchor chain was stored. There would be no exit there. To each side there was an under-decks corridor running the length of the ship, so if a rat had got aboard, and had gnawed or wriggled its way through into the locker, it could easily come and go. Maybe I should bring Cat down later.

I was just turning to go when I realised why I was uneasy. This locker should smell of canvas and wood, but overlaid on that was the smell of cigarette smoke, not recent smoke, as if someone had lit up in here, but the sour smell you'd get in the house of a habitual smoker. I wrinkled my nose and came forward to the suitcases, sniffing each in turn. One of them obviously came from a smoking household, but the smell was faded, not quite what I'd sensed from the middle of the floor. I stepped back and turned round, flaring my nostrils, but it wasn't coming from any particular direction. A trainee who'd thought to come and smoke down here, instead of on the designated bench, then been scared off by Mona coming?

I gave a last look around, then climbed up the ladder. The prickling sensation in my back increased so much as I bent over to fit the boards to the space that I turned to stare behind me at the door to Erik and Petter's cabin. I knocked gently, then swung the door open, but of course there was nobody there, although the smell lingered here too.

I frowned to myself, and headed back up the stairs to the main deck.

* * *

41

Word of Johanna was good. They'd let Anders in to see her, and she was groggy but relieved of pain. The doctors were talking of sending her home tomorrow, he announced over dinner, with no trace of being awed by the mahogany table, velvet curtains, glooming portraits of royalty and assembled ranks of gold shoulder bars that had intimidated me into silence on my first dinner in the officers' mess. Her parents would collect her, and she was determined to join us in Belfast. She'd offered him her cabin, too, so he asked me to move her clothes to free up one drawer, and squeeze a space in the hanging locker. I felt a bit awkward about doing that, but less than Anders would have, and she kept her clothes so tidy that it was a simple matter of lifting and shifting two piles of immaculately ironed T-shirts.

The wind was from the north-east, a perfect sailing wind, but dead on the nose. The trainees stayed on deck as we left Kristiansand, watching the shore slip past: the opera house, the dark trees of the sheltered land, white wood houses with their own landing stages, then Odderøya lighthouse, square and white with its conical hat. As we came to the coast pounded by the wild North Sea, the green gave way to curves of polished rock rising up from the ocean, with small pines clinging with knuckled roots to the darker line of seaweed-rich earth. Grønningen lighthouse, a cluster of buildings on a rocky island, appeared to port, the red-ringed tower of Oksøy lighthouse came on starboard, and Kristiansand was left behind.

Ah, but it was good to be at sea again. My forebodings blew away. It was a most beautiful evening, glorious sunshine, with a clear blue sky above the sparkling ocean, the hills on our right, the sea horizon on our left. *Sørlandet* forged steadily forward, the engines chugging gently, the swell lifting her bowsprit and the waves curling with a sloosh and suck under her stern. I stood under the triangle of ratlines on the aft deck and looked out at the ocean, and felt myself at home once more.

My watch began at eight. Below me, on the main deck, the watches were mustering. The outgoing white watch stood on the windward side (so that they could 'hand' the wind over to the oncoming watch) and my own blue watch lined up to leeward. I did a quick head count; two short. They'd soon learn that the outgoing watch wasn't dismissed until the oncoming one was all present, and the grumbling of their fellow trainees at being made to stand and wait for them would do far more than we officers could to encourage punctuality. Erik consulted his list, and sent the named watch positions – lookout, safety, helm and standby – off to their stations. The lookout went forrard and the others came up to the aft deck: Ellen on helm, Sindre beside her on standby and Dimitris on safety. I gave him the laminated list of things to check, a full tour of the ship each quarter hour. 'You also ring the ship's bell. Just stick your head in the cabin here for the time. *Ding* for a half hour, *ding ding* for a full hour, so two and a half hours gone is *ding ding, ding ding, ding*. The first one you'll ring will be eight o'clock, the end of the previous watch – four double dings.' He nodded.

I installed Sindre by the wheel, with a choice of standing on the leeward side or sitting with his back against the captain's coffin, explained the compass and wheel to Ellen, and waited with her until I was sure she had the hang of it.

At last, a full five minutes after Dimitris had rung eight bells to signal the end of the white watch, the last straggler of the blue watch came out on deck. '*God vakt!*' the white watch chanted. '*God vakt skal vaere!*' my own replied: a good watch it shall be.

It was a quiet watch. The ABs got out the miniature sail and showed the trainees how to tie and untie the gaskets, the lines that held the sails fastened up to the horizontal yards, then took the climbers up the rigging while the light was still good. This time they went out along the yards, stepping off the safety of the metal platform to edge along the foot-wires, bellies resting over the curved wooden yard, so that their weight was centred there, feet seemingly swaying in air, and untied the gaskets, then tied them up again. Dimitris reported four times that all was well, then headed for standby, Sindre took over the helm – he was, I gathered, a keen fisherman, and well able to steer a straight course – while Ellen went forward to lookout. The lookout, Gabriel, came back to safety, and I had to do the briefing spiel about bells all over again.

The main problem was smoking. It seemed almost all of the ones from Social Services smoked, and couldn't manage a whole hour without a cigarette, so that the safety watch was prolonged by a smoke break each time, and I'd glance aft to find the standby on the helm while the real helm was below at the designated benches, the smoke drifting up to our aft deck. Yuck. It reminded me that I must get Jenn to re-emphasise smoking areas on the next muster.

Gradually, the sky darkened, and the moon thickened from a transparent honesty penny to the colour of old brass, poised in a diamond of rigging. The coast of Norway became a dark line on the horizon, punctured by winking lighthouses. I stood under the triangle of spider's web ratlines and ticked them off as we passed: the top-heavy bulk of Songvår, then the three Mandal lighthouses, Ryvingen, Hatholmen, Lindesnes.

The last half hour of a watch was always the longest. On deck, the trainees were beginning to yawn and look longingly at the banjer stairs. The first star sharpened to a steel-blue point. I was just contemplating the delicate traceries of rope against the cobalt sky when Anders came up beside me. 'She sounds good, doesn't she?'

44

He meant the engine. 'Chugging away nicely.'

'Now you have a salary, you could think of changing your old Volvo in *Khalida*. She too could sound like this.' He considered for a moment. 'Well, no, since it would be a much smaller engine.'

My *Khalida's whole hull* could fit twice into *Sørlandet's* engine space, with enough room left over to throw a party for the ship's crew. 'A touch smaller,' I agreed. 'Are you settled into Johanna's cabin?'

'I like the *Chief Engineer* on the brass plate over the door. It will please Rat and Cat too, to be so close.' He looked ahead, eyes narrowing. 'I thought they had been told about smoking.'

He was looking at a dark shape up on the boat deck: a man, broad-shouldered, hunched over the rail. His back was to us, but his hand moved with a tell-tale red glow.

'I will tell him again.' Anders went swiftly down the stairs and across the deck with authoritative strides befitting the gold on his shoulder. *Give a man a uniform*, I thought, amused. The dark shape turned. I saw the red spark arc over the rail and hiss into the water. The man circled in a quick movement, like an otter cornered under a jetty, slid to the rail and swung downwards, climbing down the far side of the boathouse while Anders was climbing up. Anders strode across to the far side of the boat deck and looked around, then shrugged and followed the stranger down the forrard ladder.

The oncoming watch was beginning to gather on deck; Agnetha came up the aft stairs and out to me, her face bleached in the silver light. 'All's well?'

'Yes.' I did the log handover and stood back while her watch relieved mine, then waited at the rail while Erik counted off the trainees. '*God vakt!*' they chorused, and headed below, where there would be a flurry of hammock-hanging by mobile phone light in the dark banjer.

Anders reappeared beside me. 'I lost him, but I think I would know the shape again. An older man – we have not so many of those on board.'

'He's not my watch. Red, or a white who couldn't sleep.'

'I will know him again,' Anders repeated. 'Are you for bed now?'

I nodded, and followed him down the stairs. As I was descending, I took a good look around at the trainees spreading out around the deck. None of them had that heavy bulk, those broad shoulders. White watch, then. I'd spot him in the morning.

Gavin's phone was switched to voicemail. *A stake-out on some damp coast* . . . I left a 'hello', then brushed my teeth, wriggled in beside Cat and Rat, and was asleep in seconds.

CHAPTER THREE

Friday 26th June

I woke at quarter past six. Cat was curled against my neck, and the sun was bright on the water outside. The waves tapped at the ship's hull and the engine throbbed. Someone walked across the deck over my head. I heard Nils give the compass course, and the helm repeat it, then the wheel clunked round and the ship moved, and settled to her new course.

Cat had spotted I was awake. He prodded at my face with one paw until I reached out for his brush and groomed the permitted bits: the back and sides of his neck, and the white owl-tufts behind his ears. On a good day he'd let me do his throat as well, but more than that was pushing my luck; he'd lay a firm paw on the brush and dare it to go any further. He was particularly fussy about his beautiful plume of tail, dark grey above and palest pearl below. Nobody was allowed to touch that.

I'd left the door ajar so that he and Rat could come and go as they pleased, and as soon as I'd finished with the brushing he used his litter tray (the downside of being at sea) and slid out to find his pal. I woke myself up with a shower, dressed in my officer gear and headed for breakfast at the captain's table.

It was very impressive, the officers' mess, rather like a well-to-do club room. The walls were panelled in walnut, with red velvet curtains masking the portholes and Edwardian-style lamps at shoulder height. On the far side were portraits of King Harald and Queen Sonja, in a glory of uniform and sash, with a carved wooden crown surmounting each. There were red-upholstered chairs round the mahogany table, where the galley girls had already laid out the morning buffet: a serving bowl of oatmeal and another of cornflakes, plates of cold meat and cheese, a basket of bread, a jug of milk and a carton of cherry-flavour drinkable yoghurt. I slipped into my place with a murmured 'Good morning' and sat quietly. We were waiting for Nils, still on watch, and Agnetha, who'd come off at four o'clock. Red watch was the worst, with your sleep broken into two sessions. Just as I was thinking that, she came in and dropped hastily into her seat beside mine. Nils came in after her, bringing a breath of sea air. Above our heads, his watch was scrubbing the decks, the brushes going *froosh, froosh*, and water sloshing from the seawater hose. Captain Gunnar said grace and passed the oatmeal round. I poured myself a glassful of yoghurt and sliced a banana on my oatmeal. Beside me, Agnetha crumbled her rye bread and took only a couple of sips of coffee. Mike was watching her too, his face concerned. I gave her a nudge with my elbow and made a *You OK?* face. She responded with a *Too sleepy* grimace, and took another sip of coffee.

I finished my breakfast with a slice of bread and *brunost*, and headed off to brush the grains of rye from between my teeth before morning watch.

We'd passed the 'corner' of south Norway, at Mandel, and now we were heading north-west. If this wind held, we'd get the sails up today. I set Erik and the ABs to teaching the trainees the ropes. To the casual eye, they were a thicket, reaching upwards into the sky from the coil around each belaying pin, but they were in a system, so that once you'd learnt the order for one mast, you knew them all. I watched from above as they formed into teams and raced to place a hand on the correct sheet or brace, with a good deal of laughter and not a little shoving. Then there was more mast climbing, and out along the yards, which took us to coffee time. I kept watching for last night's smoker, and thought I glimpsed his broad shoulders from out of the corner of my eye a couple of times, but when I turned to look properly he wasn't there. It was an uneasy feeling, rather like the climber's hallucination that there's one more person there than can be accounted for.

Agnetha came out onto the aft deck for coffee, yawning and clutching her scarlet jacket around her, but with a touch more colour in her cheeks than she'd had at breakfast. '*Ouf!* The red watch is hard work.'

'The hardest,' I agreed. My blue watch could sleep from twelve to seven, and the white watch from ten till four o'clock in the morning, and both watches tended to have an afternoon nap, but the hammocks were cleared for breakfast at seven and lights not turned off until ten, so the red watch, on duty from twelve till four, got the least sleep. 'You're OK, though?'

She shrugged and turned away, so that I couldn't see her face, but the answer came lightly. 'I'm having to catch up with a straight-after-lunch nap like an old lady.' She was a head taller than me, and very fair, that typical Scandinavian look; it was hard to imagine anything less like an old lady. *Mind you*, I thought, looking at Ellen, coming up the stairs to take over standby helm, a cup of coffee in each hand, *old ladies aren't all after-lunch nap types.*

Erik and my ABs left the trainees enjoying their coffee and biscuits, and came back aft. I was still getting to know Mona and Petter. Mona was great: lively, enthusiastic, experienced. I found Petter harder to talk to. If we'd been in America I'd have called him 'preppy'. *Aristokratisk.* He oozed privilege, even in his regulation uniform. Every time he paused by the rail, he looked like a men's clothing advert. He was good on deck, but his real love was gadgetry, and he always had the latest watch, tablet and phone, paid for by his parents, I presumed, for the ABs were volunteers. I went over to lean on the rail beside him. 'They're going to be a good team, don't you think?'

He gave a half-turn so that his back was on the rail, gave me a shy, sideways glance, then looked straight across the ship, face turned away from me. 'I think so. Several good climbers – Johan will be a real asset – and a strong deck team, with the two fishermen.'

'Is this your first season as an AB?'

He nodded, and answered defensively, 'But before that I was in the navy cadets, and I have had two seasons as a trainee.'

'Oh, it's obvious you know what you're doing,' I said. I didn't understand why he should be so quick to think I was criticising. I smiled at his unresponsive profile. 'What's your winter job?'

He didn't move, but a tide of red crept up his neck. 'Oh, a bit of this and that. My father's in a law firm.'

It didn't quite answer the question. 'You're lucky,' I said. Whatever idea he had of me as a dyed-in-the-wool sailor who'd look down on lesser jobs, I decided to get rid of it. 'I funded my seasons aboard by double shifts of waitressing in a sleazy Edinburgh cafe.'

He gave me a quick glance at that, but didn't reply. I left the silence unbroken. At last he gave me another look, then drank the end of his coffee and straightened himself up on the rail. 'Well, man-overboard drill?'

'To time,' I agreed, and watched him walk away as if he'd escaped unscathed from ten minutes in the lion's den. I felt rather hurt; normally, I thought, I got on well with everyone, and I certainly didn't see myself as intimidating. Maybe he was really shy under the superior air . . .

The man-overboard boat was an inflatable dinghy stowed, naturally, on the boat deck, the central raised area above the banjer. The drill took up the rest of the watch: fitting everyone with life jackets, attaching the dinghy with straps to the swing-around pulley, hauling it out so that it hung clear of the ship's side, lowering it. The team had a couple of shots, sorting themselves out into who was best doing what, then Erik timed them for their third shot. 'Two minutes dead!' he called out, and there was a triumphant cheer. Erik congratulated them all, then came aft to talk to Agnetha. He put his hand on her upper arm, a gesture of concern. She shook her head, and he leant forward to her, talking persuasively. She stepped back, shaking her head again, and shrugging his arm off, stalked off towards the stairs to the main deck.

Olav, coming up to make his last report, gave them a narrow-eyed look. 'Are they a couple?' he asked me. 'I'm still trying to sort out who everyone is.'

I shook my head. 'Just friends.' We didn't need that kind of gossip aboard. 'Erik's married to a South American lady, Micaela. She came to see him off, with the children – did you notice her? She's really beautiful.'

He pursed his mouth, and nodded. Then I remembered Agnetha's closed door yesterday, and how she had arrived only just on time for morning muster. Erik had come out of that corridor too, when he should have been on the gangplank . . . of course, he could have been fetching something from the other ranks' mess, or making himself a cup of tea in the pantry. There was no reason for him to have been with Agnetha. The thought was ridiculous. All the same, it made an uneasy nest for itself in the back of my mind. *Complicated, Agnetha had said* . . . So many marriages suddenly ended in a suddenly discovered affair, and everyone said, 'I would never have expected that . . .'

Twelve o'clock was lunchtime, and there was a savoury smell of soup drifting along from the galley. My watch said their *'God vakt!'* and stampeded below to fling off oilskins and line up at the banjer serving hatch. At a guess, the soup would incorporate leftover spaghetti from last night's tea, and there would be bread, cold meats, cheese and pickled herring laid out along the tops of the lockers. I tidied my hair in my cabin, tickled Cat's and Rat's bellies, and joined Captain Gunnar and my fellow officers in Edwardian splendour.

Jenn had a yoga class at 13.30, so I spent half an hour up on the boat deck doing down dog and warrior lunges, with the sea sparkling around us and the coast of Norway slipping slowly by in the distance. When that was over, it was banjer cleaning time, and Jenn headed below with a detachment of the red watch to turf the blue and white trainees upwards. I waited on the boat deck, watching for the broad-shouldered trainee, but he didn't appear. He had to be red watch after all then, busy mopping.

As soon as the banjer was finished, there was a bustle of activity. Captain Gunnar had ordered the sails to be made ready, and the red watch got busy in their teams, hauling each heavy yard around to a close-hauled starboard tack. Then they headed upwards into the rigging. I wasn't surprised to see that Sean was the first out along the yard, feet swaying on the wire, hands busy untying the gasket. Once everyone was back down they formed teams again and released the buntlines to let the sails fall, then moved to the clews to tighten them into a bonny curve. The whole process took an hour, but at last there she was, under sail, with acres of tautly curved canvas reflecting the grey sky. Captain Gunnar, watching from the aft deck, nodded to Anders. The motor gave a cough and fell silent.

Suddenly there was no sound but the grey waves stroking the ship's hull, the gentle creak of the rigging, the sharp mew of a seagull curving overhead. The wind was soft on my cheek. I was standing just forrard of the ship's wheel, with the two ratlines making a triangle above my head, and my sky was filled with white canvas. *Sørlandet*'s pennant fluttered above the mainmast. The wooden deck moved under my feet and the afternoon sun glinted on the horizon.

Anders came up to stand beside me. His face reflected mine, his eyes alight at the solemn joy of being here, caught between wind and water. His chest rose and fell in deep breaths of the soft air. We didn't speak, just stood there, side by side, and absorbed it all.

Most of the trainees had come on deck when the engine went off. Now they were lounging about, leaning against the rail or sitting on benches along the mid deckhouse sides. The Greek boys had gathered up on the foredeck looking out, with even lively Dimitris awed into silence. A knot from my watch were amidships, checking where we were on their mobile phones and pointing out distant landmarks. I glanced at the plotter, then up, clocking the square bulk of Søndre Katland lighthouse, which showed the entrance to Farsund. The red-brick tower of Lista, with its slightly wider top, like a chess piece, was faint on the corner of the headland.

I stood up there for a long time, just watching the sea go by, until my back grew stiff with standing and the low clouds that left moisture on my upper lip became a gentle drizzle that darkened the canvas sails. The midships area cleared as the off-duty watches headed below. At last I headed below too, made myself a cup of tea and joined Cat and Rat on my bunk, to lie back, hands crossed under my head, and listen to the pad of feet above my head, the waves at my ear, the ship forging forward. Every so often a wave flicked around the porthole.

I would be on duty at eight, and there was an all-crew muster at 19.30. I filled my hot-water bottle straight after dinner, then realised my clean nightshirt was still down on the washing line in the galley stores area. I'd just have time to go and fetch it. I shrugged my jacket on and headed down into the banjer. The trainees were busy finishing their meal and searching for jackets, hats and gloves. Slipping through the chaos and into the black hole of the narrow stairs down to the centre of the ship, I gripped the handrail and felt my way down.

I met the first washing line, strung across the ship just above head height, as soon as I took a step from the bottom of the stairs. My items were on my right. There was enough light for me to see the white star pattern of my nightshirt among the flutter of T-shirts and socks. Switching on the light would spoil my night vision. I stood for a moment, waiting until my eyes got accustomed to the dimness.

In the silence, I heard a soft movement somewhere in the dark with me, and smelt that stale tobacco. My heart thumped. I felt out with one hand, along the wall, and switched the light on. The washing sprang up in front of me, glaring white against the dark tunnel.

Behind it, something moved.

I couldn't see who. The brightness had dazzled my dusk-accustomed eyes and I was still wincing away from it when a large, dark shape rushed towards me, knocked me aside so that I staggered against the wall, gave me a second shove onto the floor, and ran up the steps towards the deck. The thudding feet slowed to a saunter on the banjer steps. I picked myself up and charged after him.

I was too late. By the time I reached the deck, it was filled with trainees in their watch lines, hoods drawn up. Jenn was already in her place, smiling, and Captain Gunnar was overseeing us benevolently from the aft deck. His eye rested on me, flushed and late, and any idea I'd had of trying to talk to him about intruders withered instantly. Not here, not now, with the whole crew assembled. Just the thought of breaking ranks made me turn cold. I slid in beside Agnetha, heart thudding, and tried to steady my breathing. She gave me a sideways look. 'Did you forget the moments of awesome?' she murmured.

I had forgotten. My stomach lurched as if an octopus was dancing inside it. 'Moments of awesome' was part of Jenn's way of moulding us into a company, and I had to say that by the end of the voyage it worked, but the first couple of musters were toe-curling. Jenn was going to name people who'd been part of 'moments of awesome'. My Shetland upbringing winced at the thought of being hauled out in public like this. She named them, one moment from each watch. For ours, Erik had nominated the younger sister, Nora, for going out on the yards. Nils volunteered a youngster who'd steered an exceptionally straight course, and Agnetha's watch leader, Jonas, clapped a hand on the shoulder of a grinning boy who, he said, had been a star in the heads-cleaning. Then Jenn asked for moments from three of us. The teenagers rolled their eyes and the adults, reticent Norwegians, edged backwards. There was silence until Mike volunteered getting the engine off.

Looking at him in the grey light, for once he didn't look like someone who was bouncing with moments of awesome. There was a strained look to his skin, and lines under his eyes as if he'd not slept well. He was actually forty-six, but usually his energy made him seem ten years younger; today, you'd guess his age at nearer fifty. I remembered Klaudina's look, and wondered if she was putting pressure on him to give up this post for a life ashore. They had two boys, aged eight and six; maybe she wanted him to be home for them. If Gavin and I became permanent, if we ever wanted children, I'd have to leave the sea . . .

I came back to earth as Jenn dismissed everyone, and realised that I'd been so busy shutting out touchy-feeliness that I hadn't looked round for the broad-shouldered man. I looked now, as the watches were dispersing. The white and blue watches broke out of their lines, but mostly stayed put; I scanned the disappearing red watch as quickly as I could, and saw nobody that resembled him.

'He wasn't there,' Anders said, appearing beside me. 'I looked, while everyone was assembled.'

'You're sure?'

He nodded. 'He was an adult, and there are not so many men. He's not there.'

'I'll talk to the captain about him.'

I went into the officers' mess and knocked on the panelling at the side of the doorway into Captain Gunnar's combined bedroom and office. It was similar to mine, except larger, wide enough to have his desk set across the ship, with a red velvet settee beside it, and matching curtains screening his cabin bed. A little door led to his private bathroom. The room was empty.

I was due on watch. I'd mention it when Captain Gunnar came up to check our course.

The wind increased during our watch until we managed 4.3 knots, a brisk walking pace. A couple of the youngsters were on helm and standby first, with Olav on safety and Ben, the younger of the two brothers, forrard on lookout. He had an important job tonight, for the grey drizzle and cloudy skies meant visibility was poor, and first a fishing boat came charging out from the murk ahead of us, then an oil vessel, five times the length of *Sørlandet*, its blazing lights appearing only at fifteen minutes to collision time.

'I spotted the mystery man at breakfast this morning,' Olav said, coming up beside me, 'and again at tea tonight.'

I looked at him blankly. 'Mystery man?'

Olav nodded as if his head was on a spring. 'That's what Ellen and I call him, because he keeps himself to himself. If you say hello, he just nods and grunts, then turns away.'

'Oh?' I tried to sound casual, but he shot me a sharp look from his little eyes.

'Do you know the man I mean? He has iron-grey hair, cut short, and a Russian face. Broad shoulders, and a dark jacket, and he smells of tobacco.'

'I think I've seen him about.' My casual tone was better this time. We didn't need rumours going round the trainees about mysterious stowaways. I suddenly remembered the man I'd bumped into at the Fiskbrabaren, yesterday morning. He had smelt of stale tobacco too. A Russian face . . . *known to the police.* My heart went cold. Olav was watching my face; I forced a smile. 'He's not on our watch, so I don't know his name. Maybe his Norwegian's not very good.'

'I thought that too, the first time, so I tried him with English. That didn't work either.'

I managed a laugh. 'Maybe he just doesn't speak at all first thing in the morning.'

'I'm not sure what watch he is on. He had his jacket on for tea, so that looked like the white watch, except he wasn't with them just now when they lined up.'

'He's a smoker,' I said. 'Maybe he'd just come in from deck, or was desperate to get out there again. It's a strange habit, isn't it?'

Olav wasn't to be diverted. 'He's a strange man. I'll keep an eye on him.'

That had me flummoxed. I didn't want to rush into saying, 'No, don't, steer well clear of him,' because that would start all sorts of rumours. I kept up the casual tone. 'I'm sure he'll open out soon. Maybe he's just shy.' Inspiration struck. 'Or seasick. People hate to admit to that, and it does make you feel awful.'

I was saved by Sindre striking two bells. I verified our course and gave it to Nora, then escaped to think it over as I scanned the radar for ships and ticked off the passing lights: Vibberodden, Eigerøy. With glasses, I could just make out the lower flashes of Grunnesundholmen in the channel behind. Next would be the two Hå lighthouses. I re-checked them in my pilot's book: Kvassheim was red, green, white directional, occulting eight seconds, and Obrestad was white, thirty seconds. I might just spot Kvassheim before handover, and soon after that the ship would tack, and head west, across the North Sea.

I was worried. If that Russian I'd bumped into was on board, if he was the man Sergeant Hansen had warned us about, then I needed to talk to the captain about him. We could still stop in Stavanger. On the other hand, if I was wrong, if the man was a legitimate trainee, then my name would be beneath mud. I spent the next hour worrying about it, but knew in the end that I had to say something. This was Captain Gunnar's decision, not mine.

When the captain came up to check our progress, I glanced around us, then murmured, 'Captain, I have a concern. Can I talk to you as soon as possible?'

He gave me a sharp look. 'The morning will not do?'

I shook my head. 'I don't think so.' I sank my voice to a murmur. 'Sergeant Hansen's problem.'

He understood straight away. 'Very well. Immediately after the change of watch.'

It was a long watch, grey and cold, and by the end of it even the keenest trainees were huddled under the boat deck, hoods pulled down. They lined up at double speed and disappeared down the hatch like puffins into their burrows.

I hung my jacket inside my cabin and knocked at the officers' mess door. 'Captain?'

He motioned me into the saloon, and waited.

'I think the sergeant's stowaway is aboard.'

His white eyebrows shot upwards. 'You're sure it's not one of the young people playing a prank by smuggling a friend along?'

I shook my head. 'An adult. Broad-shouldered, strong. One of the trainees described him as Russian-looking. He wears a dark jacket, and I think he's lurking down in the tunnels.' I explained what had happened, and Captain Gunnar listened, one hand tugging at his moustache. When I'd finished he was silent for a moment, then he looked straight at me, eyes stern. 'You are sure of all this?'

I nodded.

His brows drew together. 'If we have to divert to Stavanger . . .'

He didn't need to finish the sentence. If we diverted to Stavanger, and no stowaway was found, my head was on the chopping block.

He gave a long sigh. 'Very well. Say nothing for the moment. I must phone Sergeant Hansen. I'll make an announcement to everyone in the morning.'

'Sir,' I agreed. I left him frowning into space and headed for the peace and quiet of my cabin. Cat lifted his head as I came in, then snuggled it down again. The waves shushed against the ship's side, and soft feet padded on deck above me. I heard Agnetha giving orders to the helm. I squeezed my feet down past Cat and Rat, and curled up around them, enjoying their warmth, then reached for my phone.

Gavin answered at the first ring. 'Cass, *halo leat*! I thought you'd be out of phone reach in the North Sea.'

'You mean you're not calibrating my mobile to see?'

He laughed at that. 'No, I don't have you on a tagging app. It wouldn't be able to cope. What's worrying you?'

'I don't only phone when I'm worried.' It was disconcerting that he could read me so accurately.

I could hear the smile in his voice. 'The worry's in your voice, like water finding a pebble in its way. Go on.'

'We're maybe going to stop in Stavanger.'

'Oh?'

I explained. I could imagine him nodding as he listened. 'So I don't know what to wish for,' I finished. 'Stowaway or not. Not, I suppose.'

'Not would be best for the ship,' Gavin agreed. 'And your captain struck me as a sensible man. He won't blame you for putting safety first.'

'Better safe than sorry,' I agreed.

'You will keep away from the tunnels?'

'No reason for me to be down there now.' I just hoped it would all turn out for the best, and changed the subject. 'How was your damp stake-out . . . ?'

TWO BELLS

Stavanger

Saturday 27th June

CHAPTER FOUR

Captain Gunnar got the whole crew together over breakfast. 'What I am about to say is confidential.' His eyes rested on Erik, who was nearest the door. He gave it a significant look. Erik nodded, and closed it behind him. Instantly the room felt too small, the air stuffy. My stomach squirmed uneasily. 'I have a disturbing suspicion,' he began, heavily, 'that we have a stowaway aboard.'

The crew glanced around each other. Mike's face was closed, unsurprised; they'd obviously discussed this earlier. Agnetha was frowning, as if she was trying to visualise all the faces she'd seen; beside her, Erik stared at Captain Gunnar, mouth open. Nils gave a sour, secretive smile.

'Unfortunately,' Captain Gunnar continued, 'this may well be more than just a teenager who thinks it would be amusing to run away to sea. I called Sergeant Hansen this morning. The man that we were warned about before leaving Kristiansand is extremely dangerous. He must not be approached. For that reason, I am not going to search the ship while we have trainees aboard. He may well be lurking in the tunnels. I do not wish any of you to go there. Remain within the well-lit areas of the ship, and do not go anywhere that is little used.'

He paused to look around us, brows drawn together. We nodded, and he continued. 'I have diverted our course to Stavanger, ETA 11.00. We will tell the trainees that we had extra time, and let them off to explore. We too will come off, and give the special forces leave to search the ship from stem to stern. Watches are suspended until they have finished. I will remain with them, to make sure they have seen everything. I would like everyone else to wait ashore while the police search. We do not want any possibility of a hostage situation.'

'I've had that feeling, now,' Mike said, 'of there being one more aboard than I can account for.' Rolf nodded in agreement. Nils remained still, watching.

'Naturally, a team of policemen coming aboard will look a little strange. If you are questioned you should say that Stavanger customs are concerned about people smuggling, and all vessels are being searched in this way.' For the first time, he smiled. 'For extra verisimilitude, you can complain about how over the top it is. Our departure from Stavanger will be 17.00, with all crew to be aboard at 15.00, and all trainees at 16.00. There will be a morning muster at 8.00, and I will announce these times.'

He nodded dismissal at the other ranks, and we officers ate our oatmeal and drank our yoghurt in a heavy silence. Cat wouldn't like it, but he'd better go into his basket until we left the ship together, just to make sure I could lay my hands on him when I needed him; Rat too. I didn't want either of them shot by a trigger-happy Norwegian special forces patrol officer.

I left the table as soon as I could, still feeling queasy. There was nothing in the ship's motion to account for it; the white watch had stowed some of the sails away in the early hours, so that we didn't arrive in Stavanger too soon, and we were rolling gently along under the two topsails on each mast. Still, seasickness was like that. You could ride out the worst of gales unaffected, then feel awful because a slight swell was hitting the ship at just the wrong angle. We'd be in Stavanger too soon for it to be worth taking a Stugeron.

I took a deep breath of fresh air and leant on the rail to look around. The sea was oily calm, wrinkled with the great sea swell that had swept all the way across the Atlantic. Looking along the coast, I could just see Feistein's imposing red and white striped tower. From here, it was pilotage rather than navigation: Mike had set our course to come up outside the Kvitsøy cluster of islands, so that all we had to do was pass them, and the next three islands, all joined by too low a bridge for our beautiful ship to pass under, until we had clear water to turn right and thread our way back into Stavanger harbour.

My watch was starting to gather on deck now. The four physicals were sent to their stations, and Olav, Ludwig and Nine headed below for galley duty. Erik began organising those who were left into sail-handling groups, one for each mast. There were clinking noises as the harnesses were put on and checked, then Erik, Petter and Mona each took a group and headed upwards into the spider's web rigging. I watched as each dark figure clipped on, then shuffled along the wire suspended under each yard. The crew went first each time, out to the end of the spar, where the sea was giddily far below, and directed operations from there – untying the bunt rope and letting it fall, then gathering up the heavy sail in folds, rolling it inwards until it was all secured, and tying it up.

While they were doing that, I checked the final passage into Stavanger, and roughed out a plan for getting out again, then the course that would take us across the North Sea to the Pentland Firth, between Orkney and Scotland. We'd leave on Nils's watch, so of course he'd change it, but it satisfied me to have done it. A fair boy from Agnetha's watch came in just as I was finishing. 'Kjell Sigurd,' he introduced himself. 'How do you like your coffee?'

'Black,' I said, 'and not too strong.'

He brought it within minutes, and a couple of biscuits, then headed off to work his way round the helm, standby and safety.

It was a good hour before the last trainee came down the ratlines. All the trainees were on deck now, in a long line along the shoreward rail, gazing at the Atlantic-polished rock and the clefts of green trees sheltering white wood houses, each with its own jetty. There was a buzz of excitement about going ashore. Far ahead, the roofs and offices of Stavanger glinted in the sun. I noticed Sean below me, checking our position on Google and sharing it with the man beside him.

Mike came up beside me. He too had a mug and biscuit in hand. 'Someone was saying that's your cousin, the dark Irishman down there.'

I nodded. 'Sean Lynch. Me dad's brother's son.'

Mike leant on the rail, looking down, brows drawn together. 'I'm thinking I recognise his face. Is it Cork your family's from?'

I shook my head. 'Dublin. Me grandda was a builder there.' I turned, and leant back against the rail. 'We used to spend family Christmases there. But of course he may have been living in Belfast since then.'

'Ah, Dublin! It's a beautiful city. I'm a Cork man meself.' He was still frowning, then he turned away, shaking his head. 'No. It's on the tip of me tongue, so it is, but I can't quite get it.' He straightened up. 'Still, we're about the same age, so we might have met as youngsters.' He flashed his smile at me, rueful. 'I was a bit

66

wild at that age, worried me poor folks ragged, until they sent me off to family in Massachusetts.'

'If you were a bit wild, you could well have met Sean,' I said.

The worry still clouded his face, but he made an effort to speak jauntily. 'All set to steer us straight into Stavanger, then?'

'Like a swallow to its nest.' I touched wood automatically, though Stavanger was *Sørlandet's* other home port, and she could practically sail herself into the quay. Bang on cue, Captain Gunnar came up to the aft deck to take over, and nodded to Petter to take the wheel. Anders stationed himself by the engine controls. Only I could see how nervous he was. I gave his shoulder a reassuring pat as I passed. Now we'd steer by visuals: a point to port, two to starboard. I'd stay by the navigation screen, but I didn't expect to be needed. Below me, Rolf was getting the man-overboard boat ready to launch so that *Sørlandet* would have some of her own crew ashore ready to take her lines. Erik began organising trainees to stand by with fenders and lower the gangplank. Faces stared at us from the moored cruise liner, cameras flashed, and I felt my usual surge of pride. Normally, coming into a port in my little *Khalida*, I was the smallest, oldest boat, and got sneered at by the gin-drinkers in their shiny white blobs; but even the most expensive new Swedish cruiser didn't outrank *Sørlandet*. She was the queen of the harbour. I was like Cat on his bench, I thought, and laughed at myself.

The port came up around us: wooden houses stretching back from the sea, white, pink, red-brown, with the glass-walled offices of modern Stavanger behind them. The man-overboard boat buzzed around *Sørlandet* like a duckling circling a swan, then headed for the quay and tied up. Slowly, carefully, we manoeuvred *Sørlandet* to the tyre-hung jetty.

A movement below caught my eye. Still looking at the quay like all the other trainees, Sean was backing away from the rail until he was clear of the others. I knew the look on his face. He was pursuing some plan. Once he was two steps behind them, he turned and went swiftly down the banjer steps. From my height on the aft deck, I saw him descend, but he didn't turn left or right into the banjer; his head kept going straight down. He was making for the next deck, the pantry, rope stores and the tunnels, where the stowaway was holed up. *I only signed on today* . . . to help the Russian get aboard, and keep him out of sight? What had my cousin Sean turned out as?

Now the ship was only two metres from the quay. Nils's ABs threw the lines ashore, Rolf and Mona made them fast on the bollards, and gradually *Sørlandet* was winched in until her white sides jammed the fenders against the tyres. I kept an eye on the door to the banjer. Halfway through the berthing, Sean came out again, hands empty, face satisfied, and sidled back to the rail, as if he'd merely changed places for a better view.

Erik and his team manoeuvred the gangplank over the ship's side and down to the quay, then there was an all-hands muster. Jenn reminded the trainees of the time they had to be back aboard and stationed herself with the passports box by the gangplank. There was a shuffling round into alphabetical order. The social workers in charge of the young people gave a last warning talk about what they weren't allowed to do ashore, and then Erik took off the 'Crew only' sign, and they filed off into the arms of the waiting customs officials.

It was a fairly cursory check, a glance at passport, face, wave on. Sean stood like a lamb, cracking jokes, then took his passport and sauntered off, hands in his pockets, not a care in the world. I knew that innocent look. The other adults followed in groups, chatting and eyeing up the coffee shops on the quay. A voice floated up to me, '. . . drinking chocolate with cream on top.' I sympathised with that one, but thought I'd resist it. I'd been feeling bloated these last few days. A walk with Cat up the hill and around the lake would be more like it.

There was no sign of the man in the dark jacket. Once Jenn had handed out our passports, her box was empty.

The police gave the trainees half an hour to get off the boat, and then they arrived, a dozen of them, dressed in black and grey jackets and black helmets with visors. Each one carried a machine gun and had a pair of backup pistols in his belt. As well as the normal red and gold police badge, they had the Delta triangle on their shoulder: the Emergency Response Unit. If our stowaway had any sense, he'd come straight out with his hands up.

They waited on the quay, faces grim, while the crew gathered together on the main deck. Anders had Rat with him, snuggled on one shoulder. I nipped to my cabin to release Cat, and carried him back up with his harness and lead on. I could see how uneasy we all felt about this invasion of our beautiful ship. We'd all seen too many action movies of the special squad bursting in, with boots kicking doors open and rifle butts smashing windows. We knew it was absurd; we wouldn't come back to find the ship trashed. No, it was an uneasiness with this world of violence suddenly breaking into our peace of waves and open sky. Erik was so white he looked as if he might be sick. Agnetha kept tugging her collar up around her chin and hunching down into it as if it could protect her; beside her, Rolf tugged his black hat down to his brows. Mike's face was drawn into long, downward lines. He went forward to Agnetha and spoke softly. She shook her head as if he'd asked her a question, and stepped closer to Erik. Nils's little eyes were darting everywhere. Anders had a hand on Rat's plush coat, as if for reassurance.

Captain Gunnar looked around us. 'Mike, Rolf: you remain with the officers at the foot of the gangplank. Once

69

the special forces have gone, trainees may come back aboard.'

The customs men weren't bothered about crew; they were already leaving as we got ourselves off the ship. Anders took Rat under his collar, I picked Cat up, and we headed down the gangplank.

'He did not go off,' Anders said.

'No,' I agreed. My throat felt choked and there was a heaviness in my chest.

Erik and Agnetha came off the ship after us, steps matching. She had her arm through his. I remembered Olav's questions, and felt a squirm of unease in my stomach. They headed up towards the town centre.

'I'll take Cat up to the lake. He can run around there. Coming?'

Anders shook his head. 'I want to phone Johanna, while we have a good signal.'

Aha! 'Say hi from me, and I hope she's feeling better.' I'd phone Gavin once the search was over.

I threaded my way upwards between white-painted wooden houses, across the main road below the twin-towered cathedral and into the gardens beyond it. They were bright with summer plantings: scarlet, orange, yellow. I unclipped Cat's lead and walked briskly up one side of the lake, with him bounding alongside, then back to the gravel sweep bordering the lake, where there were flocks of pigeons for him to scatter. A little bandstand overlooked the lake, its pitched tile roof topped by a supercilious seagull. I followed Cat around the back of it and sat down on the warm stone surround, legs stretched out towards the lake. Traditional houses ran along one side of the water, turned now into one restaurant/cafe, with tables on a balcony and the Norwegian flag fluttering against the white wall, all picturesque and peaceful. I breathed the land-scented air deeply and tried not to think about the intruders aboard *Sørlandet*.

Cat crouched low on the gravel and began stalking his way around the bandstand. His tail waved as he pounced. There was a flap and rattle as the pigeons rose into the air, then Cat went charging past me into the bushes. He was moving too fast for me to be sure, but I feared there were wings flapping from his mouth. I rose and went after him. I didn't want to spoil his fun, but I liked to know where he was, in case he got his harness hooked on something. There were agitated sounds from the undergrowth. A branch waggled, as if something had jumped against it. I sighed and went around to sit on the grass, near enough to see Cat coming out again, but not close enough to hear any crunching noises. In front of me, the fountain sparkled in the air, making a rainbow shower. A flock of seagulls bobbed around it.

I was just contemplating the lavender bushes in the little beds between me and the lake, and wondering if I should interfere with Cat, when I heard Agnetha's voice, clear and defiant. 'I'm not going to change my mind.'

It seemed to come from right behind me. I twisted my head and saw two pairs of cargo breeks at the other side of the bush, standing, as if they'd strolled down to a good view of the lake, and were going to talk there. Now what could I do? I was tensing myself to rise up and come around the bush with a cheery '*Hei!*' when I heard a choked sob. Agnetha spoke again, her voice muffled. 'Oh, never mind me, my hormones are just all over the place. It's not surprising.'

'But it does show,' Erik said, 'that you're not happy about it.' His voice made it clear that he wasn't happy about it either. 'Look, you have plenty of time to really think it over. A baby's a big decision.'

'It's not a baby yet.'

'But it's not a nothing either. Look, I've had kids; I know. You

71

have no idea . . . that first scan, when we saw Alexander's face, he was only five months, and yet that was him already. We look back now and see his features.'

'Another child.' Her voice was bitter. 'So what do you say to your wife? "I've been having this affair with a woman on board ship, and she's pregnant." That'll go down well.'

Eric's voice remained level. 'Of course it won't. But if it has to be done . . .'

'It doesn't have to be done.' Her voice muted as she turned away. 'I'm not turning into a housewife with playdates and mother-and-toddler groups, and stepkids every second—' She broke off in a rustling of leaves and flapping of wings as the pigeon took off across the gravel, with Cat in hot pursuit. I stumbled to my feet and hurried forward, back bent until I was safely out of earshot and could straighten up to casual contemplation of the lake. Cat stalked back to the bandstand, obviously thinking poorly of a deity that gave food the unfair advantage of wings, and focused on the pigeons once more.

I needed to forget I'd heard this conversation. In just ten minutes, I'd be back at the ship. I needed to meet Agnetha with a clear look. I kept my back turned to them, only checking up on Cat from the corner of my eyes, until at last I sensed them moving away, and turned to see them heading back up the slope and round the square-towered corner of the cathedral. Erik's hand was on Agnetha's shoulder, but she walked apart from him, arms swinging free.

I let Cat chase pigeons for a bit longer, then I began to stroll shipwards, up past the creamy yellow house with the grey window frames, past the fuchsia-pink rhododendrons, an ivy-covered tree, a black iron lamp post, and over the top of the hill to see the harbour spread out below me, the cruise ship on the left and

Sørlandet's masts soaring on the right. We sauntered back down via one of the old cobbled streets, with red-tiled roofs pitching down over wooden walls and yellow poppies thrusting from the cracks between wall and pavement. At the end of it, the bridge raised its double triangle of rigging. Cat trotted ahead of me on his lead, plumed tail held high, pausing every so often to prod a drain with his paw or pat a piece of paper in the gutter.

I was determined not to think of Agnetha and Erik, but of course I couldn't help it. Agnetha's peakiness at breakfast time was explained. I wondered how far on that made her. I had a vague notion that some women were sick all through pregnancy, while others didn't suffer at all. It was going to be hard for her over the next few months. I supposed the ship would be in her winter quarters by the time the baby was actually due, but what then? Was Erik really going to leave Micaela and his other children? Yet Agnetha hadn't sounded as if that was what she wanted. I remembered the scorn in her voice: *Playdates and mother-and-toddler groups* . . . Was she planning to continue as ship's officer, baby and all? I supposed she'd get the standard maternity leave, but then what? The baby could be with her in her cabin at first, I supposed, as she walked the after-deck, no further away than a child in a bedroom cot while its mother cooked in the kitchen. It would depend on how Captain Gunnar's successor took it. But once it could crawl, then toddle, it wouldn't be easy. Perhaps she could employ an au pair to live aboard. If she was determined to hold on to her job, then she'd arrange things somehow – and I knew she would be that determined.

And Micaela . . . I understood her air of concealed worry now. Erik was her world, he and the children and their house by the sea, with its little jetty and productive garden. Even as I tried not to think about it, I didn't believe it. If Erik and Micaela weren't proof against separation, then no relationship was. I felt a cold clutch at my heart. Could Gavin and I manage, somehow, to forge a joint life with me at sea much of the time, as Erik was, or was it just not possible?

We came out into the harbour space. Anders was still sitting at the cafe table. He saw me coming out and raised a hand. Cat started off towards the ship's gangplank. I picked him up and slid into the seat opposite Anders. 'How is she?'

'Home now, and feeling much better, though sore around the stitches. She says hi.'

I nodded my chin at the ship. 'Have they come off yet?'

Anders shook his head. 'Nearly. They're working from stem to stern.'

I listened, and heard thumps and clanks as paint pots were moved in the forrard store, followed by heavy feet on the ladder down to the anchor locker. A voice asked a question, and another replied. There was a long pause, then tramping on the decks, and the men appeared from under the foredeck and gathered in the waist of the ship. Their black uniforms were flecked with dried paint and greyed with dust. Their leader went up to the aft deck, where Captain Gunnar was waiting. I felt an uneasy feeling in the pit of my stomach. There was a low-voiced conversation, with a good deal of shaking heads.

The long search had found nobody.

CHAPTER FIVE

The squad marched down the gangplank and headed for their rank of black vans. At the table next to us, Nils and his ABs rose. I let Cat off his lead and he bounded ahead of them back on board, jumped up on a bench and began washing his paws. Anders and I headed for the officers' galley, where Anders made a sandwich while I buttered myself some ryebread, and added a couple of slices of ham and cheese and a gherkin. 'D'you want to bring it into my cabin?'

He nodded, and followed me through. I gestured him to the table, but he shook his head, and we sat side by side on the cushioned bunk-settee, plates balanced on our knees. I put some ham in Cat's dish, and he and Rat shared it, then swarmed up together onto the berth and cleaned whiskers in a contented huddle. 'They like being together,' Anders said.

I nodded, absently, and we munched for a while in silence. 'He *was* on board,' I said, at last. 'And he didn't get off. We both watched the trainees leave.'

'He didn't get off,' Anders agreed. 'All the others did. They all behaved perfectly normally, except for . . .' He gave me an awkward glance.

'My cousin Sean. I know.' I frowned. 'He was up to something. Hiding something, maybe? *Someone*? I watched him go below. He went right down to the pantry area.'

'You think that he might have something to do with this man?'

'I don't know. But if he was hiding him, how did he manage to spirit him off the ship?'

'Could a boat have taken him off during the night, unseen?' We considered that one, looking at each other, then both shook our heads. 'I don't see how,' Anders answered himself. 'For a start it's light enough all night to see something approaching, and we were sailing, so we'd have heard it too.'

I agreed. 'If he was taken off by a boat, the lookout deserves keel-hauling. To say nothing of all the people on deck.'

'As we arrived in port, when everyone was looking the other way?'

'Maybe . . . there were other boats coming in and out of the harbour. If he doubled a rope around a ratline to shin down to water level, I suppose he could have got off like that. He'd have been seen, of course, from the other boats, but they'd just think it was one of these things tall ships do.'

'The man was certainly aboard,' Anders repeated. 'We were both sure of that.' He ate his last piece of bread and rose. 'And now he is not, so we can relax and have a peaceful voyage to Belfast. I must check they've done nothing to our engine.'

Our engine; his and Johanna's. 'See you later.'

I shifted Cat and Rat enough to lie down on my bunk myself, and got my mobile out. Five bars, and it was half past one in Scotland now; definitely Gavin's lunch hour, if he was having one.

He answered on the first ring. 'Cass, *halo leat*!' His voice warmed me. 'Did they find the stowaway?'

'Oh, Gavin, I'm in the doghouse. A squad of Special Force men just searched from stem to stern, and found nothing.' I felt my voice rising, and lowered it. 'He didn't go ashore, so the only thing that I can think of is that he somehow got off the ship before she landed.'

He was silent for a moment. 'Tricky. But, Cass, the captain will have thought of that too. You acted for the safety of the ship.'

'I know,' I said, drearily. 'And I suspect my cousin Sean is involved somehow.' I described the way he'd slipped below just as the ship had docked. 'He was just so casually furtive, you know. Butter wouldn't have melted.'

'Would it be helpful if I had a look for him in our computer system?'

I thought about that for a moment, with memories of all the trouble he'd got into in our teens galloping through my head. 'No. No, don't. He's family. If the Irish police are after him, they can get him when we reach Belfast – if they can catch him.'

Gavin's voice went serious. 'If he's wanted by the Northern Ireland Constabulary, it won't be for a parking ticket.' He paused, and I thought for a moment he was going to remind me I'd be an accessory, but he went straight to the important bit of the dilemma. 'The Troubles are far from over in Ireland. Do you want a death on your conscience?'

'No.' I thought of things Sean could be involved in: gun-dealing, drugs, planting bombs. He was family, but if he was involved in something like that, his innocent victims had to take precedence over kinship. 'No. Look him up. But if the police are going to be waiting on the quay, then don't tell me. You know what a poor liar I am.'

'I do indeed. Give me two seconds.' I heard his fingers click on computer keys. 'E-A-N or with an H?'

'S-E-A-N.'

'Nothing so far. Hang on.' The keys squished again. 'Nothing. No. I don't think he's there.'

'He just hasn't been caught yet,' I said, but I was relieved.

'Is that all the worries?'

I cast a quick glance at the curtain hanging in front of the door space. 'Agnetha, you remember her? Second mate. Tall, fair.'

'A high-flyer.'

'Yes, that's her. But it's something I overheard. I didn't mean to listen; it was one of those awkward things.' With another glance at the curtain, I lowered my voice. 'It sounded like she's having an affair with Erik, you know, my watch leader, and she's expecting his baby. It's all horrid.'

There was a pause while he considered that. Above my head, footsteps padded softly. 'She looked like a career girl to me, and Eric and, what's his wife, Manuela?'

'Micaela.' They'd invited us up for a meal while Gavin was over, seven weeks ago, Micaela's best fiery cooking.

'They seemed like a devoted couple. Are you sure you haven't got the wrong end of the stick?'

I turned my head away from the door, and spoke softly. 'She said she wasn't going to change her mind. That was the first thing I heard. Then she said something about her hormones being all over the place. Then he said that she had plenty of time to think it over, a baby was a big decision. Neither of them sounded happy. He was speaking about his children, how you could see their faces in the scan, and then they spoke about telling his wife. He said it had to be done, and she disagreed. She said she wasn't going to turn into a housewife with a toddler.'

'Sounds more like she wants to bring the baby up on her own.'

'That's what I thought. He wanted to tell Micaela and move in with Agnetha, and she didn't want that.'

'Or that she wanted to have an abortion.'

I hadn't thought of that. Now Gavin had said it, it was blindingly obvious. I tried the conversation again in my head, and nodded. 'Yes. She's headed for captain level. But would she want her career that much?' Even as I asked the question, I heard the answer in my head. Yes, she did.

'Some people really do see a baby as a collection of cells until it's born. Well, not quite that, perhaps, but as something that isn't properly alive yet.' He considered that for a moment, then added, 'Well, a lot of people. The whole developed world doesn't see abortion as murder. It's an in-out clinic visit.'

I'd never been in the situation, so I hadn't thought about it. I'd taken the church's view for granted: a child had a right to protection from conception onwards. 'I'd never thought about it.'

'But you're not one of the "it's my body" women?' He was trying to keep his voice casual, but I could hear it mattered to him. I thought hard before answering, trying to imagine a child growing like a seed within me.

'It is my body, of course, but it's the child's body too. I don't have rights over that.'

Gavin said, tentatively, 'I'd like to have a family.'

It was strange how it was easier to talk on the phone. In Shetland, I'd regularly looked after my best pal Inga's three-year-old, Peerie Charlie. I tried to envisage myself with a tribe of Peerie Charlies tumbling around my feet. Life ashore, in a house, with regular meals, and a story at bedtime. *Playdates and mother-and-toddler groups* . . . Maybe in a few years I'd be ready to give up wandering and become normal, the selkie wife giving up the sea to live ashore with her fisherman. I knew what had happened to her; she'd pined for the sea, and when she found her skin she ran off without a second glance. I tried to answer as honestly as I could. 'I'm not against it, in principle. I enjoy messing about with Peerie Charlie. I think I'm good with young people. I'd just never imagined myself living ashore. Give me time to think about it. I've only just got home. A few more years of wandering.' Even as I said it, I remembered I was thirty. In five years I'd be in danger of leaving it too late. 'Two or three years anyway. Let's talk about it when we're together.' I tried to lighten the tone. 'Are you still all set to join us in Belfast?'

'All set. All annual leave being cancelled doesn't happen as often in real life as it does in detective stories. Until then, I'll follow you on the Sail Training website, and wave as you pass the nearest point to me. Are you coming between the islands?'

'Between Orkney and the mainland, then between the outer Hebrides and Skye.'

'The Pentland Firth and the Minch, Scotland's two most notorious stretches of water.'

'It's a shorter way.' I smiled. 'The Viking way to Ireland.' I changed the subject. 'What's the news with you? How's the growth in the fields?'

'Och, it's good.' His voice quickened as he talked of his land world, and I listened, and heard how much he loved it. The hills were in his bones as the sea was in mine. His grandmother's croft was ready and waiting for his summer holidays. I hadn't yet seen the cottage, but he'd described it: simple, pine-lined rooms, lit by Tilley lamps. I could imagine him there, steadying the boat for a pair of russet-headed kilted boys to clamber into. I thought I would like them to be mine too; just to be sure, I tried imagining another mother – his Shetland sidekick Sergeant

Peterson, for example – and was startled by the wave of rage that swept through me.

He paused for breath. 'Have you got the sheep clipped yet?' I asked. I did know about sheep; the Shetland sheep population was ten times that of the human.

'Last weekend, so that I'd be free to come to you. Well, good luck.' His voice warmed. 'Don't worry, Cass. Your captain knows you're good.'

I felt better for his faith in me. 'I'll speak to you in a couple of days, once we get near enough to Scotland.'

'Yes, I'll speak to you then. Have a safe journey, Cass. *Beannachd leat, mo chridhe.*'

Blessings on you. I replied in broad Shetlandic. 'Tak care o deesel. Spik tae dee shune.'

I put the phone away and lay back, feeling restless. They hadn't found the man. He'd got himself off somehow. Agnetha and Erik weren't my problem. Sean was. I could go and look down below, to see if there was anything out of place, any sign of what he'd been up to. I swung my legs down, ignoring Cat's faint growl at being disturbed, and headed towards the banjer steps.

Several of the trainees had come back on board and were making themselves at home. There would be a lot of items in Jenn's 'left lying about' bag before the ship set sail: mobile phones complete with charger cords, a couple of towels, a book, a hat and gloves, a jacket. I said hello to the group of card players around the table nearest the hatch as I passed, and headed down the pantry steps.

The light was already on, so that I could see the two rows of washing in the corridor crossways to the ship, and the long tunnels stretching into blackness each side of her. I felt a reluctance to go down there, and a shiver down my spine as if I might still be being watched. They'd found nothing, I reminded myself, and focused on my cousin. What might Sean have been doing below here? Hiding something, was the obvious conclusion, something he didn't want to be caught with on his way ashore, and something he didn't want to leave in his locker, in case the customs searched those. Something pocket-sized; he'd gone and returned empty-handed.

I sighed and cast a look along the port tunnel. There were dozens of places to hide something: the long rows of wide shelves, stuffed with spare sails, canvas and rope, the grey-fronted boxes, the lidded lockers beneath. Still, everything would have been securely stowed for a ship at sea, liable to tilt on her beam ends at any moment. I should be able to see if something had been disturbed. I began at the far end of this section, and peered at each shelf. A thin layer of dust lay over most of it. Beyond the Rope Store door, the shelves were narrower, but without lifting every coil of rope I couldn't see what was at the back of them. If it was something small he'd hidden, we'd need to take the ship apart to find it, without even knowing what we were looking for.

All the same, I had no feeling of anything being disturbed here, and the bulkhead leading forward to the carpenter's store would have been closed while we were at sea.

The pantry next. This was a neat, narrow room running across the ship, shelved around, and in constant use with the galley girls coming up and down to collect stores, or slice cold meat and cheese. The shelves were stacked with tins, jars, cartons and packets of rice and pasta, with not an inch to squeeze anything between. Openwork crates of bananas covered the floor. I had a quick look in the cupboards below the shelves, but I didn't expect to find anything here. Sean hadn't known that the crew too would be chucked off the ship to let the men in black search; he'd have expected the galley girls to be making lunch as usual, and we all knew that routine by now, with plates of meat and cheese and vats of pickles and herring being brought up the stairs. No, he wouldn't have put anything in here.

The pantry led into the cold store. I opened the door, walked in and closed it behind me. The shelves here were stainless steel, floor to ceiling, filled with all the perishables a ship's crew would need for a week: potatoes, onions, carrots, cauliflowers and courgettes, watermelon and apples; long blocks of cheese and cardboard boxes of the cherry drinking yoghurt; buckets of pickled herring, onion, sauerkraut; condiment jars. I went around slowly, checking everything. There were four white boxes, unlabelled, like expanded foam wine crates. I couldn't open them without taking them out, but a hand under them suggested they were light enough to be empty.

The only place left was the walk-in freezer. The door was stiff, and it took me a couple of tries to get it open. The cold flowed towards me, glittering in the air. He wouldn't have lingered in here, or risked the door closing on him. I looked quickly at the shelves within arm's reach, keeping the door open, then backed out again.

That left the starboard tunnel. The passage this side was wider, the shelves so narrow that you could see the ship's white sides behind them, patterned by rows of 'widow-makers', the heavy pulleys that halved the load on the ropes. I walked slowly along the shelves, looking. Nothing, nothing, until, at the very end, there was the shadow of a smear in the dust, as if a sleeve had brushed it. I reached in, feeling between the wooden blocks, and touched metal. My fingers groped over the smooth barrel, the cross-hatched grip, then closed around the handle and drew it out into the light.

I would have taken it for a child's toy if it wasn't for the deadly weight of it in my hand. It was black metal, lighter along the top, darker below, with *LOCK* underlined in a circle, then *17 AUSTRIA* stamped along the barrel. There was no obvious round chamber for putting bullets in, which I supposed made it an automatic. I also supposed it was loaded.

It had no business aboard. Just looking at it made me feel sick. I felt the scar on my cheek burn. If my lover, Alain, hadn't insisted on having a gun aboard, he couldn't have shot at me, halfway across the Atlantic . . . if he hadn't had the gun, I'd have found some way to calm him down. He'd still have been alive. My heart thudded as if I was still out there, in the grey waste of sea, with Alain's gun pointing at me, his voice telling me to leave his ship. I never wanted to see a gun again, ever. This *thing* was going into the harbour as soon as I got upstairs, into the sea, where it could do no harm. My cousin Sean could whistle for it. Holding it by the handle, with the barrel pointing away from me, I'd got as far as the steps when I realised what a sensation going outside with a gun in my hand would cause.

I stopped and took several breaths, until my heart rate steadied. I needed to be sensible about this. Another couple of breaths made me realise, reluctantly, that I couldn't just get rid of it and say nothing. The right thing to do was to give it to Captain Gunnar . . . and a pretty set of explanations that would be, especially after the stowaway search that had found nothing. I squared my shoulders, and prepared for life to get difficult. I made a face at the heavy gun dangling from my hand. It wasn't going in my pocket. There'd be something in the pantry that I could carry the thing in.

I was just putting it into an empty herring tub when I heard footsteps above my head. Someone was coming down to this level, not one of the galley girls, but someone with a purposeful, heavy tread. I straightened up quickly, heart thumping. I had no real excuse for being in there, but there was no way out except the door I'd come in. I decided to brazen it out. I was looking for something for a late lunch. Potatoes and cheese, a jacket potato, done in the aft galley's microwave. I dodged back into the cold store, picked out a potato of the right size and returned to the door, lidded bucket carried over one arm, brandishing my alibi before me.

The footsteps stopped at the pantry door, waiting. I could imagine the person looking around, up the tunnels, to see where I'd gone. Then the feet began to move towards the cold store. I jerked open the door, and found myself nose to nose with Captain Gunnar.

He was as startled as I was. We each fell back a step and stood for a moment just staring at each other. I could see he wasn't in a good mood. The jovial Victorian captain was gone; his white brows were drawn together, his mouth a steel line. I murmured 'Sir,' and stood back to let him pass.

He regained his composure with an effort. 'Cass, what are you doing down here?'

I opened my mouth but couldn't find the words to begin.

His dark eyes considered me, moved down to the potato in my hand, flicked behind me to the storeroom, travelled round and returned to my face. 'The police found nobody.'

'I know, sir. I'm sorry.'

He didn't ask me if I was sure the man had been aboard, which comforted me a little. 'We're not popular with Special Branch. Nor with the office. A diversion for nothing.' His eyes flicked behind me again, looking at something down in the corner where the unlabelled white boxes were, then flicked back to the herring tub. 'Potato and pickled herring for lunch?'

'No, sir.' Hell's teeth, why did this have to happen to me? I was going to have to explain, and he wasn't going to believe I'd found a gun, just like that. He'd think I was mad, not the sort of person you'd employ on board a sail-training ship with young people. I took a deep breath. 'It's a gun, sir.' His white brows rose. 'I found it, along the tunnel.' I jerked my chin starboardwards. 'It was hidden behind the widow-makers.'

'*You* found it.' The emphasis on *you* reminded me that the whole ship had just been searched by professionals.

'They were looking for a man,' I said lamely.

'And you were looking for a gun?' He glanced down at the tub, and back at my face, and I could see he didn't believe a word of it. I felt the tide of scarlet running up my neck. 'You need to explain this, Cass.'

For a wild moment I thought of trying to keep Sean out of it. My brain half-formed something about Cat going missing, and looking for him among the shelves, but I knew I couldn't make it convincing. No. I had to tell the truth. I did my best: my cousin's stealthy withdrawal, his slipping downstairs and back up, and how I'd come to search and found the gun. Captain Gunnar watched me as I spoke, face expressionless. I couldn't tell whether he believed me or not.

'And what were you planning to do with it now? You were not bringing it to me.' His glance slashed like a sword. 'I will not have firearms on board. You know that.'

'I was going to throw it overboard,' I said passionately. It was rare that I acknowledged my scar to others, but I touched it now, bullet-straight across my cheek. 'Guns cause accidents.' My voice was rising again. I took a deep breath, and tried to control it. 'Then I realised it had to come to you . . . I didn't know it was you on the stairs. The potato was my excuse for someone else – for whoever it was coming down.'

He looked away from me at that, considering. Then he lifted the gun out of the tub and examined it. I could tell he was used to firearms; he would have done National Service, and many country dwellers in Norway went shooting. His brows rose. He looked back at me. 'A Glock automatic. This is a serious weapon, and loaded. You should not even be carrying such a thing.' He gave the plastic tub a contemptuous glance. 'The bullet would go straight through this.'

'I didn't know whether it was loaded or not. I just wanted to get rid of it.'

Captain Gunnar sighed. He spoke quietly, but I could hear anger simmering under his voice, like a tide eddy under a calm sea. 'Cass, this is all too sensational. I understand that you have been involved in investigations these last months, with your friend the policeman, but this is a sail-training ship. We do not need to create these excitements.'

I gripped my hands tightly together behind my back, digging my nails into the palms. There was a heavy weight on my chest. He hadn't believed me, and there was nothing I could say. 'No, sir.'

'I will lock this in my cabin until it can be appropriately disposed of.'

I nodded.

'Have you worked out the navigation plan for after we leave here?'

My breath caught in my throat. Surely he wasn't going to relieve me of my command. 'Yes, sir. It's all ready in the nav shack.'

'Good.' He allowed a weighty pause. My heart hammered. 'I will ask Mike to supervise your watch with you.'

Not fit to be in charge of a watch. It felt like he'd struck me. I spread my hands, but couldn't think of any way to explain. 'It really isn't my gun, sir.'

His face didn't change. 'Go back upstairs. There is no need for you to be down here. This is the galley girls' world. If you want something, ask them.'

'Yes, sir,' I said, and escaped.

I paused to look back at the top of the stairs. Captain Gunnar was standing below, the gun still in his hands, watching to make sure I'd gone.

I went.

CHAPTER SIX

I went straight to the rail and stood there, hands clenched on the smooth wood, gazing across the harbour and fighting the humiliation. Then, as the trainees began to gather on deck, I went down to the engine room. The familiar smell of diesel oil and hot grease closed around me as I clambered down the iron ladder. Anders was in his green boiler suit with a stained rag in his hands. He took one look at my face, wiped his hands with the rag and came forward to meet me.

'What's wrong?'

'My cousin Sean had a gun.' I tried to remember the name of it. 'A Lock. A black thing, weighed a ton. He hid it down among the widow-makers, and I found it, but then Captain Gunnar came and found me with it.'

'And he did not believe your explanation?'

I shook my head miserably. *We do not need to create these excitements.* The words burnt too much to repeat. 'He thought I was getting bored, after being involved in investigations with Gavin.'

Anders pulled a sympathetic face, and put an arm around my shoulders. 'But he knows you are not like that really. He is just annoyed about looking foolish in front of Special Branch.'

I shook my head. 'It's worse than that.' I was annoyed to hear my voice tremble, and took refuge in a burst of swearing. Anders' arm tightened. 'He's putting Mike on watch with me,' I managed. 'He doesn't think I'm fit for command.'

I stepped away from the comforting arm and began to pace back and forth across the engine room. There was nothing to be said, and Anders had the sense not to say it. After a moment, I rubbed my eyes with my hand. 'I'll go up to my cabin.' I took a deep breath, and tried to convince myself. 'It'll blow over. Like you said, he's annoyed at having been made to look foolish. And the gun . . .'

'I don't think you need to worry too much about that,' Anders said. 'Everyone knows how you feel about guns.' His hand clasped my shoulder, and let me go again. 'The captain knows too. He will come around.' He glanced at the engine-room clock. 'Back on duty at four?'

It was ten to three. I nodded. 'I'll go and tidy up.'

I had just splashed my face with water and re-plaited my hair when the curtain at the door twitched. Cat and Rat vanished under the bedclothes in a flurry of waving tails and Sean came strolling into my room. 'Sure, Cass, this is the height of luxury you have here, and me squashed into a berth a foot too short.'

I turned to face him. He was looking too laid-back, speaking too casually. My senses went to red alert. This wasn't the tearaway teenager I'd followed into trouble fifteen years ago. An adult self-assurance had taken the place of faith in his luck. He moved with the easy grace of someone whose body was in tune, ready to react to trouble. *Dangerous* . . . I didn't know what he did now, but it sure wasn't a desk job. He prodded my mattress, and gave his old smile. Above the curving mouth, his eyes were watchful. 'This looks just the job. You wouldn't care to change places, now?'

'I would not,' I said. I tried to think where I'd place him on a ship of mine. *Not at all,* my mind replied, but then I had a vision of him in an emergency situation, gun at the ready, keeping order in a panicked scramble for the life rafts, his blue eyes cold and narrowed. *This boat's full. I'll shoot the next man who tries to push his way on board.* I banished the picture, and made my voice as casual as his. 'What're you up to in the posh end of the ship?'

'Oh, just paying me cousin a visit. I had a stroll round Stavanger, then got bored and came back to the ship. I'd have gone to the pub, but I'm not a millionaire yet.' He sat down on my chair and looked round. 'It's real Edwardian elegance, this.' One finger slid along the polished wood of my berth. 'Is that mahogany?'

I nodded. 'Those were the days. And if you think this is grand, you should see the captain's cabin. Maybe you've seen it already?'

He gave me a sharp glance, then shook his head. 'Not for the likes of me, dining with the captain.'

It wasn't quite what I'd asked. 'Not respectable enough?' I said coldly.

'Oh, I'm a reformed character now, with a steady wage coming in.' His eyes danced. 'As sensible and stable as yourself.'

Exactly. 'Me mam and dad wouldn't agree with that one.'

'Ah, parents are only happy if you end up a doctor or a teacher. Look at our Seamus now, and him the head of his department in the high school in Dublin. Mam's so proud of him her apron strings are like to burst, but all the fun's gone out of him entirely.'

'Until you go and liven him up.'

He laughed and conceded that. 'Though a day at the TT races is the best his wife will allow him. Well, as sensible and stable as your stately captain, then, God bless him.' He stretched his legs out until they almost touched the opposite cabin wall. 'It's funny the way the ship's marked out, like. I wouldn't have expected that, in this day and age.'

'Marked out?'

'Oh, you know, the areas that belong to different people. Here I am, making meself at home in the officers' quarters, but normally we trainees wouldn't be allowed to put our noses into the corridor. Then there's the decks above here, where you all congregate, while we trainees keep to the middle bit. You never come down into our cabin-cum-dining room. Then there's the bit below that.' If I hadn't known him so well, I'd never have heard in his voice that this was the important bit. 'Where the pantry is, and all the ship's stores.'

'Galley girl territory,' I agreed. I tried not to see Captain Gunnar's face, nor hear his voice: *I will ask Mike to supervise your watch with you.* 'And of course the trainees who're helping out.'

'I've not had to do that yet.'

'Don't worry, your turn will come.'

'They go up and down too, do they?'

'As required. The pantry's down there, remember, with all the stores. Other people too – Jenn had washing hung down there. And the safety patrol go down.'

'Of course. I've been down there meself on safety patrol. Do those tunnels run the length of the ship, now?'

'All the way. But people don't use them for that.'

'No. No, they wouldn't. And of course your sailmaker would go down there, for his bits and pieces of canvas, and your spare blocks are there too.'

'All the repairs stuff,' I agreed blandly. I feared he could read me as easily as I was reading him.

'For all he's stately, though, your captain looks a good man in a pinch. I'd go to him if I had any kind of problem.'

Like finding a loaded gun down among the sail blocks. He must have seen us coming out of the banjer steps together. 'I'd do that,' I agreed. Very well, then, cards on the table. I looked Sean straight in the eye. 'Anything I found that was bothering me, he'd get it straight away.'

I saw his leg muscles relax. He gave me his most dazzling smile. 'Very wise. That's what higher command is for.' He stood up, stretching his arms sideways and yawning. 'So, we head out at five, and straight across the North Sea. Over the top of Scotland, down the side, and home.'

'Ah, my home's a travelling one now.' I had a sudden pang of longing for *Khalida*'s little cabin, with my narrow quarter-berth running aft under the cockpit seats, and the simple cooker on its gimbals, and the brass fish gleaming against her mahogany bulkhead. Now we were embarked on *Sørlandet*'s summer season, I only had time to visit her quickly, check all was well, and return to my other ship, like a man with a wife and a demanding mistress.

'You always had a touch of the gipsy about you. Well, I'll go and see what's doing on deck.' I thought he was about to say something more, eyes calculating, then he seemed to dismiss the thought, nodded, and headed off.

I listened to his footsteps, soft on the polished floor. He paused at the captain's door for so long that I was tempted to go out and see what he was up to; then at last the steps moved on, out into the open air.

* * *

I wasn't on duty once the ship had left harbour; it was Nils's watch. He threaded us out on his amended version of my course, through the little islands and on until the white tower of the Kvitsøy lighthouse was to the south of us, the red hat of the Geitungen lighthouse to the north, then westwards straight out to sea. Tea was a hurried meal before the all-hands muster. I had no appetite for it anyway. It was obvious that the captain had spoken to Mike, from the sympathetic look he gave me as we came into the room together, and he must have spoken to Agnetha too, for she gave me a speaking glance. I writhed inwardly, and left half of my stew hidden under a piece of bread.

There was an edgy feel in the air, and it was obvious from the muttered conversations on deck around me that several people had seen the special forces squad come aboard, and drawn the most melodramatic of conclusions. Olav's mystery man had become a semi-mythical figure. 'He was a Russian hitman, on his way to assassinate the British prime minister,' Nine breathed to Anna, who promptly passed it on to Maria and the Greek boys. 'They didn't find anyone,' Sindre told the Ethiopian boys in Norwegian. 'He slipped down a rope from the ship and swam ashore while nobody was looking.' Captain Gunnar came out himself to spread reassurance: 'We feared that there had been a stowaway aboard, but the ship was searched, and nobody found. You may now all relax and enjoy our journey across the North Sea.'

Sean was at the back of his watch, on the aft end of the line, detached from the nearest group of youngsters, and looking around him so casually that I was instantly suspicious. As Jenn's 'moments of awesome' began, he began to slide sideways, face still turned towards her as if he was just shifting position. He'd slid a good two metres along the rail when he looked up and saw me watching him. His eyes narrowed, and we stared at each other for a drawn-out moment, then he leant back once more, body slanted towards the crowd on the deck. Whatever he was planning to do while everyone was amidships and the captain's cabin was deserted, he'd save it for another time. I relaxed and looked back at Jenn, then back to where Sean had been. He was gone. He'd slipped away like a cat, without moving the air round him.

I wanted to go after him. I was just moving from my place when I caught Captain Gunnar's eye on me, and subsided. I was in enough trouble. I stood there, fretting, as the long moments passed. Jenn was just rounding off the session when Sean slipped back, as unobtrusively as he'd left. The people nearest to him would have sworn he'd never moved. Only a suspicious cousin sensed his air of satisfaction. Whatever he'd gone for, he'd got it.

We had ten minutes before we were due on duty. I made myself a mug of drinking chocolate and took it up to the nav shack, watching as my trainees assembled below. Nils met me with a grave face. 'What's this story about you waving a gun at the captain?'

'Nonsense, of course.' I managed a laugh. 'I found a gun on board and gave it to him.'

I could see he was going to ask more, and turned away, busying myself over the chart until Mike slid in beside me, his eyes not meeting mine. 'You've got the course all worked up? Good.'

By now my watch was lined up on deck. Samir was feeling sick, Erik announced. I gave a quick glance around, and saw him by the rails, instead of in his usual place in the front row, raring to go. 'I need a volunteer for galley duty.' Erik looked hopefully at the young men, but none of them offered. Olav stepped forward. 'I'll do it.'

'Good man,' Erik approved. 'It'll only be half an hour, just to clear up.' That sorted, he went over to Samir, and asked a question. Samir nodded gloomily, and Erik sent him aft towards the sick bay. Sadie, our MO, would give him seasickness pills. I made a face; we were losing one of our best climbers.

The forecast had been for mist, and now it had blown from the land, grey as cobwebs all around us. There was a breath of wind to curve the sails, but the sea was oily, studded with jellyfish, brown with a spirograph pattern or starred with sunflower yellow in a clear bell: *brunmaget* and *glassmaget*.

Sailors hate mist. It blinds your sight and deadens sound, the two senses that first warn you of trouble. We were moving away from the Bergen shipping lane, but there were still vessels all around us, moving blips on the electronic chart. I clicked on one and found its details: the *Bright Star* (UK), steaming at fifteen knots on a heading of 312 degrees, destination Lerwick, ETA Monday 01.00, ship type: fishing. It was only half a mile away, yet I could barely make out its lights. We could do with an extra pair of eyes on lookout. We'd also need to stow these sails soon. Who were my non-climbers?

Just as I was looking, Olav came out of the banjer hatch. He had an air of excitement that made me uneasy; a man with news to share. He made straight for the aft steps and had just climbed to deck level when Captain Gunnar materialised beside me. His face was still closed against me, but his voice was less cold, and although he flicked a glance at Mike, it was to me he spoke.

'Cass, I think we should stow the sails on the foremast now. We will need an extra person on lookout, one of the adults, to back up the younger ones.' He turned to see Olav hovering. 'You are on this watch, are you not? Please go and join the foredeck lookout. We have to switch the radar off while the sails are stowed, so it is particularly important that you watch and listen. For the time that the radar is switched off, our safety depends on you.'

Olav nodded, and went, with a last glance towards me. I'd find out what he wanted at the first opportunity. Mike leant back against the nav shack as I called Erik up and began giving instructions: teams up the rig, with the foremast sails to be stowed first, so that the radar could go back on as soon as possible. 'And Olav came up as if he wanted to speak to me just now,' I finished. 'While everyone's getting their harnesses on, could you send Petter or Mona forrard to see what he wanted to say? Thanks.'

The silence was eerie. The topsails were lost in cloud, the grey sails hanging like emanations of mist stretching down towards us. Cold drops clung to the ratlines, and clouded the bright brass of the handrail; the ropes were dark with water. Below me, the trainees were getting their harnesses on, backs to the still water, but with the occasional uneasy glance over a shoulder. Even their bright jackets were dulled by the dim air. Forrard, the grey mist coiled over the boat deck, and the foredeck was wreathed in it, so that Ludwig, Ben and Olav were just dark shadows, and frighteningly vulnerable. If something rammed us, they'd be the first to go overboard. I looked around me and found my standby helm. 'Nine, can you nip down and tell Mona to get the lookouts to put lifejackets on.' Beside me, Mike nodded approvingly. 'Thanks.'

I watched her go down the aft steps and speak to Mona, who made a thumbs up and headed up to the boat deck to get life jackets, then went on forward, with three slung by the armhole along her arm. Her blue jacket dimmed to a silhouette. I saw arms lifting as each jacket was put on, then Mona's shadow returning, ready to lead her team up the foremast.

Ahead of me, ten metres in the air, the radar arm stopped

revolving. The blips on my screen disappeared. Now we were crawling blind through the greyness, all senses alert for the sound of a foghorn or a distant light through the murk. There had been nothing within ten miles of us when we'd switched the radar off, and in theory no responsible captain would be hammering his ferry or cargo ship at twenty knots in this dimness, but not all captains were in a position to resist the demands of their company that the ship keep to its timetable whatever the conditions.

My job was to delegate. There was no sense in making my own eyes hurt. We had two sharp youngsters and a responsible older person in the bows. I focused on my own work. The ship was on course, heading straight across the North Sea towards the Pentland Firth. Erik and Mona were leading the trainees up the forrard ratlines, a handful of people on each side. As I watched, the first swung up and over onto the platform, and began to edge along the yard. Petter was watching from on deck. They were doing the upper topsail first, then the lower one. It would take them a good three-quarters of an hour to secure both, then we'd need to square up the yards. An hour of creeping forward blindfolded.

It felt a long, long hour, with everyone staring upwards at those dark figures spread along the yard, reaching over to gather the canvas and bundle it upwards, reaching again to pull up the gasket and secure it around the sail, tying it, then moving on to the next one. Three bells rang as they were climbing back to the lower topsail. That reminded me that nobody had come to tell me what Olav had wanted to say. He was off duty now, so he'd likely come up to tell me himself.

He didn't. I couldn't see who was on lookout now; they were lost in the dimness. Maybe he'd stayed there. Then, at last, the trainees began climbing down, and Mike went to switch the radar back on. The arm began to turn, and the blips reappeared on the screen. Nothing close; an oil supply boat was within a mile of us, but heading away, and a ferry would cross behind us. I let out a long, relieved breath.

Petter came up as the trainees prepared to start on the mainmast. His fair hair was damp with drops that sparked in the ship's lights. 'I spoke to Olav.' His voice was curt, as if he resented being used as a message boy. 'He wanted to tell you that the "mystery man" in the dark coat is still aboard.'

A cold chill ran down my spine. 'He saw him?'

'He came for dinner with the last of the white watch. He wasn't wearing the coat, he had a sailing jacket on, and a woollen hat pulled down over his brow, but Olav was sure it was him. He took a good look at him, and recognised his face.'

Still aboard . . . 'But they found nothing,' I said.

Petter flushed. 'I did think of one hiding place, when Olav said he was still aboard.' He glanced from me to Mike, as if he was expecting we'd tell him off for not mentioning it sooner. 'We found it as we were clearing up during the winter, Rolf, Erik and I. There's a cargo space down under the engine room, right at the back, under boards, so inaccessible that we couldn't think of a use for it.' He straightened his head and added, defiantly, 'But he couldn't have been in there while they searched, because you couldn't put the boards back from below.'

'But he could have hidden there if someone had helped him,' Mike said.

Petter looked directly at me, startled, pupils wide in the dim light. 'Hidden him there? But how would they know? Visitors aren't allowed in the engine room—' He thought about it, and flushed. 'It would have to be one of us, wouldn't it?'

I glanced towards the engine-room door. The Russian could easily have been shut in this morning, while Anders was at breakfast. *Rolf, Erik and I* . . . I gave Petter a sideways glance. Surely he wouldn't come and tell me about the place if he himself had put the Russian there? Unless it was an elaborate double bluff, or unless he was now afraid of the man, and wanted him found?

'Should I tell Captain Gunnar about the hiding place?'

'I'll tell him,' Mike said. 'For now, don't mention it to anyone else, and don't go down there.'

'I won't,' Petter said. He turned away, then back to me. 'Olav said he'd come and speak to you himself when he came off duty.'

But he hadn't; and when the red and blue watches formed their lines, we were one person short. Olav was missing.

Of course we searched. The banjer first, then the heads and the pantry. He was nowhere to be found.

The last time anyone had seen him was at the end of his trick as lookout. They hadn't spoken much, Ludwig and Ben said. They'd all been too busy staring out into the blankness. They'd left the foredeck before him, coming down the starboard steps. Ben had an impression of someone going up the port steps as they came down, but 'People were always coming and going. I didn't take any notice.' The next lookouts, Ellen and Naseem, had said hello to him as they passed, heading straight for the bow, to stand one each side of the headsail sheets, staring out into the greyness. They hadn't noticed what he'd done behind them.

We dismissed the watch, whispering speculations to each other. It would be a while before they slept. Then Mike went down to tell the captain while I went to the foredeck. The life jacket Olav had worn was lying on the coil of anchor rope as if he'd dropped it there, but there were no signs of a struggle: the coil itself lay in a neat circle, and the ropes hung in their usual places.

I stood where Olav had last been seen, at the top of the narrow stairs leading down to the main deck. Ludwig and Ben had gone down the starboard side, and they'd thought Olav was following. On my right hand, the ship's rail that protected the foredeck crew stopped, and there was a gap between that and the ratlines leading up the foremast. I imagined coming up behind someone here, catching them from behind, silencing them in some way and then lifting the body over the side, between rails and ratlines, letting it down by the arms and dropping it that last metre to the water. If you were strong enough to lean over yourself, between the extra metre of your arms and his, his feet would almost touch the water, so that when you let him slide downwards, the splash would be no louder than the curling waves beneath the ship's forefoot.

Olav took a good look at him, Petter had said. No doubt the Russian had noticed. He'd hoped to slip back to being thought of as a member of another watch, but here was this person on galley duty staring at him, making sure he'd know him again.

He'd been small, Olav, and slightly built. It would take only a few seconds for a combat-trained man to catch him from behind, smother him or break his neck, and lower him overboard. I shuddered at the picture. Could the Russian really have done that unseen?

I looked forrard. The lookout, only fifteen metres away, were focused on the grey mist ahead of us. Back along the ship, the trainees were gathered midships, and the corridor between the galley and ship's side was empty. During my watch, the trainees up in the rig had been looking only at their handholds on the folds of sail and hanging gasket lines, and Petter, on deck, had his head tilted up, looking at them. The other trainees were smoking in their corner or chatting under the shelter of the banjer roof overhang. Aft, as the bell had rung, I'd been checking our course, ready to direct the new helm, and the other physicals had been changing over. It was a risk, of course, but it had paid off.

I leant over the side, and thought there was a dark smear on the lip of the single porthole immediately below me, black in the green of the starboard light. It could be blood.

I came slowly back along the main deck and up the steps.

'No sign?' Agnetha asked. Her face was drawn in the dim light, with lines of a woman thirty years older. I shook my head.

'Now what?' Erik asked. Like Agnetha, he was pale and tense. 'We've never lost someone like this. They'll blame us for not keeping count. Only seventeen on the watch, and four of us. "How come we didn't notice sooner?" they'll ask.'

'You and Mona were up the rig,' Petter said. 'I was the one on deck; they will expect me to have seen.'

'No,' I said forcefully. 'Don't start allotting blame. We have the ship routines, and they've always held good.' I looked them straight in the eyes. 'I carry this can. You head off to bed. I'll report to Captain Gunnar.'

I glanced at my watch. Five to one. On heavy feet, I headed to his door and knocked. It was opened straight away; he and Mike stood there, grave-faced. He motioned me in.

'Take me through your watch, Cass. When was he last seen?'

I made as short a tale of it as I could, only explaining at the end that Petter had said Olav had recognised the man in the dark coat. The captain held up a hand to stop me.

'No, Cass. Mike has also told me this, but I will not have it. An accident on board the ship is bad enough. I will not have your conjectures about mysterious men.' He sighed. 'Very well. I will inform the police. This is a matter for the helicopter. There is no point in us turning back; where he was last seen is three hours behind us now.' He bent his bushy brows towards me. 'They will ask why he was not missed sooner.'

I'd been working out my answer to that since Erik had asked the question. 'Why would he have been?' I said simply. 'Our focus was on the crew up in the rig; we weren't worrying about an adult on deck. We only muster the crew at the end of each watch.'

He knew that, of course. He nodded heavily, and gestured towards the door. 'Go to bed now, Cass. The police may need to talk to you, but that can wait. If they insist, I will wake you.'

I nodded, and left them to it.

My berth was empty. Cat and Rat must both be curled up beside Anders. I wanted to speak to Gavin, but the signal symbol on my phone was blank. I wouldn't be able to talk to him again until we reached Scotland. Above my head, Agnetha walked the deck. The bell rang; the trainees on helm duty changed over. I heard the creak as the great wheel turned, the new helm getting used to the feel of the ship. We'd left squaring up the main and mizzen yards to give the next watch something to do, and now there was the pad of several sets of feet immediately above me, and a series of slaps as coils of rope were taken from the belaying pins and dropped on deck.

I wanted company but there was no sense in me going up on deck again. I had a watch to lead in the morning, a ship to steer across the North Sea. There were tears pricking behind my eyelids. I'd had enough of this. I didn't want to see Olav's face in that split second as the man in the dark jacket came up behind him, or imagine his body slipping into the water. I didn't want to hear the captain's voice, or see Mike's look as he stood beside me on the aft deck. I shut my eyes and pretended with all my strength that I was aboard my own *Khalida*, in my narrow quarter-berth. If I opened my eyes, I'd see the engine box, with my heavy brass candlestick on the top step, and the book I'd been reading beside it. Then I heard Cat's soft paws landing on the settee-step and felt him arrive on the bed beside me. He patted my face with one paw, then curled himself into the space between my shoulder and chin. I freed a hand to stroke the soft fur behind his ears. He began to purr, and the soft rumble comforted me. I buried my face in his side, and slept.

THREE BELLS

The North Sea: Stavanger to Scotland

Sunday 28th June

CHAPTER SEVEN

Things always feel better in the morning. I woke hoping that Captain Gunnar would have calmed down, that his knee-jerk reaction to the gun would be modified by remembering my record. Then the evening rushed back on me: the search for Olav, the smear of blood, the captain's reaction. He'd called the police. I'd have to tell them what I knew, no matter how it annoyed Captain Gunnar. *Keep quiet*, a voice inside me urged. Making a fuss couldn't help Olav now. I had no real evidence that the Russian was still on board, hidden in that cargo space under the engine. I wished I could talk to Gavin, but the waves curled with that slow, rolling motion that told me we were now well out at sea. We'd been thirty miles from Norway when I'd signed off six hours ago, and we'd have doubled that now. I'd have no phone signal until we reached Scotland.

It was Sunday. I was just reaching for my battered scarlet missal when I heard a soft, angry voice speaking through the wall.

I couldn't hear the words, just the vehement tone. That side joined Mike's room, but the voice was female. Then there was the sound of someone retching into the sink on the wall, a metre from me on the other side. Agnetha's voice came clearly through the wall, right at my ear. 'I won't have it.'

Agnetha? Agnetha and *Mike*? My brain spun, trying to visualise this unexpected combination. I couldn't hear Mike's reply, but the tone was soothing.

'I *won't*,' Agnetha repeated. She stopped and was sick again. My own stomach curled. 'You can't force me.'

Mike's reply was sharp, and Agnetha's retort sharper still. 'Do that, and I'll go to the captain. You're my senior officer.' Her voice was sour. 'Fifteen years older than me. You'll never work on a tall ship again.'

This time his voice came across clearly. 'Nor will you.'

I'd heard enough. Was this how affairs ended, two people who'd once loved scraping each other raw? I curled away from them, pulled the downie over my head, and waited until Agnetha moved away from the wall, and the voices returned to murmurs. Then Mike's door snapped open and closed again.

An abortion, Gavin had said. Agnetha's voice echoed: *I won't have it.* It wasn't Erik's baby, but Mike's. I'd got completely the wrong end of the stick. *If it has to be done*, Erik had said, not *If I have to tell her.* Agnetha had replied, *It doesn't have to be done.* An abortion would solve everything – except that Mike, brought up in a country where abortion was still illegal, didn't want her to have one.

Five bells rang above my head and echoed from the foredeck. Half past six. I took a deep breath and dismissed everything but the day ahead from my thoughts. I had a shower, dressed in a crisply-ironed shirt and clean cargo breeks, and went out on deck.

The fresh air hit me, cold and salt-tanged, with a touch of dampness in it. Nils's watch had just finished scrubbing the decks, turning the wide teak planks from grey-brown to dark red. The varnished handrail gleamed against the two ochre funnels. The whole ship had that extra sharpness of rain-cleared air.

The yards had been squared overnight, but the sails were still furled. I turned my head until I felt the wind soft on my right cheek. We could carry full sail. I strolled over to the nav screen box and lifted the lid. The dot flashed, not quite a third of the way across. Two hundred miles at six knots; thirty-three hours. We'd be approaching the Pentland Firth in the early hours of tomorrow morning. I'd need to calculate more precisely, to make sure we were still good for the tricky tides going through.

'You'll need to check the Pentland Firth tides,' Nils said over my shoulder. 'It's a difficult stretch of water.'

'Yes,' I agreed.

'You lost a trainee last night.'

I turned to meet his toffee-brown eyes. He'd been on board this ship for five years – did he know about the hidey-hole? Yet it didn't seem in his rule-stickler character to smuggle a man aboard. 'So it seems.'

'We have never had an accident aboard.' His tone suggested I'd somehow caused this one. 'Come, you will be late for breakfast.'

I closed the lid, squared my shoulders and headed for the officers' mess, with Nils behind me like a prisoner's escort. Anders was already there. I slid in beside him. He gave a quick look at my face, and his hand stole to touch mine under the table. The ship's gossip chain was obviously on overdrive; I could see he'd heard all about Olav's disappearance.

Captain Gunnar was looking particularly grim. As soon as we were all assembled and he'd said grace, he began to speak. 'There was an unfortunate incident last night. It seems a trainee was lost overboard. He was on extra lookout duty, and did not rejoin his watch. It was a foggy night, and I conjecture that he stumbled coming down the steps to the foredeck and fell overboard. Nobody heard him cry out, or heard a splash, so my belief is that he had a heart attack, and did not cry out.'

He paused to give a stern look around us. 'The police will of course investigate all this. There is no point in us turning back. The Belfast police will come on board when we arrive. They will take statements from those on watch, while the police in Norway will talk to his family and doctor and find out if a heart attack was likely.' I could see that Captain Gunnar had persuaded himself of it. A heart attack didn't reflect on his ship. 'A helicopter has been sent from Norway to search the area, in case his body can be recovered, but he was not wearing a life jacket. It is not likely that he will be found. I depend on you all to minimise this unfortunate accident.' His eyes bored into mine for a moment. 'I will call a muster at the change of watch, and make a statement to all crew and trainees. After that, we must get on with the voyage, and make sure the trainees enjoy themselves. We also need to turn them into an efficient crew. We have a race to win in the next leg, do not forget.'

I had forgotten, although we'd discussed it endlessly in the evenings before we left. Our fellow Norwegian ships, the *Staatsraad Lemkuhl* and the *Christian Radich*, had both won prizes in previous years, and we were determined that we'd be in the top three this year. We'd need luck with the wind, of course, and spot-on navigation, but we also needed the crew to be slick with turning the yards and trimming the sails. I drank my yoghurt and ate my oatmeal, considering. More rope work, so that my watch went unhesitatingly to the right ones when Erik said, 'Trim the main lower topsail.' They'd need more practice up in the rig to be able to furl the sails quickly, and it shouldn't take us two miles to tack.

Anders nudged me. 'You're not allowed the cat o'nine tails for last down the rigging.'

'Was I looking that grim?'

'I'm glad I'm not on your watch.'

'Rope training,' I said. 'Rig practice.'

Captain Gunnar nodded approvingly, and my heart lightened. 'She could carry sail now.'

I took that as an order, and headed out. My watch was beginning to muster, and I could tell straight off that the captain's hopes of keeping Olav's death quiet didn't have a chance of being fulfilled. The youngsters were buzzing with tensed-up excitement, and even the older people were exchanging grave-faced gossip, with the occasional sideways glance at the empty sea around us. A spot of yard-shifting and mast-climbing would do everyone good.

The ABs of Nils's watch headed below to round their trainees upwards, and once the whole crew was lined up in their three sides of a square on the main deck, Captain Gunnar came out and talked to us all. He did it well: it was a regrettable and unusual accident which stressed the need for care aboard the ship at all times. He had sent the sympathy of the whole crew to Olav's family.

Eight bells chimed above our heads. Our watch had begun.

I was determined to keep everyone busy. I got Erik to start with a bit of rope-learning. Mike came up for a moment, said, 'Good idea,' checked our course, then returned below. I hoped that meant I was back in command. I was leaning at the rail watching the trainees racing round the main deck to lay hand on the correct halyard, brace or sheet when Anders came up beside me.

'I had a thought,' he said.

111

I turned my head to look enquiringly at him.

He looked around to check that the helm and standby were properly focused on their duties, and the safety watch was off on his round. 'You know the captain caught you down in the galley.'

I didn't need reminding. I made a face.

'Well, what was he doing there?' He gave a pause for that to sink in. 'He told you off good and proper, and said it was the galley girls' territory. So what was he doing poking around down there?'

My mouth fell open. I'd been so busy worrying about keeping my job that it had never occurred to me.

'For example,' Anders continued, 'had he perhaps seen you go down and followed you? But that in itself would be suspicious. Why should you not go below?'

I shook my head at that. 'I'd been down a good while before he arrived. He might have seen me go down and wondered why I hadn't come back – but you're right, why should he follow me?'

'And to tell you off so severely. Does that not suggest he wanted to distract you from what he was doing down there?'

'There was the gun,' I conceded. 'It's not the sort of thing you want your crew wandering about with.'

'You were carrying a loaded Glock in a plastic bucket.' Anders' voice curled with affectionate scorn. I remembered that he'd spent his teenage years helping his uncle hunt bears. 'It was obvious it was not your gun. Nobody who'd ever shot would do so stupid a thing.'

'I don't like guns,' I retorted.

'I know. Anyway,' Anders said, 'you have been warned off good and proper, and you're on duty besides. I'm not on duty. I'm going to go down and get myself some biscuits and cheese to have with my morning coffee. Was there anything particular you noticed down there?'

I shook my head.

'Nothing in the galley?'

'But everyone's down there all the time. The girls, Henrik, the trainees. It would be a lousy place to hide anything.'

'*The Purloined Letter*,' Anders said. 'It is a story about a letter which is hidden from the police among all the other letters. Hidden in plain sight.'

'You mean there's something hidden down there – inside a herring tub, or a tin that's been opened and sealed again?' I tried to remember if it had been the herring tub that Captain Gunnar had reacted to. No. He'd opened the pantry door, and almost walked straight into me. He'd only noticed the tub as he was dismissing me. 'But what could it be? Do you think Captain Gunnar is involved in anything underhand . . . smuggling – well, drugs, or something?' I tried to envisage it and shook my head. 'No.'

'No,' Anders agreed, 'but I am sure there is something. What did he do when first he saw you?'

I tried to remember. 'He looked over my shoulder, around the cold store.'

'Not at the freezer?'

'No. Behind me.' I frowned. 'He did seem to look down in the far corner. The starboard aft corner. There were these four boxes, about this by this' – I indicated with my hands – 'I tried to lift one up to see what it was. Expanded foam, painted white. By the weight, and the feel, it was empty.'

He smiled at that. 'The size of a twelve-bottle box. The captain's private stock of drink.'

'Four boxes. Forty-eight bottles.' I was used to France. I thought about the bottles of wine that stood on the table at every meal in my cousin Thierry's house. 'That wouldn't go far.'

'He would have to declare it on our arrival back in Norway, and pay tax.'

Sailing friends on the English coast regularly brought supermarket trolleys of wine back into the UK. I knew nothing about the Norwegian alcohol import laws. 'How much are you allowed to bring in?'

'Oh, nothing like that. One bottle of spirits or six bottles of wine, I think, and some beer, but you can't use the beer quota for more wine. You can only change downwards: spirits to wine, wine to beer.' He pushed himself off the rail. 'I'm off to look. Do you want a biscuit?'

I didn't usually eat biscuits at this time of day, but I suddenly felt a ginger snap would go down well. 'A handful of ginger nuts, please. *Pepperkaker.*'

'I know. The ones you break into three using your elbow.' He headed down the steps. I watched his silver-gilt head cross the deck and disappear into the darkness of the banjer stairwell, and hoped he wasn't heading into trouble.

The trainees had finished their rope drill and were taking a breather. I nodded down to Erik. 'Let's set one yard, then put them in teams to square the rest up, a team to each mast.'

I checked our course and then, while the trainees drank their coffee, Erik, Petter and Mona shifted the top yard on each mast until it was at roughly the right angle for sails to catch the wind. My hands itched to help them, to stand shoulder to shoulder again, hauling the rope round, but it wasn't my place. I stood with my palms on the satin-smooth handrail, watching, and nodded when I reckoned it was right.

Then it was all hands to the ropes. Soon the aft deck was a mass of hauling bodies. The higher, lighter yards were easy enough, and they tended to swing them round too far, then have to work them back; the lowest yards were great telegraph poles that took a dozen people to shift, even with a system of blocks on each rope.

They were in the middle of doing that when Anders reappeared. He swung up the steps and pressed a handful of ginger nuts into my hand. I gave him two back and crunched, looking at him expectantly. He shook his head.

'There was nothing like the boxes you described in the cold store, nor in the pantry. So I had a small snoop around. Nothing. Whatever they were for, they have been moved. In the starboard corner, aft, there was a plastic crate of watermelons.'

I stopped crunching to stare at him. 'Not there?'

'No.'

Our eyes met.

'Odd,' he said. 'Don't you go back down there to check. Take my word for it.'

'I am.' We'd sailed together, Anders and I. If he said they weren't there, then they weren't. But why move empty boxes, and fill the space they'd been in? Because word had gone round the ship that Cass, the policeman's girlfriend, had been snooping around down there . . . ?

'I must go to our engine.'

He swung back off down the steps, leaving me thinking. *The captain's private wine store* . . . I didn't see it. But maybe someone else was taking advantage of the cover a tall ship gave to smuggle drink into Norway.

The heaving backs around me stopped, straightened. I tilted my head back and looked up. For a first shot, it was pretty good; the outward end of each yard was within a foot of a straight line from the topmost one down to the sea. Now it was rig time, to drop the sails we were going to set, and then back to the ropes, for the deck crew to pull them tight, followed by a last trimming to the wind by shifting the yards again until each sail bellied out in a perfect curve.

As I'd hoped, it took all their attention. The tension slipped from the young faces, and by the time they mustered for the end of watch, flushed from exertion, Olav's death had been accepted as a regrettable accident that was now over.

I tried to forget the morning's discovery as I handed over to Agnetha. There was more colour in her cheeks than there had been this morning. Her lips were set in a determined line as she climbed the steps, but she smiled as she came up to me. 'All sails, Cass?'

I nodded. 'I've left your watch to finish them.' I touched the nav screen. 'And we're nicely on course for the Pentland Firth.'

Captain Gunnar came up beside us to watch as the trainees lined up, and nodded approval. My heart lifted. 'That is good,' he said. 'Now they will have lunch, and feel even better.'

I felt ravenous myself. Lunch was the last of yesterday's pork with pasta twirls, and the usual wonderful rye bread. I ate heartily and headed up on deck for a few breaths of fresh air. Ah, it was good to be out at sea again, really out at sea, with the horizon a smooth line all around us, and nothing existing in the world but this ship, so large and stable beneath our feet in this calm weather. The sails arched above me, tier after tier; the masts creaked in rhythm with the ship's slow surging roll. Around us, the sea was the colour the word 'aquamarine' was invented for, reaching up to touch the ship's white sides, then curling away in a shoosh of snowy foam. We were almost in Shetland waters; I was breathing my native air. I stood there for ten minutes, lightly balanced so that I rolled with the ship, just enjoying the salt tang in my face and the glacier colour of the sea, the lace patterns of the foam. A solitary fulmar flew over us, then landed on the water. He fluffed out his feathers and settled himself comfortably, watching us with his beady black eyes.

I took one last deep breath then headed below. Cat and Rat had made themselves comfortable on my berth, but they were pleased to see me. I gave Cat a brush around his ears, then lay back. I wished I could talk to Gavin. I really wanted his take on what I should do when the Belfast police questioned me; I wanted his endorsement for 'Tell the truth, even if your job is at risk'.

Then I heard his voice, clear in my head: *Hearsay.* I frowned, thinking about that one. Hearsay. Of course, what Petter had told me wasn't evidence. I was off that hook. Petter himself had to tell the police that Olav had said he'd seen the man in the dark jacket.

It wasn't really a huge weight off my mind, because I'd still have to speak out if Petter didn't, but it felt like it. I shifted Cat and Rat enough to lie down, and let the movement of the ship take me. I was out at sea again . . .

I was just dozing off when there was a stir at the door curtains. Cat and Rat vanished down the back of the berth in a flow of black and white and grey fur. I raised myself up and swung my legs over.

It was Captain Gunnar. The approving look was gone, the white brows drawn together again. He spoke abruptly. 'Cass, you have not taken your gun back again?'

I shook my head. I hoped the blank look of surprise I could feel on my face was convincing.

'I locked it in the drawer of my desk,' Captain Gunnar said. 'Now it is missing.'

CHAPTER EIGHT

For a moment I couldn't catch my breath. 'Missing?' I repeated stupidly.

'It has been stolen. You know nothing about it?'

I shook my head, and thought he believed me; and then, at that moment, the memory of Sean stealing away from the all-hands muster that morning came back into my head. Captain Gunnar's face changed, eyes narrowing. 'You have thought of something.'

I rubbed one hand over my face. 'My cousin, Sean. He was the one I thought hid the gun. He slipped away from this morning's muster. I didn't want to go after him, but he was standing at the aft end of his line, so it was this way he came.'

He used to pick a pretty lock, my cousin Sean. He'd showed me how, but I'd never got the knack of it the way he and Seamus had. A locked drawer in the captain's desk would be child's play.

Captain Gunnar sighed. 'Cass, why would your cousin be

travelling with a loaded gun on board a sail-training ship? What is his job?'

'I don't know,' I admitted. 'I haven't seen him since we were teenagers.'

'And why would he then steal it back? Why not come to me directly and say, "That is my gun"? No, Cass, it will not do. If you have that gun, I wish it to be returned to my custody immediately.'

'I don't have it.' I could hear my voice was sullen as a teenager's. I tried again. 'Captain Gunnar, I don't have it. I didn't take it. It's not my gun.'

His face was closed against me. 'Please do not put me to the embarrassment of having to search your cabin.'

It took an effort to keep my voice level. 'You're welcome to search, sir. I don't have that gun.'

He gave me a last sharp look. 'Your cousin, he is the tall, dark man on the red watch?' I nodded. 'I will talk to him.'

The curtain swished closed behind him. I slammed my fist into my pillow. Damn, *damn*. I just hoped Sean would be more open with Captain Gunnar than he had been with me.

Then I was struck by another thought. The captain had threatened to search my cabin. What if the gun had been planted on me? My heart began thumping uncomfortably. If it was found in here, nothing would save me from cabin arrest now, and dismissal the moment we tied up in Belfast.

I stood up so quickly that my head spun for a moment, then began with the desk, checking each drawer. The bookcase next, looking behind and inside each file. Nothing. My clothes cupboard. My clothes weren't in such neat piles as Johanna's, but it was still possible to lift each drawerful out in a lump, and feel the weight. Still nothing. My jacket pockets were empty.

There was nothing behind my toiletries, or above the sink. My breathing slowed to normal. I was being paranoid; why should it be planted on me?

And if it wasn't here, where the hell was it? It would almost be better to have it here and face the music than to have a loaded gun astray aboard the ship.

I would have to tackle Sean; except that if Captain Gunnar saw me talking to him, then he'd take it I was asking him to cover for me. Another black mark. It was like one of those nightmares where whichever way you run or hide, the monster with slavering jaws confronts you.

Two bells rang above my head. One o'clock. I wanted to go somewhere, do something, but I was sailing in a fog. If the man in the dark jacket was still aboard, it definitely wasn't a good idea for us to try and find him, especially if he was prepared to kill someone just for looking at him too closely. What the captain had said, approaching Stavanger, about not going into dark tunnels, applied even more now; but the captain was determined not to have a mystery man on board.

I didn't see my cousin Sean co-operating either. If he was going to admit whatever he was up to, he'd have gone to the captain, explained, and asked for his gun back. Stealing it back meant he wasn't telling anyone anything.

There was one thing I could check, though it wasn't really done. I could look at the crew forms, and see what information he'd given about himself. It would be in Jenn's office, on the ship's computer.

I walked straight into a row between Nils and Mike. I was through the curtain and in Jenn's office with them before I realised anyone was there. I hadn't heard any raised voices, but the air was thick with tension, like blown spray hanging over the sea in a gale.

Mike was sitting in front of the computer, half-turned to face Nils, who was leaning over him, brows drawn together in an angry line, mouth twisted. They both turned and stared as I came in, and I was about to make an excuse and back out when Nils straightened and flung past me.

There was an awkward silence that seemed to stretch for ever. I took a deep breath. 'Sorry. I just wanted to check something.'

Mike swivelled back to the screen. His eyes were black with fury and he was breathing heavily, but he managed a normal voice. 'Sure, I'm just finished.' He flicked a glance at me, and closed the window he was looking at. Another click, and Maria's dark eyes smiled at me from the screen. 'I was just trying to match names to faces. I'm pretty good on the adults, but I don't know all the youngsters yet.'

He had an amazing memory for names and faces, Mike. By 'pretty good', he meant that after only two days he could greet each of the adult trainees by name and chat about their home ports with them. Seeing him frowning over the computer gave me an uneasy feeling down my spine. He was looking pale, with worry lines creasing his cheeks. I remembered the row I'd tried not to listen to, and felt a pang of sympathy. Whichever way he went, he'd created trouble for himself, whether he left his wife to be with Agnetha, or left Agnetha to have her abortion and continue her career. I couldn't imagine what it must be like to know that your own child was about to be pulled out of its safe womb to die drowning in the air like a fish. It had to be worse if you already had children, as he did. He'd be imagining how it would have grown up: a baby in his arms, a toddler with gold curls like my friend Peerie Charlie, a little boy going to school, a girl in her first party dress. But it would be just as bad for Agnetha, even though it was her decision; no, perhaps worse, because it was her decision. Surely every year, she'd be remembering her baby would now have been one, two, three; she'd look at the children of others, and be stabbed by the sharp pang of 'My child would have been like this.'

Or could Mike overrule her? I had a memory at the back of my mind of a test case in the British courts, where the mother had been determined to have an abortion and the father had wanted to keep the baby. It had gone against him, I thought, but maybe it would be different in Norway. Was that what they were threatening each other over? If he took her to court, she'd tell the captain about their affair?

Mike looked up at me then. There was another long silence. I could see in his face that he knew I'd felt the hostility between him and Nils, but not how much I'd heard. His mouth opened as if he was going to say something, then closed again. I wanted to reassure him, but I couldn't frame the words. I tried for an everyday tone. 'I was wanting a look at them too. It's harder learning them when you're up on the aft deck, a step removed. I'm OK on my own watch, but I wanted a look at the other ones.'

The grim look left Mike's face. He nodded, and stood up with a *Be my guest* gesture. He hesitated in the doorway, then headed out. I heard his footsteps recede along the corridor and clatter briskly up the stairs to the nav shack.

It didn't take me long to call up Sean's details, but the file didn't tell me anything new. Sean Xavier Lynch gave his address as 31 Leinster Road, Dublin, and Seamus Lynch as his next of kin. Job: marketing. He had no medical conditions, and no dietary requirements. I was just going to snick the computer off when I wondered what Mike had been looking at. I scrolled down the list of 'last opened', and looked at the one before Maria. Sean Lynch. He'd been looking up my cousin. *I'm thinking I recognise his face*, he'd said. *Is it Cork your family's from? I was a bit wild . . .* What sort of trouble might they have shared? I didn't want to think about that one.

I called Cat and went out onto the main deck. It was raining now, light drizzle that darkened the dry decks and smudged the dulling brasswork. All the trainees were huddled under the overhang, waiting to be allowed back below once Jenn had finished her banjer cleaning. Happy hour, she called it, but my watch were looking particularly unhappy. After four hours on duty and a rushed lunch, they'd have preferred to lie in their hammocks reading a book, listening to music or just enjoying the rolling feel of being at sea, the long slow surge as the bow rose and fell, the sloosh of translucent water curling round the portholes, the rhythmic creak of the masts. I went to stand among them, exchanging greetings, and Cat let himself be admired. He'd been stand-offish with the trainees at first, not being a cat who liked casual caresses, but now he seemed to enjoy strolling across the deck, king of this moving kingdom, and hearing the compliments aimed at him. I answered the usual questions: yes, he used a litter tray and stayed below in bad weather; no, he didn't seem to be seasick.

I was just standing chatting when the galley door opened, and Henrik came out, scowling. This was his domain. The cooking area opened out from deck level – right by the rail, for fire safety reasons – and the benches by it were generally reserved for the galley staff to chop carrots on, or take a breather when the galley became too hot for comfort. He was Norwegian, Henrik, from Bergen. I'd noticed in my travels that ship's cooks came in two breeds: round, cheerful and accommodating, or sour, skinny and pernickety. James, the steward, and Elmer, the cook were both the former, and Henrik was definitely the latter. In particular, he didn't like having Cat aboard. Goodness knows what he was saying about Rat. I gave him my best smile and said cheerfully, 'North Sea weather.'

He grunted, and glared at Cat. 'Don't encourage that animal to come near the galley.'

'Of course not,' I said. 'C'mon, Cat.'

I moved three paces forwards and leant on the rail, looking out at the grey water, brooding. It would be good to think that the missing drink boxes belonged to Henrik, that he was a secret toper, but I didn't believe it for a moment. He was far more likely to be strict TT, and his sour expression suggested a box-of-Rennies-a-day habit. Nor did I see him selling wine on the black market once we got home. He was a law-abiding citizen.

When four bells sounded, the cleaning team came out from below and my watch bolted back down. The novelty of being aboard a tall ship under sail gave way to comfort and dryness. There'd be no deck yoga today. I strolled back to the aft door, giving a slow glance round the galley as I passed, but there was no sign of the white boxes. Cat went inside, shaking his paws fastidiously, and I headed up to the chart plotter. We were still bang on: another twenty hours like this and we'd be nicely off Orkney, ready to change course for going through the Pentland Firth.

I leant against the rail and looked at the watch below. They were spread along the rail now, with Sean just below me, hood up. I looked down at him, considering. I had to risk talking to him. If it was his gun, and he'd stolen it back, at least it was in experienced hands, not being gloated over by a wayward teenager, which would be a crumb of comfort. I wished I'd been quicker, yesterday; the wretched thing could have been rusting in Stavanger harbour, with no trouble to anybody. Still . . . I sauntered down to deck level, and propped my elbows on the shining wood beside him. 'Hi.'

'Now then, little cousin.' He looked down at the top of my head. 'Do you know, you've barely grown at all.'

My lack of inches was a sore point. 'Better than growing like a weed,' I retorted. I moved closer to him, and took the bull by the horns. 'I don't like the idea of a loaded gun loose aboard ship.'

He raised one eyebrow. 'Loose?'

I looked him straight in the eye. 'I'd like to be sure that it's back with its owner. Preferably somewhere that none of the trainees can get hold of it.'

'Ah.' He didn't pretend to misunderstand me, which I was glad of. 'Yes, you can be sure of that.'

That was something. 'I suppose if I asked why the owner was carrying it, I wouldn't get an answer.'

He turned his back to the sea and leant again, arms folded. 'I'd agree with that one, now. Little girls shouldn't ask questions, as Da Patrick used to say, God rest his soul.'

I wouldn't let him rile me. 'Can you assure me there'll be no accidents with it?'

Sean shrugged, and put on the country bumpkin accent that used to annoy Granny Bridget. 'Sure, I haven't a clue what you'd be talking about at all. Your captain's already asked me if I know anything about a gun, and I told him I didn't. That seemed to be good enough for him.'

I straightened my shoulders. 'Very well.' My voice was icy. I shot a glance towards the other trainees, and softened it to casual chat. 'Your business is your own. But you'd better make sure nobody else gets hold of it.'

Both brows went up this time. 'Well, who'd have thought my little cousin would have turned out such a spitfire?'

I went back to being family. 'You would. Don't you remember trying to kiss me, and getting a slap in the face?'

Now he was laughing openly. 'You let me kiss you at New Year. I didn't think you would object at Easter.'

'It wasn't a good Easter.' Maman had gone, and instead of me going to her French family, where we'd always spent Easter, Dad had sent me to Dublin while he recce'd out the job that would later take him to the Gulf and send me to inland France.

Sean held out his hand. 'Forgiven?'

We shook hands. 'You do realise, though,' I said, 'that Captain Gunnar thinks I'm creating excitement to liven up life aboard? He's threatening to search my cabin for the gun.'

He grimaced. 'That's hard on you.' He gave me a sympathetic glance. 'Good thing you're tough enough to take it.'

No help there, then. Whatever he was up to, whoever he was working for, he wasn't going to step in on my behalf. I leant back on the rail. 'The other thing I was going to ask you was if you know—' I stopped dead. If Sean knew Mike and hadn't let on to him, he wasn't likely to let on to me. If Mike knew him from some shady incident in their past, and Sean didn't know Mike, then it might be safer to leave it that way.

Sean's head had whipped round. 'If I know *who*?' I didn't like the look in his narrowed eyes.

I substituted lamely, '. . . if you know the sail locker. I think that's where the stowaway started his hideout.'

There was a long, charged silence. 'Someone aboard thinks he knows me?' His eyes searched my face. Then his light manner returned. 'Ah, I'm a well-known man about town, so I am.' Around us, the other trainees straightened up as Nils's ABs called them forwards to the centre of the deck. Sean nodded at me. 'Now, if you'll excuse me, I've duties aboard this ship.'

He lounged after them. *Damn.* I'd given away far more than I got in that little encounter. I waited for a moment, looking out at the shifting sea, then headed back to my cabin.

CHAPTER NINE

Nils did the handover briskly: course, distance from the Pentland Firth, no oil rigs in the way. I could see it took him an effort to say '*God Vakt*', then he headed below, steps hard with simmering anger. Whatever was wrong between him and Mike, it was just as well Mike hadn't come up to supervise. He still didn't appear as the watches lined up. I took that as a good sign. Perhaps Sean had explained to Captain Gunnar about his gun after all . . . then the captain himself appeared, checked our course and heading with me and went to stand in front of the nav shack, looking down over his ship.

The youngsters were restless. They huddled together when they formed their line, with frequent glances over a shoulder or across the deck at the shifting waves. Ellen was my first standby helm. 'What's got into them?' I asked her, nodding downwards, once I'd sent the safety watch on his rounds and got the helm, Gabriel, steady on his course.

She sighed. 'Nonsense, of course. One of the boys was remembering an old photo he'd seen, with the heads of two drowned shipmates in the water, following their ship.'

I knew the one she meant, a black and white image of two faces looking up at the ship's side from the waves. I'd seen odd things at sea, but that particular picture hadn't convinced me – the faces looked too big, for a start, and the rigging framing one didn't join the ship's side. However, from a starting rumours point of view, it was perfect.

'Then one of the others looked out,' Ellen continued, 'and said he'd seen something in the water, like a face, and then the girls became all excited, and started looking for it, and, well, you know how easy it is to see something you're looking for.'

I did indeed. 'So now there's a rumour that we've got a ghost following us.'

'They're enjoying scaring themselves,' Ellen said comfortably.

She was right, of course; they'd enjoy the thrill of it, but once that tension was aboard the ship, panic wouldn't be far away. I hoped, how I hoped, that Olav had been mistaken, that the Russian had indeed got off in Stavanger and that Sean would keep his gun safe. We needed a positive distraction – and then the sun came out from behind the last grey rags of cloud and poured warm beams over us. The hanging sails went from smoke-grey to creamy white, the water dazzled in a gold pathway stretching from us to the western horizon. The last lumps of cloud at the edge of the sea could easily have been Tír na nÓg, the fairy land.

The sails were doing us no good now. The wind had fallen. I set my trainees to furling them up. Then, of course, there was rope coiling. Erik, Mona and Petter went around, encouraging, and Mike appeared on deck, but he didn't come up to supervise me, just went round the trainees, exchanging a word with everyone. Sean appeared from below and began chatting to Erik.

Suddenly, there was an excited shout from the lookout. '*Delfiner!*' An arm waved, pointing downwards. A grey and white torpedo burst upwards in a roll of foam, curved its sickle fin over the waves and dived under again. Rope coiling was forgotten as all the trainees crowded to the sides to watch. There were three of them, white-sided dolphins, playing on the bow wave of the boat, diving up and under her prow, slipping back along her side with the wave, then speeding forward again.

It wasn't correct ship's practice, but dolphins were a great treat for trainees, and on a day like this it would do no harm to have one experienced person at the wheel for ten minutes. I went forward to Captain Gunnar. 'Sir, may I take the helm to let the trainees on duty go forrard and watch the dolphins?'

His eyebrows drew together. There was a long pause, as he thought about it, then he nodded. 'Permission granted.'

I went back to Ellen and her standby. 'On you go, they're worth watching. I'll take her.'

They hurried down to the waist of the ship, leaving me alone at the great wheel. I braced my feet and took a firm grasp of it, feeling the movement of the ship beneath me. The masts stretched above me; the dolphins played on the turquoise sea, so joyous in all their movements that it felt like they were welcoming us as fellow travellers in their element. I watched them diving and twisting, swift and lithe, and felt the wind on my cheek, and smiled at the misty horizon.

The moment stretched on. Nils came up the nav steps for a last look round before bed, and ducked down again. Mike and one of the trainees came up the starboard steps and passed aft, Mike pointing as if he was indicating Shetland, Fair Isle, Orkney; just to the north of us. I forgot I was Cass Lynch, Officer of the Watch, and returned to my first time on board a tall ship, standing at the wheel with the ship alive under my feet, and the embarrassment of trying to fit in with fashion-conscious French teenagers behind me. With the ruthlessness of sixteen, I'd blanked out Maman's worry at finding me gone. After all, I'd left her a note. She knew where I was: I'd taken a tall ship to Scotland. After a year in exile fifty miles inland, I'd been back where I belonged, with the grey waves of the North Sea tumbling about me and the salt tang in the air.

As abruptly as it had begun, playtime was over. A last jump, a twist under the bow wave, and the dolphins were gone, leaving the glimmering sea empty. Ellen came back to her post. I handed over the wheel reluctantly, and checked our course again. Below me, Erik coaxed the excited trainees back to clearing spaghetti, but most of the younger ones were too elated to listen; they were comparing photos and describing what they'd seen to each other. The adults worked steadily away, foremast, mainmast, mizzen, coiling up the long ropes and hanging them up on their belaying pins.

The sun was setting by the time the decks were clear. Above it, long skeins of cumulus reflected their scarlet tint back to the water, so that we were sailing in blood-red waves, with the path to the sun brighter gold. The horizon dazzled, too bright to look at, then turned creamy yellow as the sun dipped below the glinting sea. The clouds faded to amber, whisky gold, and back to grey. On the other side of the sky, the first star peeked out through the rigging.

Six bells; eleven o'clock. The last hour of watch was always the hardest, with everyone's thought turning bedwards. Mine too; I covered my yawn with a hand. Below me, Erik, Mona and Petter were gathered in the centre of the ship with the trainees spread in groups around them, leaning against the railing or sitting on the benches. Drowsiness clouded over us, slowing our movements and softening our voices. I shook myself out of it and went to check our course, re-instruct the helm and write up the log.

I'd just finished doing that when Agnetha came up the nav-shack steps and out on deck, a mug in each hand. 'Here, Cass.'

I clasped my hands round the warmth, dipped my nose to it and smelt the rich chocolate. 'Thanks. That's welcome.'

We leant companionably against the nav shack. The ship's lights had come on now, green on starboard, red on port, white at masthead and stern, darkening the blue sky, dimming the stars. We were our own little planet in this endless sea. Beside me, Agnetha's coffee smelt rich and sharp. She drank about half of the mug, then cradled it to her chest. 'I don't suppose you've seen Mike about?'

Her voice was tense in its striving for a casual tone. I shook my head. 'Not for a while. He was about earlier, on deck, talking to the trainees.' I frowned, trying to remember. He'd been down in the waist of the ship, then come up aft with someone in a red jacket. 'An hour ago, maybe – no, more than that. About the time we saw the dolphins.'

The worried lines about her mouth deepened, but she only said, 'I'll catch up with him later.' Her voice became more natural. 'The trainees always enjoy seeing dolphins. It makes the trip for them.'

I smiled. 'For us too. I've never got over the thrill of a close encounter.'

'But they must feel very far down on this ship, compared to your yacht, where you could reach out and touch them.'

'Far down is exactly what you want when it's a pod of killer whales. I came up with a dozen of them off Shetland, every one of them the length of my *Khalida*. All I could think of was this video I'd seen on TV of them reaching up to take seals off rocks.' It had been amazing, of course, thrilling to be so close, but my heart was pounding like I'd just run a marathon, and I'd never been as relieved as I was when they swam off.

She laughed at that, face lightening. I wished there was a way I could say, 'I know, and you have my sympathy,' but there wasn't. The only way I could support her was by keeping everything normal. 'We're nicely on course for the Pentland Firth. We should spot Fair Isle and Orkney during blue watch tomorrow morning.' Shetland would be just too far to the north, unless it was an exceptionally clear day. I felt a pang at my heart. I loved the Norwegian scenery, the soaring hills, the fjords with their spread-out houses, each with its own little jetty, the conical hat lighthouses, but Shetland had become home once more. Sometimes, waking up to another rain-washed morning between forest-green mountains, I longed for the low, brown heather hills around Brae, and the little sheep crunching along the shoreline, the white tirricks diving, then rising with a flirt of their forked tails, and the marina seals sculling round. I'd been a whole year at home; I'd watched the first daffodils open along the roadsides and seen the burns become yellow with marsh marigolds. The shalders had arrived, peep-peeping along the shore, then the Arctic terns, white swallows of a Shetland summer. The heather had bloomed purple and faded again, until the hills were rust auburn, then the snow had dusted them white. I'd got used to land colours around me, the subtle colours of Shetland, where there were few trees to usher in autumn in a blaze of scarlet or greet spring with a rush of new green. The colours were in the bones of the land and the tints of the sea.

Agnetha drank the rest of her coffee, and took my mug from me. 'I'll go and get on my thermals for night watch.' She paused, and I thought she was going to say something like, 'If you see Mike, can you tell him I was looking for him?' Then she sighed, closed her mouth again, and headed below.

I wouldn't be able to tell him, if I saw him. There was nothing I could do to help them with the mess they were in. But the watch wore on, and I didn't see him. That wasn't surprising in itself; he often did come out to chat with the trainees for a bit, then go back below. It worried me that Agnetha had looked below and not found him there either. The thought of Olav lay heavy on my mind.

Seven bells, followed by silence except for the throb of the engine. Captain Gunnar came up to check our progress, but Mike wasn't with him. When Agnetha came up, the anxious look had settled into her eyes and I saw her glance around the decks, searching each adult figure. Her manner was too carefully normal. 'Well, here I am, all set to take over. Three layers of thermals.'

'Even on a bonny summer night like this,' I agreed. I felt her anxiety tug at my heart too. If she'd really been looking for Mike, she'd have found him. He might have been having a shower the first time she'd looked, but not the second, or the third. He wouldn't be in the banjer with the trainees at this time, when half those below were sleeping, ready to get up at four, and the other half were scrambling into their full overalls. There was no reason for him to spend more than five minutes in the galley or the boat stores area. A cold shiver ran down my spine at the thought of the tunnels below decks. He might be in the carpenter store, fixing something, but Agnetha would have thought of that.

She'd have looked everywhere before drawing attention to herself by asking me. I was pretty sure she wouldn't ask Captain Gunnar. Her hand was tense on the rail, the knuckles bunched.

I told her the course, and showed the log book, then watched as my trainees lined up, yawning, already starting to pull off hats and gloves, unwind scarves, to be quicker in bed. Opposite them, the red watch was straggling into their places. Sean was among them, alert as if he'd never been asleep. I saw him give a quick glance upwards; he was watching me as closely as I was watching him. He was on duty now, while I was a free agent, yet I didn't know what I could do. I couldn't go to the captain and say Mike was missing;

he'd just think I was creating more drama. And suppose Mike was just absent on his own concerns? My mind baulked at the idea of two girlfriends aboard, but it would be hugely embarrassing for everyone if he was found in someone else's bed.

I didn't want to cause trouble, but I didn't want to do nothing either. Mike might not be . . . gone, my mind substituted for the 'dead' that sprang to my thoughts, but injured somewhere that was off-limits to the usual safety patrol.

I watched my trainees file off, said goodnight to Erik, Mona and Petter, and waited until they'd finished in the crew galley before I knocked gently on Anders' door and slipped into his cabin. There was no need to start up a new lot of speculation.

He wasn't asleep, just in bed, propped up on one elbow, reading a magazine. The bedside lamp turned his hair to guinea-gold, and gleamed on his brown shoulder. Cat and Rat were curled up in the crook of his knees; the two heads lifted as I came in, then snuggled back.

Anders put the magazine away hastily, though not before I'd spotted the spiked writing and sword-brandishing warrior on the cover. His hobby was war games, and I knew that somewhere in the cabin was the roll of green baize with little pockets in which he carried his army, ready for meetings with fellow enthusiasts. I suppressed a smile, closed the door behind me and came in to sit down on the settee by his bed. 'Anders, *jeg er bekymret.*' *I'm worried.*

He reached out one bare arm for a T-shirt and pulled it on, then put an arm around my shoulders. I leant against him, and was comforted by the warmth. Cat stretched forward to pat my cheek with one soft paw, then swarmed his way down into my lap. He was warm too. I stroked his side, and felt a rumbling purr. 'What are you worried about?'

'I think Mike's gone missing now.'

'Were you looking for him?'

I suddenly realised I couldn't tell the whole story. Some instinct of female solidarity held me back from betraying Agnetha, even to somebody I trusted as wholeheartedly as Anders. 'Someone else was.'

He gave me a sideways look, but made no comment.

'They'd looked for him, and hadn't found him.'

The arm round my shoulders gave me an affectionate shake. 'Cass, you do not listen to gossip. The whole ship knows, except perhaps the captain, for I think he would have put a stop to it, since Mike is a married man. And Nils is his brother-in-law, and at his throat for the way he is treating his sister.'

I gaped at him, feeling very stupid. Anders shook his head at me and continued. 'So . . . Agnetha was looking for him, and could not find him, and she asked you.'

'I'd seen him earlier, around nine o'clock, but not since.'

Anders considered this. 'He would not be missed, of course, until breakfast. So, what do you want to do? You're unpopular enough with the captain already.'

I sighed and nodded. 'But suppose he decided to . . . oh, I don't know, follow up some clue or something. Look by himself for the man in the black jacket. I'm worried he may be lying injured somewhere. I feel we ought to look.'

'No.' Anders' voice was unexpectedly firm. 'No, we should not.' He let go of me and turned so that we were face-to-face. 'Cass, you believe – no, *we* believe – that there is a dangerous man on board. He is probably armed, since the man who chases him is also armed.'

'Man who chases him?' I echoed.

'Your cousin.' Anders gave my shoulders a gentle shake. 'Wake up, Cass! You are not usually so slow on the uptake. Of course it's likely that the two things are linked. A dangerous man stowing away on the ship, and another man who carries a gun. Either one is helping the other, or following him. Since he is your cousin, I will let him be on the side of the angels.'

When he put it like that, it was blindingly obvious, and I felt stupid for not having seen it before, although I wished I could share his belief in which side Sean was on.

'So you wish to search the places he might be hiding. No.' He looked me straight in the eyes. 'I'm serious, Cass. If he has really harmed Mike, he has less and less to lose. I will not help you search the ship, and if you try alone, I'll go to the captain.'

I could see he meant it. His mouth was set in a determined line, and his eyes were steel-grey. I felt as startled as if Cat had turned and bitten me. 'But—'

'No.'

I took a deep breath and persisted. 'But if Mike is injured somewhere, and we leave him, it could be too late. The man in the dark jacket wouldn't be hanging around someone he thought he'd dealt with.'

'No, but it is very likely he would have dealt with him somewhere he was hanging around. Somewhere Mike had cornered him.' His hand cupped my cheek for a moment. 'Cass, it is good that you feel you should do something, but now is a time for wisdom.' His voice teased. 'What have you always said about the girl who goes into the lonely old house?'

'But if there is even a chance that we could help him?'

'Then go to the captain, and have a proper search put underway.'

I shook my head.

'*Cass.* Listen. You are not alone here, investigating. This ship has a hierarchy. If you are worried enough, go to the captain, and risk causing a huge fuss. Otherwise, leave it alone.' He spread his hands. 'Promise me you will do one of these two things.'

I wasn't happy, but I knew determination when I saw it. I knew sense too. The girl who went into the lonely old house and climbed the stairs usually came to a well-deserved sticky end. I sighed, and nodded. His point gained; Anders knew better than to say any more. I rose. 'Goodnight, then. Come on, Cat. Bedtime.'

I went out on deck to brush my teeth. The ship's lights cast a silver glow over the aft deck, slanting down over the faces of the helm and standby, and sharpening Nils's beaky nose . . . Suddenly, I saw the resemblance that had eluded me. Mike's wife, who had come to see us off, had just that nose, those cheekbones, that sullen cast of mouth. If Mike was Nils's brother-in-law, no wonder there was that sense of bitterness between them. And if Nils had overheard Agnetha this morning, as he passed along the corridor to breakfast, he had good cause to feel bitter.

I retreated to my cabin, and lay awake for a long time in the dusk of the northern summer night, with the ship rolling below me and the soft pad of feet above my head. It wasn't until after the first sunlight had touched the water on the eastern horizon that I finally slept.

Four Bells

The North Sea, the Pentland Firth, the Atlantic

Orkney to Cape Wrath

Monday 29th June

CHAPTER TEN

I awoke with that sense of something wrong, then the events of yesterday came flooding back: the quarrel in the morning, the tension between Nils and Mike, the missing gun, Agnetha's anxious face as she'd asked if I'd seen Mike. I swung my legs down, ignoring Cat's growled protest, caught up my towel and headed for the showers. The hot water woke me up, but there was still that lingering nausea, so I headed up on deck for a breath of air before breakfast.

Sea still surrounded us, but the turquoise colour was gone; these waves were the cold grey of my home waters. Shetland was just seventy miles away, over my right shoulder, and we'd soon see Fair Isle, then Orkney. The wind had fallen away completely, and we wouldn't want sails in the Pentland Firth anyway, so I'd need to consult Erik and my ABs on ideas to keep our watch occupied. Scrubbing would be greeted with initial groans, but everyone enjoyed messing about with our wide sea-water hose. The white watch were busy right now, rubber-booted and woolly-hatted, cleaning the decks; my watch could do the houses.

That settled, I headed for breakfast. Agnetha was there before me, white-faced, her hands twisting the napkin in her lap. She saw me noticing, and stilled them, but her fingers clenched on the white paper until she brought both hands up to lie one each side of her plate. Anders gave her a quick glance, then looked at the table again. Gradually, the others filed in: Jenn, Rolf, Henrik. Nils, fresh from on deck, with his mouth drawn down in sullen satisfaction. Captain Gunnar. Only Mike's place remained empty. The captain noted it under drawn-down brows, and looked down the table at Rolf. 'If you please, Rolf, the captain's compliments to the chief officer, and we are ready for him to join us at breakfast.'

Rolf nodded and slipped out, while the rest of us waited in silence. We heard a knock on the door, a pause, then the door opening. Rolf's voice called, 'Mike?' There was no answer. The door closed again.

Rolf returned, a worried line between his brows. 'He's not in his cabin, sir.'

'Very well, we will start without him.' The captain said grace, and we reached out for our breakfast preferences. I had a cold feeling in the pit of my stomach that drained my appetite. I poured half a glass of cherry yoghurt, but the flavouring seemed suddenly artificial. I pushed it away to finish later – Henrik had strong views on waste – and forced my oatmeal down.

'We will arrive at Orkney today,' Captain Gunnar said, 'so perhaps, Cass, you could do your talk on the links between Orkney, Shetland and the Viking world.'

I nodded. 'Sir.'

'Three o'clock. I look forward to it.'

I saw Anders' brows rise. I certainly wasn't the obvious expert.

I'd picked up a bit at Easter, helping guard the Viking sites in Unst, and found more in a guidebook, but it would take only one question from a real expert to floor me. I just hoped there wasn't one on board.

I cleaned my teeth, then headed up to the aft deck. Nils handed over with the minimum of words. On the chart plotter, the line pointing from the ship's bows was still bang in the middle of the opening to the Pentland Firth. Sea crossings were like that: you chose your course, and steered it. I glanced down at Agnetha, standing by the rail midships, face white. She'd chosen her course too. *It would be easier for her without Mike*, a voice in my head pointed out. I wanted to ignore it, but I could feel the thought ticking on. Without Mike, she could go ahead with the abortion she wanted once we got back to Kristiansand, and continue working her way up the ranks to first officer, chief officer, captain.

I shoved that thought away and concentrated on what I knew. Mike had been looking at the photos on the ship's computer. He'd checked out Sean. That meant, I hoped, that he'd believed my version of where the gun had gone. Then what? He'd been on deck, chatting to the trainees, then come up aft with someone in a red jacket. I tried hard to focus on them in my head, but they'd been on the edge of my vision as I'd looked forward at the horizon. They'd come up, gone behind me. I hadn't noticed them coming down again, but that wasn't significant. I'd been focused on steering, then once I'd handed the helm back I'd moved forward to the rail. He could have gone down the nav-shack steps behind me and gone to talk to Sean, or to the Russian, if he'd seen him on deck, or gone right below, as I'd first thought, and investigated the tunnels for himself, and met the Russian there.

I was just contemplating that when Captain Gunnar came

143

up to me. 'Cass, when was the last time you saw Mike?'

I hoped he wouldn't think I was suspiciously ready with my answer. 'During my watch yesterday, sir. He was down on deck, talking to the trainees. Then he came up the steps.'

'With a trainee? Of which watch?'

I shook my head. 'I didn't notice, sir. He wore a red jacket.' I tried again to remember, and had to shake my head. 'I wasn't looking.'

'There was no reason why you should be. And the time?'

At least I could answer this. 'It was while we were looking at the dolphins. The exact time will be in the log – I noted the dolphins. 21.18, I think.'

He frowned at that, and was silent for a moment. Then he sighed, and nodded. 'Very well, Cass.' He looked out and around him, as though he was drawing strength from the sea, and squared his shoulders. 'We should see Orkney soon. You could let the trainees climb the rigging and look, if you wish.'

'Yes, sir.' Land-spotting always raised spirits, and even if most of low Orkney was only a smudge on the horizon, they should see the higher land on Hoy.

'What time do we need to enter the Pentland Firth?'

He had it all in my detailed passage plan, but he needed to know that I knew. 'The tide turns with us at High Water Dover plus 1.15, sir.' High Water Dover was 9.47 today; I'd already done the arithmetic. '11.02 BST. It'll take us four hours to get through, and we'll be through the passage between Stroma and Swona and past the Merry Men of Mey before the full force of it hits us. 3.5 knots as we're coming out on the other side.'

'Current ETA?'

'11.00, sir.'

'Good.' My spirits rose at the word. Captain Gunnar turned away, then paused, and turned back. 'Your friend who came on one of the fjord trips, he is a policeman, is he not?'

'Yes, sir.'

'Detective Gavin Macrae?'

I nodded, stifling the hope that leapt in my breast like a dolphin bursting from the water. We were in Scottish waters, Gavin's patch. If the captain was going to call for official help, it would be natural for him to ask for a name he knew.

Captain Gunnar turned away and headed back down the nav-shack steps. I waited until the last buckets and scrubbing brushes were stowed, then beckoned Erik up and gave instructions for a climb to see land. There was a jingle and chink of harnesses being put on, then the steady clamber aloft. Johan waved from the second platform, and called downwards, 'There. Over there.'

It was funny, seeing land from sea. Even only passing it, I could feel it reaching out to claim me. Half an hour later, there was Fair Isle, a lump on the horizon. I'd sailed by it on Old Year's Day, returning from Gavin's loch. Then Orkney came suddenly over the horizon, unexpectedly close, long and low, with the humps of Hoy grey behind the long masses of Mainland, Burray and South Ronaldsay. As we came closer, we began to see the land colours through the mist, the green of pasture punctuated by white houses, hazed still with distance. Last night's clear sky was gone; now there was a grey fleece stretching from the horizon behind us and over the mastheads to blanket the Orkney hills. To port, the Pentland Skerries lay low and ominous, a graveyard of shipping topped by two white towers. Behind them was the lower coast of the north-east tip of Scotland: Duncansby Head, looking like a separate island, Dunnet Head, Scrabster.

We came into the firth bang on time. As soon as the tide caught us, our speed began to rise: six knots, seven, seven and a half. I went back to talk to the helm, Samir. 'Keep her as bang on course as you can, now. See these two islands ahead? We want to be well clear of the left hand one, Stroma. There's a nasty point, the Swilkie. Keep the ship two-thirds of the way across the channel.'

He nodded. I'd watched him helming yesterday, and had confidence he'd steer a straight course. Anders was on deck at the engine controls, face set, eyes narrowed in concentration. 'Don't let the tide take us over eight and a half knots,' I told him. 'But keep good steerage way.'

He nodded.

Satisfied, I went back to my post. Now, on starboard, the pool between the islands was beginning to open out: Scapa Flow, where the British Navy had anchored during the war; where the *Royal Oak* had been lost, and the surrendering German officers had scuttled their fleet. I could just distinguish Flotta's jetty, with a tanker lying at it, and the circular gas and oil tanks behind.

Below me, the watches were beginning to muster. Agnetha came up beside me. Her face was bone-white, with dragged circles under her eyes and a long line running down each side of her mouth. The eyeshadow she'd put on didn't quite disguise the red rims to her eyes. Involuntarily, I put out a hand to her. 'Are you sure you're well enough to stand watch? I can keep going.'

Her eyes brimmed full of tears, but she shook her head and moved away from my touch. 'I'm fine. I'd rather be busy. What's our course?'

'288 degrees. Just keep well off Stroma, and be ready for the Merry Men.' I had the pilot book ready at the right page. 'Here.' I checked the plotter, marked our course and scribbled the log entry. '*God vakt.*'

'*God vakt skal vaere.*'

But it wouldn't be, I knew. I waited there until she'd instructed the new helm and standby, then we went below together to lunch.

Captain Gunnar waited on his feet until we were all present, and then closed the door. 'I have something to say to you all.'

I could feel everyone trying not to look at Mike's empty place.

'We are fortunate that Mike is not a member of a specific watch, so that his absence has not yet been noticed by the trainees. I beg of you all, do not mention it anywhere outside this cabin. We do not wish a panic.' He sat down in his place, letting himself fall heavily, an old man at the end of his career. He had been almost twenty years on the *Sørlandet*, and loved her as a sailor came to love the ship that took him flying though the waters, that sheltered him in storms and brought him safe to port. He was doing his best to lead us through this, but it was a situation he'd never foreseen, and the damage it would do to his ship's reputation was breaking his heart.

'I have talked to you all. Mike was seen at various times earlier in the evening. He was at Jenn's muster. After that, he went below for a while, to his cabin, but then he came out and was on deck, chatting to the trainees. He was last seen coming aft with a person who has not yet been identified.'

I felt the words cold in my breast. Captain Gunnar gave us all a long, steady look. 'Two people missing. I would like to say that it is a second tragic accident, but I cannot believe it. Mike was not one to have a heart attack and fall silently overboard.' His dark eyes went around us. 'I have contacted the police.'

There was silence, like an indrawn breath.

He looked round us all. 'You will remember Gavin Macrae, who joined us on the first fjord trip of this season.' If it hadn't been so serious he would have smiled. 'The Scotsman who climbed the mast in his kilt.'

My heart thudded.

'Macrae is an inspector in the Scottish police. I called him directly. He passed me on to his superior officer, but I stressed the international nature and youth of the crew, and the unfortunate media coverage that might create, as well as diplomatic difficulties. I made a good case that DI Macrae's familiarity with the ship would be of help in investigating Mike's disappearance. I have asked that all be kept as discreet as possible, but—' He shrugged, and gestured with his hands. 'I beg you all, let us do what we can to minimise the damage to the ship's reputation.'

'How can we keep it from the trainees,' Nils asked, 'if we have police here?'

'He does not look like a policeman, and I suggested that he could be sent aboard in a pilot boat.'

Aboard? A full four days before we expected to be together . . . I had difficulty keeping my face impassive over the leap in my heart. He was coming, and soon.

'A routine customs inspection of the ship,' Henrik suggested. 'The trainees will not know how very far from routine it is.'

'Say nothing unless you're directly asked. If you are . . .' He paused for a moment, one hand stroking his moustache. 'No, not customs. It is a police visit to do with the death of Olav.'

'But won't he need to interview the trainees?' Nils asked.

'I will allow that only if it becomes necessary,' Captain Gunnar said. He didn't know Gavin. Interference with the investigation wouldn't be allowed, as I knew from my own attempts. There could be an interesting clash of authorities here. My spirits were rising by the second. Gavin was coming, we'd have professional backup at last, and I'd be able to tell him about the Russian, about Sean and the gun, and be believed. 'Inspector Macrae has asked that you do not discuss what you saw yesterday evening with each other. Think for yourself where you saw Mike, and when, but do not talk about it. In particular, think about his state of mind – if he has seemed worried to you, or depressed. The inspector will interview you when he comes aboard.'

We all nodded.

'And if anyone asks where Mike is?' Henrik asked.

'Say vaguely that he is somewhere about, and ask if you can help, or offer to give him a message.'

We all nodded, and the captain rose, picked up an apple and headed into his cabin, closing the door behind him, and leaving silence in the mess room. We were all struggling to take it in. This kind of thing didn't happen aboard a tall ship. We were braced to deal with storms and whales, cold-water showers and grumbling trainees, but two unexplained disappearances were outside our experience. I knew I should be used to death, because I'd seen enough in the past year, but it still came as a shock, a blankness in the mind, that Mike had been here with us yesterday and was gone today.

I was glad Gavin was coming.

None of us had any appetite now. We left the table and headed about our duties. I went to stand on deck for a moment, greeting the trainees mechanically as I moved among them. Orkney was to starboard, with the red cliffs round the west of Hoy just starting to come into view; we'd be able to see the Old Man of Hoy soon. On port the north coast of Scotland was spread out, a long line of humped hills, grey as the fretted clouds above them, with the opening to Scrabster and Thurso just visible. Seeing the land reminded me I'd get a signal now. I fished out my mobile and dialled Gavin. 'Hey.'

'*Halo.* What on earth have you been up to?'

I glanced around me at the trainees lining the rail, mobiles in hand. 'I'll tell you all about it when you get here. When will that be?'

'It's not that easy. Your captain suggested a pilot boat, but he doesn't know our Highland roads.' In the background there was that echoing bustle of an airport, and a bing-bong announcement. Gavin paused to listen to it. 'That's us. 13.40 to Stornaway.'

I visualised my map of Scotland. Stornaway was on Lewis, in the Western Isles, and at least a day's sailing away. 'Why Stornaway?'

'They talked of a pilot boat from Scrabster, but by the time I get there, you'll be coming up to the Cape Wrath light. A bit of a trip. So my boss talked to the coastguard helicopter instead. The government closed half the stations, but Stornaway is still open, so all I have to do is get there, and then they'll fly out to you and land us right on the deck. Hopefully avoiding the masts. Hector – he's the winchman – sounded quite excited about it. He says he's never done a drop on a tall ship before.'

'You sound quite keen yourself.'

'I've never done a helicopter drop before.'

I thought about being dangled from a spinning bird in the sky and felt my stomach lurch. 'You're welcome to it. So when do you hope to get here?'

'Arrival in Stornaway, 14.25 . . . say an hour to get to the chopper and get all organised . . . then we have to fly to you. Not before five o'clock.'

'I'll be glad to see you,' I admitted. '*Beanneach leat*, safe flight.'

Up on the boat deck, Jenn was assembling her troops for yoga. I went up to join them, and spent the next half hour twisting myself into odd shapes, with the water rolling grey below us. As I placed my hands, my mind was writhing too. The captain had sent straight for Gavin, and pulled rank to steamroll his objections. Perhaps that meant he thought I was in the clear. Or, I thought gloomily, manoeuvring myself so that I was on my side, balanced on one leg and one hand, more likely he had me in the frame for everything, and hoped that Gavin would minimise the publicity for my sake. Not that a public arrival by helicopter could be called unobtrusive . . .

On the aft deck, opposite us, Agnetha was on duty. Her face was still pale, but she was moving on her round of nav shack, chart plotter and helm as briskly as if nothing had happened. I looked across at her from under my braced arm, and she spotted me and lifted a hand. I moved into the position we'd nicknamed 'the crab', levered up on backward twisted arms, and saw her wavering upside down. Pregnancy must have upturned her world, stealing all her certainties for herself: her life aboard, her career, her ambition to be the first female master of a tall ship. I lowered myself back to the deck and lifted again. Upside down . . . my plait swept the deck. Jenn counted to eight, and I collapsed, thankfully. I'd thought I was fit, but this used muscles I didn't know I had.

My talk on the Vikings and Orkney/Shetland was at three, so I headed below, my whole body glowing, to check over my notes. I hated public speaking, but it was part of the job. In this case, I was planning to take the trainees through the Norse/Shetland history, starting with the first Norse settlers in Unst in the eighth century. They'd spread down to the rest of Shetland, then to Orkney, Caithness and the Scottish and Irish coasts. I talked myself through it in my head. The early homesteads, the kleber industry, the fish trading enterprise at Jarlshof for the Norwegian longships heading south or west. Shetland had stopped being a Norse colony in 1469 with the marriage of Christian I's daughter to James IV, although the treaty pawning it to Scotland insisted on maintaining the Norse laws and language, ready for it being redeemed again. The Scots crown wangled their way round Denmark's many tries. The links continued through the Hanseatic League, with a series of booths in Shetland supplying best quality salted fish to traders from Germany, Flanders, the Baltic, and Norway. It ended with the Union of Parliaments in 1705, when an act was made to stop Scotland trading with anyone but England, followed by a heavy tax on imported salt. It was Shetland's bleakest time. That should take twenty minutes of my half hour. After that, I'd talk about how aspects of modern Shetland reflected our Viking heritage: the double-ended boats, the spread-out settlements and narrow fields stretching down to the water, the long, low croft houses that were being replaced everywhere by Norwegian wooden 'kit houses', the place names. I'd finish by reciting a poem in dialect.

It was pleasant out on deck, dry and calm, so I got Rolf to lug me out a whiteboard and the trainees gathered round. Cat came out and sat on one of the benches, washing his whiskers and smoothing out his plumed tail. It took me back to summer, teaching the Brae bairns, with them crowded round the shed whiteboard and Cat presiding from the top of one of the boats, though talking about Viking Shetland was a far cry from reminding my Brae trainees about the no-go area and five points of sailing. I suppressed the pang of homesickness and busied myself drawing a rough map of Shetland, Orkney and Norway.

It all seemed to go fine. I talked as clearly as I could, and used the slowly passing scenery of Orkney to illustrate some points, and tried not to listen for the sound of a helicopter which couldn't be here for two hours yet. The adults nodded their heads, and the teenagers took photos and winged them back to Norway. I answered a few questions, then my audience dispersed, and I headed to the aft deck to join the others in a well-earned cup of tea. 15.40. An hour and twenty minutes to go.

The aft deck was busy with the off-duty crew gathered together over flasks of tea and coffee. Kjell Sigurd brought me a coffee, exactly as I'd asked for it last time. I watched him go on round the crew and realised he'd memorised everyone's preferences. The boy was a star. The galley girls must have decided we needed cheering up, for today there was a plate of meltingly gooey chocolate brownies. Anders was still on engine duty, but from the chocolatey look of Rat's whiskers, he'd already had his share. I helped myself to one, as good as it looked, a crunchy crust with a toffee-soft inner.

'That was interesting,' Erik said, leaning on the rail beside me, mug suspended in the air above the glinting water. His voice was too cheerful; I shot a quick look at him and saw that he was pale under his tan. The hand holding the mug shook slightly. Quickly, he cupped the mug in both hands and raised it to his lips, then held it on the rail. 'You must guide us when we come to Shetland at the end of July.'

'Oh, no,' I said. 'I've got a much better guide lined up for you: my friend, Magnie. What he doesn't know about Shetland isn't worth knowing.'

'I'll look forward to that. Once this voyage is over.' He turned his back to the trainees and lowered his voice. 'How soon do you think Gavin will get here?'

'An hour or so.'

'But what can he do?' Erik drained the last of his tea and cradled the empty mug. 'He's surely not going to search the ship himself. After all, if this mysterious stowaway the trainees talked about . . .' He paused, biting his lip, then continued. 'If this man killed Mike, he's not just going to come out with his hands up for one policeman.'

I certainly hoped he wouldn't try to arrest the Russian single-handed. 'Captain Gunnar's just trying to do the right thing.'

Erik nodded gloomily. 'I wouldn't want him to get hurt, hunting this man.' His eyes were unhappy, his tone bitter. 'Sometimes doing the right thing causes a lot more trouble than if you'd done the wrong thing straight off.'

I gave him another look, under the cover of resettling myself on the rail. I wondered if he was thinking of Mike and Agnetha's affair, though it was too late now to say what the right thing was; leaving his wife or abandoning Agnetha both felt like wrongs to me. Erik flicked a speck of loose paint over into the water, and echoed what I was thinking. 'Or maybe it's just that what felt like the right thing was actually wrong after all, and then trouble multiplies from it, and you're left with a choice of wrongs.'

'Mike and Agnetha?' I said softly.

He started at that, as if he'd forgotten I was there, and looked behind him again. His voice echoed my murmur. 'Did Agnetha tell you too?'

I shook my head. 'I overheard something. Is there anything I can do to help?'

'Not if Mike's gone.' His barely audible voice was heavy with grief. 'There's nothing anyone can do.' His shoulders straightened, his voice hardened. 'Except get the bastard, whatever it costs.'

I didn't like the emphasis he put on the last words. *Whatever it costs*. I hoped he wasn't going to try any heroics. 'Remember Micaela, and the children,' I said awkwardly.

His eyes blazed at that. He shot out a hand to grasp my wrist. 'What do you mean?'

I stared at him. 'I was just worried that you were going to get him yourself.'

'Oh.' He drew the sound out long. 'No. No, I won't try to do that.' He let go of my wrist and turned away, walked off without another word, leaving me staring after him, disquieted. Something was wrong, but I didn't know what. I had a sudden memory of Micaela's anxious face as she waved us off. *She still expects a sudden knock on the door*, Erik had said. I wondered if that was what was at the root of her fears: not an affair on board ship, but the fear that someone would come for her while Erik was away. Maybe their marriage didn't automatically make her a Norwegian citizen . . . My next thought was to wonder how she'd got out of the repressive regime. A student visa, which had long since run out? If she was an illegal resident, the nightmares were understandable. Furthermore, if she was illegal, I wasn't sure what the children's status would be. It was all so complicated nowadays.

Something was wrong, for Erik to blaze out like that; but I didn't see how Micaela's nationality or status could be relevant to what was going on aboard. Erik and Mike were mates. If Mike had known Michaela was illegal, he wouldn't go threatening Erik. I didn't believe that for a moment. Besides, Erik could just have countered with threatening to tell Captain Gunnar about Agnetha's pregnancy, since he was in her confidence.

I thrust the thought away. Agnetha. Nils. My cousin Sean, if there was some past history between him and Mike. I wondered if his gun had a silencer. The stowaway, if he was still aboard, was the most likely of all. Even if Captain Gunnar refused to believe in him, Gavin would.

CHAPTER ELEVEN

I went to see if Agnetha wanted a coffee refill. She was still on duty, checking the chart plotter, giving instructions to the helm, then turning to receive the safety watch. Her eyes were red, but she was holding herself together well.

'More coffee?'

'Oh, yes please, Cass.'

I took her mug, refilled it, grabbed the last brownie and took them over. 'How're you doing?'

She flicked a quick glance at me, and I remembered that I wasn't supposed to know about the baby, about Mike. 'Good.' Her voice was determinedly normal. 'Steaming steadily towards America. We'll turn the corner during your watch, about ten o'clock.' She nodded at the red cliffs on our right. 'There's your Old Man of Hoy.'

I looked, and saw the sandstone column jutting up above the cliffs. 'You wouldn't catch me climbing that.'

'Yes, people do odd things,' Agnetha agreed. The ghost of a smile touched her lips. 'Nothing like a nice safe mainmast.' She tilted her wrist to check her watch. 'Ten minutes.'

Below us, the trainees were starting to gather to their sides of the ship. Nils drained his mug and came over to us. 'Course?'

'Steady as she goes,' Agnetha said. 'We're out of the tide race now.' She went into the nav shack with him to do the handover stuff, then came out and linked her arm through mine. The gesture was friendly, but the arm was bar-hard, and shaking. 'So, your Gavin's coming aboard to sort us all out.'

'Something like that,' I agreed.

'You'll be glad to see him.' She gave me a sideways look. 'Won't you?'

I smiled. 'A whole four days before I expected him.' I felt the tension in her arm, and wondered if she needed a chance to talk. 'Come and collapse.'

'Good idea. Your place or mine?'

'Either,' I said.

'Yours is nearer.' She led the way across the passage. The two heads, black-and-white and grey, lifted as we came in. Rat yawned and snuggled down again, but Cat disentangled himself, stretched, and came down to settee level. I sat down and lifted him onto my knee. 'Good Cat.'

Agnetha shut the door behind us and sank down on the settee beside me. 'Oh, that's good, after standing for four hours. Hallo, Cat. *Hei, Rotte.*' She leant her head back against the mahogany side of my berth, and closed her eyes. I sat beside her, and waited. She was tough, Agnetha, and proud; she wouldn't break down in tears. I tried to imagine what she was going through, but the thought of Gavin going missing, believed killed, made an iron hand clench around my heart. I thrust the thought away. That was different. There was relief as well as grief in Agnetha's rigid face. She'd lost Mike, and she'd give the world to have him back in it, even if it meant giving him up, but losing him also meant the end of the deception, each meeting being stolen from her duties or his wife. It meant she'd be free to have an abortion, if that was what she'd decided.

The moment drew out. The last waves of the Merry Men overfalls slapped against the side of the ship. Then suddenly Agnetha's control broke. She gave a gasping sob and buried her face in her hands, her whole body shaking. She wasn't crying; her breath came in harsh rattles. Tentatively, I moved along and put an arm around her shoulders, lightly, giving her human contact, if that would comfort her. To do any more would feel an intrusion.

We sat like that for a good five minutes and then she took a deep breath, and straightened, and I drew back from her. 'Sorry,' she said. 'Making an exhibition of myself. I needed that, though. I've been controlling myself all day. Since last night, when I looked for him, and couldn't find him.'

I nodded.

She turned towards me, face shadowed. 'You knew. Didn't you?'

'Only since yesterday morning.' I picked my words carefully. 'I heard your voice in his room.'

Her eyes flew to mine, then flicked to the wall behind her. 'When I was at the washbasin.'

'Yes.'

'So you know about—' One hand indicated her stomach. There was no time to think of a lie. 'Of course you do.' Her gaze hardened, as if I was suddenly an enemy. I stared back, puzzled. 'Well, don't start preaching. The choice is mine.'

There was nothing I could say to that. She was an adult who could look up all the latest medical thinking about what a foetus

158

was: a joining of cells that gradually grew a head, a backbone, limbs. When it became a human being was where we differed.

Agnetha held out a hand to clasp mine. 'I'm sorry, Cass. I'm all on edge. Hormones.'

'Grieving,' I said. 'Shock.'

'Yes, those too. He was ten times more alive than anyone else. I can't believe he's gone. I keep thinking I hear his voice, or expect to see him when someone walks along the corridor.' Her eyes filled with tears. 'And the worst of it is: we parted on a quarrel.'

I didn't know how to comfort her. 'You'd have made it up, if he'd lived.'

She shook her head. Then, suddenly, as clearly as if she'd said it, I saw her remembering who I was: *the policeman's girlfriend.* She managed a smile. 'Yes. You're right. Of course we would have.' Her voice rang out as false as poor-quality copper nails under a carpenter's hammer. 'In fact, that's why I was looking for him, to say sorry, and make up.'

Her sky-blue eyes were peering sideways at me as if she was checking that I was swallowing this. 'It wasn't a serious quarrel – well, you heard. I was just feeling wretched, and taking it out on him.'

I wanted to tell her that I hadn't heard the words, but I knew how bad a liar I was. I nodded. Agnetha changed position. 'It's hard, this. Hormones everywhere, and feeling bloated and sick.' Her eyes were on my face. '*You* know.'

For a moment I didn't know what she was talking about. Then, suddenly, it all rushed together, like blood to the head. The way I'd been feeling bloated and lethargic, which I'd put down to too much rye bread and not enough exercise, and the queasiness in the mornings. My mouth fell open. I couldn't think of anything to say, just sat there gaping at Agnetha like a guillemot panicking at an approaching boat.

Her eyes were still guarded. 'You hadn't worked it out?'

I shook my head. My brain was doing sums. Seven weeks since Gavin had been aboard, on the fjord trip. Could these changes happen so quickly? I'd missed a period, but I wasn't particularly regular anyway, so I hadn't worried about it. The time we'd been together before that was in March. That was too long ago; surely I couldn't be a whole three months gone and not have known it. And we'd been careful . . .

'Morning sickness can start at six weeks,' Agnetha said, reading my thoughts. 'And last till twelve weeks. I've been looking it all up.'

'I suppose,' I said slowly, 'that I'm seven weeks.' *But how*, my brain was saying, *could it be*? We'd had so little time together . . .

'Too late for the morning-after pill, but plenty of time to get rid of it.' Agnetha's voice was flat, as prosaic as if she was talking about throwing away an old jumper. 'It's no big deal.'

She made it sound so easy. Instinctively, my hands moved to clasp my abdomen, even as my head was going, *Of course, that's the easiest way out.* Suddenly it was hard to breathe. What was I going to do? Gavin and I had barely begun to know each other, and I'd just got back to sea; I couldn't bear to leave it again . . . and yet inside that curved space under my fingers was my child, a tiny living human being, already dependent on me. I hadn't meant to create it, but now I had to live with the consequences.

'I'll have to leave *Sørlandet*,' I said, slowly. My heart wrenched, like a fish trying to escape a hook. 'But only for a while. When she turns into an academy, I could leave for those two years, while she's a teaching ship, and then return.'

Agnetha shook her head. 'Only if you've got a devoted mother who's prepared to raise the child for you.'

I tried to imagine Maman taking on a toddler. 'No.' I didn't want even to think what she would say about me giving up my career so soon. My brain began scurrying ahead, trying to make plans. *Khalida*'s cabin would be fine at first, while it was at the carrycot stage, but what about when it began to toddle? I tried to remember the arrangements of netting on the guard rails that I'd seen used by other parents, and caught myself up on the word 'other'. I was thinking like one already.

'Or if you have a house-husband.' Her eyes were steady on mine. 'Would your Gavin give up his career so you could keep yours?'

I shook my head. It wasn't just that he was proud of his role as part of the Police Scotland serious crimes team. I knew that being in work mattered to him in a fundamental way. You couldn't reconstruct a thousand years of Scottish male breadwinner bloodline with a mere thirty years of women in equal roles. Could I give the sea up more easily? A knot of panic gripped me at the thought. Yet he'd want his child to grow up ashore . . . *I'd like to have a family*, he'd said. Were we somehow so in tune that he'd felt my body changing?

Agnetha spoke over my thoughts. 'You see, I've considered it all, over and over. It's just not possible. Sure, you have plenty of time off, and that's all very well when the child's sleeping, but if it's a wild day and you're on duty, you can't expect other people to amuse your child below. Or if it needs you at night while you're on watch, you can't abandon your post to go below and soothe it, or read an extra story because it can't sleep, or whatever. No. Captains can have their children aboard because they bring their wives to do the actual caring. Cruising couples can take them round the world, the family together, and good luck to them. But for us, no. The child or the career. The choice is that simple.' She rose. 'Look, I can see this was a shock to you.

I know how that feels. I'll leave you to get used to the idea. See you later.'

I slid to my bunk and swung my legs up. Cat and Rat came to cuddle in; Cat in the crook of my shoulder, Rat on one arm. The engines throbbed reassuringly, and the sea curled around the porthole with a soft shoosh. Above my head, Nils went aft to the helm; I could just hear the murmur of his voice. It would be steady as she goes until we were well clear of Cape Wrath.

I felt as though I'd received a crack from a flying block. My brain had simultaneously accepted the news and rejected it. I knew I was pregnant, yet I didn't believe it. A ridiculous voice in my head was saying triumphantly, *See, you weren't seasick!*

Seven weeks. I reached for my laptop, then remembered that of course there was no Internet. There was a basic medical book on the captain's shelf, ready for a quick consultation when the ship's hospital cabin was locked. I checked nobody was about, nipped through and brought it back to my cabin, heart thumping. *Pregnancy.* The picture showed that the baby inside me was well past the collection of cells stage, well past being a tadpole. It had a misshapen head, with bumps where the features would be, and stumpy arms with tiny webbed fingers. According to the text, it was the size of a blueberry. I couldn't honestly say it was recognisably human, but if you had to guess, human would be the most likely.

What it looked like didn't matter. The church taught that it was human from the moment of conception, and I felt that too. I couldn't see any other defining moment where you could say it went from being a collection of cells to a person. I put the book back and came slowly into my cabin again. I felt sick. There was a tiny human being growing inside me. I laid one hand on my stomach, feather-light, and tried to imagine the little heart beating under it.

What was I going to do?

What Agnetha had said made sense, of course. I couldn't have a baby and the sea too, or not this life, aboard *Sørlandet*. I'd still have *Khalida*, though, with her sails bent on, ready to take me out into the ocean. It would only be the end if I let it be. Once he or she was born, I'd work out how we'd live. I was young, and strong. We'd do it somehow.

That 'we' reminded me that Gavin was in this too. His promotion meant he was no longer stationed at Inverness, although that was his base, but might be sent anywhere in Scotland. If he wanted to be a hands-on father, that wouldn't fit in so easily – and I was sure that he would want to be, although as I said it so certainly to myself, I felt as though a cold hand was gripping my breastbone. Maybe, when it actually came to it, he wouldn't want to be involved. Maybe a here, there and everywhere girlfriend was one thing, and a wife and baby quite another. I suddenly realised that we'd only ever talked about when our joint schedules would let us meet up. We'd never seriously discussed how our separate lives could be twisted to make one.

I was looking at the white wood ceiling and thinking about it all when I heard another noise swirling through the wind: the chop of helicopter blades, the sound rising and fading as it turned. Gavin! I shoved the apprehension away under thankfulness. Whatever was going wrong aboard this ship, now we'd have professional help. I rose, ignoring Cat's protests, hauled on my boots, and headed up on deck.

The helicopter was still a mile away. I glanced at my watch: ten past five. Not bad timing. Captain Gunnar was on deck, talking on a hand-held radio to the pilot. 'The aft deck, then. I'll make sure it's cleared. *Sørlandet* standing by.' He clipped the radio back on his belt and turned to us. 'They'll land Macrae and his sergeant on the aft deck. Nils, make sure all trainees and crew are off the aft deck for now, and put your watch leader on the helm.' He glanced round at me. 'Cass, tell the trainees the helicopter's going to land a couple of men. There'll be a lot of wind, so although they're welcome to take photos, they'll need to watch they don't lose cameras and hats overboard.' A sweeping glance round us all. 'Get all hands on deck. Go round making sure everything is stowed securely. White watch: midships; blue watch: boat deck; red watch: foredeck.'

I gave a quick glance round for my team. Yes, Erik was there, Mona, Petter. 'Erik and Petter, you go for the boat deck, and Mona and I will warn the trainees and check the main deck.' Loose items didn't stay long aboard ship, so everything should be lashed down, but it wouldn't hurt to check. I went down to deck level and found a bunch of my youngsters watching the helicopter. It was close enough now to see the chevrons on its underside.

'It's a coastguard helicopter,' I told them. 'They're dropping a couple of people off. It'll be spectacular to watch, but keep a tight hold on your phones; the down-draught's fierce. Can you pass the word round?'

I did a quick headcount, nipped below to get the last stragglers on deck, and grabbed four of the reliable ones. 'Can you go round the ropes making sure they're all fast round a belaying pin. Thanks.'

'Line up the watches!' Rolf yelled from the aft deck. I repeated it below, and the blue watch came into its place. The chopper was coming downwards now, circling the ship. The hatch in its belly opened and the winchman began to descend with another person strapped to his chest. I saw the flutter of Gavin's kilt, a corner of plaid tugging loose from the climber's harness.

The noise was horrendous, and the down-draught far worse than I'd expected. It was like being in the centre of a hurricane.

The air sucked at my jacket and tugged my hair from its plait, and my ears hurt with the deafening throb that started overhead, then echoed from all around the ship. It got louder, wilder. The double spider above us descended on its thread, growing to become a man in orange, with goggles and white helmet, and Gavin, also helmeted, kilt fluttering around his bare knees. A moment with legs flailing, and the winchman talking into his helmet, then the pilot dropped the pair of them dead centre of the space aft behind the captain's coffin. Gavin undid the buckles and straps, handed the helmet back to the winchman and came forward, looking as trim as if he'd stepped on board at the quayside. I knew he'd spotted me from the air; a quick nod, then he headed for Captain Gunnar, standing straight and stern on the captain's promenade.

Gavin wasn't tall, but he carried himself with the upright bearing of a Highlander, alert as a golden eagle on a crag. He was wearing his second-best kilt, the green hunting Macrae, teamed with a faded green tweed jacket whose pockets bulged, due to his habit of carrying a little tin of fly-making equipment. He had green wool knee-socks with a little dagger in the top of one, wood-handled to match his plain leather sporran. Behind me, phones flashed as our young Norwegians sent photos of this Scottish native home. The down-draught from the helicopter ruffled his dark red hair, cut short enough to discourage its natural curl.

He and the captain shook hands as the winchman returned upwards, and waited together for the sergeant to be buckled on. The twin burden came out of the hatch and eased downwards. I saw a flash of gold hair tugging free from under the helmet and a familiar dark trouser suit, and felt my jaw stiffen. What was *she* doing here? I must be mistaken . . . but as she descended, it became clear that I wasn't. There, suspended with the winchman, was Sergeant Peterson from the Shetland force, she of the mermaid-green eyes and calm indifference to human oddities. The last time I'd seen her, in the Viking treasure case, she'd accepted that I was on the side of the angels ('For once,' her raised brows had added), but she'd still banished me to tea-making once things got interesting. Civilians, her calm dismissal had made clear, particularly disreputable civilians who'd been the prime suspect twice over, weren't allowed into confidential police business. I supposed that was fair enough, but I didn't have to like it.

My next thought was dismay. I'd expected some anonymous sergeant who could be pushed off to the lower ranks mess. I was never going to manage to talk to Gavin, really talk to him, with Freya Peterson hanging around, determined to be top sidekick.

She landed on deck, took the helmet off and stood there, neat and lean as a cormorant on a skerry, pale beak tilted up to the sun. Not a hair was out of place. She gave a quick look around, establishing the layout, then she too walked forward to Captain Gunnar. I lip-read her greeting. 'Sergeant Peterson, sir.'

The winchman jerked upwards, the chopper rising as it reeled him in, then it spun sideways and headed back south-westwards. As the noise faded away, I became aware of my ears ringing. Around me, my watch was chattering and comparing photos. Rolf stepped forward once more. 'White watch, back to your stations,' he called from above our heads. 'Blue and red watches dismissed.'

That included me, of course, and however much I might want to stick my nose in, I knew my place at sea. Gavin would come and find me when he got the chance. I was just heading for the passage to the officers' quarters when Captain Gunnar called Agnetha and me up. Inwardly sticking out my tongue at Freya Peterson, I went smartly up the steps. 'Sir?'

He turned to Gavin, very formal. 'The other officers of the watch: Second Mate Solheim, and Third Mate Lynch.'

Gavin held out his hand to Agnetha first, then to me. 'Gavin Macrae.'

'Sir,' I said, in my best no-nonsense manner.

His grey eyes gleamed with amusement. He wasn't good-looking, my Gavin; or perhaps he was, but in a plain, Scottish way, with a square jaw, a long, rather wooden mouth, a nose that had been benkled by too much rugby in his youth, and level, uncompromising brows over eyes the grey of a misty sea. A good bloke, that's what he looked like; a mate who'd lend you a fiver in a pinch, or who could be trusted to take your girlfriend to the pub when you had to stand her up. Not somebody who'd be cleverer than a murderer; definitely not. If he wasn't convinced a suspect had got that idea yet, he brought out his battered tin and tied flies. *Nobody can remember what lie they're telling when they're busy watching my fingers*, he'd told me once. 'When do you go on watch, Ms Lynch?' he asked, blandly, as if he didn't know.

'Eight till midnight, sir.'

'Then I'll talk to you in the morning.' He turned to the captain. 'May I talk to you first, sir?'

The captain nodded, and gestured him towards the nav-shack steps. Descending back to deck level, I caught a buzz of Norwegian speculation among the youngsters in the smoking corner: 'Don't be stupid. The police could easily wear kilts as a uniform in Scotland.'

'He didn't have a gun.'

'Yes, he did. I saw the bulge of it, strapped under his jacket.'

Full marks for observation. I'd missed that one. Police Scotland must be taking this very seriously, if they were allowing an armed officer aboard a training ship full of youngsters. Still, if somebody had to have a gun, I'd prefer Gavin to my cousin Sean.

'See?' Dimitri crowed. 'I said they were police. They're investigating the mystery man in the tunnels.'

'Do you think there'll be a gun battle?' Sindre turned to flick his fag-end overboard, and saw me. There was a sudden silence. I murmured '*God dag*,' and tried to pass on, but was instantly surrounded.

'Is it true we have a stowaway aboard?'

'Did he kill Olav, because he saw him?'

'Are they the police?'

Captain Gunnar wouldn't want me to answer any of these questions. I did my best. 'The Norwegian Special Branch searched the ship in Stavanger, you saw that. There can't possibly be a stowaway aboard. However, there are formalities to do with losing poor Olav overboard like that.'

'Is he a policeman?' Nine persisted.

I nodded. 'DI Gavin Macrae of Police Scotland.'

'His kilt's really cool,' Anna said. 'It's a much more interesting uniform than ours. Why doesn't the woman get one?'

'They're both in plain clothes. DI Macrae wears the kilt because he likes it.'

'Don't his legs get cold?' Sindre asked.

I shook my head. 'He's got a treble thickness of best wool cloth round his upper legs, compared to your single thickness of denim, and his socks are wool too.' I gave up on heading below, and went for my Scottish Tourist Board badge. 'Did you notice the knife?'

Some heads nodded. 'In the top of his sock,' Nora said.

'That's called a *sgian-dubh*. The sheath's under the sock. And the leather pouch thing's called a sporran.'

Someone had to ask. 'What does he wear under his kilt?'

'I'll leave you to ask that,' I said, and escaped. Four bells rang out over my head as I gained the quiet of my cabin: six o'clock. An hour till dinner. My constant hunger was explained now too. The baby inside me was grabbing all the nourishment it could get, planning to grow from blueberry size to plum size over the next week. Surely I'd have a bit of time before it showed . . . enough time to tell Gavin, and my parents. My heart plummeted at the thought of the trouble ahead. Dad – well, Dad's reaction would depend on Gavin's. He still had the belief that what a woman really needed for happiness was a husband and a skirtful of bairns, and if Gavin wanted that too, then all would be congratulations there – except that I didn't want that. I didn't want to become the Old Woman in a Shoe, with a good Catholic family that would sit between us in the pew, in descending height order. I didn't want to be like Maman, longing and longing for the music she'd lost until she could bear it no longer and just ran. Maman would understand that I didn't want to get married and have six children when the sea was still calling me . . .

I made a cup of tea in the crew's galley. The captain's door was closed, but a steady sound of voices came from within. I was carrying my mug back to my room when the door opened and Sergeant Peterson came out. 'Cass. I was just coming to look for you.'

That was my lie-down gone. I followed her into the room.

CHAPTER TWELVE

They were seated round the captain's polished table, with Captain Gunnar at the head of it and Henrik at the other end. On the far side was an open laptop, policeman's notebook and pen that I took to be Sergeant Peterson's, then Gavin, with Jenn and Rolf beside him. Agnetha was facing Gavin, with Sadie and Anders on each side of her, and Nils had been called down from on duty. Gavin nodded gravely at me and indicated the spare seat opposite him. 'Thank you all for joining us.'

Formality was obviously the order of the day. I glanced quickly at his green jacket and saw the bulge my sharp-eyed youngsters had spotted. We all nodded, murmured variants of 'You're welcome', and waited for the inquisition to begin.

'I've called you all together to get an overview of what information we have. We'll then do individual interviews. Now, with regard to this suspected stowaway.' He nodded at Sergeant Peterson, who sat down behind her laptop and began to tap instructions into it.

'While I was waiting to come aboard, I got in touch with the police in Kristiansand for more information about the man they warned you about. They sent a photograph and description.'

Sergeant Peterson turned her laptop around. There, bang in front of me, was the man I'd bumped into in the fish market: the cropped hair on that bull head, the flared nostrils. I gave an involuntary 'Oh!' and Gavin looked across at me. 'You recognise him, Ms Lynch?'

'I saw him in the Fiskbrabaren, the morning that we sailed. He was dropped off by a motorboat, and I walked straight into him. That's why I remember his face so clearly.'

'Alexander Viktor Bezrukov. Wanted in several countries, traced as far as the Warnemünde district of Rostock, right on the Baltic Coast.' He turned back to me. 'What sort of motorboat?'

'An Aquador, maybe thirty foot.' Anders nodded; it was the sort of boat that could have come across from the Baltic. 'I didn't take any notice of registration or name. It was just one of those fibreglass hulls, white and cream.'

'He's a very dangerous man. That's why we've been sent aboard.' He spread his hands: tanned hands made for use, not ornament. 'Now, there's not a lot we can do about him at the moment. Can we establish that he was indeed on the ship?'

Anders leant forward. 'There was someone similar to this. I saw him the first day, on deck. He was wearing a dark jacket. He smoked on the boat deck.'

Gavin's gaze moved to me. 'I can't swear it was the same man,' I said. 'But the man I bumped into, this Bezrukov, smelt of tobacco, and the day we sailed, someone who smelt of cigarettes had been lurking in either the sail locker forrard or Erik and Petter's cabin.'

'Did you see the person?' Sergeant Peterson interrupted.

I shook my head. 'But the smell didn't come from any of the

suitcases. On Friday, Olav – the first man to go missing – spoke to me about a Russian-looking man.' I tried to recall his exact words. 'He called him a "mystery man" because he didn't talk, just nodded and turned away. He described him as having "iron-grey hair, cut short, and a Russian face. Broad shoulders, and a dark jacket." He'd seen him at meals.'

'And it was Friday you were knocked over by somebody in the tunnels.'

I nodded. 'It was all too quick for me to see who. Big and strong, and smelt of cigarettes.'

'Then on Saturday the ship was searched by the Special Police.'

'They found nothing,' Captain Gunnar said.

'But Petter remembered a hiding place which they might have missed,' I said. I looked sideways at Anders. 'In the engine room, in a corner, floorboards which lift up and lead to a cargo space.'

'He didn't look there?' Gavin said quickly.

'I don't think so.'

'Good.' Gavin looked around us all. 'I must emphasise to all of you that we don't want heroics. I'd rather this man got away than have a multiple shooting aboard this ship. If this man is still aboard, then don't approach him, don't draw attention to him. Keep well away from him.' His gaze went to Anders. 'Do you know of this hiding place, Mr Johansen?'

Anders shook his head.

Gavin's grey eyes travelled round us. 'Is it a hiding place that would be known to all the crew?'

Henrik frowned, as if he was trying to remember something. Nils and Agnetha shook their heads. 'I don't know it,' Agnetha said. 'But then, I wouldn't be in the engine room, except for safety checks.'

Gavin's gaze moved to Jenn and Rolf. 'Not my area of the ship,' Jenn said.

'I think I remember,' Rolf said. He flushed, as if he thought he was incriminating himself. 'I forget why we were down there, but I did know about it. When you said Petter, I remembered. We were down there, Petter and Erik and I. I think we were perhaps talking about using it for storage, but it was so inaccessible that we decided not to.'

'But it's not somewhere obvious to, say, people visiting the ship while it's in port?' Sergeant Peterson asked.

Rolf shook his head. 'Oh, no. The engine room is off limits while there are visitors aboard.'

'So,' Gavin said, 'it's unlikely that the man could have explored the ship beforehand, on an open day, and spotted that hiding place?'

Erik and Rolf spoke almost as one. 'Very unlikely.'

Erik continued, 'He could perhaps have found it if he'd known what to look for. The engine room is made off limits only by a chain across the door. It's not locked. He could have waited for his chance and ducked under.'

'So you think that somebody who did know of the place showed it to him.'

Reluctantly, Rolf nodded.

Captain Gunnar stiffened. 'You are accusing one of my crew of smuggling him aboard?'

Erik flushed, Rolf opened his mouth to protest and Petter looked down, uncomfortably.

'I didn't draw that inference, sir,' Gavin replied. 'I presume the ship's hull is worked on over the winter. A carpenter or caulker in the yard could have found that space, and remembered it.' He nodded to Sergeant Peterson, and she turned the laptop back and rattled her fingers on the keypad. 'Now, to the voyage since Stavanger. Is there any evidence he is still aboard?'

I took a deep breath. Captain Gunnar wasn't going to like this. 'Yes. On Saturday, in the mist, Olav came up to speak to me, and Captain Gunnar sent him forrard as an extra lookout while the radar was off. I asked Petter to find out what Olav had wanted, and he came back to say Olav had told him that the mystery man in the dark coat was still aboard. Olav had been on galley duty, helping prepare and serve meals, and he recognised the man's face.' I paused, then kept going. 'The last time Olav was seen was at the end of his shift as lookout.' I remembered the smear of blood I'd seen, but couldn't force myself to declare it. It was too melodramatic.

Gavin flicked at glance at his notes. 'Olav Olsen, who went missing between ten and midnight on Saturday.' He looked at me. 'Your watch, Ms Lynch?'

I nodded.

'On the face of it, it seems astonishing that someone could be killed on board this ship, filled with trainees, with nobody noticing.'

'I agree,' Captain Gunnar said. 'A deliberate killing is most unlikely. Of course, an accident is also unlikely. But if the man suffered a sudden heart attack and fell, silently, when nobody was looking at him—'

Gavin nodded, and returned to me. 'Ms Lynch?'

'I've thought about that,' I said, reluctantly. 'It was a misty night. The off-watch trainees were almost all below, and the wind was blowing on the side he presumably fell from – the steps he was about to go down when he was last seen – so the on-watch trainees were on the other side of the banjer, having a breather from taking sails down. The lookout pair, who were nearest, were focused on what they could see forwards, and paying no heed to anything behind them.'

'That explains very well,' Captain Gunnar said swiftly, 'why nobody saw him fall.'

Gavin nodded, and left that one there. 'If you can give me the names of the last people to see him, I'll talk to them. An investigation of a person lost overboard is a perfectly legitimate excuse for me to be aboard.'

'He was watching with Ludwig and Ben,' I said, 'and the relief lookouts were Ellen and Naseem.'

'Your watch? Then I'll borrow them from you this evening, and get a quick statement from each of them.' He looked round us all again. 'It could very well have been an accident, of course, though accidents are unusual aboard *Sørlandet*.' He smiled. 'I've looked up your record.' Captain Gunnar bowed his head in acknowledgement of the compliment. 'All the same, I don't like the coincidence that has Olsen disappearing immediately after believing he's seen our possible stowaway.' He flicked the pages of his notebook again. 'Now, Mike Callaghan, your chief officer. If you could think, please, about when you last saw him, and with whom. I would ask you, as your captain has already asked you, not to discuss your memories with each other. Now, the white watch is on duty currently, and then the blue, immediately after the whole-crew muster?'

Captain Gunnar nodded.

'If you'll permit, sir, we'll talk to the non-watch officers first.' He checked a list. 'The chief steward.' He looked up and Henrik nodded. 'The medical and liaison officers.' His gaze flicked to Sadie and Jenn, moved on to Rolf and Anders. 'The bosun and the chief engineer.' He turned to face Agnetha. 'Then the officers of the red watch.'

Agnetha had herself well in hand, and neither moved nor changed colour. All the same, I saw Sergeant Peterson shoot a look at her, then fire a clicking of words into her laptop.

'There's one thing about Mike which might be relevant,' I said. 'He had a wonderful memory for faces and names.' As I'd hoped, Sergeant Peterson diverted her attention from Agnetha to me. 'Yesterday, before I went on watch, I went into Jenn's room and found him checking the trainee photos on the computer.' I looked at Gavin. 'Rolf photographs every trainee on board, when they arrive. I wondered if Mike had spotted the odd man out, and was checking that he wasn't a trainee.'

'Possible,' Gavin agreed. He looked back at Agnetha and continued, as if I hadn't spoken. 'Depending on the time. Do you usually have a sleep before your watch?'

'I do,' Agnetha said, 'and one of my ABs does. My watch leader and my other AB are night owls, so they stay up till midnight, then have an extra sleep after breakfast.'

'Then if it's before nine o'clock, we'll speak to you and the other AB first, and the night owls after that.'

Agnetha nodded agreement.

'The white watch tomorrow morning, after breakfast, and the blue in the afternoon.'

There was a short silence, broken by six bells ringing above our heads. Henrik leapt up. 'You must excuse me. Detective Macrae, now is the time that our evening meal is served.' He made a sweeping gesture at the table.

'Of course.' Gavin nodded at Sergeant Peterson, who began putting her laptop away.

'You will of course eat with us,' Captain Gunnar said. 'Rolf, show Sergeant Peterson to the other ranks' mess, and bring an extra chair here.'

Ha! Below the salt. I tried not to grin as Sergeant Peterson was shown along the corridor. It had probably been arranged so that she could assess the other ranks as Gavin assessed us.

It was a subdued meal. From the blue watch point of view, that was partly because I didn't have time to talk, if I was to be on deck booted and spurred – that is, with full evening watch gear and teeth pre-brushed – for Jenn's pep talk and 'moments of awesome'. Naturally, the helicopter descent was voted the most awesome, but the view of Orkney got a vote from the older trainees.

We were still chugging along the north of Scotland, with Cape Wrath off our beam. It wasn't yet time to make the 90 degree turn that would take us down the Minch, but we could start shortening the distance with a bit of slant. I checked the course on the plotter and took it back to the helm, Nora. '270 degrees.'

She repeated it. '270. Right.' She looked as if she was struggling with the weight of the helm; on the other side, Jan-Ole, the stalwart fisherman, leant against it. I waited till they were on the new course, then went back to check the chart plotter for other vessels. None within ten miles.

It was a grey evening: grey fleece skies, grey hills spread out in the distance, grey sea. It was strange to be sailing this route again. I'd done it in my *Khalida* just six months ago, going down to Gavin's loch for Christmas. I'd sailed in the dark, steering by compass from lighthouse to lighthouse. Now we were in the light nights, even this far south, with only a couple of hours of twilight after midnight.

On the thought, Gavin came to lean over the rail beside me, his green sleeve touching my black mid-layer. 'This was the way you sailed to visit us at Christmas.'

'I was just remembering that.' I leant against his shoulder and felt the warmth of him, close to me, caught a breath of Imperial Leather soap. I felt a surge of love for him that shook me. I wanted to cuddle close, but I was afraid he'd read the rising panic within me. When, how, was I going to tell him? His hand clasped mine on the rail, let go again. 'Your captain's put me in the hospital cabin. I'm to keep strictly to the book on this one.'

'I know.' I straightened up again.

'I'm still compromised, so Freya will do your interview.'

I made a face, but swallowed the 'What's *she* doing here anyway?' that sprang to my lips like a three-year-old. 'OK.' I remembered the blood. 'I couldn't come out with this one in front of Captain Gunnar, because he'd say I was being melodramatic, but I was sure I saw blood on the porthole in the easiest place to throw someone over.'

'Where?'

I nodded forward. 'To starboard, where the steps from the forrard deck come down, in the space where there's no rigging. There's a porthole just below there. It'll be clean to the naked eye now, with the sea washing it, but your forensics experts might get something, come Belfast.'

'They might, but blood's not evidence of murder. He might have scratched himself falling.' He turned around, making a space between us, his back to the sea, and looked upwards, then turned to smile at me. 'Have you been allowed any mast-climbing?'

'We officers are too dignified. Maybe in Belfast, when the trainees aren't looking.' If we weren't going to get to be together, then I'd have to wait till Belfast to tell him. A jolt of relief ran through me, followed by apprehension. I couldn't keep it from him through all those sea miles; he was too quick. He'd know something was wrong.

'Well, I'll go down and start these interviews. You just behave now, tomorrow, when Freya talks to you.' He glanced around. 'I'm hoping that if our man is coming out among the trainees, he'll go back underground when he hears them talking about police officers on board.'

My heart gave a terrified bump. 'You don't think he'll try to take you out?'

He gave me a reassuring smile, and shook his head. 'Not unless he's cornered, and I'm not going to go anywhere near that situation.'

He strolled away and wove his way around the trainees amidships, where Erik and Mona were taking them through the names of the sails in Norwegian English and (with help from Dimitris) Greek. Erik had got out chalk, and was busy drawing a diagram of the sails over the deck. We'd be popular with the red watch tomorrow, come scrubbing time. I listened to the litany that breathed Drake, Spanish galleons, romance, royals, topgallants, upper topsail, lower topsail, foresail. They'd do the square sails first; then the staysails, the triangular sails suspended between the masts, would come easily. *Røyl, bramseil, merseseil, stump, fokk.* I peered down at the writing on the deck. βασιλική πανί, *topgallant*, άνω top πανί, χαμηλότερες top πανί, προσκήνιο πανί, Dimitris had written. πανί was sail – I knew that much Greek from my days teaching children in the Med. Good improvisation; the boy would go far.

The wind had turned bitter, but it was a bonny enough night. Erik organised races to reach the right sail first, then they began racing to its ropes. Lena, the trainee in the Bob Marley jacket, whose mutinous face I'd noticed on the dock, came up from below to join in, even though it wasn't her watch. She was flushed and laughing, the delight of being at sea glowing in her face. Slowly, at a gentle jogging pace, we crept across the wrinkled waves. I looked ahead on the chart and began drawing angles. Another half hour and it would be time to turn, ready for the run straight down to the Minch.

Jan-Ole had moved from standby to helm when I went back to give the order. '205 degrees. Right.' He began to spin the wheel, and it jammed. He looked up at me, frowning, then tried again. I put out a hand to stop him; he was strong enough to do serious damage. 'No, don't. Steady as she goes for the moment.'

We were, of course, right in the middle of Scotland's fishing grounds. The chances were we'd picked up a great lump of net, which the wash from the propeller had sucked into the gap between the rudder and the skeg it was hinged from, wuppling the rudder so that it couldn't move.

Jan-Ole was thinking along the same lines. 'It'll be a net in the rudder.'

We exchanged a *That's a pain* face. The rudder stretched down to ten feet below the surface of the water. Fixing it would be a wetsuit job, and of course we'd have to switch the engine off while the diver was down, so we'd be wallowing. I gave the mountains of Scotland a measuring glance. We were well offshore. We'd have searoom to do this now, so long as it was a straightforward cut-it-off job. I just hoped it was rope or net, and not something with wire in it.

Check the obvious first. There was no reason why anyone should have shoved anything on top of the cogs and shafts of the steering mechanism in the captain's coffin, but people could be incredibly lazy about taking life jackets back where they belonged when there was an apparently handy locker to shove them in. I'd look there first.

It was called the captain's coffin from its shape, six feet long and with a raised top like an old-fashioned coffin, double-lidded. The word *Sørlandet* was carved along each upright side. I came around Jan-Ole and lifted the port side.

I knew then, of course. On my side the long, threaded shaft

stood out clear, but it was jammed by something on the other side: a curl of hair, an arm's length of navy jumper with one limp hand dangling, navy trousers dim under the pointed lid. I felt the deck sway around me and closed the lid, hanging on to its raised edge with my fingertips until the world had steadied again.

I was glad I had two adults on the helm. The youngsters didn't need to know about this if we could possibly keep it from them. I turned and met their eyes. They could see something was wrong. I squared my shoulders, and spoke calmly. 'There's been an accident. No, don't look. Aage, could you go and tell the policeman in the kilt that the captain wants him here. Go down the nav-shack stairs. He'll be interviewing in the captain's cabin.' I looked at them imploringly. 'Don't say anything to anyone else. *Please.* We don't want the youngsters to get all panicked.'

'We will say nothing,' Jan-Ole agreed. He swept a glance around the deck. 'It is the chief officer who is missing, no?'

I nodded. Aage set off down the steps, leaving Jan-Ole and I staring at each other. 'You will not be able to keep it from them for long,' Jan-Ole said, practically.

'As long as I can,' I said. 'Keep as you were.'

It felt a long two minutes before Gavin and Aage came clattering up again. A pause, then Gavin came strolling forward beside Aage, the pair of them as casual as sea-gazers on a beach promenade, with Sergeant Peterson behind them.

'I've found Mike,' I said. I jerked my chin towards the captain's coffin. 'In there.'

Gavin's brows drew together. 'What did you touch?'

'The lid, this side. He's under the other side.'

'OK. Can we leave him in situ until we can get forensics out here?'

I shook my head. 'He's fouling the steering. That's how I

181

came to find him. We can't turn the wheel, and we need to.'

'Have you told the captain yet?'

'No.'

'Right. Freya, you go and do that now.' He checked his watch, and looked at Jan-Ole and Aage. 'You two are on the wheel until . . . ?'

'Another twenty minutes, then there will be a new standby.'

'Twenty minutes. That should do it.' He waited beside me until Sergeant Peterson reappeared with the captain behind her. They went straight to the far side of the captain's coffin and lifted the lid. I turned my head away, but not quickly enough. Mike had been shoved under the lid, scrunched up to make him fit, so that his face was canted at an odd angle, and there was a dark bruise on his nose where the lid had pushed it down. His eyes were open, staring in blank surprise. I gave a quick glance around to make sure Agnetha was safely below. She didn't need to see this. Whatever the Russian in the dark jacket had done to him, she didn't need to know the details. But it was a strange sense of humour that had left him here, in the captain's coffin. How could Bezrukov have known that was what we called it? Why not just throw him overboard? Was he hoping for a panic, to cover his leaving the ship in Belfast? But surely a dead body would only bring the police aboard in swarms.

Gavin closed the lid again. 'Normally, sir, we'd leave everything until forensics can get here. However it's obvious he's been placed here, rather than this being where he died, so I have no objection to his being moved. Can he be taken to your cold store without being carried across the deck?'

Captain Gunnar frowned. 'Down the nav-shack stairs and through the tunnels, yes. I'll organise crew to do that. Erik, Nils and Rolf should be able to carry him between them.'

I looked down at the main deck. My watch was having a breather from racing around from sails to ropes. 'If I get Petter to bring the rope bag out, my watch could tie knots up forrard, under the shelter of the banjer, on the far side from the nav-shack door. That way we might be able to lift him out without too much attention.' The captain nodded approval, and I went down to call Petter up and explained what I wanted him to do, without going into why. 'We need to keep their attention off the aft deck for half an hour.'

It took ten minutes to get them all settled; some had to have a smoke first, of course, others had a quick swing from the bars along the side of the banjer roof, but eventually they were all lined up along the furthest half of the main deck, heads bent over pieces of rope, learning reef knots, bowlines and clove hitches. Cat went along to join them; he always enjoyed rope work because there were dangling ends to chase. By that time Rolf had found a spare piece of canvas, and he, Erik and Nils were standing by. I sent my safety watch youngster off to do his rounds. The captain gave the trainees a last look, then nodded. 'Go.'

They'd just started to lift the lid when Agnetha came up the nav-shack steps. I saw by her face that she knew something was wrong. Swiftly, I tucked my arm in hers and drew her forward to the railing in front of the nav shack that looked out over the main deck. 'Don't look. We need to mask what's happening behind us.'

She heard the urgency in my voice. I felt her sag against me, but she had the self-control to keep her voice soft. 'What's happened?'

She would have to know sometime. 'We've found Mike.' I felt her instinctive jerk forwards. 'He's dead. Don't turn.' I could imagine how he would look as they brought him out, frozen in that scrunched-up position, with the hand that should be dangling as stiff as a dead starfish. 'They're taking him below.' It would be like

183

manhandling a statue down the narrow, curved nav-shack steps, down the stairs to the next level and through the tunnels. Gavin had gone ahead of them. I wondered if he would take his gun in his hand before entering the below-decks region.

There were several soft thumps and knocks as they got him around the corner and down the stairs, elbows and feet banging the wood as they passed, followed by the scuffling of feet negotiating the corner. The closing of the lower door cut off the sound. We stood there in silence, imagining it. The shuffling along the corridor and down the next stairs. Edging their way through the tunnels, one man at Mike's head, the other two at his feet, all on the alert for the least sign of movement. I suddenly thought of *The Phantom of the Opera* and pushed the idea of deformed monsters lurking in the darkness away.

The moment dragged on. They should be getting to the galley now, ready to open the door into the freezer. Trainees didn't go in there. Erik and the others would make sure he was swathed round with the canvas, then they'd leave him to Gavin and Sergeant Peterson. I thought Gavin would say a prayer in his head, and joined him silently, my eyes on the tracery of rigging against the darkening sky: *Eternal rest grant unto him, O Lord, and may perpetual light shine upon him . . .*

My hands were shaking. Delayed shock, I supposed. Agnetha put her hand on my shoulder. 'Was it you who found him?'

I nodded.

'I'll get you something hot. Tea, coffee?'

'Tea.'

She hesitated before going into the nav shack, then squared her shoulders. I heard her footsteps descending. On deck, we seemed to have got away with it. The toorie-capped heads were still bent over their knots. I just hoped that Jan-Ole and Aage were as reliable as they seemed. From lazy races aboard my Shetland friend Jeemie's Starlight, I knew all about what men could do in the way of gossip.

To work. There was no point in standing here watching the banjer door for Gavin and Sergeant Peterson to come out. I checked our course again, and went back to Jan-Ole. 'Go for 205 degrees now.'

The wheel turned smoothly under his hands. Slowly, the ship turned until the mountains of Scotland were stretched along our port horizon. Ahead of us, a grey headland stretched out, with a humped island crouched before it: the point of Sandwood, and Am Balg. The great lump of mountain with its high peak wreathed in cloud and a lower peak to the side was Beinn Dearg.

Agnetha returned, and slid a mug of tea into my hands. I clutched it gratefully.

'Was he,' she said softly, 'in . . . *there*?' Her chin tilted back behind us.

I nodded.

'What had been done to him?'

'I couldn't see.' I put a hand on her arm. 'Try not to think about it.'

She jerked away. 'I can't help but think about it,' she hissed, and clattered down the nav-shack steps, leaving me feeling foolish. Tactless. I looked bleakly out at the grey water.

'It's done,' Erik said, in my ear. He came to lean on the rail beside me. 'We laid him out in the cold store. The police want to look at him, then they'll put him into the freezer until we reach Belfast.' His voice was chilled, as if the cold had entered it. His hands clenched on the rail. 'We have to do something about this.'

'Two whole days till Belfast,' I said. 'We should arrive there about midnight on Wednesday.'

'Two days is too long. We need to find the bloke and confront him.' His voice was shaking with anger. 'Deal with him.'

'You know we can't.' I nodded down at the trainees. 'Our first duty is to them.'

Erik's voice was savage. 'We failed in our duty to Olav, didn't we? And what about Mike?'

There was nothing I could say to that. Erik waited beside me for a moment, fingers rattling a tattoo on the varnished rail, then he flung away, clattered down the steps to the main deck and began to do a tour of the ropes, tightening some, freeing the others which had been secured for the helicopter's arrival.

I sympathised with him, but I was with Gavin on this one. There was nothing we could do now to help Olav or Mike except make sure we caught this man without further loss of life. We weren't in the theatre, to take blazing torches down into the bowels of the ship. We were a little wooden world out in the Atlantic. The nearest city with a squad of arms-trained police was Glasgow, through the islands and up the Clyde; we could reach Belfast as quickly, and with less need for wondering about the change of destination on the part of the trainees. Some were leaving the ship in Belfast; they'd have flights booked. All in all, it would cause less fuss if we could keep going. Once we got to Belfast the ship could be cleared of all her crew and swept by the police. This time, they'd get him.

My safety watch came back from his round, reported that all was well and rang four bells. Halfway through the watch. Aage took over from Jan-Ole, Naseem came up as standby, Jan-Ole took over safety and Sindre headed for the foredeck. Cat came up to see what was going on and sat on the bench by the nav shack, looking out at the grey mountains as if he remembered them from our voyage at Christmas. Rolf came with tea and coffee all round, and insisted on putting two spoonfuls of sugar in mine.

It was a long two hours. Instead of enjoying our progress through the flat sea, with the mountains creeping by on the horizon and the glimpses of moon through the fleece-grey clouds, my attention was on the banjer door, waiting for Gavin and Sergeant Peterson to come out. They'd not go back through the tunnels, with just two of them; they'd come up the galley stairs, and so I watched the opening like Cat at a suspected mouse hole.

Six bells had just rung when they came out at last. You would never have seen in either of their faces that they'd spent the last hour dealing with a dead man: bagging his hands and feet, I supposed, removing the items in his pockets, covering him with clean plastic so that any traces of DNA on him would be left as uncontaminated as possible. Finding the cause of death. Gavin was brisk and upright, making a smiling comment to Sergeant Peterson as he came out on deck, then turning to join the trainees and inspect their knots. He took a length of rope and tied a reef knot, a bowline and a clove hitch in quick succession, then seemed to be answering questions the trainees were firing at him. One must have been about his gun, for he took it out, tipped the bullets into his palm and let them pass it around. You could see the country youngsters were used to handling firearms, squaring up and sighting through it knowledgably; the town ones, as I had with Sean's gun, exclaimed at the weight.

Sergeant Peterson strolled along the deck, exchanging greetings as she went, leant for a while admiring the view, then came up to the aft deck and looked down at the chart plotter, with the little circle that was us flashing in the middle of the screen. She took a moment to match the map before her to the real world, looking down and up again. I nodded out to the right. 'As the light dims, we should just pick up the lights on the Butt of Lewis and Tiumpan Head. Three o'clock.' I touched the screen and drew the headlands out. 'What I like about this programme is that it shows you the flashing pattern you'll see. The Butt of Lewis is visible for nine miles.' I was chattering, and knew it; I fell silent, and left her staring out into the grey mist of the horizon. If she wasn't going to tell me what had happened to Mike, I wasn't going to ask.

Then she turned around, staring aft at the wheel and the captain's coffin behind it. 'It would take some strength to lift someone the size of Mike into that.'

I hadn't thought about it yet. I remembered trying to lift the half-weight dummy in my fire-fighting course, back in Scalloway, before I'd been shown how. 'You think he knew how to do a fireman's lift?'

Her eyes flashed green. 'Do you know how?'

'Yes.' All the officers would, for the fire certificate was part of the Officer of the Watch course; but I wasn't going to say that. 'That explains what had puzzled me.'

She looked an enquiry.

'How the person managed to put him in the coffin without me hearing. If he was on their shoulders, they just had to open the lid softly and lower him in.'

'The coffin?'

'The captain's coffin. That's what the steering box is called.'

I could see her focusing on that. 'Appropriate name. D'you think that's why he was put there?'

I shrugged at that one, and she turned away, back to her interviews. The evening dragged on to mustering and handover time. Eight bells. Undress. Bed.

I managed a quick goodnight to Gavin in the galley. 'I wish I could join you,' he murmured into my hair. There was something odd about his manner, as if he knew something he couldn't share with me, yet wanted to.

'No compromising suspects,' I agreed, and he gave me a sharp look as if I'd hit a nerve.

'Sleep well. Don't worry about it; just tell Freya what you saw.'

It took me a while to settle. I was too conscious of Gavin moving on one side, in the sick bay, and the silence from the other side. Mike's cabin. Only two days ago, Agnetha had been there with him. Now she was walking the deck above my head, knowing that he was lying covered in the cold store. I wondered if they had told his wife yet. Probably. A Norwegian police officer would have gone to her door. At least the ship could spare her the grief of identifying him; Captain Gunnar could do the formal ID. I wondered if she'd fly over to meet us at Belfast, to take his body back to Kristiansand, or if he'd be buried in Cork. The old seamen used to wear gold rings in their ears to pay for their burial abroad . . .

Suddenly, in the stillness, I heard a hand brush over my door. I lifted my head, watching, as the brass handle dipped down and the door eased open. A dark shape stood in the dimly lit corridor, silhouetted by the light.

My first thought, with a surge of pleasure, was that it was Gavin; that wanting to be with me had won out over duty. But as he stood there, listening, as if he was checking that I was asleep, unease crept up my throat, followed by panic as he took a stealthy step into the room. I swung my legs down, took two steps to the wall, lifted my fist and hammered on it.

The shadow jerked back. My door was pulled closed. I leapt for it and yanked it open. Gavin was already in the corridor, dressed only in his kilt, torso and feet bare. 'What's up?'

'Someone came into my room. You didn't see anyone in the corridor?'

He shook his head. 'Missed him.' He drew me back into my room and glanced at the fastenings of my door. 'Lock yourself in. Have a think about why anyone would want to threaten you. Maybe you saw something you didn't realise you saw.' His hand was warm on my shoulder. I wanted to ask him to stay, but I wasn't going to let a faceless thug make me all clingy.

'I'll do my best.'

'*Beanneachd leat.*'

'Night night tae dee.' I locked the door behind him, and set myself to think, but nothing came to me. A person in a red jacket . . . had there been anything about the walk, the jacket, that I'd recognised? I did have a sense of familiarity, but then, if Bezrukov had picked up a jacket from the banjer, of course I'd have seen it before. No inspiration came, and it was three bells of the red watch before I finally fell asleep.

FIVE BELLS

The Atlantic: Cape Wrath to Tiree

Tuesday 30th June

CHAPTER THIRTEEN

I was woken by Cat, mewing indignantly at the locked door. It took me a moment to surface, then it all came back: the stiff figure under the polished lid of the captain's coffin, the men carrying their shrouded burden down the nav-shack stairs, Mike laid out in the cold store. The dark figure in the room, reaching out for me. Then being pregnant rushed in as well, almost as an afterthought that blotted everything else out again. I lay still for a moment, bracing myself against the day. It was all too much to cope with, but not coping wasn't an option. Cat miaowed again. I yawned my way to the door and opened it, then reached for my watch. Ten to seven! I rushed for the shower and toilet, cursing. It was nearly twenty past before I got on deck, flushed and out of breath, but officer-neat, and with only a medium queasiness to remind me of my tiny passenger. It seemed the worst of the shock was over; the jolting *I'm pregnant!* that had dogged my mind yesterday had softened to surprised acceptance. A body can get used to anything, even hanging, as my Granny Bridget used to say. It wasn't going to be easy, any of it, but I could do it. One step at a time. I'd tell Gavin first, then worry about Maman. All the same, I warned it silently, as I kept prudently by the rail until the nausea had passed, *You needn't think you're going to keep this up. You'll be growing up around boats, so get used to it.*

It was a fine day. Cat had come up with me for his early-morning constitutional, and sat himself by the chart-plotter pedestal, where the sun was warming the decks. The mountains of Scotland were still on our port side, closer now but misty in the spray-laden air. Sunshine glinted on the water. Ahead, the sea was slashed with white crests from a stiff breeze. Great Atlantic breakers rolled along the ship's sides, changing colour with each movement, pale green, grey, silver. My spirits rose at the sight of this gleaming wilderness.

Gavin was up already, talking to the foredeck lookout, his kilt fluttering in the breeze. The white watch was busy erasing the last remnants of Erik's sail diagrams with brushes and the seawater hose. Up here on the aft deck, Nils was checking the plotter, ready for handover. I went over to join him, taking care not to cast a shadow over Cat. 'A straight run towards Skye, Cass. We should be level with the north coast around 9.30. 230 degrees, to dodge the Shiants, then straight down the middle of the Little Minch.'

'Tides?' The Minch was notorious.

He gestured at the nav shack. 'Your paper's in there.' There was something odd about his manner this morning, almost wary, with his narrow eyes looking sideways at me from behind the beaked nose. *The policeman's girlfriend . . .* I went in to look, and he retreated quickly to talk to his helm.

I'd written it up in my best handwriting. The north-going stream began at HW Ullapool -3.45 and turned south at HW Ullapool +2.40, running at 2.5 knots each way, with the Skye side being slightly stronger. High water Ullapool, 6.34; low 12.57 and high 18.54. ETA for the narrowest piece was 14.00. I checked my arithmetic one more time. Yes, just as I'd planned, the tide would be with us from our first sight of Skye, sweeping us downwards, then we'd go through the narrows just as it slackened and get the last of it as the sea opened out before us again.

I cast a long look around the glinting, shifting sea, taking deep breaths of air. The sickness had steadied now. Mind over matter. I wasn't having Gavin guessing and worrying before I got a chance to tell him properly. On the thought, he glanced at his watch and began making his way aft. I called Cat and joined him in the companionway door. '*Halo leat.*'

'*Madainn mhath.*' *Good morning.* He gave me a sharp look. '*Ciamar a tha thu?*'

I didn't know the Gaelic for 'slightly sick due to early pregnancy', and it didn't seem quite the way to break the news. I shrugged. 'A bit short of sleep.'

'No more disturbances?'

'Only Cat being indignant at being shut out.' The ship's bell rang out above our heads, and I quickened my steps. Cat trotted in ahead of me and made himself at home on the red velvet settee. The seating around the table had been altered slightly; Henrik had been moved up to Mike's place, with Anders on one side of him and Gavin on the other, which ranked him above us mere officers. There was something odd about the way Henrik was looking at me too, as if he was assessing my height, and Rolf's manner was distant, preoccupied. *No compromising suspects . . .* but I'd been on the helm. Surely Mike's death wasn't going to be pinned on me. I remembered the captain catching me with Sean's gun in the herring bucket, and felt another wave of sickness pass over me. I tightened my teeth and fought the mouthful of vomit back down.

Bezrukov was still aboard. There was no need for us to suspect each other.

Captain Gunnar came in promptly on the seventh bell and said grace. I sipped my yoghurt cautiously, and noticed Gavin's eyes on me. Damn. I threw caution to the wind, sent the ship's newest crew member a stern motherly warning, and took a couple of slices of rye bread, some cheese and an apple. At least I'd have something to sick up, if that was going to be the way of it. The movement of the boat, engine against waves, gave me an excuse.

I escaped upwards as soon as I could, taking the apple with me, and stood on the aft deck, gulping long breaths of the sea air. The fresh breeze was livening everyone's spirits. My watch lined up with ruddy cheeks and heads held high. 'A general tidy up,' I suggested to Erik, 'and sail practice again, then how about splicing, since they did so well with knots yesterday?'

I watched from above as the physicals and galley duty were sent off. Rolf had been sent to oversee me this morning. He seemed slightly awkward, as if he just happened to be hanging about the aft deck, his eyes avoiding mine. When Captain Gunnar came up and nodded dismissal, he shot off down the stairs as if he'd heard an all-hands emergency call. I tried not to think about it, but the sting was cold in my breast.

Erik had just got them re-coiling ropes when Gavin appeared beside me. 'Don't forget Freya's interviewing you straight after lunch. Try not to think about it. Just answer.' His hand was light on my shoulder. 'Make with the words.'

The pit of my stomach jolted again, but I wasn't going to be nervous of Sergeant Peterson. 'No time to think about it,' I replied briskly. I didn't look at Captain Gunnar, upright and dignified on his gold-footed cane as he talked to the trainees at the helm, but forward at the white prow plunging in the waves, the black ratlines against the shifting water, and squared my shoulders. 'Right now she's my ship.'

He stood for a moment watching me. 'Don't move. Keep looking up.' He pulled out his phone and took a photo, then turned the phone to show it to me. 'Cass, in the middle of the ocean.'

It wasn't the face I saw in my mirror. This woman was smiling, head up. One strand of dark hair had tugged loose to make a crazy corkscrew on her flushed cheek, and her blue eyes shone. She wouldn't want to call the king her cousin, Granny Bridget would have said. I looked at Gavin, wondering if that was how he always saw me, and couldn't think of anything to say.

He put the phone away. 'One o'clock, in the officers' mess.'

'OK.'

His hand touched mine on the rail. 'Are you all right?'

I wasn't going to spin an elaborate set of lies that I'd have to kick away later. We needed to trust each other. 'Mostly. I'll be fine.' My fingers turned to curl round his. 'Will we still get time together in Belfast?'

'Hope so.' He turned his back on the trainees and made a face, mouth turning downwards. 'You know how it is. If we can clear this up.' He smiled at me, then pushed away from the rail and balanced upright, swaying easily to the ship's movements. 'Where have we got to?'

'Your own world.' I gestured at the mountains spread along the horizon.

'Quinag, Ben More Assynt, Canisp, Cùl Mòr, Suilven. Aye.' He nodded at them as if they were old friends. 'And a bonny fresh day too. I'm glad I don't seem to have lost my sea legs.'

'What will you do today?'

'A watching brief as Freya interviews. I'll write up my report on your chief officer and email it to the CC, if I can get a signal on the laptop. If not, I'll have to use the captain's satellite phone.' He gave me a sideways look. 'I've spotted your cousin Sean, in among the red watch.'

'The tall Irishman,' I agreed.

'I'll maybe have a chat with him about firearms.'

'He'll be happy to lead you as far astray as possible.' On our returns from various exploits, Sean had been spokesman, as he was particularly good at telling the truth in a way that made it sound as if we'd been behaving like holy angels.

It was a quiet watch. Below me, my trainees went round the ship's bulwarks, tightening and re-coiling each rope, and then did more sail-naming and racing for the ropes of specific sails. They were getting good. Bells rang, and the safety watch went round. Once we were past the top of Skye, we came into lobster-pot marker territory. I sent an extra watch forrard and the pair were kept busy from then on, ringing warnings for port, starboard, straight ahead, and indicating half-submerged plastic buoys trailing lengths of propeller-tangling rope.

Just at coffee time, a set of sails appeared on the horizon, a gaff-rigged ketch with tan sails and a long bowsprit, enjoying a rollercoaster ride through the waves. My watch lined up against the rails to take photos, then Mona got the rope bucket out again and the heads bent over the intricacies of the eye splice and monkey's fist. My standby helm, Anna, already knew the eye splice, so I showed her the end splice, for finishing off a fraying piece of rope in the days before heat-sealed nylon.

All through it, Gavin's photo stayed in my mind. It was strange to see myself looking the way I felt on board: at home, joyous. Even with Captain Gunnar watching me, this shifting, sparkling mass of water and the breeze tugging at my hair gave me that feeling: *this is what I was made for.* I was so fortunate that I had this. Some people never found their niche, but worked year after year in an office, enduring boredom for the sake of the pay packet and the weekend. I wondered how Captain Gunnar had felt, all those respectable years in the classroom, teaching the properties of light and growing beansprouts, and knowing that this was waiting for him. I took a deep breath of the salt air. 'You'll like it too, little crew member,' I assured the tiny person within me. 'A few years inshore, then we can go adventuring together.'

By eight bells I was my normal ravenous self, ready for anything Henrik was willing to offer. I dismissed my watch and headed below for two bowls of soup and three slices of rye bread, all good nutritious stuff. I'd have to find out about vitamins. The breeze had given everyone an appetite. Gavin tucked into his soup, chatting amiably to Henrik about fly fishing. Anders tore into rye bread and pickled herring. Only the captain was silent, picking at his food, his face drawn.

Once the galley girls had cleared away, Sergeant Peterson came back from her below-the-salt lunch and set up her laptop and notebook. Gavin came in silently behind her, and settled in a corner, just out of my direct line of vision. 'Now then, Ms Lynch.' She gave a smile that had all the warmth of a statue. 'I need to take you through what exactly you saw on Sunday evening. I want you to tell me everything you can remember about that watch, in as much detail as you can. Don't leave anything out, and don't worry about boring me. Don't try to think about what's important and what's not, just spill it all out, and we'll sort the wheat from the chaff. What seems to you a piece of puzzle not worth mentioning may be the corroboration we need.' She snicked a hand-sized recorder on, and gave her name, Gavin's and mine, the date and time. 'Now, Ms Lynch, just tell me all about it. Let's start with the moment you noticed the dolphins. Close your eyes and imagine you're there on deck. Where are you?'

Make with the words. I closed my eyes and felt the smooth rail under my hand. 'At the front of the aft deck, looking forwards. The trainees were spread over, then someone – one of the sisters, I think – shouted "*Delfiner!*" All the trainees crowded to the rails to look, and people came up from the banjer as well, so that the rails were crammed all the way along from forrard of the mainmast. There were several up on the foredeck as well; I wasn't so happy about that, as it's lookout territory, but it wouldn't be for long, and Erik went up there to keep an eye on them. I checked it was OK with the captain, then I went back and told Ellen and Ismail that they could go and look, I'd take the helm for a few minutes. It was about then that Nils came out of the nav shack, looked out forward, and went back downstairs. Then Mike came up, with someone in a red jacket, and they went out of sight, behind me. I don't remember them coming down as I was helming. Then Ellen came back, and I gave her the helm and went forward again, into the nav shack, to log the dolphins.'

Sean had been on deck too, just below me, talking to Erik just before the dolphins came. I'd lost sight of him when I'd moved aft to take the helm. He'd been wearing a navy jacket then, but it was only ten steps to the banjer entrance, with the array of jackets hanging there. I shoved the thought away. It had been Bezrukov . . .

'OK.'

I thought that was it, and half-rose, but she put out a hand to wave me down again. 'Try to focus on Mike. When did he first come into view?'

'As they came up the steps.' *Make with the words*. 'I saw Mike coming up first, with the other person behind him, in a red jacket.' My mind caught a flash of reflector tape. 'A sailing jacket, I think, with reflector bands on the sleeves. I couldn't see his face, it was behind Mike's back. Mike waited at the top of the stairs, and the other person came up on the far side of me . . . Oh, he had a hat! A navy one, faded navy, with ear flaps and a velcro under-the-chin strap. They went behind me, and I just caught Mike gesturing out of the corner of my eye, as if he was pointing out where we were. You know, Shetland, Fair Isle, Orkney.'

'Hold on to that image. Where was the other person then?'

I tried, but I could only see Mike's navy-clad arm flung outwards. 'Behind him, I think – I couldn't see him.'

'Try going backwards, as if you were back-reeling a film. Start with Mike gesturing.'

I tried. 'The gesture caught my eye. Before that I was looking forward. There was a long, grey cloud with a back and snout like a crocodile that I was steering by. I'd just noticed it before they came up, and they walked in front of its snout. The man moved stiffly . . . he was clumsy on the steps, as if he hadn't got his sea legs, but I didn't worry about that, because Mike was looking after him.'

'Can you see anything of his face?'

I shook my head. 'His head was turned away from me, and the peak and flap of the cap came down.'

'How about height?'

I tried to re-visualise the person walking behind Mike. Mike had waited at the top of the steps, and they'd walked aft together. 'He or she was not quite as tall as Mike. It's hard to say, with the hat, but three inches shorter, I'd think. The top of the hat was level with Mike's eyebrows.' I was swept by a sudden wash of relief. Sean was as tall as Mike. He was cleared of this, at least.

'Good. That's very helpful. You're doing well, Ms Lynch.'

Keep encouraging the witness, I thought. Straight from the training manual. She glanced at her notes. 'A scarlet sailing jacket and a faded navy hat. So far, you've only described Bezrukov in a dark jacket. Where might he get other clothes from?'

Olav had seen him in a sailing jacket and hat. 'Oh, that's easy. The trainees all hang their wet gear at the top of the banjer steps. He'd only need to reach in and pick something off a peg.'

'The banjer steps.' She made a note of it. 'OK, imagine now that instead of being on the helm, you're on the forrard deck looking aft. Try and think about who you can see on the deck.'

I tried it. 'Me, on the wheel – no.' I visualised again. 'It's hard, I'm not used to being forrard. I don't think I'd see me, because I was behind the nav shack. Captain Gunnar was in front of it. Nils came up to the rail and went down again. There were all the trainees, and Erik went up on the foredeck with them. Mona was by the port steps to the foredeck, the Greek boys were leaning a bit too far over, and she drew them back. Petter . . .' I tried to think where he'd been, but drew a blank. He'd been on deck. 'Maybe he was forrard, behind the front of the banjer, where I wouldn't see him. Oh, Henrik came out from the galley to look over the starboard side. He watched for a little while, not as long as they were with us, then went down to the banjer. None of the trainees were up on the boat deck, but one of Agnetha's ABs was, and Rolf, with his camera. And Jenn was on deck among the trainees. She came out, oh, not long after the call. She was taking photos too.'

'Could you draw me a map of them?' She passed me a piece of paper. It took a while, but as I drew the faces came back. I labelled each X as best I could, and passed it back to her. She scanned it, nodded, then returned to the questions.

'Go back to that shout of "Dolphins!" What did you hear after that?'

I closed my eyes and tried to listen. 'All the trainees repeated it, and there was a scuffle as everyone went for their phones. Ellen went "Oh!" in an excited voice, and that's when I asked Captain Gunnar if I could let them go and look. There were oohs and aahs from forrard, and the trainees saying, "Did you see that?" to each other, and that winding electronic noise as they took photographs. Then . . . the steps of Mike and the other man – the other man was uneven-sounding, that's why I thought he was clumsy. Then I just got caught up listening to the waves, and the chug of the engine, and the flag fluttering, and the wind on my cheek.' I paused for breath, feeling as if I'd been wrung out, like a dish-cloot. I was surprised I'd remembered so much.

'You're doing really well, Ms Lynch.'

I gave her a rueful grin. 'I think that's it, though.'

'Just to finish off. How long did the dolphins stay with the ship?'

'Oh, five, maybe seven, minutes. Not very long – well, long in terms of letting everyone see them, but sometimes they stay and play for ages.'

'Could you see them from where you were?'

'Not really. A fin or white gleam when they came further out from the ship's side. The action was immediately under the bow, that's why I sent Ellen and Ismail forrard.'

'How did you know when they were gone?'

'Oh, I could see that – the trainees looking down and around, and gradually breaking away from the rail, and comparing photos.'

'And were Callaghan and the other person still behind you then?'

I shook my head. 'I suppose so, because they hadn't gone past me. Then I gave Ellen back the helm, and went forrard to the rail again.'

'Who did you think the other person was?'

'I didn't think about it. I just took it to be a trainee.'

'Why would he be taking a trainee aft like that?'

'I really didn't think about it.' I spread my hands and leant forward, trying to explain. 'Mike was my superior officer. Whoever it was, he was responsible for them, so they weren't my problem. If it had been a trainee going back on their own, I'd have noticed.'

She scribbled something in her regulation notebook. Her eyes flicked at Gavin, and returned to me. 'Several people on deck also saw Callaghan going upstairs with the person in red, but nobody saw either of them come back down.'

I felt the pit of my stomach judder. Then I had been the last person to see them. I considered the implications of that in silence. If someone had taken the cover of the dolphins to kill Mike, it had been done behind me, while I was on the wheel.

She gave me a moment to absorb that. 'Now, about the disposal of the body.' Her voice was as calm as if she was talking about putting a black bag out. I braced myself. I knew it wasn't going to sound good. 'Which side of the helm were you standing on?'

'Starboard.' I didn't need to think; I could feel the helm under my hands, and the wind in my hair.

'Starboard. The right-hand side.' Her voice was casual. 'The side the body was found on.'

'Yes.'

Her eyes flicked across at Gavin, and back to me. 'Ms Lynch. Are you asking us to believe that someone lifted the lid not a half metre behind you, put a body in the box and closed the lid again without you hearing them? Right behind your back, so close they could have reached out and touched you?'

I could hardly believe it myself. 'It must have taken some nerve,' I agreed. 'But he really was right behind my back, so I couldn't have looked without turning my head right round. If he'd put Mike in the other side, I'd have been more likely to see.'

'One squeak of the hinge and you'd have turned round to see what was going on.'

I was beginning to get rattled. 'There are no squeaking hinges aboard this ship,' I retorted. The flash of satisfaction in her eyes warned me. I leant back in my chair, and had another shot at explaining what felt so obvious. 'It was Mike behind me. My superior officer, showing something to a trainee. I was helming, looking forward. That was my business, and what he was doing wasn't. If I'd heard the lid, and I don't think I did, I still wouldn't have turned around to stare.'

'Why dispose of the body so elaborately? Why not just kill him and drop him overboard?'

I'd had a chance to think about that one. 'I wondered if it might be because I'd have spun round straight away at that.' Mike falling from the aft deck, the highest point of the ship, would have made an unmistakeable 'man-overboard' splash. 'That would have cornered the man who'd just thrown him over.'

She nodded and said, almost casually, 'You're making it sound like a crew member who knows the ways of the ship.'

I hadn't thought of that. My mouth fell open. I raised startled eyes to her face, as calm as if she was asking about the weather. 'You think it might not have been Bezrukov?'

'We're considering all possibilities,' she said smoothly. 'So?'

I tried to think. Certainly all the crew had some kind of foul-weather gear, and several of them had a scarlet sailing jacket, scarlet being the most visible of the colours on offer. Charcoal grey was all very trendy, but if you fell into the sea, you didn't want to be camouflaged against the hungry waves. 'We only wear our oilskins at night, or in poor weather, but often enough that I think I'd have recognised the person in it. I'd have thought, even subconsciously, "Oh, that's Mike and whoever going to confer aft."'

'How about the hat? Faded navy, you said, with a brim and ear flaps.'

'Fleece. I have one. They're pretty popular; there are several on board.'

'Belonging to trainees or crew?'

'Both.' I frowned. 'Again, you know, I think I'd have recognised him if it was someone who habitually wore that hat, especially teamed with its usual jacket. Looking along the length of the ship, you get used to knowing people by their general shape and profile, and the hat's part of that.'

'You keep saying "he" and "him",' Sergeant Peterson observed. 'Can you tease out the reason for that?'

I thought about it, and couldn't. 'I can't pinpoint anything. I suppose I was assuming it was Bezrukov.'

Her gaze sharpened. 'You didn't think it was Bezrukov at the time.'

'No,' I agreed. Time to remain silent. I stole a look at Gavin, grave and quiet in his corner, and wasn't reassured. *A fellow crew member . . .* I looked across at the plan I'd drawn, and saw the people I knew couldn't have killed Mike: not Erik, Petter or Mona, not Rolf or Agnetha's AB, not Jenn. They'd all been in my sight. Henrik had come out and gone back in, and Nils had returned downstairs before Mike and the other man had come up. Nils, Mike's brother-in-law.

She nodded, then lifted her head up again. Her green eyes were boring straight into me. 'Are there any crew members who might have a grudge against Callaghan?'

Nils. Agnetha. My expression must have changed, for Sergeant Peterson's whole face sharpened. She leant forward. 'Yes, Ms Lynch?'

I shook my head. Nils had a scarlet jacket. He'd had time to realise I was alone on the helm, go down the nav-shack steps, get it from his cabin, and come out to draw Mike away from the others. Agnetha's overalls were white, with a navy and yellow flash, and her rarely worn hat was a yellow toorie-cap; I wouldn't have expected to see her in scarlet. The height had been about right, and she could easily have crossed the deck, picked up a jacket at random from the rail and gone over to Mike. Her voice echoed in my brain: *I won't have it . . . Do that, and I'll go to the captain . . . You'll never work on a tall ship again . . .* I could hear Mike's rejoinder: *Nor will you.*

It wouldn't have taken her five seconds from that first shout of *Delfiner!* to know what I would do. She'd seen the face Gavin had shown me on the phone, the woman so absorbed in her ship that she'd see nothing behind her. She knew the name 'captain's coffin' as Bezrukov didn't . . .

'Ms Lynch?' Now there was a hard note in Sergeant Peterson's voice, like a keel scraping on rock. 'I can see you've thought of something.'

Agnetha was my friend. I wasn't going to believe she'd killed the father of her child without much better evidence than this, and I did know that one word from me now would blast the career she'd worked so hard to build. I wasn't going to say anything. There was no point in lying. I looked Sergeant Peterson straight in the eye. 'Nothing that I'm prepared to tell you.' I took a breath and went on. 'Mike was very well thought of on board the ship. He had all the skills needed for his position, and was particularly good with the trainees.'

For a moment we stared at each other, chins up, like Cat meeting another cat on the pontoon. If we'd had tails, they'd have been lashing.

'I'll put down that you do know of some disagreement, but are not prepared to tell me about it.' I watched her scribble it down, and thought that was the end of it, when she flung at me, pencil still moving, 'Was that disagreement with you?'

My 'no' was out before I had time to think. Her pencil added 'with another person' and dotted the full stop with precision. She raised her head.

'You're putting yourself in danger, Ms Lynch, if the person who disagreed with Callaghan knows you know.'

I wasn't going to be tricked twice. The 'she doesn't' Sergeant Peterson was hoping for stayed firmly behind my closed lips. There was a mutually hostile pause. I contemplated the portrait of Queen Sonja, and waited. I could do silence as long as she liked.

It was she who spoke first. 'Do you carry a knife aboard, Ms Lynch?'

I raised my eyes to her face again, computing this. If Mike had been killed, silently, behind me . . . I nodded, and fished out my Swiss Army knife on its lanyard. It lived in my pocket, but the cord attached it to my belt so that it wouldn't fall from a height onto someone, if I was aloft. Basic ship precautions. I unclipped it and laid it on the table. 'We all have a knife.'

She turned it over, opened the blade, closed it again. 'This doesn't lock. What do you need a knife for?'

'Neatening off rope. Twisting awkward screws and shackles, or undoing seized knots. Anything your fingers can't quite manage.'

'And would they all be of this type?'

I tried to think what I'd seen other people carrying. Several of the Norwegians had businesslike clasp knives that would probably be illegal in Britain, and there were various multi-tool gadgets going around. 'A variety, I'd say.'

Anders' knife had a ring that went around the neck to hold the blade open, and most of the Norwegian ones looked similar to his:

a businesslike wooden handle, with the blade folded inside. The younger crew members preferred a multi-tool.

'May I take this?'

I made a *Go ahead* gesture that covered the feeling that I was an officer surrendering my sword. Handling it by her fingertips, she dropped it into an evidence bag and labelled it.

That she was asking about knives answered the question I hadn't asked: how Mike had died.

CHAPTER FOURTEEN

Sergeant Peterson dismissed me then. I left her and Gavin to it, and headed for my own cabin, then, on a thought, turned towards the open door of the hospital cabin. There was one officer I hadn't seen at all last night: Sadie, the ship's medical officer. She had her own cabin, but normally you'd find her in here, where she kept all her medicine stocks and medical files. I knocked on the door jamb and went in.

The hospital was a slightly larger cabin than mine, with bunk berths instead of my berth and settee arrangement, so that Sadie could stay with a patient overnight if need be. Gavin's backpack lay on the lower bunk. Sadie was at her desk, writing in one of her ledgers. She lifted her head as I came in and automatically put a piece of paper over the page. 'Seasickness. The swell's getting to several of them.'

I was relieved to see her face friendly and welcoming as ever. Maybe my own self-consciousness had exaggerated Nils's edgy suspicion, and Rolf's awkwardness. She was in her mid forties, the same age as Mike had been, softly spoken, with a striking face that suggested Native American ancestry: high cheekbones and huge, dark eyes in beautifully moulded sockets. Her brows were as dark as her eyes, and her hair a surprising dark copper, long and straight. She'd been bitten by the sailing bug young – she'd grown up in Rochester, on Lake Ontario, and had spent her youth messing about in dinghies. She'd trained and worked as a nurse, but had grabbed this post when she heard of it.

'How's Samir doing?' I wanted my rig star back for the race, and anyone on medication had to stay at deck level.

'He's fine now. How about you?'

'Me? Fit as a fiddle,' I answered before I remembered it wasn't quite true; but then, I supposed, I was doing fine for someone in the early stages of pregnancy.

She gave me a sharp-eyed glance, but didn't pursue it. She wasn't looking too well herself, with her smooth skin pale under the tan and dark circles under her eyes. Her hands smoothed the paper over her writing mechanically, as if it was a cat she was persuading to lie still.

'I was just wondering if you fancied a cup of tea. I'm making.'

'Amazing.'

'Milk, no sugar, right?'

'Right.'

I whisked back into the corridor. Two minutes later, and I was back in the hospital with two mugs of tea and a handful of biscuits. I hoped the ginger nuts weren't too big a giveaway. Her medical training, I consoled myself, was aimed at injuries and surgical emergencies, like an appendix; pregnancy would be low down on the list of shipboard worries.

Sadie'd had time to put the file back and lock the cupboard.

She motioned me to the other chair, and leant back. 'So, what's all doing up on deck?'

'A stiff breeze. Sunshine. Skye on one side, and the Outer Hebrides on the other.' I was going to continue that I was wondering how she was doing, when I realised that it would look like a request for information. A ringside seat on the action; *trying to make things more exciting.* Captain Gunnar's words still burnt. I thrust the thought away. 'The trainees are all livening up: sunshine now, and Belfast tomorrow.'

'Apart from the ones that are feeling sick.'

'All the others on our watch looked fine.' I tried to think. 'I didn't see anyone being peelie-wally or uninterested.'

'Oh, sure, your guys are great. There are a couple on red watch, one of the African girls, and the tall Irishman.' She seemed suddenly to notice the names. 'Hey, Sean Lynch, he's not related to you?'

'My cousin,' I said, adding precisely, Shetland fashion, 'me dad's brother's son.' If there was one thing I was certain of, it was that Sean had never been seasick in his life. 'Was he feeling queasy?'

'More like some kinda stomach bug, I'd say. I gave him soda bicarb and told him to come back if he didn't feel good in an hour.'

Worse and worse. The Lynch family was known for its cast-iron stomachs. Elmer's cooking might not be hugely exciting, but there was nothing about it to upset any Lynch interior. I wondered what Sean was up to. Checking out where the medicines were? Wanting a night alone with the files? Or finding out where Gavin was sleeping, so that he could keep an eye on him?

'It's awful about Mike,' Sadie said suddenly. 'I had to go down and look.' Her face was bleak. 'Officially declare him dead. Take photographs for the inspector.' She glanced up at me, then turned her eyes down to the tea slanting in her mug. You got used to everything being on a slant on board ship, until liquid reminded you what horizontal was. 'We went back a long way, Mike and I.'

'I didn't know that.'

'Oh, yes. We were both on *Ernestina,* back in the nineties.' Her reminiscent smile suggested they'd been more than friends.

My breathing juddered and started again. 'The fishing schooner from Massachusetts?'

'That's the one. *Effie M Morrissey*, that was her real name.' Her face was soft with memory. 'Only forty-six metres long, but she spent twenty years in the Arctic, cruising Greenland. Now she does educational cruises up and down the New England coast. Mike and I signed up after her big restoration in 1994.'

I did a quick bit of arithmetic, and reckoned that must have been once she'd finished her training. 'As the MO?'

'No, no, as paying trainees that time, then we came back as ABs. We were on her, oh, several summers, with Mike rising through the ranks each time.' Her face was warm with the memory. 'We kept in touch between summers.' She smiled, and kept talking, as if it was doing her good. 'Well, we were "an item", I suppose you'd say.' Her eyes lifted to mine. 'You know what it's like, when you're shipmates.'

I nodded.

'Then he met Klaudina, and he was bowled over by her. He's like that, Mike.' Her voice sharpened. 'Enthusiasms.' She caught herself up, lips quivering. 'He *was* like that. I can't believe it.' She shook her head, and resumed. 'If Klaudina hadn't been after him it'd have fizzled out – he told me that. Well, she's not a sailor. She can only share half his life.'

'Maybe that's what he wanted,' I suggested. 'Two separate lives.' I understood that too: the exhilaration of being out here, on the waves, and then the security of the marina, with the storms raging past the harbour mouth. A house where there was space, and no knee-high lip at the toilet entrance; a wood-lined cottage by a bay fringed with rowan trees. But, I reminded myself, Mike's two separate lives had included a woman in each: Klaudina on shore and Agnetha aboard *Sørlandet*. I wanted to ask Sadie if she'd known about Agnetha, but it wasn't my secret. *Everyone knows*, Anders had said. The light in Sadie's face suggested she'd stayed keen on Mike. I wasn't going to ask how she'd felt about his having an affair under her nose with somebody else, especially if he was offering that someone else a whole life together, afloat and ashore. Especially if that someone else was turning it down . . . but in that case, wouldn't it have been Agnetha who'd died?

Maybe not. What was that old quote about *like love to hatred turn'd*? I tried to hear the scansion in my head. *Revenge hath no spur* . . . something like that. If she'd still cared, and he hadn't, and made it obvious . . .

Sadie's carved face grew bleak again. 'It doesn't feel real. He was always so alive.' Suddenly her mood changed, became brisk, as if she feared she'd said too much. She rustled her papers together. 'Thanks for the tea, Cass. I need to get back to work.'

'No problem,' I said, and gathered up the mugs. 'See you later.'

The verse jingled in my head as I washed up. *Revenge hath no spur* . . . no, that wasn't right. Captain Gunnar had an *Oxford Quotations* in his bookshelf, because he knew how irritating it could be to have half a phrase trapped in your head. I put the mugs away and headed for the officers' mess. It was easily found: Restoration drama, Congreve. *Heaven has no rage*, that was it: *Heaven has no rage like love to hatred turned*, followed by that often-quoted old chestnut: *Nor Hell a fury like a woman scorned.*

I didn't like the way my thoughts were going. If Sadie and Mike had remained an item on board until Agnetha came along, the *real thing*, the one he was going to leave his wife for, well, that could well turn love to hatred: to have waited all these years, playing second fiddle in the hope that one day he'd cut free of his shore life and give you everything, only to find out that you were second best after all.

I hadn't seen Sadie on deck the night Mike died. She didn't stand watches, so I didn't often see her in oilskins, but I had a feeling her jacket was scarlet. She could easily have drawn him aside, with a murmured excuse about needing a private word about one of the trainees. She was a nurse, used to lifting people. And if a knife had killed him so silently, surely that suggested some kind of medical training?

I headed up on deck and leant on the rail, looking out gloomily over the dancing water. My opinion of Mike was changing. I'd only looked at the excellent seaman, the enthusiast, good with the trainees, part of the team. Some historical tag was tugging in my brain, brought up by the Congreve quote: someone who'd boasted that he'd never lied to a man nor told the truth to a woman. How did it come about that we were a separate species? Of course, in Congreve's day they were still arguing about whether women had souls or not, but this was now. We'd had the vote for a century. We had equal rights and some of us even had equal pay. Well, in the developed world, anyway. So how was it that men like Mike, good blokes, all these loving husbands who had affairs, could still, somehow, put their relationships with women into a different box? I didn't get it.

'Penny for them,' Gavin said, appearing suddenly beside me.

I shook my head. 'Too expensive. I was just brooding on the oddity of the male race.'

His shoulder leant against mine. 'A propos of the way you held out on Sergeant Peterson?' He smiled. 'After doing so well, too.'

His voice teased. 'You managed more words than I've heard you say in all our time together.'

I wanted to respond to his teasing, but my very bones felt weary. 'Can we pretend you've given me the lecture about priorities?'

'Only if you want to turn me into a yes man.' His voice had a warning edge to it. I thought about that one, and knew I didn't. The sudden sharp edge to the conversation frightened me. I shook my head and slipped my arm through his.

'Sorry. I'm so tired. Look, will you give me a chance to think about it?' I shot a sideways glance at him, and saw his brows were still drawn together, his eyes the dark grey of a winter sea. 'I'm not putting myself in danger.' I gave his arm a hug. 'I promise I won't make appointments with a possible suspect on the lonely deck at midnight.'

'There isn't a lonely deck at midnight, or any other time.' He looked down at the swarm of trainees, and let the subject drop. 'Word's got round about there being a body in the cold store. The young ones are having fun hearing strange knocking noises from inside there, and the folk on galley duty are high as ponies on a windy day. Not wanting to go downstairs alone, that sort of thing.' He straightened up. 'Well, I'll keep on with my watching brief.'

He walked away, leaving me feeling suddenly unprotected, alone. I drew myself up to my full five feet two, and gave myself an indignant scold. I was perfectly capable of looking after myself.

Word's got round . . . I looked round the trainees. Yes, that air of unease had returned, the tendency to gather in groups, a slightly higher note to the voices. A faded navy cap caught my eye, one of the trainees from the white watch. Reminded, I looked around, and realised, now I was looking, that there was nothing like the jacket I'd seen. Only one trainee had an obviously new scarlet sailing suit. There were a couple of red jackets, but outdoor jackets, not sailing ones. I strolled across to the banjer door and looked in. There were only a handful of jackets left on the pegs, all variations of dark. If it had been Bezrukov, then he'd stolen a jacket from elsewhere; from a crew cabin. I thought that through. He'd come into the aft corridor. There was Anders' cabin first: a white sailing suit, like Agnetha's. The sick bay: locked. The next cabin was mine, with just that combination of scarlet sailing jacket and faded navy hat, hanging inside the curtain, all ready to be snatched up.

The breath left my lungs as if someone had punched me. The clothes the person had worn looked familiar because they were my own.

I needed peace to think about this. I headed for the crew galley and found Anders there, making a cup of tea, Rat on one shoulder. He looked up as I came in. 'Drinking chocolate?'

'Please.'

'I need to go back down to my engine. Come and keep me company.'

I followed him down the narrow ladder, mug in hand. The warmth and the diesel smell were reassuring. Anders gestured at the makeshift settee in one corner. 'Make yourself at home. I just need to run through these checks.'

I hunkered into the seat while he went along the gauges and fiddled a lever or two, then he came and sat down beside me. His face was grave. 'So, how's it going?'

I pulled a face. Anders was a fellow sailor, and definitely above suspicion; at least, the only sure things in life, as Granny Bridget used to say, were death and taxes, but Anders was a newcomer on board, not involved in ship relationships. I could talk to him about it. 'I think it might have been my own jacket and hat that I saw. That the person who went aft with Mike was wearing. I've been looking at all the trainees, and none of them has one like the one

I saw, a scarlet jacket with reflective tape on the sleeves. No, Samir has, but it's shop-new. I'd have noticed that.'

His fair brows rose, then narrowed. 'Someone – Bezrukov – reached in through the curtain and picked them up from your cabin?'

I nodded.

'You realise how much that narrows things down,' Anders said.

I gave him a blank look.

He gestured at me with the hand that wasn't holding his mug. 'Cass, are you sure you're well? It's really not like you to be so slow. You are usually charging ahead like a rogue elk.'

'A bit under the weather,' I conceded. I wasn't going to share my little passenger even with Anders. 'Go on then, Holmes. Dazzle me.'

He made the gesture again, and I got it. Size. I preferred not to think about being knee-high to a grasshopper, but in this case, I should have. 'Mine are small men's,' I said. Women's gear seemed to bring out a manufacturers' obsession with shades of pastel blue, or pretty pink flashing, so I bought the small men's size and velcro'd the cuffs out of the way.

'If they were yours, it was not the Russian,' Anders said. 'He has shoulders like the side of a house. There is no way he'd have fitted in a small man's jacket. And that means . . .'

He looked bleakly across at me, and I nodded. One of us.

Anders swirled his mug in both hands, staring gloomily into the coffee. 'I was hoping that it would all be decided. They would catch this Russian in Belfast, and that would be that.' He looked across at me. 'You had no idea who it was? From the height, the walk?'

'He was clumsy, not like someone used to being on board. None of us would walk like that. Height, not as tall as Mike. Three inches shorter, maybe.'

'My height or a shade taller.' Anders considered this. 'Not Henrik, then, he is six foot, and Erik is tall too. Rolf would be that height, but he's broad-shouldered. Nils, Petter, either of Agnetha's ABs, any of them could have worn it. The women, of course, but are you sure about the height?'

'Pretty sure.'

'Then Mona would not be tall enough, nor the girl on Nils's watch. Nor the younger galley girl, what is her name?'

'Laila. Ruth would be the right height. Jenn as well.' I'd never seen Sadie standing beside Mike. I tried to think of her standing beside me. Yes, she would be the right height too.

Agnetha. I suddenly realised that I was off the hook. I could go to Sergeant Peterson with this. The relief blazed, dazzling, through me. The forensics lab would take my jacket and hat – that would be a nuisance, bang in the middle of the season – and test them for hairs, or skin cells, or whatever modern forensics could come up with. There could well be hairs on the cap. Fingerprints on the stiff collar of the jacket. If Agnetha had done this, they would find the evidence. If she hadn't, there would be no scandal aboard the *Sørlandet* to spoil Captain Gunnar's last season.

I rose. 'I'll go and tell Sergeant Peterson.'

His hand caught my arm. 'No, wait.' He frowned across at the engine then turned his eyes to me. 'Cass, this is not looking good for you. Gavin will not be allowed to tell you, of course, but I don't like what I'm hearing. Do you realise you're chief suspect?'

I turned back to him as if I was caught in treacle, moving slowly. My lips framed the word 'Why?' Then I realised. I hadn't recognised my own jacket and cap because I wouldn't expect to see them on anyone but me. My crewmates would have known them, and assumed it was me inside them.

'This is what I've heard.' He set his mug aside. I sat down again.

'I've been thinking about it, trying to make sense of it. There were four people who saw the person that you saw, the person in red. Rolf was on the boat deck, and Nils on the aft deck. Henrik was by the galley door.' I remembered my map, and nodded. 'Jenn was coming out of her cabin, and saw the person at the end of the passage, going out. She thought it was you, although she didn't see the face, and when she thought more she wasn't sure the person was small enough. When she came out, she was looking at the trainees enjoying the dolphins. She did not look for the person. Nils was looking from above as the person went over to Mike. He was certain it was you.'

'He would be,' I muttered.

'He went downstairs then, and did not watch them come up, but Henrik saw them on the deck. He thought that it could be you, except that you looked taller, compared to Mike, than he would have expected. Rolf said he only glanced over, but took it to be you.'

'So,' I said slowly, keeping my voice steady, 'the theory is that I got rid of the helm and standby, nipped down the nav-shack stairs to get my jacket, went out on deck, brought Mike up on some pretext, and killed him while everyone was looking at the dolphins.'

Anders nodded.

'Leaving the *helm*,' I stressed. 'They thought I would leave the helm unattended?' In the days of Nelson, I'd have been keelhauled. Nowadays, being confined to quarters until your court martial would cover it.

'To commit a murder,' Anders said. It didn't sound a good enough excuse to me. 'But I have thought about this. The people who were sure it was you, Nils and Rolf, they are both accustomed to seeing you in your foul-weather gear. You have worn it in the evenings and at night until now. They would have said "Cass" and not looked further.'

It was what I'd said to Sergeant Peterson. I nodded.

'And Nils, who was the most certain, was immediately above Mike and the person in red. He could not judge relative heights; nor could Rolf – the person was a step behind Mike going up the stairs. But the two who were not sure, Henrik and Jenn' – he gestured with one hand – 'they were both on deck, level with the person, and they both thought it was taller than you, relative to Mike.'

Most people were. I remembered my map again. Erik, Petter and Mona were cleared. Jenn or Rolf had been there, Henrik was too tall. That left Agnetha, Sadie and Nils.

'Does the ship grapevine have any information about how he was killed?'

Anders nodded. 'They have been looking for a possible weapon. Rolf told me. They were searching the carpenter's shop, looking at his smaller chisels. The sergeant had a piece of paper for comparison, which they showed him. It looked, he said, like a shallow diamond. Not like a normal clasp knife, more like a dagger. Naturally she did not say anything more, but there was no blood on the deck, so we're thinking he was stabbed, perhaps in the back, which would not bleed much.'

Our own knives were personal, recognisable, and attached to us. It would be too incriminating not to be able to produce yours, when asked, and everyone knew these days that the smallest traces of blood would be found. You'd go for something that had no connection with you, that you could replace at your leisure. *More like a dagger . . .*

It was those words that did it. I gave an involuntary laugh. Anders turned to stare at me. I took a deep breath. 'This is crazy. This is too Agatha Christie.'

He raised his brows. 'Explain.'

'Captain Gunnar has a silver paper knife. A little dagger, sharp, with a cross-section just like that. He keeps it in the rack above his desk.' I stood up. 'I'm going to have to go and talk to Sergeant Peterson.'

'*No*,' Anders said. He pulled me down again. 'No, I think you should not. Keep your head low; do not go volunteering the weapon. She will find it for herself. If someone is framing you by wearing your clothes, do not give her more evidence against you.'

I tried to think about how it would look if I came forward, suggesting the weapon, and conceded that he was right. 'All the same, unless it comes on really foul, I'm not going to wear my jacket and hat until they've been examined. As far as I know, nobody but me's worn them. Just one hair that shouldn't be there . . .'

'She will take it for examination soon enough.' His hand rested on my shoulder, then he rose, and dropped into Shetlandic. 'Lass, geng du and hae a sleep, until dy brain wakes up.'

CHAPTER FIFTEEN

I met Sergeant Peterson at my door. 'I was just coming to look for you,' she said briskly. 'Would you mind me bagging up your jacket and cap for later examination?'

'Go you,' I said, gesturing towards them. I didn't touch them.

'When did you last wear them?'

'I wore the jacket three, no, four nights ago; the misty night. I only wear the hat when it's raining or very windy, so I've not had that on since, oh, two weeks ago.'

'I brought evidence bags. Hang on.' She rummaged in her briefcase and brought out a pair of blue plastic gloves, then a clear bag, just big enough to hold my hat. Cat watched with interest from the berth as she turned it in her hands. The light from the porthole glinted on two short, silvery-fair hairs. Nils, Rolf and Agnetha were all fair. I thought of Sadie's long copper hair, and wondered if that cleared her. Sergeant Peterson wrote a label, stuck it on and sealed the top. The jacket, of course, was too big for a bag.

'I have a dry-cleaner's bag over my dress jacket,' I offered.

'Better than nothing.'

We swapped them around, with Sergeant Peterson holding the jacket gingerly by the shoulder seams, and she took jacket, hat and herself off. I swung myself up into my bunk, feeling suddenly weary. Cat curled up in the crook of my neck, and sighed. 'You and me both, boy,' I said. I lay there, listening to the waves slapping at the hull, the padding of feet on deck. A thread of tune from Sindre's mouth organ drifted on the wind. I dozed for a bit, then got up, refreshed, and went off to find Gavin.

He had no inhibitions about invading the captain's space, and was happily sitting back on a red velvet settee, drinking tea under the portrait of Queen Sonja. The captain's cabin door was closed: do not disturb.

'You're looking cheerful,' he greeted me. 'I looked in as I was making tea, but you were dead to the world.' He gave me a sideways look. 'Nothing like confession for clearing the mind.'

It hadn't quite been confession, but I'd set the wheels in motion to catch the guilty. I leant against him, and was honest. 'If my jacket gives you the evidence you need, I don't have to share my suspicions.'

'We do understand confidentiality, you know.'

I nodded. 'It's not that. It's – it's trust between shipmates.' I turned to look straight at him. 'I can't. Really, I can't.'

He didn't move, but I felt as though he had. There was still a gulf between us. My allegiance should have been to him, or to the forces of law that he represented here, not to the ship. I was in the wrong and I knew it, and until I got myself back in the right, we'd be as separated mentally as we were physically. There was a silence that seemed to drag out for ever. I felt a chill running down me. Was it so easy to lose a relationship? Part of me wanted to turn to him now and tell him everything, but some dogged loyalty kept me silent. Playground mentality, I told myself, not telling the teacher even when she should be told; not wanting to be the copper's nark.

Four bells rang out above our heads. Six o'clock. I looked bleakly at Gavin, and he stretched his hand to mine. 'Either it was you, or it was someone who was prepared to see you take the rap.'

'She's got the evidence now.' I thought of the glinting hairs on my cap.

'If it was your jacket and cap. If it was, if usable traces have been left, we'll know a couple of days after we arrive in Belfast.' His fingers curled tight around mine. 'Cass, you're too important to me to risk. You know now, none better, what a murderer will do if he or she feels threatened. I'll tell you what I know about Callaghan's killer. It's someone who's quick-thinking, decisive, ready to snatch the opportunity that's offered. It's someone who's prepared to take risks. Organised. Someone with those qualities could have come in and snatched up your jacket while everyone watched the dolphins, then gone out to waylay Callaghan. They were knowledgeable enough to kill him silently, and strong enough to put his body where it was found. They were daring enough to do it, in spite of you being less than a metre away.' He paused, grey eyes searching mine. 'But there's no reason why any of the trainees would do that. He didn't know them, he wasn't working closely with them.'

I nodded.

'So I'm looking at one of your shipmates. Organised, clever, ruthless. Ruthless enough to frame you by using your jacket. Cass, do you really want somebody like that fearing that you might have something on them?'

'I know you're right,' I said. 'I *know*. But I don't believe the person I'm thinking of killed Mike. If I was to tell you what I know, it would cause all sorts of complications that couldn't then be undone.

I can't spoil their reputation, their career, with my suspicions.'

He sighed and looked around, then rose, pulling me with him, out of the room, across the corridor and through the curtain into my own room. We sat down on the settee together, and he put his arm around my shoulders. 'Cass, I do understand. You don't get on with Freya Peterson, and you do get on with your shipmates, one in particular – I'm already beginning to learn about people dynamics on board – and you don't want to betray your friend.' He reached into his sporran and drew out a letter, sealed in a clear evidence bag. I recognised Agnetha's handwriting, saw the words *desolate without* and turned my head away before I could read any more – *you here* . . . my brain finished off.

'It was in a book in Callaghan's room. So, you see, we know about the affair now. Freya will be talking to Agnetha again as soon as she comes off watch.' He looked me straight in the eyes, hand gripping my shoulder. 'You won't warn her?'

He was trusting me enough to risk his career. I knew he shouldn't have shown me the letter. I slid my hand into his, and shook my head. 'No.'

If she was innocent, interrogation wouldn't hurt her. She could say as little or as much as she liked. I reckoned Agnetha was a match for Freya Peterson: two strong-minded career women, determined on their upwards path. If she was guilty – but I wouldn't think about that.

'Is what you don't want to say evidence that we could use?'

Was it? I considered that, and shook my head, eyes on the letter. 'Not more than you've got.'

I felt like I'd just been to confession; absolved. It was alright again. I curled down into the curve of Gavin's shoulder and turned my head, my mouth searching upwards for his. We kissed passionately, arms tight around each other, my hand curved around the muscles of his shoulder, and wanted each other. He pulled back from me. 'I'm still on duty.' He smiled. 'How soon do we get to Belfast?'

'Won't you still be on duty there?'

'It's not my jurisdiction. I'll hand Mike's body over, and update them on my findings, but the Northern Constabulary will take over the investigation, and we can be together.'

'Good.' I withdrew my hands from his, and checked my watch. 'Dinner time. I'd better tidy up.'

'Dinner at the captain's table.' Now he was teasing me. 'No evening dress?'

'Evening dress aboard this ship is all the thermals and outerwear you've got,' I retorted. 'Which I've given to Sergeant Peterson.' I glanced out through the porthole. The sun was still dazzling on the grey sea, and the long rollers had subsided as the wind had fallen. It shouldn't be too cold. I laid an extra jumper ready to put on between leaving the warmth of the officers' mess and heading up on deck, and I'd have my fleece-lined mid-layer jacket on top. That should do me.

It was a glorious evening. The full moon came up fine on our port bow, the pale-gold of polished brass, dodging behind the clouds to dazzle out in an orange spotlight on the water, bright as tongues of fire, or sailing from behind them to make a dancing pathway stretching from us to the horizon. We were clear of lobster-pot territory now, but although the wind was from a better quarter, it was too soft to make it worth setting sail. We motored on into the dusk, with only the occasional glint of light from a passing ship to break the velvety blue dimness of the sea horizon.

This would be an extra long watch, for we needed to get the ship back to Blighty time, and Captain Gunnar had decreed that the blue watch would stand an extra hour, till one, then the ship's clock would go back to midnight, and the red watch would do their usual midnight till four, BST. The dimness closed to navy, then black, the moon's light shrouded by the clouds, the ship's rigging lit only by the deck lights. It was lucky that the nav was easy, for I was stumblingly tired by the end of the watch.

All the officers of the blue and red watches were spread around the aft deck, just above the companionway down – a steep flight of a dozen steps with a varnished handrail on each side – with Captain Gunnar slightly further over, in the centre of his bridge, ready to declare it midnight again. I'd handed over to Agnetha and said a general goodnight. I was starting down the stairs, one hand on the midships handrail, when something caught at my ankle, yanked at it, and before I knew it I was falling.

It's at times like these you realise what a puny thing the human body is. I slammed against the handrail with a wallop, and attempted to grab at it, but my grasp was weaker than the force of my eight stone being pulled by gravity. My shoulder banged painfully against the handrail and I tried again to grab, but now I was in freefall, catapulting towards the solid deck ten feet below.

It was my other foot that saved me, catching on the step it had been about to stand on. It dragged for just long enough to pull my falling length back towards the step, instead of forwards, and just at that moment the bow went up over the long Atlantic swell and tipped the ship backwards. I paused in mid-air; truly, I felt myself pausing, for everything seemed to be in slow motion, inevitable as a car skidding. Then the friendly, hard steps came up to meet me, and time speeded up once more. I hit them with a force that slammed the breath out of my lungs. A hard edge bashed my chin. My hands grabbed the steps and I was slithering down, cheek scraped against one step, shoulder thunked again by another, until I ended in an undignified heap at the bottom, somersaulted over myself and lay still. Green stars sparked around me.

The stairs rang as my fellow officers clattered down to me. 'Cass, are you OK?' Erik's voice.

'Yes,' I said, loudly, to show I was conscious. I didn't move yet, but I opened my eyes to look up at the concerned circle standing round me. 'Give me a minute to check.' I flexed my fingers experimentally, then moved my arms. Nothing broken. Toes and legs, ditto. I was pretty sure I hadn't banged my head as I'd come down. Lucky. Louisa Musgrove had come off far worse. Gradually, the stars subsided.

Someone must have called for Sadie, for she was on deck now, feeling down my spine, pelvis, arms and legs, checking my ears. 'Bring her into the hospital.'

I reached for Gavin's hand and let him support me as I eased myself into a sitting position. My shoulder hurt worst. It had had two bashes. I'd have a bonny bruise in the morning. I ran my other hand over it. It felt as it should, and there was no bone pain.

My head was spinning. I could hear the trainees on watch chattering, relaying the story round the people who'd missed it: *Fell right down the stairs, concussion, just tumbled right down, hit the deck, nearly fell overboard* . . . I'd be lucky if twenty phones weren't already winging the photos of me sprawled on deck to Norway. I leant on Gavin, staggered through into the hospital cabin and folded myself into the chair. My eyes closed. 'Don't go to sleep,' Sadie said. 'Cass, don't go to sleep.'

I opened them again. 'I don't think I hit my head on the way down.' I managed a laugh. 'Everything else.'

She shone a light into my eyes. 'Pupils even, but keep an eye on them.' That seemed to be at Gavin. 'Pulse.'

'Tumultuous,' I murmured. I was beginning to feel light-headedly cheerful. 'I thought I'd had it there.'

'How on earth did you come to fall?' Sadie asked.

'Tripped. An extra hour of watch did for me.' I flicked a glance at Gavin. His mouth was grim. I could see he didn't believe me, but he wasn't going to question me in front of Sadie.

'No serious damage. You were lucky.'

'Luck of the Lynches,' I agreed. Luckier than she knew.

'I should maybe keep you in here, in case of delayed concussion. But—' She looked a question at Gavin.

'We'll stick together,' Gavin said.

My heart gave a hopeful leap. Being together was worth falling down stairs for.

Sadie looked relieved. 'Listen for unusual breathing. Check her pupils.'

'I'm going to have some beautiful bruises tomorrow.'

'And scrapes.' She opened her cupboard and brought out a bottle of antiseptic and a wad of cotton wool. 'This may well sting. Sorry.'

It did sting. It burnt like fire on my cheek and chin. I gritted my teeth and endured, remembering a childhood of grazed knees: '*Non, Maman!*' Her beautiful face, very calm above me. '*Il faut.*' No more argument, even from my mutinous six-year-old self. When Maman said '*Il faut*' like that, then it had to be done. My hands next, well grazed on both palms, with a bonny slice cut across my knuckles that was oozing improbably vermilion blood. Funny how humankind had got to the furthest reaches of the galaxy, but not managed to invent an antiseptic that didn't sting. 'Thanks,' I said, once it was over. 'I'll do now.'

'Tough, you sailing types.' She shook her head, laughing. 'It was a spectacular fall.'

'Probably on Facebook already,' I agreed. 'Thanks, Sadie.'

'No worries.'

We left her putting away the bottle and headed for my cabin.

Peace. Quiet. I lay back on my bed and felt the rise and fall of the ship soothe me. Gavin closed the door behind us, then sat down on the settee, facing me, one arm over my midriff. 'Well?'

'I was tripped.'

'I'd already deduced that.'

I started to shake my head, and was stopped by another burst of green stars. 'No, accidents do happen on board ship, even to the most sure-footed of us. But this wasn't one. Someone caught at my ankle as I lifted my other foot, and I went over.'

'How do you mean, caught at your ankle? Bent down and grabbed it?'

'Not with fingers. Hard, like the edge of a shoe. The foot nearest the rail, the centre of the ship. Hooked their foot round my ankle, maybe? I'm not sure. I just felt the tug, then I was falling.'

His arm tightened across my waist, and I thought of my little passenger, and hoped the fall hadn't hurt it. 'Who was there? Above you?' I could see him already thinking back, visualising.

'All of us. We'd just changed watch and declared midnight. Erik, Petter and Mona from my watch. Rolf – I think he tried to grab me as I fell. Agnetha. Her ABs were below, organising the watch, but Jonas was there, her watch leader.' Suddenly, behind him, I saw my cousin Sean, beside the helm.

'Sadie?'

'I don't think so . . . why would she be on deck at that hour?'

'She said it was a spectacular fall, as if she'd seen it.'

Rolf. Agnetha. Sadie. I hadn't seen Nils; he'd be sleeping, ready to get up for 4 a.m.

Gavin leant forward to lay his head against my side, gently, not letting the weight fall on me. His hair tickled my cheek; he smelt of salt air and Imperial Leather soap. 'My heart stopped as you went over. I was down midships, and trying to get to you, to catch you.' He lifted his head so that he was looking at me. 'I knew I wouldn't manage it. In that instant I thought of all the dead bodies I'd seen, and feared you'd be the next.'

I brought my hand up to hold his. 'We Lynches are much harder to kill than that.'

'So someone is finding.' He leant back, and smiled. 'Well, are you going to bed?'

I returned his smile, and tightened my grip on his hand. 'Are we?'

'I wasn't wanting to push my luck.' He gestured at the settee. 'I'd be fine here.'

'From the official point of view, that would compromise you just as much. You should be sending Sergeant Peterson in, to lose her night's sleep.'

'Be damned to that.' He stood up and took his jacket off. 'If you're sure you're not too shaken.'

'All in a day's work aboard a tall ship,' I said, and reached forward to kiss him.

I woke in the night and felt myself bleeding. The child that I'd only known I was carrying for half a day was leaving me, and with the wash of relief I felt a sadness sharp and sudden as standing barefoot on a thistle.

When I slipped back into bed, Gavin turned towards me without waking, his arm curving over me, his soft breathing undisturbed. His skin was warm against mine, but I had never felt so alone.

232

Six Bells

The Irish Sea: Tiree to Belfast

Wednesday 1st July

CHAPTER SIXTEEN

I woke up at my usual half past six, Norwegian time, and was confused for a moment as I heard only three bells sound above me, then I remembered Captain Gunnar nodding at the safety watch to ring eight bells again. Half past five, British time. I was curled into the curve of Gavin's body, with his arm over my waist. His breathing was soft and even, warm on my shoulder, barely audible over the shoosh of the water on the ship's side. I snuggled closer, smiling, and his arm tightened around me. Cat was on the other side of me, determinedly holding his place on the berth, paws braced on the wood lip, in spite of the double-person pressure on him to move towards the cold metal porthole shelf. He opened one yellow eye as he felt me stir, greeted me with a yawn, expanded into the extra centimetre of space I'd created and curled his tail back over his nose.

Falling. I remembered the hard tug at my ankle, then the graceless cartwheeling into the air, the slam as I hit the deck. Several bits of me hurt: my cheek and chin, my shoulder, the cut along my hand. My hip. My stomach. I felt the emptying space inside me, and bit my lip. The child I had wanted to protect was gathered back into nothingness – no, gathered back to God, for us to meet again in our next life. Yet even as I was grieving, relief was pushing its way into my mind, along with a resolve that I'd go on the pill as soon as I possibly could. I wouldn't yet have to choose between the sea and a child – but the choice to be made lingered still in my mind. I pushed it away, and said a prayer for the little soul that was leaving me. My cheek was warmed by Gavin's shoulder. I wouldn't have to tell him now, or force him to make choices. It was all over, and I had to face him with clear eyes when he woke. I moved my fingers down to my stomach in a farewell caress, then set myself to bring the day into focus.

Who had tripped me? I tried to visualise it again. I'd handed over the watch to Agnetha, and she'd got her new helm settled on course. Sean had been on standby helm, but I thought I'd have noticed him forward among the crew, and he couldn't have caught at me from the side of the steps with a boathook, say, because Captain Gunnar had been standing there. Mona had stayed down on deck, but Erik and Petter had come up after they'd dismissed the watch. Now I was thinking about it, they had been standing together, directly behind me, and Erik had motioned me in front of him. Either of them could easily have hooked a foot round my ankle.

I couldn't rule Agnetha out either. Her watch leader and two ABs would have been down on deck, but she'd been right there, standing by the corner of the stairs. She could have done it. Erik, Petter, Agnetha. Sean. But what did I know that had made me such a danger?

I thought about that one for a bit. I knew about Agnetha's

pregnancy. I was certain that Erik and I were the only ones who knew about that, unless Sadie had guessed. If I was eliminated . . . No. I stopped myself there. I'd had a nasty fall, but if somebody really wanted to eliminate me there were surer ways. I'd had a chance of a broken neck, but a broken arm or leg were more likely. No. Somebody just wanted to throw me off my stride, give me something else to think about for a bit. Get me off the ship, maybe? I'd be able to manage with a broken arm, but I'd be no use aboard on crutches. Reduced to galley duty, like Long John Silver . . . I contemplated that for a moment. If it was Agnetha, she wouldn't want to kill me, but if I was put out of action she could go ahead and have her abortion, then deny everything. But now Mike was gone, she could do that anyway. I didn't see how me being out of the way would help her.

If I'd been airlifted off yesterday evening, what would I have missed? I started thinking ahead.

Wednesday. We'd be arriving in Belfast late today. There'd be all the customs inspections – tomorrow morning, probably, rather than today, by the time we'd docked. Then we'd be free to explore the city *en fête* – at least, the trainees would; we crew would be on duty that evening for an on-board party for some corporation that wanted to join in the tall ships experience. It was one of the ways *Sørlandet* kept afloat. Friday was the big crew parade through the city centre; all hands on duty again, in our best *Sørlandet* T-shirts. That would be followed by a prize-giving, and speeches, then some sort of party.

I couldn't see any reason why anyone would want to make me miss all that fun. Granted, I wasn't at my best in social situations, but I could talk about the ship to slightly drunk executive types with the best of them. Perhaps it was the customs inspection, with everyone on board lined up to be checked; was the person who'd worn my jacket and hat afraid I'd know them again? I considered that for a bit. Erik, Petter, Rolf, Agnetha. Erik was too tall, but the others were the right height, just shorter than Mike. Agnetha had slimmer shoulders than the men, but I reckoned any of them could have got into my jacket, and it would have been quicker for Petter to grab it from my cabin when the dolphins arrived than to get his own from his cabin beside the sail locker, forrard and down a flight of steps.

The stumbling block with that was that I knew them. They'd have no fear of the long, alphabetical customs line snaking round the deck as each person was taken into the officers' mess and scrutinised. To worry about that, you'd have to be somebody I didn't know. One of the trainees who wasn't on my watch.

I could rule out Sean. He'd know I knew him, and besides, he had the Lynch height. Somebody else from the red watch? Bezrukov? But I thought I would have noticed him on deck last night.

I couldn't see any pattern to it, but I had no doubt there was one. I lay for a bit longer thinking about it, then turned over towards Gavin. I'd need to be getting up soon. Cat leapt over us both, and landed on the floor with a soft thud. Gavin's head lifted.

'Only Cat,' I assured him.

He curled his arm around me again. 'How are you feeling this morning?'

'Sore. I need to be getting up.' Five bells rang as I spoke. I let the clang echo into silence. 'Breakfast at seven.'

'Mmmm.' He sat up and stretched. 'Can you stay in here while I shower?'

'I can't be kept under guard all day,' I pointed out.

'As much of it as I can manage,' Gavin said. 'Until we get safely to Belfast, and forensics. I want evidence.'

'I was thinking about that,' I said. 'I wondered if the person who tripped me wanted me out of the way for the customs line-up. In case I recognised them.'

'Maybe. But unless there's something really important you're not telling us, or something you know that you don't know you know – that old one – I'm inclined to think someone's trying to be clever.'

'At my expense?' I moved slightly, and winced.

'I just have this feeling. You know, as if a conjurer's trying to force a card on me. You're being made too obvious.' He lifted his head to look over me. 'Is that the time? I must get up.' He buckled his kilt around him in one swift movement, caught up one of my towels and headed out, closing the door firmly behind him.

I felt that shock of grief again as I moved. I had to try not to think about it. I got on with dressing, wincing every time I tried to raise my arm. My right arm, for a mercy; at least I'd be able to keep the log book. There was a nasty bruise on my hip, and a purple and yellow scrape on my ankle bone. I lifted my foot onto the settee to look at it more closely. Yes, it was where the person had hooked round my ankle, a defined circle, as if the point of a shoe had dug in, then a scrape backwards. The point of a shoe, or a boathook. I remembered the hard feel of it. If it had been a boathook then it had to be from where Agnetha had been standing, on the side of the bridge. Agnetha, my friend . . . I didn't want to believe it, but my brain kept ticking on. I was the only one who could give her a real motive for killing Mike. Only she knew about the child that had been growing inside me. Maybe she thought a miscarriage might get me off the ship . . . she could have her abortion, and deny everything . . . Agnetha, my friend . . . I wanted to cry like a bairn.

I was dressed and in control of myself by the time Gavin came back, head damp. 'Do you ever get used to having to step over a knee-high lip into any room with water?'

'Normal life on board.' My shoulder hurt too much for me to be able to do my usual French plait; I ran a brush though my curls and bundled them back with a band. My face was a sight: a graze on one side, to balance my scar on the other, and a mass of scab on my chin. There was more than a suspicion of black around one eye.

'Maybe we'd better not go out together in Belfast,' Gavin said. 'I'd get taken in charge.'

'Sure, and he's my man, and a fine sowl when he's not at the drinking,' I said, in my best Dad accent. 'You leave him be; I'm not after pressing charges.' I straightened my shoulders. 'Ready?'

'Ready.'

One look at Jenn reminded me it was Canada Day: she had a Canadian flag blazoned on her sweatshirt and a maple-leaf transfer on each cheek. She pressed one into my hand. 'You've got one whole cheek left. How're you feeling this morning?'

'Fine,' I said. I dipped the transfer into her bowl of water and clapped it to my cheek, remembering the childhood thrill of peeling off the paper to see the vivid colours.

Agnetha had already applied hers, scarlet on her pale skin. 'Hold on to it, Cass, it takes longer than you think. Let me see.' She put her hands up to the paper and I felt a stab of disbelief that I could even think of her as Mike's killer, peeling the backing off so gently. Her blue eyes met mine, clear and unshadowed. 'There. Don't touch it.'

Breakfast was a quiet meal. Anders gave me a concerned look, and I nodded, and shrugged with the shoulder that didn't hurt. He nodded back, then flicked his eyes towards the captain's cabin. I followed his gaze. The captain's silver letter opener gleamed in one corner of the wooden rack above his desk. I should have told Gavin about it while I had him to myself. Captain Gunnar asked how I was, then focused on his oatmeal and raisins, lifting his head only to announce that the ETA for Belfast would be around 22.30. We'd spend the day making ready for port, please: touching up rust, brass, the usual.

It was a bonny morning. The wind was light, the sea moved only by the long Atlantic swell. The sun played chase with the turtle-back clouds just as the moon had done last night, spotlighting the sea with a pool of polished silver, then turning to a dazzling pathway snaking to the horizon. A Canadian flag waved at the mizzen cross-trees, and when I gave a swift glance into the banjer, there were maple leaves slung all along the front of the galley. To port was a long, low, grey island, Islay, with the Paps of Jura just visible behind it.

'Islay,' Nils confirmed. He seemed slightly less abrupt this morning. Maybe my damaged cheek and stiff movements were getting a sympathy vote. 'You should see Ireland soon.'

We hadn't far to go; less than a hundred miles now. 'Course?'

'190 degrees at the moment, changing to 110 when we enter the Irish Sea.' He hesitated, then gave me a sideways look. 'I don't suppose there's any truth in the rumour that you were pushed?'

He hadn't been there. He shouldn't have been there. His watch began at 4.00, and most folk on that watch slept early, then dozed in the afternoon. I hoped my sudden sharp suspicion wasn't visible in my face. *Your voice gives you away*, Gavin had said to me once. I tried to keep it amused. 'Pushed? The rumour mill's working overtime.'

'There have been too many strange happenings on board.' He shot a glance forwards to the banjer. I knew he was thinking of the cold store below, where Mike lay shrouded.

'Belfast today.' They would take Mike away, and if Bezrukov was still aboard, he would presumably leave too, and cousin Sean, whatever he was up to, and we would have peace again.

Rolf had been sent to watch over me. His manner had changed too. Yesterday, he'd been a fellow crew member set to an awkward duty. Today, there was an odd sympathy in his manner, not quite patronising, but as if he felt I needed to be looked after until they got me safely ashore. I clenched my hands on the rail, and set my teeth, and endured it.

I set my watch to scrubbing off rust with a wire brush and painting over with anti-rust hardener, meanly leaving the brass for the red watch. The sun was warm on our backs, on the wooden decks. The Paps of Jura vanished into mist, Islay darkened from mist grey to slate, with a sharp cliff at one end, then slipped behind us. 'Whisky,' Jan Ole said wistfully, watching it retreat.

Halfway through, Rolf handed over to Captain Gunnar. He had that same paternal air. 'Not long to go now, Cass,' he said encouragingly, and took up his position on the nearest we had to a bridge, upright, beard neatly trimmed, one hand on the rail, the other on his staff, surveying his kingdom.

Not long to go till what? I wanted to ask, but didn't dare.

He went back below when Agnetha came up with the mid-morning teas. She brought mine forward and leant on the rail beside me, looking out. She echoed my thoughts. 'Belfast. They'll catch this man, and then we'll all be safe.'

'I hope so,' I agreed. 'Oh, I do hope so.'

'And Captain Gunnar will relax.' Her hand rested on my shoulder. 'You'll see. He won't really dismiss you in Belfast.'

My throat closed. I couldn't look at her. 'Is that what they're saying?'

Her head bobbed downwards in the corner of my eye. 'But it'll all blow over. You'll see.'

Dismissed. The word rang round my head like a blow. Captain Gunnar thought I was unstable. *Trying to create excitement* . . . I was the scapegoat for the stowaway, for things going wrong. I remembered Rolf's careful consideration. Then the pain turned to anger. 'Agnetha, how long have they been saying that I'm not right in the head?'

She looked uncomfortable at me putting it so bluntly, but she'd begun the conversation. She couldn't back off now. 'The first time I heard it was that morning.' Her face twisted. 'The last time I saw Mike. The morning we quarrelled. Somebody mentioned you at coffee, that the captain had caught you with a loaded gun and taken it off you.'

Nils had heard that rumour. I remembered him asking me about it.

'That same evening,' I said slowly, 'someone dressed in my jacket and hat killed Mike, as everyone was watching the dolphins, when I was alone on the aft deck.'

Her mouth fell open, stretching the maple leaf on her pale cheek into a scarlet smear, like a bloodstain. 'You think someone is setting you up to take the blame?'

'I'm sure of it.' The anger was warming. I felt my brain beginning to work. 'I found that gun in the block store. I don't know why the captain followed me down there.' I couldn't ask him if someone had sent him after me, but Gavin could. 'That was in Stavanger. If someone had seen me then, the gossip would

243

have been round straight away. Someone set it going the day Mike died.'

I turned to face her, and saw her thinking it through.

'And the man in my cabin, two nights ago,' I said. 'He was gone before Gavin arrived.'

Agnetha bit her lip. Slowly, she nodded. 'I heard about that too. That you'd said someone had come into your cabin.'

'The only people who knew he was there were Gavin, me, and him. I haven't said anything, and I don't suppose Gavin would have. So why would that person spread it around, except to make it sound as if I was imagining things?' I could hear it in my head: *Oh, Cass said there was a strange man in her cabin. Nobody else saw him, of course.*

Agnetha ran her tongue round her lips. 'But who of us would do such a thing? *Why?*' Then she saw it, and flung up a hand against me. 'You're not thinking that—' The hand curved round to touch her chest.

I shook my head. 'No.'

My safety trainee appeared at my elbow then: Gabriel. 'I'm off to do the safety round.'

'Good. Thank you.'

Agnetha was silent, watching him go down the stairs. 'You would only have had a motive if you were mad. You had no quarrel with Mike.'

I thought I heard a courtroom voice say *Unbalanced by pregnancy*, and shuddered.

Agnetha kept talking, soft-voiced, eyes darting round to make sure nobody was listening. 'But you're not mad. And I quarrelled with him. That sergeant tricked me into admitting it, though I managed to keep *why* from her. But I didn't kill him.' Tears glinted in her eyes. She shook them away. 'Who else might have had a motive? He got on with everyone.'

244

I laid my hand on hers. 'Belfast. The police there will find this stowaway. They'll investigate. It's not our job.'

She pulled her hand away. 'They always get it right, of course. No, that sergeant has one of us in her sights. You, because it looked like you, or me, because I have a motive.'

'She might; Gavin doesn't.'

She shoved herself upright. 'Oh, Cass, don't be so naive. Your Gavin will get you off. At my expense. Here, give me your mug.'

She snatched it from me and slammed it on the tray. I heard her feet clattering down the steps, and felt as though she'd slapped me.

I spent the next part of my watch mulling the thought over. *Forcing a card*, Gavin had called it. Someone was setting me up. The gun had been Sean's, but someone had seen me find it, and sent the captain after me. That was a good start to making me look unbalanced. I was sure it had been Sean who'd nicked it back; if that same someone else had wanted to blame me, they'd have hidden it in my cabin. Still, it added another charge against me. Mike's death, when only I was aft. The person had taken a huge risk. If Mike had cried out, I'd have turned – the thought made me wonder, with a shudder, exactly how he'd died. A knife. If he'd seen the knife, he'd have struggled, and he'd been strong and fit, likely to be able to hold a wrist and perilously sharp knife away from him for long enough to shout for help. No, if it had to be done silently, the old pirate movies would be the only possible way: a hand over the mouth, a knife in the back. In the films, it was quick and clean. I didn't think it would be so easy in real life. You'd have to know exactly where to strike. I thought about that for a minute. We'd all done first aid, of course, but it dealt with hypothermia, airways, breathing, and consciousness, rudimentary bandaging and splinting. It didn't say where you'd stab the spine to kill somebody so quietly that another person standing four metres away would hear nothing. Only Sadie, among us, had medical knowledge – but that didn't mean it was her. You'd find it on the Internet . . . except that when Mike died, we hadn't had any Internet connection since Stavanger, which meant someone had looked it up beforehand. Not a sudden fury, but premeditated murder.

I wished I could try talking this through with Gavin. I caught sight of Nils's fair head on deck below, and wondered how long he'd known about Mike and Agnetha, about Agnetha's pregnancy . . . except, I suddenly realised, he couldn't have overheard the quarrel I'd heard. He'd been on duty. He could have heard them talking another time, though. I shook my head. It still didn't work. However protective he was of his sister, killing Mike wasn't going to help her. If it had been Nils, he'd have killed Agnetha.

Then there had been the person in my cabin. Someone who wanted to silence me, in case I'd recognised them? Or just another makeweight for madness?

My safety watch came back, handed over and headed for lookout. Now we were in the shipping lane. A container ship passed us, with a great extended deck and a white tower stuck on aft. Just after five bells the lookout spotted the first signs of Ireland, a low grey blur off the starboard bow, then Rathlin Island came into view, the same dark grey as the shadows on the clouds. Phones flashed and the trainees lined up on deck, enjoying the sun and the glinting sea, and watching the land come closer. The deck was alive with that air of excitement that you always get when port is creeping nearer; but it seemed to me there was an extra eagerness this time. There had been too many rumours flying round, of a dead man's face peering up from the water, and a corpse knocking from inside a locked door. My bruised cheek and chin had got curious glances. *Pushed* . . . They hadn't got to panic stage yet, but it was just as well we were coming into port. Land was safety to them.

I hoped it would be safety for me as well.

CHAPTER SEVENTEEN

I'd been vaguely looking forward to hot soup, but I was out of luck; Henrik was starting to clear the galley for tomorrow night's party on board. I ate my fill of rye bread, pickled herring and *brunost*, and headed back on deck to gaze idly at the red watch polishing brass.

'Thanks,' Agnetha said, looking at them. Her manner was back to normal. Life on board a ship was like living in a village; you couldn't indulge in quarrels or hurt feelings. You just had to get on with everyone.

'It'll be us next time,' I promised her. 'Or we could shuffle it off on Nils.' I glanced down at the trainees. 'They don't seem to mind. It's quite a satisfying job, if you don't have to do it often. And then Rolf's going to do the singing, at 15.00. They always enjoy that.'

Enjoy it they did. Gavin and I watched from the aft deck as they lined up along the sides, backs against the ship's rails to keep as far as possible from any embarrassing participation, but as Rolf launched in, they relaxed. He'd hung a whiteboard from the banjer roof, for scrawling the words on, and chosen the simplest possible shanties, starting with 'What Shall We Do with a Drunken Sailor?' He explained how the shanties, as well as being work songs to get everyone pulling in time, were the crew's chance to be rude about the officers with impunity, and checked for where Captain Gunnar was before launching into a particularly scurrilous verse about the captain's daughter. Ten minutes got them all laughing and joining in with 'Heave away, haul away, and we're bound for South Australia'. By the end of the half hour, they were ready to tackle whole choruses of 'Liverpool Packet' and 'Strike the Bell'. When Rolf stopped, red-faced and hoarse, they thanked him with a hearty round of applause and walked away laughing and humming to themselves.

'That's a very good effort,' my cousin Sean said, appearing suddenly at my elbow.

Involuntarily, I moved nearer the centre of the rail, towards Gavin. 'I'm not sure I heard you singing,' I said. Gavin and I had joined in everything.

Sean leant back on the rail, entirely at his ease. 'Ah, I never had the voice. I only croak.'

'You don't need a voice for "Strike the Bell",' I said.

'I approve the sentiments. Sure, the last half hour of a watch lasts for an eternity, and the last ten minutes of it's even longer.' He looked towards Gavin, and went into embarrassing family mode. 'So you're the man who's going to tame this wildcat?'

I glared at him, but Gavin took it entirely in his stride. 'I wouldn't dream of it.' His shoulder was firm against mine. 'She'll tame herself or not, as she pleases.'

Round one to us. 'Well, good luck to yez.' Sean's gaze swept down my face. 'You came a bit of a cropper there, last night. You alright?'

'As always. We bounce, we Lynches.'

'We do that.' He lifted one hand and turned my face up to the light, tilting it to check my chin. 'Down one of the steps here, a fella on me watch was saying.'

'That one there.'

'Sure-footed as a mountain goat, so you were. D'you remember that time we fell foul of that old fella in the pub, and had to take off over the roofs? It's a good thing Granny Bridget never found out about that one.'

I remembered it very well, the frantic climb up someone's outhouse and over slates wet with rain. 'Our narrowest shave.'

He turned around again to look out at the deck. His voice came back, softly, 'The fella on me watch was after saying someone pushed you.'

I shook my head. 'Just tiredness, with the extra hour's watch. I stumbled. Careless.'

His expression said he didn't believe me. 'Still, nearly in Belfast. That'll quieten things down a bit, surely. What's the drill once we get there?'

I couldn't think of any reason why he'd want to know, but I could feel the tension in his arm, and knew that this was what he'd come over to ask. 'We'll get a pilot from the outside of the harbour, and there'll be a tug to guide us to the berth. Then we tie up, and customs put a guard on us until we've had our passports checked.'

'Tonight?'

'Morning, probably.' Customs offices liked paying overtime no better than anyone else.

'Whereabouts will we be berthed? In the inner harbour there?'

'It depends what other ships are arriving.' The pilot book showed Belfast Harbour as three rectangles, with the southernmost one almost in the centre of the town. 'But there'll be a water taxi or a shuttle bus to get to where the action is. These tall ships host towns vie with each other to give us all a good time.' Beside me, Gavin grinned, and Sean turned to look at him, and abandoned the inquisition.

'Ah, still the life and soul of every party going, is she?'

I'd had enough of this man-to-man over-my-head baiting. '*She*,' I reminded him tartly, sounding exactly like Granny Bridget, 'is the cat's mother. And she has work to do.'

I didn't, but I headed down to deck level. Mona was just finishing off the last touches of rust-covering hardener, leaving every white part of the ship gleaming, and Erik was busy removing the tape markers from the braces and putting fine cord around them. I paused by him, vaguely disquieted. He was whipping the lines as neatly as I'd have expected, but there was a tremble in his hands as he wound the cord round and it took him three goes to get the needle thrust under the whipping. He turned to me, smiling, but there were strain lines around his eyes and at the corners of his mouth. 'Just thought I'd neaten these up a bit.'

'Tape's apt to pull off,' I agreed. 'This'll be much better when we're racing, to make the midships point as we pull the yards round.' I leant against the rail. 'Have you been to Belfast before?'

'No. You?'

I shook my head. 'I spent Christmases in Dublin as a child, but we didn't cross the border.'

Erik eased his needle into the next whipping. 'I'll be glad to get there. This voyage has been jinxed from the start. Never again.' The last two words were a vehement undertone, so that I wasn't quite sure I'd caught what he'd said. 'They'll take Mike ashore?'

'Yes.'

'What about shipping him home?'

I shook my head. 'I'm not sure. Yes, but maybe not soon.'

'Do you know if they've told Klaudina yet? I wanted to phone, but I wasn't sure.' He grimaced. 'I knew Mike better than I know her. I didn't want to have to break the news, not like that, over a dodgy phone connection from miles away.'

'They'll have sent police officers. It'll all be done as gently as they can manage.'

'What about catching the man who did it? The Russian. Is your policeman any further on with that?'

It was natural that he should be anxious about it, but I thought there was an extra strained note in his voice. I shrugged. 'He wouldn't tell me. Confidential police stuff.'

Of course, Erik was below the salt. The whisperings that Cass was unbalanced were captain's mess only. I changed the subject. 'What shall we do with them this evening?'

'How about touching the top of the mast? Particularly for the ones that are leaving us at Belfast.'

'Couldn't get a better day for it,' I agreed.

'It's a plan.' Erik bent his head back to his whipping and I watched him for a moment, then headed up to the aft deck, where Kjell Sigurd was dishing out tea. He pressed a mug into my hand. I took a handful of ginger nuts, and went forward to join Agnetha at the rail. '*Hei! Pepperkaker?*'

'Thanks, Cass,' she said. We each took a couple, and leant on the rail as the watches assembled below.

'They're coming on,' I said, looking down. 'Almost straight lines, nobody leaning on the rail, and it looks like all Nils's trainees are present and correct, instead of having to be hauled up on deck.'

'Yes, they've been a good bunch. It's been fun having so many youngsters on board.' She watched them for a moment, nodding in approval at the enthusiastic '*God wakt!*' that echoed up to us.

252

Then she turned back towards me, face averted still, and spoke softly. 'I've been thinking. About . . .' Her hand touched her belly. I nodded. She gestured with one hand. 'Well, in so far as I can think. And I know it's crazy, and I know I'll change my mind back and forward over the next weeks, but I think – I want . . .' She paused, moistened her lips. 'It's all that's left of Mike, you see. I don't know if I can bear . . .'

There was a long pause. She closed her eyes for a moment, then resumed, in a more normal tone. 'I was thinking, you see, that we could manage with two of us, on different watches. One on duty, and one in charge of the children.' The colour flooded up her neck, rose-pink under her fair skin. 'If the captain would allow. I'd need to look up the legislation about employers' duty to childcare, but I think we might be able to swing it, if we were both determined.'

I didn't know what to say. I opened my mouth and shut it again, then turned to look at her. 'The fall . . . I lost it.' For a moment there was anger in her face, and envy. The policeman's girlfriend, having all the luck. *It wasn't luck*, I thought, from my grieving space, and I was going to try and explain this when Nils came up beside us. His voice was as soft as Agnetha's had been, but with an iron sound, like the first harsh cut of a saw.

'I don't care what you do,' he said, in Agnetha's ear. 'That's your business.' He glanced sideways at me. 'Nothing to do with me.' His gaze went back to Agnetha. 'But I'm warning you now. Klaudina knows nothing about you. I don't want her ever to know.' His voice bored into us. 'Not ever. D'you understand?'

Agnetha flushed scarlet.

Nils gave a moment's pause, then, when she didn't answer, he stepped back from us both. 'This is my watch. I'd like you off my deck.'

Agnetha headed for her cabin in silence, and I went for a lie-down. I'd thought Gavin might come and join me, but there was no sign of him or Sergeant Peterson, just a murmur of voices from the officers' mess. I tried to read for a bit, with Cat on my chest, but I couldn't concentrate. There were too many different things spinning round in my mind: Agnetha, thinking that Gavin would focus on her to get me off, word going round that I was unstable, and Captain Gunnar's encouraging smile. *Not long to go now* . . . Agnetha's new idea, to keep both ship and baby. I didn't want to ask myself whether this turnaround gave her less of a motive, but my brain kept ticking round anyway. If she didn't want an abortion, she had no motive to kill Mike – but she had wanted one, most desperately, at the time of his death. Nils's anger . . . *I'd like you off my deck.*

I shook myself mentally and tried to think. Somebody was setting me up. What did I know about them? Well, they'd seen me with Sean's gun. That made it someone who'd been on deck and followed me down. A cold shudder went down my spine at that thought: one of my shipmates lurking in the shadow of the tunnel, watching me find it. Anders and I had wondered how the captain came to find me there, but now I thought he'd been tipped off. Someone could easily have gone to his door and suggested . . . what? That they were a bit concerned about me, and that I was down in the tunnels, seemingly searching for something.

It was too long ago. I couldn't even begin to remember who might have been around. Focus, Cass! It had been just before my watch, so Erik, Mona and Petter would have been there. Just before four, and we left at five, so everyone would have been on board. That didn't help.

Then, that night, Olav had died. I tried to fit that into the pattern of framing me, but it didn't go. I couldn't be blamed for his death, because Mike had been watching me. No, Olav had made his interest in Bezrukov too obvious, and Bezrukov had killed him. Then the next day Sean's gun had gone missing. The captain had blamed me, but I was certain it was Sean who had taken it back. That was separate from framing me too.

Then, that evening, Mike had died. Forget who for the moment, I told myself, and think about why. Agnetha had a motive: she wanted an abortion, and he wanted to stop her. Nils had a motive: he'd quarrelled with Mike over the way he was treating Klaudina. I wasn't convinced that either of these were very good as motives. I didn't know how injunctions worked, but I couldn't see what could stop Agnetha going to a private clinic and having her abortion if she'd wanted to. Killing Mike wouldn't help Klaudina; the police investigating would certainly ask her if she'd known about Agnetha. I shook my head. No, I didn't believe Mike's affair with Agnetha had caused his death.

Bezrukov was much more likely. Mike had found out who had smuggled him aboard. He'd tackled that person about it, and the person had decided Mike had to go, before he told the authorities.

I couldn't imagine Agnetha people smuggling, but I wasn't certain about Nils. I remembered the map I'd drawn for Sergeant Peterson. Nils had been about, Jenn, Rolf, Henrik. Erik had been with the trainees, and Mona, and Petter. The thought pulled me back on myself. I'd assumed Petter had been forrard, but now I came to think about it, I hadn't actually visualised him when Sergeant Peterson was taking me through them. I'd seen him earlier, so he was in my mental picture as being there. He could easily have come forward and caught up my jacket. Petter, who always wore designer polo shirts and had the latest gadget. What my friend Magnie would call *the likely o' him* had made me assume he had rich parents, but maybe he was creating his own income by people smuggling; not in bulk, just the occasional person who wanted to get into another country without passing through customs. Drugs sprang to mind, of course. A mule, carrying half a million pounds worth of whatever the latest craze was. Terrorism: a backpack full of detonators. It would be naive to say he wouldn't have those kind of contacts. Anyone, these days, could make those contacts if they wanted to.

Very well: Petter. Only Mike found out about it. He'd looked at the pictures, and then, later – probably not long before his death, because if I was Petter I wouldn't want to give him the chance to tell anyone else – he'd seen Petter talking to the man who shouldn't be on board. He'd tackled him, and Petter took the first chance he could to kill him: when the dolphins were focusing all eyes on them.

I tried to see Petter in my head. Tall, but not as tall as Mike, with his fashionably cut fair hair, like the hairs that had glinted silver on my hat. That air of privilege, with his Lacoste shirts and well-cut trousers. The latest in all-singing, all-dancing watches on his wrist: tacking angle, GPS, distance to waypoint. The idea of him doing drugs at a party didn't surprise me. He was sharp enough to come up with the framing me plan at the last minute, and agile enough, bold enough, to carry it through.

Part of me wanted to jump at that solution. Gavin would arrest him in Belfast, and all would be well. The other half of me was going, *wait.* It just all felt too complicated, too dependent on the coincidence of him having seen me go below, followed me, so that he could tell Captain Gunnar about the gun, of Mike speaking to him just before the dolphins gave him the opportunity to kill him, of him knowing that I'd take the helm and be so caught up in my own world of wheel and sails and sky that I wouldn't hear murder being done behind me. *Clever, bold, ruthless,* Gavin had said. Somehow I didn't see Petter like that . . . and it was all too rigged somehow, and my brain was tired. I curved a hand round Cat's soft side, and closed my eyes.

I was just dozing off when I heard soft voices outside my door, two men speaking in Norwegian. One was Henrik; I knew his voice, because he usually spoke to the galley girls in Norwegian.

'It's all arranged.'

The other man sounded slightly further away, as if he was in the doorway of the officer's mess, with Henrik in the corridor. I couldn't place his voice. The sound was familiar, of course, but it had to be someone who habitually talked to me in English, which didn't help, as most of the crew did. 'Where did you put . . . ?' The voice faded, as if he was leaning in. Henrik answered equally softly:

'In my room, for the moment.'

'And the delivery of the merchandise?'

'As planned. Thursday.'

'Good.'

I heard footsteps walking away as Henrik returned to the galley. I lay back. Henrik! *The delivery of the merchandise* . . . were they talking about Bezrukov? Henrik was well-placed to shelter a stowaway, with his own domain in the middle of the ship. He'd been amidships at the time of Mike's death, and anyway he was too tall to be the man I'd seen, but who was the other one? This made better sense than the timing of Mike seeing Petter and Bezrukov. Henrik was equal to him in rank. He could have persuaded Mike not to go to the captain straight away, giving him time to start rumours about me. If there were two people working together, that made it easier. Henrik and Petter? Henrik to be clever and ruthless; Petter to be bold, to wear my jacket and kill Mike.

The merchandise . . . it was an odd thing to call a person. The

257

scenario I'd come up with for Petter, where the smuggled person carried drugs or bombs, made more sense.

I didn't know Henrik very well. He kept himself aloof from the sailing side of things, and hid his face behind shades at mealtimes. He disapproved of Cat. The galley girls jumped to his bidding. Other than that, well, he was heading towards his sixties, I supposed, and as far as I knew had no family. He'd be high on the pay scale, but perhaps he needed a decent sum to retire on. He could be a compulsive gambler, or a collector of expensive china. I could imagine him with a fussy, old-maid house, whose sofa, carpets and curtains were changed every year. Perhaps, because he wasn't a sailor, his commitment to the ship was less – because that was what I found hardest to believe, that one of us who loved the ship, and worked her, and cleaned her, and rejoiced in her white sails and speed over the waves, would betray her for money. We were all part of her crew, she was our ship, and it would take the strongest of motives to do something that would bring her into such disrepute if it was found out. I could just imagine the headlines: *Tall ship used to smuggle drugs.* The funding we scraped and wheedled for would be cut off instantly at the least hint of wrong-doing, and the sponsors would find another ship to fly their banners. As for her becoming an academy, the deal that would keep her solvent for the next two years, that would be off instantly.

I shook my head and headed for a breather on deck before preparing for dinner and Jenn's 'moments of awesome' gathering. It was longer than usual: she had a great list of instructions for the evening, particularly whether people would be able to go ashore the moment we arrived (no), and the activities people could sign up for over the weekend. The paintball and laser quest were instantly popular, but there was also a bus tour of Belfast, bodhrán playing and a tour of the Belfast *Titanic* museum.

Gavin nudged me. 'Shall we sign up for that? I've been told it's good.'

'OK,' I said, and signed our names on the sheet as it came round. '14.30 tomorrow.' Of course it depended on us both being free. I meditated gloomily on the double meaning of that for a moment, then headed aft, ready for eight bells to ring.

CHAPTER EIGHTEEN

It had become a most beautiful evening. The sky was whisked with skeins of teased grey fleece, tinted gold by the sun behind them. The land had taken shape from misty shadows to wooded hills punctuated with white houses, soft and enchanted in the mellow light. The sea was like grey velvet under *Sørlandet*'s white sides.

Now the land world was closing around us. There were other ships around: cargo ships, yachts coming to join the fun and two tall ships behind us on the shining sea, masts just visible on the horizon. I clicked on their dots on the chart plotter: *Christian Radich*, the largest of our Norwegian fleet, and the Polish *Mir*.

It would take a while to get into Belfast. All the pilotage was within my watch, so I'd read up as carefully as I could and studied the harbour on the chart plotter. The actual berthing wasn't my problem, as the pilot and tug would do that between them, and as Belfast was a wide shipping channel, there was no difficulty from the nav point of view.

Eight bells. The four physicals were sent off to their duties, and Nils handed over to me. We had an hour to go before our turn into Belfast Lough, so there was plenty of time for mast-climbing. I watched from above as Anna and Nora lugged out the harness basket, and everyone began strapping themselves up. Petter was talking to Ellen, who hadn't climbed yet because of her replaced hip; she looked up and nodded, and soon he was helping her into the harness. Erik checked each person's straps were tight enough, then they set off upwards, spiders climbing up their webs, black against the glowing sky.

I could imagine the view they were having at each platform. First, the deck falling away, with the people on it turned to dots of shoulders and head-tops. Now Mona and the leading trainees were in a world of spars and grey canvas, the heavy, dark wood arms stretching round them like a playground climbing frame. At the next platform the spars were lighter, with the sky filling the spaces, and then, as they came to the top, where the ratlines were only just wide enough to squeeze a sideways-turned foot into, the spars were all below you, and you were suspended in the air, poised between sea and sky.

Samir made it first, and patted the top of the mast with a triumphant shout. Anna was after him, then Nora. Gradually the whole watch ended up in the rig, spread out along the yards or sitting on one of the platforms, drinking in the evening and watching the land coming towards us, with the non-climbers swapping with climbing physicals to let them go up, and only Erik keeping a watch on them from deck level. Ellen made it too, Petter behind her; she didn't risk the swing-up-and-over at the first platform, but remained just below it, looking out, flushed and triumphant.

At two bells, Captain Gunnar took over the navigation. Mona

took the wheel from the trainees and sent them back to the main deck. Slowly, Belfast came into view, the rows of houses an alien mass after so long at sea. The lamp posts were flicking on ashore, spoiling the soft evening light. As we came around the last point, the bay stretched round in a glitter of lights, like arms pulling us in. Involuntarily, I shuddered, and caught Gavin's quick glance at me.

'Land,' he said softly.

I didn't want it. The jumble of shore colours, the noise of the cargo ships passing, the crowds of people come to look at the tall ships, all the jostle and blare of a fairground . . . a whole five days of it before we could put to sea again, and be lost in the blue-grey silence of the Atlantic.

We'd radioed the pilot boat, but the man-overboard boat was on the side it would come in at, so I recalled my watch from the air and set them to shifting it. Once they'd done that, they set up the flight of steps amidships and rigged fenders to keep the black-hulled pilot boat off our white sides. Anders came up to take his station at the engine, hands steady on the gear lever. A crackle of the radio, and the pilot boat announced they were coming out. Erik and Rolf took up their stations by the steps, and we watched, trainee phones flashing, as the red and black boat roared up to us, stopped dead ten metres away, then glided forwards. The pilot stepped aboard, with Erik and Rolf standing smartly at ease, and was ushered up to join Captain Gunnar on the monkey deck, the rail-enclosed roof of the nav shack. He looked down at Anders and I, ready on station. 'Now, Chief,' he said to Anders, 'just take her steady as she goes. Three knots is plenty. Navigator, you sing out the course and speed every five minutes.'

The engine rumble became a purr. My world shrank to the numbers on the screen. Though I had no time to look at them I could feel the lights drawing us closer, until we were in the channel, with the neon orange stifling us. The daylight had dimmed now, the water darkened to coal-black. We passed under great four-legged cranes with reared necks like metal-boned horses, then by a dock where piled-high containers were being swung onto a freight ship. The garish colours and dancing lights shouted at me. In and in, with the land arms closing.

We paused to pick up a tug at the harbour mouth and proceeded through the dark bulk of container piles and industrial sheds looming over us. We were to moor in the northernmost of the docks. We inched onwards towards booming music, coming from a square tower outlined by a string of white lights. Past it was a jostling of coloured-light-outlined stalls with an entrance in the form of a spindly-legged pirate, legs white, head bent forwards, sporting a red kerchief.

As we came closer, the tower resolved itself into *Guyas*, with lights strung from bow to mast tops and down to the stern. A calypso band was giving it laldy on the aft deck. Beyond her were white marquees, an orange-canvassed bar area with tables and a string of little stalls with neon-lit names. It was empty of people now, but it would be heaving all weekend. Still, I hoped to be out of it with Gavin for part of the time.

The channel had become a dead end. The ABs and Rolf were standing by with the shore lines. Slowly, carefully, the tug and her own engines manoeuvred *Sørlandet* alongside.

It took fifteen minutes to get her bound to the dock with a network of plaited hawsers. The trainees were jumping with impatience to get ashore. Captain Gunnar and the pilot disappeared below for the traditional dram, sweeping Anders with them. Gavin was busy talking on the phone, presumably to Belfast police. Rolf and Erik got the gangplank ready. Jenn went off to talk to the immigration official waiting by the door of our fenced-off area, and the trainees swarmed after her to photograph each other setting foot on our permitted ten metres of British soil. An anonymous white van pulled up ten yards from the gangplank, and Gavin went to confer with the people in it, then they unpacked a rigid orange stretcher from the back and headed down the banjer steps with it. Mike. The Belfast authorities would be keen to get him ashore with the least possible fuss, so as not to spoil the party.

I was the only one on deck looking away from the shore, that garish mass of earth-fastened canvas and waving feather banners. Across the dock from us there was a schooner like a pirate ship, yellow and black, with a carved figurehead. I was just trying to read her name when a series of ripples stole across the water. I looked aft. A dark inflatable was creeping alongside *Guyas*. It dodged into the shadows of the space between us, then disappeared under our bow. Curious, I moved to get a better look. It came up alongside us, and stilled. The men aboard were wearing black clothes, made of fleece that didn't reflect any light. If I hadn't seen the ripples, I'd never have spotted them.

Of course, I recognised the tall figure standing ready at the forrard steps, dressed in equally dark clothing. My cousin Sean wasn't waiting to talk to immigration, or take part in any police investigation over Mike's death. He leant forward to catch a rope thrown upwards, flung it around the rail, shinned down and was in the boat before I could even think about stopping him. The music blaring from *Guyas* drowned the roar of the engine as it pushed off, bows in the air, and sped away.

My first impulse was to phone Gavin. I was reaching for my phone when I realised there would be no signal down below the banjer, and definitely not one in the cold store, with its tin walls. Besides, he – they – were gone. Unless the police were very quick with a launch they'd not catch them now. Professionals. Let them go.

I was tired, with a heavy feeling at my heart. We'd been a bird skimming the waves, a cloud catching the wind, out in the beautiful bareness of the sea, and now we were tied to this noisy land, with the beat from *Guyas* thumping through the hull. If I'd had a child, I'd be forced away from this life I loved – but my child had gone back to God. The grief would subside. Life would be normal again.

They would be bringing Mike out soon. I went over to Agnetha and slipped my arm through hers. We stood together in silence as they brought him up the banjer steps. There was nothing to see, just the shrouded figure strapped on the orange stretcher. Gavin and Sergeant Peterson followed, heads down. The bearers snicked down the wheels, rolled him rapidly around the corner and onto the gangplank. Agnetha's hand tightened on mine. The doors of the van were flung open. They wheeled him in, the doors closed, and the van took off, turning quickly round on the quay then heading towards the city.

I brought my arm up to Agnetha's shoulders, rigid under my touch. 'Tea?'

She shook her head, then turned to me, eyes bleak with tears. 'The last time we spoke, we quarrelled. I wish . . .' Her voice trailed off.

'I know,' I said.

She sighed. 'Midnight. I'll try and sleep.'

'Five nights of normal sleep patterns,' I reminded her. Night watches were suspended when we were in port.

'Yes. Night, Cass.' She slipped away. I waited there for Gavin to come back from the quay and join me. He looked around, spotted me and came aft.

'I'll need to spend tomorrow morning with the Belfast police, filling them in on all that's gone on.'

I leant my shoulder against his. 'I'll be busy on board. The ship has to look her best for visitors.'

'Are you off duty now?'

I nodded. 'Gone midnight. Ship secured. Sleep.' I yawned, and remembered what I had to tell him. 'Listen, Sean's left the ship. A rubber boat came for him.' I described what I'd seen, and he nodded.

'Dodging the customs.'

'Why?'

Gavin spread his hands. 'I can tell you this much: he's not known to be a member of the paramilitary, on either side. Other than that, they drew a blank on him.' His arm came up in a brief hug. 'Listen, you get to bed.' He nodded at the nav shack. 'I'll be in there, phone in hand, waiting for Bezrukov to leave. I warned Anders not to go down again once we were berthed.' He hesitated. 'I'd feel happier if Sergeant Peterson came into your cabin until I can join you.'

I made a face, but didn't demur. 'Be careful.'

'Don't worry. My job is simply to phone the word the minute he shows his face.'

I headed below. Anders must be still in the captain's mess, for Rat and Cat were curled together on my bunk. I turfed them both off and changed quickly into the thermals that did duty as pyjamas before Sergeant Peterson appeared. To do her justice, she wasn't obtrusive. She brought her laptop and installed herself in the chair while I brushed my teeth and clambered into bed. Cat came to curl in his usual place, in the angle between my neck and shoulder. I felt as though I ought to stay awake, sharing Gavin's vigil above-decks, but I was just too tired. I closed my eyes against the glow from Sergeant Peterson's screen and let sleep take me.

I felt as though I'd been fathoms deep when a noise like firecrackers from the dock awoke me. For a moment I didn't know where I was. The chair scraped as Sergeant Peterson sprang up. Cat dived down the back of the berth. I shot up, reaching automatically for my black jacket. Footsteps ran above my head and clattered down the steps. The sound came again, a series of bangs then a single sharp crack, then another. By then I was on my feet, pulling my jeans on. Instead of leaping upwards to see what was happening, Sergeant Peterson stayed put, blocking the doorway. She held back a 'stop' hand, fingers spread. 'We stay put here. DI Macrae's orders.'

'That was gunfire!'

'All the more reason to obey orders.'

The only way she was going to let me past would be if I wrestled her physically. I hung my jacket back up, put on a jumper instead and sat on the bunk. Cat reappeared from below and slid onto my lap. I stroked him mechanically, listening. Silence, until a couple of cars parked somewhere among the cluster of stalls on the pier started up and drove off. Then I heard footsteps in the corridor, and a knock at the door. Gavin called softly, 'Cass? Freya?'

Sergeant Peterson stepped back to let him in. 'Sir.'

'We lost him.' Gavin shook his head in frustration. 'As soon as it was quiet he came up on deck and jumped down onto the dock. I phoned the Belfast officers, but there was just too much cover for him, with all the sideshows. Then someone started shooting.' He frowned. 'Men dressed in black, who arrived from nowhere in a black car.'

Men dressed in black . . . I remembered the rubber boat that had taken Sean off.

'My cousin Sean?' I asked.

Gavin shrugged. 'A reception committee. They might have winged him, but the Belfast officer I spoke to thinks he got away. They have men sweeping the place now – they're armed here – but I don't think they'll find him. Or get him if they do.' He made a face at me. 'It's not like in the movies, Cass, where the crack shot hits a moving target, just like that. Anything over ten metres is sheer luck.' He hung his tweed jacket over my black one. 'Thanks, Freya. No bother here?'

'None.' She lifted her laptop and headed for the door. 'Goodnight.'

The door closed behind her. 'Bed.' Gavin held out his arms. 'Don't spoil it by telling me breakfast is still at seven.'

'I won't,' I said, and didn't.

Seven Bells

Belfast

Thursday 2nd July

CHAPTER NINETEEN

I woke to greyness filtering in through the porthole. We had sailed out of our clear northern light. Gavin was still asleep, his breath warm on my cheekbone.

The sharp grief had subsided to an ache, and smouldering anger. I hadn't wanted a child, but we'd created one, Gavin and me, and it should have had a chance to live. We'd have worked out something, somehow. It shouldn't have been killed by a fall down a flight of steps. I gritted my teeth. I was going to help Gavin find out who, and why, and make sure they were held responsible.

Something had changed in me too. For those hours I'd known about the child, I'd had to confront where Gavin and I were going. Just drifting, meeting up when we could, wasn't enough for a relationship. If we were to become a couple, the time would come when I'd have to make the choice: the sea, or a family. Deep inside me, I'd wanted that child. I wanted there to be others, Gavin's children, with russet heads, dressed in miniature kilts; not immediately, but not too far in the future either.

I felt his arm tighten around me. A kiss on the back of my neck, then he reached over me for his watch. 'Creator Lord, is that the time?' A hug, then he rolled out of bed, and buckled his kilt around him in one swift movement. 'I must shower.'

I followed him into the shower, grateful not to feel sick any more, and managed a proper breakfast. The same feeling of relief that had hovered over the trainees was here in the officers' mess too. Bezrukov was gone from the ship, and Mike's body was in the hands of the land police. It wasn't our problem any more.

There was a whole-ship muster at eight, the last for the trainees who were leaving today. Jenn reminded everyone who was going on what activities, and explained which bus each group would get. Then it was customs time. Captain Gunnar welcomed the three officials on board, and a fourth stood guard over the re-lowered gangplank. I thought of Sean's exit down the ship's side, and Bezrukov's jump to the dock, and grimaced to myself as we all lined up alphabetically, crew and trainees in one long snake round the deck.

That over with, we set to work on our beautiful ship so that she would be immaculate for visitors. The yards had to be squared, and I was just starting our work party on the aft mast when a van arrived with a team of SCOs and forensic officers, all set to go over the steering gear and inside of the captain's coffin. Naturally, our trainees were far too busy gawking at them brushing for fingerprints and picking hairs off with tweezers to pay proper attention to the line of the yards, but we managed to get it done not too horribly behind the speed of the other two watches. I'd clean and grease the steering gear later.

After that, all the watches tidied up the spaghetti of ropes they'd left behind them, and departed for their individual scrubbing duties: the decks, the heads, the banjer. By the time they'd finished that it was lunchtime, and they departed like bairns released from school towards the city tour of Belfast, laser quest, paintball or generally hanging about the town centre and checking out the shops. There was no sign yet of Gavin returning. Our tour of the museum started at half past two, and I hoped we'd make it.

On my way to lunch, just out of interest, I stopped at Jenn's room and logged on to the ship's computer. She should have a list of all the trainees and crew, the one she'd given to the customs officers. *Belfast arrival.doc* looked likely. I opened it and scanned down the list. Fredriksen, Hansen, Iversen, Lynch, Kristoffersen. My eye jumped over it, and back. Lynch, Cassandre. I was the only Lynch on board. I closed the file, frowning, and opened *Watch lists Krist Belf.doc.* There he was, large as life, in the middle of the red watch: Lynch, Sean.

I closed the machine down. It would have been child's play to sneak in here and delete a name from the customs list. It was a gamble, of course; Jenn might have been so efficient that she'd printed them out before the ship sailed. But then, so what? Sean's name was on it, but he'd been long gone by the time customs arrived. The passports were kept in a locked drawer, but he'd managed to get his gun back from one, so I didn't see that as a problem.

So what had he been doing on board? Setting aside political involvement, I thought it had to be Bezrukov. What had Gavin said, the police computer had drawn a blank on him? Well, if he was MI5 or MI6 or whatever real James Bonds were, 'they' wouldn't say, would they? Suppose he'd been chasing Bezrukov. He'd found out he was going to be on board, maybe even seen him slip on board, and booked his passage. I heard his voice, airily, *I went down to the office and signed on this very morning.* Maybe his orders were to watch him, not to interfere. Follow him onto Belfast soil, and dispose of him there.

After lunch we dressed our shining ship. We didn't have fancy lights, but we hoisted a line of signal flags stretching to each mast top, with the pennants of all the tall ships races she'd taken part in going from her stern to the mizzen top. The courtesy UK flag waved at one cross-tree, and the Norwegian flag was at the other. Lidl were one of the sponsors of this year's race, and their executives were the people partying on board tonight, so we strung up two of their flags as well. That done, we were ready to open to visitors. Only the crew on watch were required to be on duty. I was just wondering if Gavin would make it back for the museum tour when my phone rang. I hauled it out of my pocket.

'Hi. I was just thinking about you. How's it going?'

'Slow. The Belfast police are being friendly, but it's taking time. I won't manage the *Titanic*.'

I made a face. 'Pity.'

'I should be free for the party.'

'You won't like it,' I warned him. 'But it ends at ten.'

'Early night, then. Or we could try for a pint of real Guinness.'

'Oh, yes please,' I said. My first half-pint, under the auspices of my cousins, had been Dublin's best Guinness, and the bottled stuff you could get on mainland Britain was never quite the same.

'I should be off in time for a bite to eat before the fun starts.'

'Good. I'm starving again already.'

'Have fun at the museum. Bye.'

We were done now. Rolf hung up the board with the information about the ship, and unhooked the 'Crew only' chain across the gangplank. I dodged the crowds coming up and walked onto the flat, heavy shore.

The dock was filled with holiday crowds in candy-coloured

clothes, and the smells of food from every nation under heaven drifted on the air: crepes, hamburgers, pizza, salsa, tikka, sickly popcorn and candyfloss. In daylight, the 'pirate entrance' resolved itself into a Ferris wheel with a toddlers' carousel below it. A jazz trio on stilts was giving it laldy just opposite the dock, moving like crickets on their extra long legs: *Lady, be good* . . . I dodged a family of ten with a T-shirted father sweating behind an ankle-snagging double buggy, and headed around the closed end of the dock, where I could check the map we'd all been issued with, and sort out my bearings.

From here, I could see all of *Sørlandet*. My heart filled with pride. With the flags from every mast fluttering in the breeze she was bright as this bonny day. The glittering water reflected her swan-white hull and the dancing pennants. How could I bear to leave her? I felt my throat close up just at the thought. It wasn't yet, I reminded myself. Sometime . . .

I pushed myself away from the railing, and hauled the map out of my pocket. It wasn't far to the water taxi, just across this dock, but the way there led beside the major road from the port into the city, with a lorry passing every five seconds. By fifty yards my face felt coated with grit. I dodged across the last roundabout and down into the cool of the dock side, where a line of private yachts was moored along a pontoon: several thirty-footers, a couple of bonny classics and a handful of motorboats. The water taxi for crews and volunteers was at the end of it, similar to the Mousa ferry at home, with rows of seats and some standing space. We clambered aboard and were taken round the end of the dock, where the open sea glittered between red-legged cranes. Four small yachts were coming in, ready to join the party. On our right, a four-lobed building glittered like an opening metal flower – the *Titanic* Belfast centre I was headed for. Further to the right again, at three o'clock, four great yellow cranes hung horizontally over the striped front of Belfast College.

Coming into the dock was like going back to the Belfast of the 1880s. We were all here, the sailing ships that had once carried cargoes round the world: first, in the outer dock, our sister-Norwegian *Christian Radich*, then *Frederyk Chopin*, with *Iskra* behind her. Beyond them were *De Gallant*, then the dark hull and merchant build of *Pelican of London*. The dressed masts dwarfed the buildings around them, a forest of waving flags. *Gulden Leeuw* had her sails immaculately rolled, but *Cisne Branco* had left hers half-furled, hanging in decorative white festoons from each yard.

The docks were hooching with people. I got along the walkway, waved my pass at the guards and stepped into pandemonium. Families with swarms of children, teenagers on skateboards or rollerblades, all eating ice cream and candyfloss, pausing to take photographs, blaring music from iPods. Off the water, the heat hit me like a sauna. I flattened myself against the barrier and let the wave of humanity flow past me until I'd gathered enough courage to press into it, searching always for the clearest route forward, my eyes fixed on the glittering building five hundred metres ahead.

Once I was out of the immediate dock area, the crowd thinned to bearable levels, though I was still moving against the flow. The world was out today, along with his wife, all their children and the family dog, coming to join the party. My map showed several markets, a Victorian play area, three fairgrounds, a family interactive zone, kite workshops and a hot-air balloon display. The gloomy thought sprang into my mind that in ten years' time, Gavin and I might be one of these families, with a buggy and a straggle of children, red-faced and constantly counting. *Never*, I swore to myself. Like a million Catholics worldwide, I'd defy the official line on contraception. Abortion was one thing, but a child a year in an overpopulated planet quite another.

I'd reached a red, black and white tugboat with a mustard-coloured funnel, set in a dry dock, and familiar from a dozen black and white photos. *Nomadic, Cherbourg* was printed on her white stern. She'd been the *Titanic*'s ferry boat, and they'd made a beautiful job of restoring her; she could have been built yesterday. I paused to admire, then walked on, into the cool of the museum.

I was the only one of *Sørlandet*'s crew on this tour, but there were several from a dozen other ships, and it took a while to get us all sorted out and issued with tickets. It was while we were waiting that I began to feel that prickle down my spine, as if someone was watching me.

I turned casually, as if I was scanning the row of ticket desks, the souvenir shop, the escalators leading up and down, the cafe entrance, the door I'd come in with the *Star Wars* droids displayed above it. Nobody met my eyes; no faces were turned towards me. All the same, there was an uneasy feeling in my breast . . . but it was a museum; it would be open and brightly lit. My fingers turned my mobile over in my pocket. Gavin was busy. I wouldn't press the panic button.

I realised my mistake as soon as I got past the ticket-taker. My idea of museums was obviously twenty years out of date. Instead of cavernous rooms lined with glass cases, there was a series of slanted walls with White Star Line posters on them, leading into a large room broken up by screens. I stared, entranced. Each screen had an old photograph of Belfast projected on it, so big that it was like you were standing in front of the reality, and crossing back and forwards across each were silhouettes of actors in costume: a lady searching in her bag as she walked, two men hurrying to work, a sweep with his cart and brushes, a governess with a pram. It felt like you were looking back a hundred years.

From the point of view of a display, it was marvellous. From the point of view of a possible quarry, not so good. The room was in semi-darkness, lit only by the photographs, and the screens were angled across, with room to walk behind. It was a pursuer's dream.

I dodged behind the first screen, heart thumping, and attached myself to a couple from one of the small pirate ships. Of course, I could be totally imagining things. A prickle on the back of my neck was nothing to make a fuss about. On the other hand, I had a selection of bonny bruises to remind me that I'd been tripped down those steps. I would try to do the sensible thing.

I looked at the photograph of central Belfast, with the horse-drawn buses in the street, and thought. I'd felt I was being watched in the main hall, and my impulse had been to look up and behind me, towards this entrance. If I had a pursuer, if he was up here, then he'd not been waiting in the corridor; the only people there had been shuffling forwards, tickets in hand. No, he'd assumed he was unobserved, and come in before me. In which case I wanted to exit again, sharpish, pleading the heat, or sickness, or claustrophobia, and head across the road to the crew centre where I could stick with other sailors in a nice cafe until Gavin was free to come and get me.

I took a long, slow look around. All I could see clearly was the moving world of old Belfast. The audience were shadows around it, blurs of a whisked ponytail, a swung shoulder, an upturned face lit white by the screens. Gradually I eased my way around the back of the screen facing the entrance, and began edging towards the ticket attendant. I had almost left the dimness of the room for the brightness of the corridor when I saw Bezrukov in the queue.

CHAPTER TWENTY

I was sure it was him. I couldn't see his face, but I recognised the broad shoulders and black workman's jacket. My heart began thudding painfully. He hadn't come in ahead of me; he'd dodged back to the other side of the hall and waited to make sure of me before he followed. If I went out again he'd close in on me.

I dodged back behind the screens and merged myself with a family group. Mum, Dad, a bored teenager with a permanently texting thumb, a lively ten-year-old who kept jumping up and down as if he'd had chocolate and fizzy juice for breakfast, and two smaller girls dressed entirely in pink. I was much the same height as the teenager. I hovered beside her as if I was one of her mates and got my phone out. Gavin. Like shortening sail, the time to call for help was when you first thought of it, not once the situation got out of control. He took so long to answer that I thought he wasn't going to, and a cold hand of panic squeezed my breastbone. Then at last I heard his voice. 'Cass?'

I took a deep breath. 'I'm in the *Titanic* museum.' I didn't dare say Bezrukov's name. 'Our stowaway has just come in after me. I felt him watching me. He's between me and the door.'

'OK. Hang on.' The pause seemed to stretch for ever, in the flickering white lights; through it, I could hear him speaking, and a jumble of voices answering. *The* Titanic *museum . . . He may be armed . . . Have you been inside that place? . . . Nightmare . . . If we had a hostage situation . . . Our chance to get him . . . Can she keep a cool head?* Then another voice came on the phone, deep and reassuring, with a strong Belfast accent. 'Now, then, Cass, I'm Chief Inspector Beattie. You're being followed by a man you think may be our suspect, is that right?'

'Yes.'

'It'll be busy in there?'

'Yes.'

'Now, we want to get you out safe, but we don't want to cause a panic, or create a hostage situation. DI Macrae tells us you've got good wits, and you'll keep a cool head.'

I was glad he couldn't see my thudding heart. 'Do my best.'

'You do that. Now, I daren't send two officers in after you in case he thinks they're after him, and the situation turns dangerous.'

'I understand.' I moved forward with the family to a wall of White Star Line posters, and heard what he wasn't saying. There were innocent people here who would suffer if Bezrukov was panicked into a shoot-out.

'Does this man know you've spotted him?'

'I don't think so.'

'Don't do anything to let him know it. Don't look to see where he is; don't avoid looking at him either. Get yourself in among other people all the time; keep behaving like a normal tourist – can you do that?'

'Yes.'

'Speed up where you can, but don't make him suspicious. I'll send officers to the museum exit. If we can get you out, and him not suspecting a thing, we can collar him as he comes out.'

'I'll do my best.'

'Brave girl. You hang up now, and we'll give you a call every few minutes. Just answer as if it was a friend, and say where you are, and you'll phone back later. Just like you would if it was for real. If you don't answer, we'll know you're in trouble. Good luck, now.'

I cut him off, and set myself to behave like a tourist. If my nerves hadn't been jangling like halyards in a wind, I'd have been fascinated. I stuck with the family into the next room, which was all about the industries of Belfast: the factories that churned out the flax, whiskey and linen that were sent all over the world, and of course the ships that carried them. The family got bored at that point and hurried through, leaving me stranded in a brightly lit room with a tabletop map of Belfast showing the docks, factories, and houses, with a model of *Titanic* under her scaffolding in the place she'd been built. I felt a pang of longing strike me. I was here, in this white model, and *Sørlandet* was moored just two handspans away, across the familiar pale blue and buff of the chart, yet I was separated from her, from safety. My heart was still thumping madly, and I felt horribly vulnerable under this strip lighting.

Then he came in. I sensed him, rather than saw him. It took all the willpower I had not to turn around. I nodded at the map, as if I was saying, *Very interesting, seen that now*, and strolled out of the room. I caught the dark shadow of his jacket out of the corner of my eye as I turned into a narrow corridor with people ahead of me. He could be closing up on me. I wriggled round my family, ahead of a middle-aged couple and jammed myself

281

between them and another family party in front. There were a couple of just-pre-teenagers with them, of my height. I infiltrated myself beside them and hauled off my jacket, hooking it inside out over one shoulder to show my red T-shirt underneath.

Then my phone vibrated, and it took a moment to fumble it out of my jacket pocket. I did my best to speak naturally, in the hushed tones appropriate to a museum. 'Hi, Agnetha! Listen, I'm in the museum; can't talk here. Call you back later.'

It was an effort to cut off CI Beattie's reassuring voice. I pressed the button and shoved the phone back into my jacket pocket. There was a surge forwards, and I found myself last to get into one of those scarily openwork lifts, set like a workmen's cradle on the outside of what turned out to be a four-storey stairwell, all painted black, with a dizzying drop back to the ground floor. *Only half the height of* Sørlandet's *mizzen*, I told myself, but the pit of my stomach wasn't reassured. There was something much nastier about a drop onto concrete.

I'd lingered too long, looking down, and now I was alone in the corridor with the next lift already creaking upwards. I gathered my wits and scuttled along after the family, through a doorway and into another queue. A warning notice said this ride wasn't suitable for people with a long list of conditions. Ride? I shot a glance behind me. The next lift had arrived, spilling the knot of people into the corridor. Bezrukov's dark jacket was among them, and here I was, at the end of the queue, all set for him to sidle in beside me and take his place in whatever little cars were waiting at the end of this railing. My breathing quickened; I cast frantic glances round me, wondering how I could get myself further ahead of him.

My queue jumped forward to a wire wall. Past it, the floor fell sharply down into a world of firelight and projections. The black cars were lining up on their rails, and I breathed a thankful sigh. Instead of the two-person buggies I'd been dreading, these were substantial cars, built to take six people. I did a quick headcount of the family. Five of them. I'd squirm in with them, rather than risk being left in a car with Bezrukov. I didn't like the way each car swung forwards into space.

He'd had the same thought, for as the queue surged forwards again he slid in behind me. One more car filled up. Another, and the family was at the front of the queue. I felt him tense behind me. As the next car drew up, I pressed closer to the pre-teens, as if I was with them, and slid smoothly into the car, as naturally as if I'd been directed by the attendant. They could hardly turn and say, 'Hey, she's not with us!' He dropped the bar over our knees, and the car jerked forwards and swung out into space.

If I hadn't been so tense with nerves I'd have been fascinated. The ride took us inside the half-built hull of *Titanic*, guided by a workman's voice, and with period film of workmen projected around us. The noise was horrendous: grinding of plates in a shower of stars, riveters hammering. We dangled all the way down to ground level, where the furnace blazed red, then rose upwards past the huge rudder fixings. Best of all, I calculated, the cars were a minute apart, and I'd be first out of this one. I could put a good distance between me and my pursuer in a minute.

We came out at frosted saloon doors with celebrating shadows behind them, raising their glasses to 'the pride of Belfast'. I resisted the urge to look back and scurried forward to the next room.

It was dazzlingly light. We were on the top floor of the building now, with a great window looking out over the whole dock area. There was an expanse of concrete that would once have been filled with workers, and was still criss-crossed with railway lines, then the dark blue water of the dock, a neon-white cruise liner, the giraffe-necked cranes, and then, beyond, Belfast Lough and the sea, my safety, calling me. To the side I could see the forest of masts, and picked out *Sørlandet* with one glance.

The phone in my pocket vibrated again. It was Gavin's voice. 'How are you doing?'

'Hey!' I said. 'I'm at the launch.' I lowered my voice. 'He's on my heels. Must keep moving.'

It was an effort to cut the connection. Fourteen years of being on my own seemed to have shrunk to wanting to be safe, with Gavin's arms around me. More than anything I wanted to get out of here. I stamped down hard on the voice that said *run, run*. If I ran, I risked the people around me. I walked briskly, with frequent glances at my watch, like someone due back at her ship.

It was too exposed in this room. I felt like an insect with a pin poised over it, and the chatter of excited *Wasn't that cool!* voices in the corridor warned me the next carload was arriving. Ignoring the overlapping voices remembering the day of the launch, I dived for the stairs and the next room, the story of how the ship was fitted out.

There was an antechamber with a screen at the end, and as I came in, the well-known picture of *Titanic* flashed up, queen of her seas: flags strung fluttering above the four raked funnels, the white layers of cabins with their long windows, the dark hull, with *Nomadic* bobbing tiny beside it. No wonder they had believed she was indestructible.

I didn't have time to stare. On my left, the room opened out to brightness again. I scurried down the steps and was caught in a blaze of light, an enormous filmed tour of the ship on three sides of me as I stood with my hand on the railing before it. This was the fancy first-class saloon, with walnut panelling, gold curved chairs and starched tablecloths. The fluted wood pillars supporting the ceiling were festooned with gilded ribbons. It was so real you felt you could walk into it. The picture slid upwards again to the grand staircase, familiar from the old photographs, except that this was shining with wood and polish, the ironwork below the bannister gold and black, the cherub figure shining. Another smooth glide upwards and we were in the bridge, fifteen times the size of *Sørlandet*'s nav shack, with the great wheel in the centre and brass-cased instruments around it. It was here that the helmsman had received his orders, and made that last, fatal movement that turned the ship towards the iceberg.

I didn't have time to stare. It was just as I was turning away that an arm flung itself around my shoulders, and a heavy hand gripped my collarbone, one finger digging into the hollow by my neck, sending a shudder of pain through it. The hard barrel of a gun prodded my side. 'Do not speak,' a voice said in my ear. He had a cold, dead voice, the kind there was no point arguing with. 'Turn.'

Obediently, I turned, and he turned with me, his arm still round my shoulders. I saw our reflection in the glass surrounding the first-class cabin, leaning together like lovers. My face showed none of the panic I was feeling. His was as I'd remembered it: the heavy brows, the flared nostrils. My eyes met his in the glass; they were as dead as his voice. He glanced round at the other people. His voice came softly in my ear. 'You scream, I shoot you first, then I shoot my way out of here. We will walk together.'

I took three measured breaths, and felt my heartbeat steady. Beyond our reflections, the cabin was upholstered in red, with hangings on the four-poster bed and a Récamier couch. First class. A lamp on the table punctured our reflections. Behind it, a filmed Edwardian lady in a cartwheel hat gave orders to a uniformed steward. There were people all around us, pausing as we were doing, then moving on. The grip on my shoulder pushed me forwards. The second-class cabin was not so very different from my own quarters aboard *Sørlandet*, with the same mahogany bed and washstand. Third class had two bunk beds, with towels hanging by the washbasin, white with a red stripe. There were still plenty of people around. I tried to think what his plan was. If he shot me here, he'd be seen, and caught. He needed to get me alone, behind a case, or in a corridor. One shot, and he'd drop my body to the floor and be out of there before the next person came.

We sauntered on, close as lovers. A case with a dinner service, festooned green and gold round the edges, and a vegetable dish with little plump legs and scrolled handles. Photographs of the pianos on board: a full-size grand for the upper classes, a simple upright for steerage. Maman would approve. The permanently texting teenager turned to look at us, then her gaze went back down to the screen in her hand. No, it had to be another teenager, for I'd left that family a couple of cars behind. My brain kept working feverishly, although my legs were trembling so hard I was afraid they might give out on me. Red velvet curtains between two glass cases. If I could get away from him, I could hide behind those. He wouldn't want to act too soon, for the minute the alarm was given they'd close the exits. There was still the iceberg to come, and the rescue by the *Carpathia*, then the recovery from the depths. It wouldn't be now.

Besides, he was enjoying this. I could feel it. He was feeding off the waves of terror I was trying so hard to control. *Angels and saints, defend me.* I sent a wordless cry up to my own particular saint, the warrior who'd dressed in men's clothes, led her troops against the English and died a witch's death in the fire. *Jeanne, pucelle, aide-moi.* The thought of her strengthened me. I wouldn't let him kill me. I tried to think clearly, ignoring that hard finger pressing into my ribs. He had the gun. What advantages did I have?

Her opponents underestimated Saint Jeanne because she was small and female. I had those advantages. I was agile with my smallness. I thought of Shetland ponies who could beat larger horses around obstacle courses, switching direction and turning on themselves while the racehorses were sorting out their long legs. I couldn't risk a chase around the cases, in these crowded rooms, but if I made a run for it I'd have an initial advantage over him. If I could get out of sight, he'd have no reason to start shooting.

We were at the end of the room now, and there was a family in front of us, filling the corridor, a short corridor, with a fire door at the end and a room to the side. We couldn't push past them without drawing attention to ourselves. I was safe for the moment. Suddenly, like an answer to prayer, I saw my way clear if I could summon up the courage to risk making my situation worse, far worse, if I failed. *Jeanne, pucelle, aide-moi.* I let him feel me relax. Now we were in the side room dedicated to the sinking, with the voices of long-dead people telling the story: the cold, the ice on deck, the judder as the ship hit. On the wall was an animation of the ship hitting the iceberg, settling, then gradually tilting forward as her bows filled so that her stern reared upward, the propellers turning in air. The family were bang in front of it; I watched over their shoulders. With a rush, the water inside her streamed forward, the stern shot skywards and she plunged down. I felt sick watching it, thinking of the people trapped below, the people on deck flung from the ship to hit the ice-hard water, only to be sucked down in the ship's wash. The voices went on over my head.

He was watching me. As the family moved onwards, past the stories of those who didn't survive – Mrs Straus, who refused to be separated from her husband, the band who played on – his hand gripped my shoulder, holding me within the room. I couldn't afford to let this old tragedy distract me. I thought again of St Jeanne in her armour, with her standard of the royal lily flowers. He was playing with me. I wasn't sure I'd really believed in evil, but now I felt it coming off him. He knew where he was going, and he was enjoying seeing how far he could stretch out my nerves. These children bouncing about two yards ahead of us were my reminder of what he could do if I panicked. Then, horribly, as if the tension between us was a phone line, I felt the thought in his head: regret that he was going to shoot me instead of cutting my throat and feeling my blood run thickly over his fingers. I *saw* it, and the thought gave me courage.

The phone vibrated against my hip. It was on the side furthest from him. I didn't react, and nor did he. *If you don't answer, we'll know you're in trouble.* I needed to save myself before they sent in the cavalry.

There was an arrow pointing to a door in the corner. The father of the family opened it to let the others through, and a waft of Céline Dion came in through the opened door, and was silenced as they let it swing to behind them. Now we were alone. If I ran, he'd expect me to go forwards. Suddenly, faster than thought, I dropped to the floor, dodged between his legs and went back, vaulting over the bench in the middle of the room to get to the door. I banged the fire door open, then, on blessedly silent feet, bolted back along the ten yards of corridor and dived behind the red velvet curtains.

I hardly dared breathe. There was an alcove behind the curtain with an internal window, just broad enough to let me croog into it, so that there would be no tell-tale bulge.

I'd got there just in time. He came pounding out of the iceberg room, head hunkered into his bull neck, nostrils flaring, looking around as if he could scent me. He glanced towards this room, then back at the fire door, slowly swinging closed on its pneumatic stop. Another long, suspicious look. I closed my eyes and prayed.

Then I heard the clunk of the fire-door bar, and my eyes shot open again. He was shoving it forwards. A glance over his shoulder, then he had his gun in his hand and he was through. I felt dizzy with relief.

I couldn't stay here. I didn't know where the fire door led to, or how far he'd go before he came back. I had to move.

The corridor was still empty, except for the texting teenager. I took a deep breath and willed myself forward, like a soldier going into battle. I dived along it on silent feet, scuttled through the iceberg room and reached the corridor beyond. A blast of 'My Heart Will Go On' met me. That would cover any noise I made. I bolted like a hunted hare between the film posters: *Atlantic*, *Cavalcade*, *A Night to Remember*, *The Unsinkable Molly Brown*, Kate Winslet standing in the bows, arms spread.

As I went I fumbled for my phone, and pressed the shortcut to Gavin. I had to let them know what was happening.

'I've got away from him,' I said, not giving him a chance to speak. Behind me, I heard the snick of a door. There was a set of stairs ahead of me. I swung down them. 'I think he's gone out of the fire exit between the cabins room and the iceberg room. He's armed. I'm getting out of here as fast as I can.'

There was a choice of doors next, and nothing to tell me which one I should go through. 'Discovery Theatre' turned out to be a film of the wreck. I scuttled through an empty row, out of the other side of it, and down more stairs to a darkened room with a glass floor above a montage of the wreck, which glowed eerily below us. The attendant was showing a family how to use machines to hone in on the objects scattered around it: a china cup, a doll, a boot. On the seabed all around the ship lay pairs of boots, leather outlasting flesh and bone. I felt sick.

Beyond the attendant was a door with the blessed word EXIT. I came out into the light, with the sun-glint on the water shining through an industrial-size window. I could hear the buzz of talk, the clatter of cups from the restaurant. I scurried down the last flight of stairs and ran the twenty yards into the bustle of the entrance hall.

Gavin was standing by the door, eyes roving round the hall. He saw me, and his whole face lightened with relief. I ran into his arms, and couldn't say anything for a moment. I was trembling as if I had the flu. He held me tight with one arm, and brought his phone up with the other. 'She's out. Safe and sound. In the entrance hall.' He nodded. 'Sir.'

'Did you get him?' My voice sounded like an old lady's.

He shook his head. 'We'll keep watching.' He put his phone back in his pocket. 'There's a police car coming for us. Straight into it.'

I could scarcely walk. His arm supported me, strong with the fear he'd felt when I hadn't answered the phone. He didn't need to say it; I knew, and gripped his hand as if I'd never let it go. I willed my legs to take me as far as the car, but when we reached it they gave way under me and I dropped into the back seat, limp and trembling. Gavin came around to the other door, and slid in beside me. 'Safe now.' His arm came up around my shoulders. 'Safe.'

CHAPTER TWENTY-ONE

I was bundled out of the car and into the police station, where they found an unused interview office, and installed me in it. I did my best to take them through what had happened, and confirmed Bezrukov's identity. Just looking at the picture of him made me cold inside.

'Once you'd given him the slip,' CI Beattie said, 'once he realised it, then he must have made straight for the outside.'

'I didn't dare phone sooner,' I said.

He gave my shoulder a pat. 'You did very well, girl, very well indeed. Trust an Irishwoman to keep her head. Now, we've not quite done with your man, but I think he'd be happier keeping an eye on you for the moment. Where do you want to go?'

I didn't need to think about it. 'My ship. *Sørlandet.*'

Gavin frowned. 'That's where he'll look for you. I was going to book us a hotel room.'

I thought of being in the neutral colours of a strange hotel, even with Gavin, and shook my head. '*No.* No. I'll be fine aboard.

I'm on duty from six anyway – this party on board. I'll have a lie down till then.' I could see he wasn't happy, and made with the words. 'I'll feel safer there. Really I will. He gave me a bad fright. I need to be home.'

He still looked doubtful.

'The crew will be there. Nils's watch is on duty now, and everyone will be about for the party.'

'We can't spare an extra man to guard her, with all these shenanigans around the docks,' CI Beattie told Gavin, 'but you've got our number. There are plenty of officers about.'

He nodded, reluctantly.

'Besides,' CI Beattie added, 'if he's watching, he'll know she's told us everything she knows. He'll know we've got his mugshot now. There's no more threat she can be to him.'

He hadn't felt that thread of hatred. I'd seen him. I'd caused the search in Stavanger. Now I'd outwitted him. On the other hand, I tried to console myself, he must have come to Belfast for a purpose, and dealing with me wasn't part of that. He wouldn't have known I'd be at the *Titanic* museum just then; that was my bad luck, to run straight into him. *When a felon's not engaged in his employment* . . . sang my head, suddenly. Why shouldn't assassins go looking at museums? *Or maturing his felonious little plans* . . . I was getting light-headed. Time I was home.

The police car ran us back through the jumble of docks and right onto the quay. The loudspeakers were blaring out thump-thump music. A stream of folk were waiting at *Sørlandet*'s gangplank, and her deck was garish with shifting summer clothes: white, pink, orange, acid green. We made our way through them, and I collapsed on my berth while Gavin boiled the kettle. Cat came straight to my chest, purring in welcome, his soft fur soothing under my still-trembling fingers. 'A close one,' I told him. He opened his mouth in his soundless mew, his yellow eyes staring straight into mine. *I've had enough of this*, I thought at him. *In the last two years I've been hit on the head, left in a Neolithic tomb, shot, nearly drowned. I'm not tough enough to take it any more.* A quiet life on a Highland farm, where the biggest excitement was the ram getting loose, suddenly seemed an attractive option. But murder had followed me even there . . . perhaps I was murder-prone, just as some people are hit multiple times by lightning, or some only have to get on a ship for it to sink. Whatever it was, I was sick of it. I didn't want to be a target. I wanted peace.

Gavin came in then with the hot chocolate. 'I made it a white one, since you were having a bad day.' He handed it to me and sat down on the settee, and gave me a sideways glance. 'You're OK? Really OK?'

I nodded. 'Scared but unhurt.'

He laughed at that. 'Oh, you, scared!' His hand lay warm on my belly. 'I told them you'd keep a cool head. All the same, a peaceful race back to Kristiansand would be just fine.'

I remembered what Agnetha had said. *Dismissed* . . . I might not be still on board. But Captain Gunnar hadn't said anything yet, and he'd had all morning to call me aside. Besides, I told myself, my ship needed me. Without Mike, there was nobody to fill my place.

'What's wrong?' Gavin said.

I made a face. I wasn't sure I could explain it in words.

'The rumours about you being mad and responsible for Mike's death?' he asked.

I nodded. His arm tightened over me. 'CI Beattie's in charge of the investigation now. Sergeant Peterson and I have handed our conclusions so far over to him.' His grey eyes looked straight into mine. 'There's nothing to link you with the crime more than anyone else. I promise you.'

Relief flooded me. 'You're sure?'

'We're sure your jacket and hat were worn by somebody else. The two witnesses who were in the best position to see were sure the person was taller than you. Your jacket and hat are at the lab now, being checked for prints and hairs.'

I felt as if my chest had suddenly filled with helium, like a balloon. 'I'm off the hook?'

'Hair matching's not a precise science yet, but I can confirm that there are hairs that don't look like yours.'

The lightness left me. 'Do you know . . . whose?'

He shook his head. I didn't know whether that meant he didn't know, or that he couldn't tell me. 'You're not completely cleared. But you're too new a crew member to have smuggled Bezrukov aboard, so your only possible motive would have been psychopathic, and you've given CI Beattie a very good example of how sane you are under pressure.'

I let out a long breath, closing my eyes for a moment. I pushed the thought of those silver-fair hairs away from me. The police would find the guilty person, and we'd have peace again. 'Then we can have fun all the way to Kristiansand.'

He gave me a teasing look. 'Fun, while your ship's racing?'

I conceded that one. 'When we're off duty.'

We stayed in the cabin in peace while the tourists clumped on the deck above us. Gavin fished his tablet out of his pocket and read, while I dozed, one hand still curved round Cat's back, his breathing warm under my fingers, one hand touching Gavin's back. From time to time we looked at each other, and smiled.

At half past four, the noises over our head changed. The excited feet of children clattered off over the gangway and were replaced by the shuffle of people carrying boxes across the gangplank. A good number of them had the sound of bottles clinking. There were heavy thuds as amplifiers were set down, and the metallic clang of a band setting up its microphones, the whoof of speakers being plugged in. I stretched and swung my legs down. 'Shall we go and find something to eat on the pier, before I change into my officer-on-parade outfit?'

Gavin nodded. Eating whatever you could snatch in passing was something police officers and ship's crew shared. I put Cat's harness on, and we went out on deck.

A human chain of black-clad waiters was passing the boxes along and piling them up beside the banjer. Henrik was in charge, pointing out where they were to go. As we waited for the gangplank to clear, a man with an air of being in charge of catering came across, directing four minions with a pair of whisky boxes each. They were set down further along, past the galley door. Henrik nodded, and gave the man an envelope. The man turned away with a wave of his hand, and Henrik himself started taking the boxes into the galley. It was all a bit odd . . . and then enlightenment dawned. *Merchandise . . . as planned, Thursday . . .*

'Spirits,' I said.

Gavin gave me a quizzical look. 'Ghosts or alcohol?'

I realised that I hadn't mentioned the white boxes in the cold store to him. That was ship's business, and if it was what I was thinking, I'd keep not mentioning it. I tucked my arm into his. 'Let's get off. I think I saw a crêpe place, if you fancy that. *Crêpe au jambon fromage.*'

He followed me across the gangplank, and took my arm again at the other side. 'Spirits?'

'I think you'd rather not know.' I'd been thinking wine bottles, but spirits cost the earth in Norway, and the ship would be giving a party for Captain Gunnar's retirement in August. If Henrik had had the bright idea of asking the catering company for this party to supply him with, say, four dozen bottles of whisky at catering prices . . . I paused to sniff the air. 'Paella?'

'No. Nor Mexican. There's a French flag over there.' He steered me towards it, and we ordered two *jambon-fromage* and two *sucrée-citron*, for pudding. We found an empty table at the open-air bar, and sat down. Cat jumped up into my lap and sniffed at the crêpe triangle. I gave him a bit with cheese and ham, and kept thinking. I should have recognised Captain Gunnar's voice, even in Norwegian. Four dozen bottles at a saving of, say, £15 a bottle, would mean he could have a send-off where the whisky flowed like water.

'Would what you're mulling over be worth killing for?' Gavin asked.

I shook my head. 'A one-off fiddle worth about £720.' The crêpe smelt like I'd bought it in France. I managed to get the cone balanced in my hand and took a mouthful of crispy edge, generously scattered with cheese. 'Mmmm.'

'Good,' Gavin agreed. He took another bite, and went into thought-reading mode. 'If it's something to do with your steward buying cheap drink, would it be a sacking offence?'

'Only if customs found out about it and there was a stink likely to damage the good name of the ship. Which I don't think there would be.' I took another mouthful and found ham, encased in cheese. I passed Cat another bit. 'A fine maybe, from customs. That could be substantial. A rap over the knuckles from the office.'

We ate steadily, and watched the caterers set up on board: tables, white cloths, rows of glasses, ice buckets. The band had installed themselves under the banjer overhang, four men in waistcoats and bow ties, with guitars. The lead singer had a Blues-Brothers hat and shades. I sighed, and negotiated the last lemony bit of my *sucrée-citron* corner. 'Time I was getting into my best uniform.'

'I haven't been invited,' Gavin said. 'I'll watch from here.'

'Have a Guinness on me.' I rose. 'Come on, Cat.'

I transformed myself into Best Third Mate, stripes and all, and headed back on deck. Erik was at the aft banjer steps, getting into his climbing harness. 'Cass, fancy a trip up the mast?'

'I'd be delighted, but why?'

'We have an acrobat.' He made a face. 'A trapeze artiste. She's just arrived, and we have to go up with her and check where she attaches her ropes.'

The crew harnesses hung at the aft steps, ready for a quick grab. I flipped quickly through them and found Mona's, which fitted me without too much adjustment. My pockets were empty. Legs, arms, front buckle, red is dead.

The trapeze artiste was dressed in a scarlet leotard which glittered with sequins. 'Celestine,' she introduced herself. She waved away the climbing harness, looped her coil of rope around one shoulder, flicked back her long hair and followed me up the ratlines.

It was good to be climbing. I felt the wind in my hair as soon as we were fifteen feet above deck level. The taped wires felt easy and familiar in my grasp, and the wooden spars were solid under my feet. Below us, a coach drew up at the gangplank, and our guests spilt out of it, men in crisp striped shirts and aftershave I could smell from up here, women with sparkling off-the-shoulder dresses, mask-like make-up and stiletto heels. They poured onto the ship, hooting with laughter as if they'd had a drink or two already, and by the time I reached the first platform they'd all got a glass in hand. The band launched into 'That's Amore', followed, predictably, by 'I am Sailing'. I clicked on for the familiar up-and-over, arrived on the platform and reached down to take Celestine's rope. She swung herself up in one fluid movement, and looked around. 'Sure, this is fine for height. Any higher and they won't be able to see me.'

The band ceased, and Henrik took the microphone to do a formal welcome to the ship, smooth as best Laphroaig. Celestine ignored him. 'I need safe fixing points for these clips, well clear of the mast here.'

I gave the yard wires an assessing look. 'What do you think, Erik?'

He had a puzzled look, one hand fiddling with the loop around his right leg as if it was too tight. He let go of it, and turned to me. 'We could put it from the fixings that hold the foot wires. They should easily be strong enough. Then a safety line to the platform.'

Celestine nodded, and watched as he slid forward along the line, her rope hooked round his elbow. Below us, faces turned upwards.

Erik had secured the lines and was making his way back to us when he gave a choked cry, as if he'd had a sudden spasm of pain. He stopped on the lines and put his hand down to his harness. His eyes opened wide in shock, and the hand came back up red with blood. Then the blood spouted out from his thigh. There was a scream from below, a panicky milling as the bright office workers moved away from the dark arterial blood that was spilling on their shining heads, into their drinks, over their shaking hands and party clothes.

I couldn't understand what had happened, but I knew we had to act quickly. I stretched out a hand to get him back on the platform, but I was already too late. The hand that was still curved over the yard slid backwards. He slumped away from the spar and dropped, feet twanging the wire as they relinquished it.

The safety harness held him. He swung below the wire, horizontal, with his head, legs, arms drooping away from the hook in the centre of his chest. His mouth was open, his eyes searching mine for understanding of what had happened. Below him, the deck ran red with blood.

EIGHT BELLS

Belfast

Friday 3rd July

CHAPTER TWENTY-TWO

'Stanley knife blades,' Gavin said, 'probably from the carpenter's shop. They were sewn into his harness, just where they would rub against his femoral artery.'

He was facing us all over breakfast. We had filed in silently and taken our places. Captain Gunnar, at the head of the table, had extra wrinkles on his face and a defeated slump to his shoulders. Henrik was crumbling his bread on his plate; Rolf's grin was quenched. Sadie kept taking her phone out of her pocket, then putting it back. Nils and Agnetha were white-faced, and Jenn looked as if she hadn't slept. Anders had Rat curled round his neck under his shirt, as if comforting him.

It felt like we'd been up all night. The shocked executives had been herded to one end of the deck, with Agnetha and I taking care of the two women who'd been directly below Erik as he fell. We'd showed them where the shower was, given them toiletries and towels, and found them spare togs to replace their blood-drenched finery.

When they'd come out, we'd given them sweet tea and biscuits and done our best to soothe their shuddering horror. By then the police had talked briefly to everyone else. There wasn't anything they could tell. None of them had been on the ship long enough to doctor a harness, but they still had to be interviewed and soothed. At last we got them back on their coach, with Erik's death already turned into a gruesome anecdote to be recounted with hushed horror to their family tonight, and with Gothic panache at their workplaces on Monday. Several had videoed it on their phones. It was probably on YouTube already. Heaven guard me from this modern land-world.

He had died from blood loss within a few minutes of falling from the yard. Rolf and Nils fixed up a pulley to lower him down to the police stretcher. Once we'd got rid of the coach party, we'd got into working clothes and scrubbed the deck over and over, until the red water ran clear. We'd just managed to finish when the first of the trainees returned.

I'd gone to bed then, exhausted. I'd had enough; I wanted oblivion. I'd been almost asleep when Gavin had come to bed at last. He slipped in beside me, and held me to him. I could feel he didn't want to talk. We'd held each other in silence until sleep took us.

Stanley knife blades . . . I remembered that picture that had come into my head in the *Titanic* museum, as Bezrukov had held me, of my blood running over his fingers, and shuddered. I remembered Erik's puzzled look, his fumbling with the thigh straps as he'd felt the prick of the blades.

It would have been easy enough to take his harness and doctor it. The crew harnesses were named, to save constant readjustment of the straps. I tried to remember when Erik had last used his. Not for several days; we'd had no sails up since approaching Orkney, and then, when everyone had been climbing on our approach to Belfast, he'd supervised from deck level. But why Erik?

Gavin was looking around us all, face shadowed, official. 'I can't go into details at the moment, but we believe that the person responsible is now off the ship.'

Agnetha moistened her pale lips. 'Did he kill Mike too?' she asked. 'Was that the person Cass saw?'

She was looking at me. I wasn't sure how to react. It hadn't been Bezrukov who'd walked up the stairs with Mike.

Gavin cut in smoothly. 'We haven't finished our investigation on that.' He spread his hands in a *That's all I can say* gesture. 'I hope that this unhappy period aboard is now finished with. There may still be some forensic investigation on board, but we'll try to be as unobtrusive as possible.'

We finished our breakfast in a gloomy silence. I was just rising at the end of it, when Captain Gunnar took me aside. 'I have phoned Erik's wife. She was naturally very shocked. I hope that the Norwegian police will send round a counsellor, but you knew her too, did you not?'

I nodded.

'You would perhaps call her after muster this morning, for the ship, and see how she is.'

'Sir.'

I'd thought all the trainees had been busy sampling Belfast nightlife, but as they lined up I saw that the story had gone round. They had a tendency to huddle together, eyeing up the place beside Mona and Petter where Erik would have stood. Captain Gunnar squared his shoulders and came out among them. He didn't go into details, simply said that there had been an accident aboard while Erik had been helping set up the trapeze for the acrobat. It emphasised the need for care in the rig at all times, he added. Then he stepped back to let Jenn take over with the schedules for the morning's activities, and then the timetable for the afternoon's parade through the streets. Henrik distributed Tall Ships T-shirts and the wristbands to let them into the party, and then dismissed them, light-hearted again and chattering like parrots about where they were going to spend the morning.

I gave them ten minutes to get away, then headed up to the foredeck, phone in hand. It was going to be a bonny, warm day. The sky was marbled with clouds, and the light breeze spread the flags. Music thump-thumped from the fairground already, lights flashed from the Ferris wheel as it turned, and the first strollers were walking along the pier, rubbernecking the boats. We would be open to visitors from ten o'clock.

I took a deep breath, then clicked on Micaela's house number. *Erik*, it said in my phone. I felt that sharp pang of unreality. There was no Erik now. She answered on the third ring. 'Cass. I hoped you would phone.'

There was the noise of children behind her, excited, as if they were about to go out on a picnic. 'Elena, Alexander, *silencio! Estoy en el teléfono.*'

There were scufflings, shooings, Micaela saying, '*Vayan al jardín!*' then silence.

'How are you?' I asked. It was a stupid question. 'And the children?'

'I haven't told them yet. Later.' She hesitated, as if she wanted to say more, then repeated, 'Later. Once things are settled.'

'Has it been on the news in Norway?'

'Only a short item, that there had been a death on board *Sørlandet*, and that the police were investigating.'

'Good.'

'Yes. They did not give his name, so I have not had any phone calls from the press.'

I was glad of that. I'd only had one encounter with the press in full cry, during the longship affair, and that once had been plenty. Micaela had enough to cope with.

'When Captain Gunnar phoned last night, it was too much of a shock. I couldn't ask all the questions . . .' Her voice wavered, and steadied again. 'Were you there?'

'Yes.'

'Captain Gunnar said it was an accident in the rig. Did he fall?'

There was no easy way of putting it. I took a deep breath. 'No. Somebody killed him.' I couldn't bear to go into the details. 'I was right beside him. It was very quick, Micaela. It sounds awful, but he didn't suffer. He was dead before any of us could do anything to help.'

There was a long, heavy silence, so long that I thought she'd put the phone down. At last she spoke again, her voice dull. 'I knew it would happen.'

She left another silence. I waited.

'He told me he had said no to them. After Mike's death. He told the Russian to tell them, not again.'

I felt a coldness in my chest. 'Erik brought Bezrukov on board?'

'All of them,' Micaela said. She hesitated. 'I did not tell Captain Gunnar, but you will explain to him. Please, tell him I am sorry. *He* was sorry. He wanted it to end.'

All of them? I waited, my mobile cold in my hand.

'You know that we met on a beach,' Micaela said. 'It was a beach in . . . well, the country does not matter. We came off the boat which had brought us from my own country. There was a patrol boat not far behind us, so we ran the boat straight up the beach, and got out, and began running for the forest behind it – palm trees and undergrowth where we could hide. There were people on the beach, a party, with a driftwood fire. They watched us as we ran. I didn't know it then, but it was a ship's crew. Not *Sørlandet* – the ship

Erik was on, *Belle Etoile*. And then I tripped. I was dazzled by the firelight, and I fell over, and I was so tired and cold and frightened that I could not get up again; my legs would not hold me. Erik came over to help me.'

She paused. I could hear that she was crying as the moment relived itself in her head. 'We looked at each other in the firelight, and fell in love, just like that. Then the patrol boat arrived, filled with men with guns, and beached itself by our boat, and the men jumped out. Erik pulled his shirt off and flung it round me, and I fumbled my arms into the sleeves, and there I was, dressed as a member of the ship. We sat down at the fire with the others. Someone passed me a tourist cap, and a tin of drink, and when the officials came over to us, I was part of the group, with Erik's arm around me. I watched as they went into the forest. I heard the shots. They brought some of them back. My uncle, and one of my cousins, and some of the others. I do not know what happened to the rest of our boatload. They punctured the boat which had brought us, and left it. Erik kept his arm around me, and when he returned to the ship, I went with him. I stayed with the ship, working, until we came back to Norway. Then I came ashore, to Erik's house. I was Erik's wife, who he'd met and married abroad. Erik got the post on *Sørlandet*, and was home more, instead of roaming the world. The children were born – I had to go to a private clinic for that; because I had no papers, I was not on the Norwegian health service, but we managed to scrape the money together. We were happy.'

Her voice hardened. 'Then the phone call came. A man who knew all about me. He threatened to tell the authorities, unless Erik would arrange to smuggle a person on *Sørlandet*. He would make sure the person got on board while he was on the gangplank, and then that person simply kept out of the way, mingled with the trainees, and left the ship at the destination port. Perhaps they were carrying drugs . . . he did not ask. After the first time, there was a payment made to our account, a hundred thousand kroner, and we did not know what to do. If we tried to go to the police, they would say we'd taken payment. Erik would be put in prison, I would be sent back to the country I had escaped, and perhaps the children too, because we weren't actually married, so we feared they might not be Norwegian citizens either. The laws are harsh. We didn't dare risk it.' Her voice pleaded. 'It was not often. One person, two or three times a year, from different ports.'

She hesitated. 'You understand?'

'I understand,' I said.

'You will tell the captain how it came about?'

'Yes.'

'And that Erik was sorry. He did not want to do it. He died because he would not do it any more. He told the Russian that.'

I heard Erik's voice in my head: *Sometimes what felt like the right thing was actually wrong after all, and then trouble multiplies from it, and you're left with a choice of wrongs.*

'I'll tell him.' I paused. 'Micaela, what about you? Will you be OK?'

'Yes. I will see you back in Kristiansand, in ten days. We will talk then. Goodbye, Cass.' She hung up, and I was left with the phone in my hand, making sense of it all. Now I understood Micaela's air of strain as she'd said goodbye. Poor Micaela, poor Erik, living with this threat hanging over them. I didn't know what I'd have done, had it been me. I tried to imagine Gavin stumbling up a beach, with armed men after him, and knew I couldn't have handed him over.

I would need to tell him. I looked around and saw him on the aft deck, leaning against the rail, talking to another man, while white-suited forensic officers clustered around the aft doorway where the crew harnesses hung. I was going to head over when I realised that Micaela hadn't said to tell the police, but to tell Captain Gunnar. This was ship's business first.

He was in his cabin, at his desk, one hand shading his eyes, a pen idle in his hand. When I knocked and went in, he looked at me for a moment as if he'd forgotten who I was.

'I've just spoken to Micaela, sir,' I said. 'She asked me to tell you – she explained that it was Erik who smuggled Bezrukov aboard. They – the gang he belonged to – had a hold over him, blackmail. She asked me to tell you how sorry he was. She said he'd told them he wouldn't do it again, and that's why they killed him.'

Captain Gunnar's white brows drew together. 'Erik smuggled him aboard?'

I nodded.

'Have you told this to the police?'

'Not yet.' I spread my hands. 'Ship's business. Micaela said to tell you.'

He lifted a paper, squared it against another, set them both down. 'So this Russian really was on board. He was the killer.' I could feel the relief flooding through him. 'Not a member of my crew. The stowaway.' He looked up at me and hesitated for a moment, then the captain I knew came back into his face: fair, kindly, encouraging, a good leader. 'I owe you an apology, Cass. You wanted to tell me about him, and I would not listen.'

'I don't suppose it would have made any difference, sir.'

'Perhaps not.' He rose. 'I will talk to the police. To the office too.' He had regained his height. 'We will need to tighten up our watch procedures in port, to make sure this does not happen again. The ship must never be left in the care of one person only.' He nodded a dismissal. 'Thank you, Cass.'

I walked back on deck to a throng of Belfast folk in holiday mood, admiring the ship, looking up at the masts and either longing for a climb or saying, 'Wouldn't catch me going up there.' My job was to mingle, so I mingled, answered questions, took photographs of families posed against the bow and gave out leaflets about our voyages. It was routine stuff, and I was glad of that, for my mind felt too full to think. Micaela's story hadn't been a shock; a hundred little things I'd never consciously noticed were fitting together in my head. It had been Erik's air of tension that had given me that sense of foreboding; Micaela's fear, as she'd seen him off. But what would happen to her now? Would she need police protection from the gang, or would she be extradited?

The ship was as full as it could hold with visitors when a wholesale truck arrived with the supply of food for eighty-five people for the next ten days. *Good timing*, I thought wearily, and went to join the human chain shifting it from pallets on the pier to the cold store and freezer. Box after box of cauliflower, broccoli, wax-skinned peppers, apples, bananas, lettuce; sacks of potatoes; plastic-wrapped trays of tins; square lengths of cold meat; boxes of fresh meat in rustling sky-blue bags. It took us a full hour just to get it all on board, and by the time it was all piled up below my arms felt like spaghetti. The last thing I felt like was a crew parade.

Gavin came over just as I was taking a breather, leaning against the banjer table. 'We're done now. I'll go back with the squad to HQ, and text you when I can get free.' He gave me a concerned look. 'Will you get a rest before this crew parade?'

I nodded. 'Muster at 16.00.'

'Make the most of it.' He bent forward for a quick kiss. 'Otherwise, stick with the crowd. See you later.'

I watched him cross the gangplank and disappear among the crowd, kilt swinging, then walked slowly to my cabin to wash my hands for lunch. Cat was curled up on my berth – he could only do so much of being admired before he headed below. There was a piece of paper under his paws. I eased it out, and unfolded it.

It was a page of notebook, with a message. *Heard about the museum. Still dangerous. Don't go the whole length of the crew parade. Slip out at the big fish. You'll be met there. Code word is O'Donoghue's.*

I knew O'Donoghue's. It was the pub we'd sneaked into, Sean, Seamus and I, all those years ago, to listen to live music. I hadn't seen Sean's handwriting for twenty years. I examined the cramped, secretive script, and supposed it looked familiar. I read the note again. *Heard about the museum* – Bezrukov. It must be Bezrukov who was *Still dangerous*. Waiting at the end of the crew parade?

I was turning it over in my hands when my phone buzzed. CI Beattie's rich voice boomed out at me. 'Cass, I was wondering if you spoke to the wife of the dead man this morning. Micaela. You moor your boat at their house, that's right?'

'Yes.'

'So you're friendly?'

'Yes. I phoned her straight after breakfast.'

'Now, there may be nothing amiss, nothing amiss at all. It's just that the Norwegian police have been around and she's not at the house, and the car's still there, though I gather it's a pretty out-of-the-way spot. She didn't mention to you that she was going to stay with a relative, or anything like that?'

'No.' For a moment my heart went cold. Could the gang have descended on that quiet house and taken Micaela and the children? Then I remembered that 'going for a picnic' air of excitement in the background of the phone call. 'Micaela doesn't have any relatives in Norway. Erik will, of course, but I don't know who they are.'

'The Norwegian police will find that out. That's fine, Cass. And how are you today? Recovered?'

'Oh, yes, life as usual.'

'That's good. Thanks for that, Cass. We'll speak again.'

He rang off before I had time to think about what to say. I sat down on my berth and stared at the bookshelf above my desk. Erik had been a planner. Suppose, just suppose, he'd decided to run from the gang, to put his family in security. They had a boat, bigger than my *Khalida* – a Colin Archer design, strong, seaworthy. Nobody ever questioned carrying bags of stuff up and down from a boat. If I'd been him, planning escape, I'd have filled her up with fuel, clothes, tins. Money, in a strongbox in the bilges. Then, when the time was right, I'd have left everything behind; I'd have walked down to the boat, without giveaway suitcases, just as if we were heading out on a day-sail. I'd point my nose to the horizon, to a country where nobody was looking for me.

Micaela was a sailor too. She'd done the RYA classes up to Yachtmaster.

It was summer, and the world lay ahead of them. Westward to Shetland, Faroe, Iceland, America. South to France, Spain, the Canaries, Africa. The wide Atlantic. The longer I kept quiet, the more of a start she'd have, to lose herself among the dozens of little boats that skimmed the world's waters.

I said a quick prayer for her and the children, for luck and fair winds, and went through to lunch.

CHAPTER TWENTY-THREE

I tried several times to phone Gavin, but got only voicemail. I didn't think they'd be doing the autopsy on Erik so quickly; Mike, perhaps. I pushed that image away, and considered Sean's note. *Still dangerous.* It felt like the classic setup. Girl is sent supposedly friendly note luring her into lonely old house. Girl is stupid enough to go. Girl meets nasty end.

I was reasonably sure it was from Sean. *O'Donoghue's* would only make sense if it was a genuine message from him to me. I didn't know what he was up to, but if he'd been on board shadowing Bezrukov, he would still be following him. He might know something of his plans. If he was against Bezrukov, he was on the side of the angels, so far as anyone ever could be in the tangle of today's politics. *Don't go the whole length of the crew parade.* If Bezrukov's plans included me – and I had no doubt he'd be coldly furious about a woman having tricked him – then whatever was going to happen was planned for the end of the parade, where we'd all be standing still, looking at the stage. Targets for a man with a gun. I needed to talk to Gavin. I tried his phone again and left a message for him to call me urgently. If he didn't get back to me in half an hour, I'd call the station and insist on talking to CI Beattie.

Slip out at the big fish. I pulled out my map of Belfast and studied it. The Big Fish area was numbered (3) on the map, with a note offering me street theatre and performers, live music, information point and official merchandise. It didn't say what the Big Fish was, but no doubt I'd spot it. *You'll be met there.*

There was still no word back from Gavin at half past three. I managed to get as far as a DI in the Belfast police, who sounded harassed, with a bustle behind him as if the office was mobilising. He said that CI Beattie was out, and he'd leave a message. *Urgent*, I said, and he promised he'd let him know straight away. *Yeah*, I thought, and didn't hold my breath. But surely Gavin would phone back soon.

We mustered on deck at four. The officers were in uniform, the trainees dressed in a mixture of *Sørlandet* T-shirts and Tall Ships ones. The sun had come out, glinting on the water and dazzling off our polished brass. Our local volunteer liaison officer had arrived, a cheerful schoolteacher with a pale blue Tall Ships fleece, and an identifying board on a long pole: *SØRLANDET*, Norway. She brought two more volunteers with her, who would stay on board to guard the ship while we partied. Henrik had more wristbands, with tear-off pieces for food and drink at the crew party, and Agnetha was carrying a bag of flags. Once we were all gathered, our liaison officer led us through the streets to the muster point on a broad side street turned into pedestrian-only by traffic cones, with a main road and flyover ahead, and an imposing red-brown civic building across from us.

It was my first parade of the season, and I'd have enjoyed myself if it hadn't been for the cold worry in the pit of my stomach. Our trainees were high with excitement, and our fellow crews were partying all around us. The crew of *Frederyk Chopin*, ahead of us, sported red-and-blue-striped rugby shirts, with white sailor caps on the men, leis round the necks of the women and Irish shamrocks painted on their cheeks. One of them was on stilts, the sort that strap on to a leg, like the jazz players had worn. The stiffness of her walk jogged a memory somewhere, something important, but it was too noisy here and I couldn't place it. There was an odd gryphon figure parroting among them – the Polish eagle, of course, the mascot of a Polish ship. They had music with them, and began dancing reels and the Macarena. The *Alexander von Humboldt* crew were behind us, until a miniature lighthouse trundled by and installed itself in front of them. They were dressed in green, and doing a circular dance. Inspired, our trainees distributed flags. Dimitris hoisted Maria on his shoulders, and she held the Greek cross above them, fluttering in the wind. Jenn took charge of the Canadian maple leaf. Several of them clustered round our large Norwegian flag, brought down from the mast, and Lena began working out a routine where the people behind ran under it, then crouched to let it pass back over them.

Still no word from Gavin. Perhaps he'd not had time to listen to his messages. I tried again. Voicemail. I had to make a decision.

I'd risk trusting family. I spoke quickly into the phone. 'I've had a message from Sean not to go to the end of the parade, but to stop at the Big Fish. Unless I hear back from you, I'll do that.' *Girl is decoyed into lonely house* . . . Of course, the flip side of that was *Girl insists on ignoring warnings*. I hauled my map out from my back pocket and checked my bearings. The Big Fish was when we arrived at the river. I'd tell Agnetha I didn't feel well, that I'd catch them up later.

314

There was a good crowd gathered now, just visible under the flyover. The blare of a brass band drifted back to us. The crews jumped down from the walls they'd been sitting on or prised themselves up from the ground, and tightened up their formations. The colourful line shuddered, then began to move.

We came out of our side road into the middle of modern Belfast, with a glass-walled office building on one side, finished with a steel tower and festooned with banners, Belfast Harbour notices and *Daily Telegraph* marquees. The sun was out now, shining from a sky of duck-egg blue, dazzling off the chrome of cars and glass of windows, and warming our faces as we marched. There was a good crowd on each side of the road, but oddly silent, not interacting with us. It took a moment for me to realise why. Only the children were looking directly at us; almost all the adults were filming us on raised tablets or mobile phones, and watching through the tiny screens. A strange world . . .

The road widened out into a square, boasting a Palladian building along one side, with a pillared front topped by a statue-filled triangle, Parthenon-style. Beyond it was a steel and glass tower with a pointed roof, and down to my left, at last, a space clear of houses, and the river gleaming willow-green between bridges. We halted, and I looked around. The Big Fish was here somewhere.

I recognised it as soon as I saw it. It was exactly what its name said: a big fish, blue-backed, white-bellied, balanced as if it was swimming, with its nose pointing towards a curved footbridge streaming with people. There was no sign of cousin Sean, but then I didn't expect to see him. He wouldn't have left a password if he was going to be there himself.

Now or never. I touched Agnetha on the arm. She jumped, as if her thoughts had been miles away, and turned a startled face towards me.

'I don't feel great,' I told her. 'I think I'll rest a bit here. I'll catch you up later.'

She gave me a concerned look. 'You OK? I mean, there's not something wrong?'

I shook my head. 'Just a bit tired, with all this standing about, then slow shuffling. Give me a good brisk walk any day.'

'Me too. See you later, then.'

I waited for *Frederyk Chopin*'s crew to launch into the Macarena again, then slipped quietly out of the parade. Nobody seemed interested in me. I retreated to the outer edge of the crowd, checked around me again, then threaded my way through a forest of bicycles to the Big Fish.

It was the sort of thing that gives modern art a good name. Close up, I could see how big it really was: a good three metres tall to the top of its back fin, and ten metres long from pointed snout to tail flukes. The staring eyes were opaque brown. It was made of ceramic tiles, all different shapes, like crazy paving, cut to create the lines of gills and fins, and printed with old photographs of the city: faces, bills and accounts, trade advertisements, letters and newspaper cuttings. The upper ones were black on navy, or navy on cobalt, the lower ones faded to smoky blue on cream. There was a large 'Do not climb on the fish' notice which was naturally being ignored by every child in sight. The temptation to clamber up its back was irresistible.

I stepped away from it and strolled back into the shadow of the trees, feeling conspicuous in my officer togs, too visible a refugee from the parade. We'd been almost at the head of it, so there was a good length to go. The crew of *Ecuador* marched past in military formation, white shirts crisp, caps at exactly the same angle, with a couple of masked creatures capering around them, scarlet masks topped with pom-poms on sticks. I turned away from my fellow sailors and looked at the people around me. Parents hauling

316

children off the fish to watch the parade. Watchers with cameras, backs turned to me. A mother with a baby in a sling around her neck. The white and black lighthouse that had been immediately behind us in the parade was also stopping for a breather. I didn't blame the person inside; it was a solid-looking construction, with chunky frames around the rounded windows, and topped by two black circles separated by a criss-cross of white two-by-two, with the light revolving in the centre. It seemed to be supported on four wheels – an old pram carriage, maybe, covered by canvas painted as foam-frothed rock – but it would still be hard work to push. Two pinstripe-shirted men walked briskly past it in long-toed shoes, each having a different conversation into their mouthpieces – or perhaps they were talking to each other, who knows? There was no sign of anyone who might have come from Sean.

The mother with the baby paused beside me to adjust the sling and peer into the folds. 'Sure, it's a grand day. Makes you feel like sitting quietly in the sun at O'Donoghue's, and having a long, cold drink.'

She said it so casually that it took a moment for the words to sink in. 'A long cold drink sounds a good idea,' I agreed, cautiously. 'Though O'Donoghue's is maybe a bit far to go for it.'

Password given and returned. I gave her a quick glance, and realised that I recognised her; she'd been the texting teenager I'd kept seeing in the *Titanic* museum. There, she'd been the complete teenager, with immaculate make-up, dyed hair strands, a row of earrings and the latest thing in baggy black overshirts; now she was an equally convincing mother, too frazzled to do more than wash her face, scrape her hair back with a band and find a T-shirt that hadn't been sicked on. I looked at the contrast between her clothes and my uniform, and felt a strange lurch at my heart, part relief and part envy.

Now what? 'We could maybe find somewhere closer,' she agreed. 'But it's a soft afternoon. Why don't you go round the other side of the Big Fish, now, and lean against it, and enjoy the view?'

Order received. 'I'll do that,' I said. I nodded, as to a chance-met passer-by, and strolled around the Big Fish, my heartbeat speeding up. It was quiet now, with the last child dragged streetwards to watch the parade. There was silence behind me, as if I was in a game of What's the Time, Mr Wolf?, and my role was to stand here motionless and blinded, while the rest of the players crept up on me from behind. I'd never liked it much in the playground, and I liked it even less now, but I knew about obeying orders from somebody who could see the whole picture.

There was a scraping noise from further off behind me, as if a roughly built door had been opened and shut. It was over to the left, where the lighthouse had been parked. My brain began working fast. Bezrukov hadn't come here into a void; he'd been expected. The people waiting for him would have made him a costume that would hide not only him but his weapons as well. I didn't even try to follow the tangled politics of Northern Ireland, but there would be political bigwigs up on that stage to welcome the crews from all round the world. The lighthouse would get him close enough to shoot, and protected enough to make taking him dangerous to all the celebrating teenagers around him – unless he could be diverted into a nice, quiet place by the chance of finishing off a private vendetta before he trundled on to the finish.

Families. My cousin Sean was using me as bait. If my Granny Bridget was looking down from heaven, I thought wildly, she'd have a few things to say to him when he got up there.

Now I knew what was happening it was easier to visualise. Bezrukov had got out of the lighthouse, and was strolling casually towards the Big Fish, gun at the ready, while everyone was watching the parade . . .

. . . and then, suddenly, he was on me, bursting around the fish's nose in a swirl of black like a striking raven, gun levelled, and I flung myself to the ground and somersaulted between its under-fin and tail and came up on the other side, to find the young mother, two of the camera watchers and the pinstriped men spreading out around the fish. The young mother was quickest around, firing as she went; three shots, with only one answering. I dragged myself up, trembling all over. I'd had *enough* of this kind of thing. I backed away from the fish, eyes on these spread-out stalking professionals, tensing myself to run again.

Then it was all over. The pinstriped men straightened and became ordinary office workers. They walked briskly to the lighthouse and trundled it away. The camera-watchers remained, one at each end of the fish, leaning casually against it, enjoying the parade from there. A white van appeared from nowhere, and curved to a halt in the cleared space. Two men leapt out with a stretcher, went round the fish's nose, returned around its tail with a blanket-covered burden and bundled it into the van, which slid smoothly away. I heard the crackle of a hand-held radio, then the young mother came out from behind the fish and nodded at me. 'Well done.'

The sling was still around her neck. 'You wouldn't risk a real baby,' I said, stupidly.

She shook her head and laughed. 'A doll. Excellent camouflage. Back to the parade, or do you need a drink?'

I needed a bloody strong drink, but I was still on duty. I gestured at the parade marching past. 'I'll just rejoin my shipmates.'

I was halfway up the parade, weaving my way in and out of the crews and crowd, heart still racing like an out-of-gear engine at full throttle, when I met Gavin coming towards me. He caught me to him and held me tight. His jacket smelt of wool, Imperial Leather soap, security. I fought back the impulse to burst into tears on his chest. I clung to him for a moment, then got a grip on myself, pulled him around and began towing him towards the head of the parade.

'You've missed the excitement,' I told him, my voice Oscar-winning steady.

'There wasn't any. That's official.'

'It was a very neat operation. I'll give my cousin Sean that.'

His mouth was grim. 'If ever I meet your cousin Sean again, there's a lot I'd like to say.'

'My Granny Bridget said it all, a dozen times.' I curled my fingers round his. 'It had no effect whatsoever, so I wouldn't waste your breath. What was he anyway? Special branch? MI5?'

Gavin shook his head. 'Above my level of knowledge. I'd just switched my phone on and found your messages when I got a phone call from a young woman saying you were safe and rejoining the parade. Then word came through that Bezrukov had been disposed of, news blackout, no paperwork, and the extra security for the speeches at the stadium could be stood down.'

'Incident closed.' I could see the green costumes of *Alexander von Humboldt* ahead of us now. 'Nearly there.'

Another five minutes of brisk dodging and we were home, among my own crew once more. I gave Agnetha a thumbs up. We filed together through the gates and found ourselves almost right in front of the stage, facing a house-high battery of speakers. A wired-looking presenter with one of those upward-pointing wedge haircuts was bouncing about on the stage.

'Right,' Gavin said. 'You're back on duty. All your watch is there, ready to enjoy the speeches and whatever else is lined up, but my trained police instincts tell me that all your fellow officers are slipping to the side, to get away from the music. Shall we join them?'

I didn't argue. We squirmed sideways and took up our stations on the low wall around the building where the crew party would be held. Jazz music was curling from inside it already – no, it was coming from higher up the steps, where the three players on stilts who'd come on board *Sørlandet* for the party had installed themselves. I watched them swaying on their grasshopper legs, and remembered what I'd noticed without seeing it.

I knew who'd killed Mike.

CHAPTER TWENTY-FOUR

The prize-giving was pretty much like every other one I'd been to. The wired presenter got the crews to shout at him, then brought on some politicians and bigwigs who all welcomed the crews, praised Belfast's proud ship-building tradition, spoke at length of the international harmony promoted by sailing and thanked everyone involved. After that there were the actual prizes – not race prizes, for this had been a cruising leg, but for colourful showing in the parade, eco-awareness, spreading the word that tall ships are fun, that kind of thing.

It passed by me in a blur. I was thinking everything through, and trying to persuade myself I'd come to the wrong conclusion.

Mike and Agnetha: that was where it began. *Everyone knows*, Anders had said. That hadn't been important, except to them; shipboard affairs were officially discouraged, just like office affairs, but they weren't uncommon. Usually they resolved themselves without fuss. A wedding, a divorce followed by a wedding, or one of the two involved moving to another ship.

Mike and Agnetha had threatened to be different. I remembered what I'd overheard. *I won't have it*, Agnetha had said. *You can't force me.* I hadn't heard Mike's reply, but Agnetha's retort had been *Do that, and I'll go to the captain.* From which, I'd concluded, he was threatening to take her to court to prevent her aborting his baby. Then Agnetha had threatened him in return: *You're my senior officer. Fifteen years older than me. You'll never work on a tall ship again.* I'd heard his rejoinder: *Nor will you.*

It had all the makings of a nasty mess. I could just see the headlines: *Senior ship's officer accused of grooming. Affair on the high seas. Tall ship's mate takes former lover to court. 'I won't let her kill my baby!' Woman fights for right to choose.* Above it all, blaring, *Scandal aboard Norwegian tall ship* Sørlandet.

I'd been thinking too hard about the personal, when it was about money. Tall ships were always news. The damage done to her reputation would be immense. The foundation about to turn her into an academy for two years would pull out; they would have to, because of all the issues around child protection, if there was any suggestion that there had been sexual irregularities aboard. Losing this new venture would be disastrous financially; tall ships gobbled money, and being an academy would keep her secure for the immediate future.

They'd spoken sharply enough for me to hear. They could have been heard in the corridor by someone taking a morning cup of tea from the kitchen back to his cabin; someone who'd loved the ship for forty years, whose life revolved around her. Someone who was only of medium height, though his upright bearing made him taller, who could easily have reached around my door to catch up my jacket and hat while I was on watch; someone who knew the ship's routines, and what noises would make me turn and look. We never saw him in sailing overalls, because he didn't stand long watches with the rest of us. The man who studied his crew, and knew how absorbed in the ship I'd be if I took the wheel. The man who could easily ask Mike for a word and lead him aft, walking past me with his head turned away, but a slightly stiff gait because he'd left his giveaway cane below. That was what the stilt-walkers had reminded me of. I'd noticed it without seeing. The ship's officer who'd been a science teacher, with a skeleton hanging in his classroom. He'd have known where to strike. The man who'd done firefighting training. The captain who wanted to leave his ship in safe hands when he retired, ready to take up her new career as a floating academy.

I thought of Captain Gunnar's kindly face. It took more than bonhomie to captain a tall ship. It took the ability to make hard decisions, quickly. He'd heard the argument in the morning, and decided action had to be taken. I'd already made the fuss about the stowaway; that had made me stand out, when nothing had been found. A good scapegoat. Only he and I knew about the loaded gun. He'd mentioned it to someone else, and the word had spread. He'd taken my jacket and hat to make himself look like me. Then, to make sure, he'd come into my cabin at night; except that I hadn't mentioned that to anyone. Only the person who'd been there could have spread that story, and the only reason for spreading it would be to make me look as if I was dramatising things. He'd been standing in just the place to reach out with the handle end of his cane and catch at my ankle. *Forcing a card*, Gavin had called it. He had been going to throw me to the police, relying on Gavin to hush everything up, and let the ship sail away.

Then Erik had died. I remembered the way Captain Gunnar's face had changed when I told him about Micaela and the gang blackmailing. Now he had a better scapegoat, one who had nothing to do with the ship. Erik was dead, and there really had been a Russian hidden aboard who was responsible. Why not blame him for everything else too?

Yes, I knew now. But what was I to do with my knowledge?

I remembered the loss of the American replica ship *Bounty*, which had foundered in a hurricane a few years back. The captain and one crew member had been lost, and the rest saved by helicopter. They'd all had to testify in the enquiry, and in spite of what they'd lived through in those boiling waters, not one had spoken against the captain who'd taken them out into the storm. The captain was the ship's heart. If you couldn't give him unswerving loyalty, you needed to find another ship.

Captain Gunnar was my captain. When I was seventeen, he'd encouraged me as a trainee. He'd let me return to the ship year after year. He'd taken me back after college, and given me these gold stripes on my shoulders. He'd taken a wrong decision for the good of his ship – I couldn't try to persuade myself that it was right, or that it was equivalent to shooting a crew member who'd gone mad and was threatening the safety of the rest of us. The decision was wrong, but he'd taken it.

But what was I to do now? The loudspeakers blared in my ears. I looked up and saw the lines of crews had been edged back by a crowd of youngsters pressing forwards to the stage. The wired presenter jumped up and down, shouting the name 'Bailey!' and the girls at the stage-front began to clap. Then, in a chorus of screams, a boy strolled onto the stage, a guitar in his hands. I blinked. He couldn't be older than his early teens.

Gavin caught my thought, and leant his head to mine. 'I'm getting old. This is their big star, and he looks about twelve.'

'Might be as much as fourteen,' I agreed. The *SØRLANDET* noticeboard began to edge away from the speaker blare, and our T-shirted crew with it. We officers rose and went to meet them, then queued together at the counter within the building.

'Food,' Agnetha said. I felt a sudden rush of gladness that I didn't need to suspect her any more, and tucked an arm into hers.

'Burgers, most likely.'

It was burgers or wraps, washed down by Heineken or a variety of fizzy stuff. I went for a cheeseburger and Heineken, as the least worst. Behind us, the dance area was already pulsing with light. I eased myself into a table beside Anders. His shoulder was warm against mine. My shipmate; but I couldn't tell him either, though he would understand as Gavin could not. I put my burger down, set my drink beside it, and announced, 'They've caught the stowaway, the Russian.'

Beside me, Gavin made a movement, as if to hush me, then leant back, waiting.

Agnetha lowered her burger back to the table, and let her breath out in a long sigh. I looked round the faces, and saw the same relief on every one. It was over.

'This is important, though,' I told them. 'He wasn't on board, nothing happened, it's all to be hushed up.'

'Mike's death, and Erik's?' Agnetha said.

I shrugged. 'They'll deal with it somehow.'

We thought about that in silence for a moment.

'I suppose,' Nils said slowly, 'that it will be better for the ship if there is no more publicity.'

'I don't see how they can hush up Erik's death,' Petter objected. 'There were far too many people there.' He shuddered. 'They won't forget it.'

None of us would; but if there was no press coverage, it would recede. It would become unreal in the telling, a Grand Guignol set piece. If Micaela ever surfaced, she wouldn't tell anyone. Olav's family had already been told that his death had been an accident.

326

Mike's wife would be told the same. She would never need to know anything about Agnetha. At the end of August, we'd raise glasses of smuggled whisky to Captain Gunnar, and wish him well in his retirement, and then *Sørlandet* would sail for America, under Captain Sigurd, setting her gold-striped prow to the Atlantic and hoisting her white sails to catch the trade winds.

She would sail under another command. Captain Gunnar would have to watch her go, without him. His new life would be retirement ashore. He would be too proud to haunt the offices, or make a nuisance of himself on the management committee; no, his contact with her would be on lonely evenings, watching her dot move across a map of the oceans on his computer screen.

Gavin's fingers were warm around mine, but I couldn't share this with him. I tried to remember what they'd called it in medieval times. *Fealty.* For now, I was still Captain Gunnar's liegewoman; but the wrongness of it hung in my throat. Mike deserved justice. The baby I'd known for only half a day should have had its chance to live.

The fingers tangled in mine tightened. Gavin leant across to me and murmured, 'Are you keen to dance, or will we get some air?'

'Air.' The thump-thump beat was already doing my head in. We rose with nods to the others, and threaded our way through the crowds and food stands towards the river. It was a warm night, the breeze blowing softly from the sea, the tide rippling the river backwards. We leant against the railing, elbows and upper arms touching, and looked out at the masts raised into the dimming sky: *Santa Maria Manuela, Lord Nelson, Morganster.* Above us, *Cisne Branco*'s sails hung in white festoons. The ebb and flow of the crowd slipped past us, pausing to exclaim, to photograph, to eat a last mouthful of burger or paella before dropping the carton in the bin, then flowing on again.

Gavin leant against me, and sighed. 'It's been a long day. How about a pint in the oldest pub in the city, then an early night?'

I nodded. 'A long, long day.' Micaela's phone call, the parade, the Big Fish. *Good luck, Micaela*, I wished her silently. *Safe landfall.*

Gavin glanced over his shoulder, as if he was checking that nobody was listening. 'They're dropping all of it. They – the big brass – just want nothing more to be said. The Belfast Tall Ships is a resounding success, the stowaway was some illegal immigrant wanting to get to Britain; it was all unfortunate. Any hairs found on your jacket will all be ones that could have got there legitimately – somebody standing beside you, say.' He scowled out at the water. 'They may well find one of Bezrukov's hairs on it. Case closed.' His voice was bitter. 'A politician's justice. Chief Inspector Beattie's not happy either.'

I wished I could help him, but I had no evidence to give. I just had to try and forget, make myself believe the official version, so that I could meet Captain Gunnar with a clear gaze. I turned my hand to grasp his. 'I'm not bothered about the pint. Let's just go home.' Suddenly, vividly, I longed for my *Khalida*. I could see her shabby blue cushions, her blue and yellow curtains, her varnished prop-leg table, and smell that characteristic mix of hot engine oil and damp.

He turned to look at me. His eyes lightened to the grey of sea polished by low sunlight. I could see he was having an inspiration he couldn't share with me. Then he gripped my hand, and nodded. 'Yes, home.'

CASTING OFF

Sunday 5th July. 55.910N, 07.541W.
Racing towards Alesund.

We had another day in Belfast, getting the ship ready to put to sea again for the race back to Norway. I felt myself awkward with Captain Gunnar, but he didn't seem to notice anything, so I supposed I was covering up well enough. Eight more weeks, then I'd be safe. We'd manoeuvred out of the harbour on Sunday morning, and set sails; then the cannon fired, and we were caught up in the excitement of starting the race, forging forwards with the other tall ships around us, sails straining, a sight to lift the heart.

The wind was from the north-west, a stiff breeze, with the ship slicing through the Atlantic swell. Islay was on starboard now, and the islands on each side of the Minch ahead of us. I could see the green sails of *Alexander von Humboldt* far off to starboard, and the white ones of *Christian Radich* just behind. I'd promoted Mona to watch leader, with Petter and Johan as her ABs. Agnetha, Nils and I were working flat out to keep our course the shortest line between two points, and the trainees were an amazing team. Captain Sigurd had joined us in Belfast, and was working as chief officer under Captain Gunnar. According to the Tall Ships website, we were lying third, behind *Frederyk Chopin* and the Czech *La Grace*.

We were standing at the rail, looking out, Gavin's shoulder against mine. My stopgap jacket was nowhere near as windproof as the one that Sergeant Peterson had taken, but when I'd asked Gavin if he could get it back, he said he'd try, but he couldn't promise. The wheels of the law ground slowly. I wasn't sure I'd want to wear it anyway. I'd buy myself another sailing jacket back in Norway.

His phone rang. He gave me an apologetic look, and turned his shoulder to me as he answered. 'Macrae.' A pause, listening, then he took several steps away from me. The conversation was short; he put his phone back in his jacket pocket and came back to me, head up, mouth set in a determined line. I looked an enquiry, but he shook his head. 'Later.' He went into the cabin corridor, phone still in hand, shutting the door firmly behind him. I waited, and watched.

When he came out, he looked like himself: the eagle on its cliff, head high. Something had shifted in him, a decision made and approved. He came back to my side and leant against the rail once more to speak softly in my ear. 'Cass, would there ever be an occasion when you'd have left your jacket lying around?'

I gave him a startled look. 'Lying around?'

'On a bench, say?'

My throat closed up. I didn't dare ask why he wanted to know. I shook my head. 'No. It'd get blown away, or slide overboard if the ship tilted.'

'How about in the officers' mess? If you came down to a meal, and just hung it over your chair?'

Captain Gunnar was a stickler about that. 'No way. You wouldn't take salty overalls near that red velvet. I'd automatically hang it up as I passed my cabin.'

'How about your hat?'

'No.'

'If it had been raining, then stopped in the middle of your watch, you wouldn't take it off and lay it down in the nav shack?'

'No. I'd stuff it in my pocket.' I spread my hands, and repeated, 'It's automatic. If you leave stuff lying around aboard, it ends up swimming. Besides, there are too many of us. If we all left things lying around, it would be chaos. No. It would go straight in my pocket.'

His eyes held mine. 'Certain?'

I understood what he wanted now. I drew a ragged breath, and tried to imagine myself in a court of law, my hand on the Bible. I couldn't lie under that oath. I met his look unhappily, and nodded. 'Swearing certain.' My hands were tight on the polished rail.

His grey eyes met mine. 'I'm sorry.'

I swallowed. 'You have to do your duty.'

Another long look, searching, as if he was trying to make sure I meant it. I felt tears in my eyes, but nodded, and put out my hand to touch his. 'Mike has to have justice.'

His hand turned to grip mine. 'I'll phone you, when I can.'

His kilt pleats swirled as he turned. He went below, and this time he was away much longer. When he came out, I could see the die had been cast.

The first bell of Nils's watch had just rung when he detached himself from the team on deck and came up to look over my shoulder at the chart plotter. He studied it intently for a moment, then took a step forward to Captain Gunnar, standing at the rail and looking out over his kingdom. My heart chilled. *Now*, I thought, *now*.

He spoke briskly. 'DI Macrae, sir, of Police Scotland. We're now in Scottish waters.' *Home*, I'd said, back in Belfast. 'My jurisdiction. I wish to inform you that a customs launch will come out from Stornaway as we get to a convenient point for the ship to stop.'

I hadn't expected that. My heart thumped. The captain gave him an outraged look. 'This is a racing leg, Inspector Macrae.'

'I regret that, sir.' His eyes met the captain's. 'We will be questioning you with regard to the death of Michael Callaghan.'

It hit him like a blow. 'Questioning *me*?'

'I'm sure that you will understand that we don't wish to ask for an extradition order.'

Captain Gunnar stood upright, giving him back look for look. 'I presume you have the authority to enforce this ridiculous request.'

'I have.'

'Have you considered that you will be leaving the ship without her captain? You are putting lives at risk here, Inspector Macrae.'

'My superiors spoke to your office earlier today. Captain Sigurd will take command of the ship as you leave it.'

I knew it was justice, yet I couldn't bear the expression on Captain Gunnar's face. 'You have thought of everything, Inspector Macrae. Am I permitted to know the evidence upon which you base this accusation?'

'Forensic evidence, sir, on the clothes worn by the person last seen with Callaghan, and on the weapon used. We'll discuss that in the formal interview, and give a full list to your legal representatives.'

332

'Very well.' He drew himself up to his full height, and spoke formally. 'Until your launch arrives, sir, I am in command of *Sørlandet*. I would ask you to leave my bridge.'

It was a customs ship, almost as long as *Sørlandet* herself, wolf-grey, with a blue-red-white stripe rising up her sharp bow. Captain Gunnar wouldn't have the sails completely furled; we used the buntlines to haul them up, and let her wallow.

He'd called all the officers on deck and assigned the gangway and fender party to their stations. The rest of the trainees were mustered into their positions amidships. Racing rules wouldn't allow us to have the engine on, of course, but Anders was ready at his post, in case safety made it necessary. The rest of us crew assembled silently into two lines, braided hats under one arm, as formal as if we were on parade. Captain Sigurd, ready at Captain Gunnar's side, gave a nod of approval.

There were no handcuffs or extra policemen. Captain Sigurd led a salute as Captain Gunnar left the ship, head high. Gavin followed him, like a Highland retainer. He didn't get a chance to say goodbye then, but I saw his face turn and his hand lift in a wave as the launch moved back from our ship and slid off in a double wash of white foam.

We didn't speak to each other as Captain Sigurd dismissed us. There was nothing to say, and I felt a separation between me and the rest of the crew that showed itself in furtive glances: a feeling that I'd known, been a part of this, while they'd been kept in the dark. We all helped get the ship underway again, then I went down to my cabin and lay on my bunk. Cat came up beside me; I buried my face against his chinchilla fur and gritted my teeth. There was nothing I could say to the others, no way I could explain. They would have to work the tug between fealty and justice out for themselves.

The curtain rustled. It was Anders, with a mug in each hand. I swung my legs down and he came to sit beside me on the couch. His jumper was rough under my cheek, and smelt comfortingly of diesel oil. I closed my eyes for a moment, and imagined I was home on *Khalida*. Cat eased down into my lap and curled himself around; Rat put his paws on my shoulder and whiffled into my ear.

I felt the mug being pressed into my hand, and opened my eyes once more. It was white drinking chocolate: the stuff we saved for particularly bad times. I sipped its sweet warmth and felt comfort spread through me.

'It was the right thing,' Anders said. He turned his head to look at me. 'He killed Mike, remember. Murder must not go unpunished.'

'No,' I agreed. Gavin had done the right thing, the only thing. In this human world, leaving justice to God wasn't enough. But I wished it hadn't happened, any of it.

Anders' arm tightened around my shoulders. I sat there, drawing strength from him. This was his world too; he understood all that I couldn't say. Then he shook me lightly. 'Now, you must drink up your chocolate, and stop grieving.'

I drank, obediently, and the cabin came back into focus. My jacket hung at a slant; the green water of the Atlantic swirled round the porthole. We were making good speed.

'Your ship and your new captain need you,' Anders said. 'We have a race to win, remember, and time to make up. You're not going to let the *Christian Radich* or the *Staatsraad* overtake us?' He took the mug from me, then stood up and held his hands out. I let him pull me to my feet. He handed me the stopgap jacket, and as I put it on I felt my strength returning. I was *Sørlandet's* third mate, and she was going to come in among the leaders of the fleet, ahead of her fellow Norwegians, if any determination of mine could get her there.

I took a deep breath and headed out into the salted air, to the slanted deck and taut-curved sails of my ship.

A NOTE ON SHETLAN

Shetland has its own very distinctive language, Shetlan or Shetlandic, which derives from old Norse and old Scots. In *Death on a Longship*, Magnie's first words to Cass are, 'Cass, well, for the love of mercy. Norroway, at this season? Yea, yea, we'll find you a berth. Where are you?'

Written in west-side Shetlan (each district is slightly different), it would have looked like this:

'Cass, weel, fir da love o mercy. Norroway, at dis saeson? Yea, yea, we'll fin dee a bert. Quaur is du?'

Th becomes a *d* sound in *dis* (this), *da* (the), *dee* and *du* (originally 'thee' and 'thou', now 'you'), *wh* becomes *qu* (*quaur*, 'where'), the vowel sounds are altered ('well' to *weel*, 'season' to *saeson*, 'find' to *fin*), the verbs are slightly different (*quaur is du*) and the whole looks unintelligible to most folk from outwith Shetland, and *twartree* (a few) within it too.

So, rather than writing in the way my characters would

337

speak, I've tried to catch the rhythm and some of the distinctive usages of Shetlan while keeping it intelligible to *soothmoothers*, or people who've come in by boat through the South Mouth of Bressay Sound into Lerwick, and by extension, anyone living south of Fair Isle.

There are also many Shetlan words that my characters would naturally use, and here, to help you, are *some o dem*. No Shetland person would ever use the Scots *wee*; to them, something small would be *peerie*, or, if it was very small, *peerie mootie*. They'd *caa* sheep in a *park*, that is, herd them up in a field – *moorit* sheep, coloured black, brown or fawn. They'd take a *skiff* (a small rowing boat) out along the *banks* (cliffs) or on the *voe* (sea inlet), with the *tirricks* (Arctic terns) crying above them, and the *selkies* (seals) watching. Hungry folk are *black fanted* (because they've forgotten their *faerdie maet*, the snack that would have kept them going) and upset folk *greet* (cry). An older housewife like Jessie would have her *makkin* (knitting) belt buckled around her waist, and her *reestit* (smoke-dried) mutton hanging above the Rayburn. And finally . . . my favourite Shetland verb, which I didn't manage to work into this novel, but which is too good not to share: to *kettle*. As in: *Wir cat's just kettled. Four ketlings, twa strippet and twa black and quite.* I'll leave you to work that one out on your own . . . or, of course, you could consult Joanie Graham's *Shetland Dictionary*, if your local bookshop hasn't just *selt* their last copy *dastreen*.

The diminutives Magnie (Magnus), Gibbie (Gilbert) and Charlie may also seem strange to non-Shetland ears. In a traditional country family (I can't speak for *toonie* Lerwick habits), the oldest son would often be called after his father or grandfather, and be distinguished from that father and grandfather, and perhaps a cousin or two as well, by his own version of their shared name. Or, of course, by a *Peerie* in front of it, which would stick for life, like the *eart kyent* (well-known) guitarist Peerie Willie Johnson. There was also a patronymic system, which meant that a Peter's four sons, Peter, Andrew, John and Matthew, would all have the surname Peterson, and so would his son Peter's children. Andrew's children, however, would have the surname Anderson, John's would be Johnson, and Matthew's would be Matthewson. The Scots ministers stamped this out in the nineteenth century, but in one district you can have a lot of *folk* with the same surname, and so they're distinguished by their house name: *Magnie o' Strom, Peter o' da Knowe.*

GLOSSARY

For those who like to look up unfamiliar words as they go, here's a glossary of Scots and Shetlandic words.

aa: all
an aa: as well
aabody: everybody
aawye: everywhere
ahint: behind
ain: own
amang: among
anyroad: anyway
ashet: large serving dish
auld: old
aye: always
bairn: child
ball (verb): throw out

banks: sea cliffs, or peat-banks, the slice of moor where peats are cast

bannock: flat triangular scone

birl, birling: paired spinning round in a dance

blinkie: torch

blootered: very drunk

blyde: pleased

boanie: pretty, good-looking

breeks: trousers

brigstanes: flagged stones at the door of a croft house

bruck: rubbish

caa: round up

canna: can't

clarted: thickly covered

cludgie: toilet

cowp: capsize

cratur: creature

croft house: the long, low traditional house set in its own land

croog: to cling to, or of a group of people, to huddle together

daander: to travel uncertainly or in a leisurely fashion

darrow: a hand fishing line

dastreen: yesterday evening

de-crofted: land that has been taken out of agricultural use, e.g.
    for a house site

dee: you (*du* is also you, depending on the grammar of the sentence
    – they're equivalent to 'thee' and 'thou'. Like French, you would
    only use *dee* or *du* to one friend; several people, or an adult
    if you're a younger person, would be 'you')

denner: midday meal

didna: didn't

dinna: don't

dip dee doon: sit yourself down

dis: this

doesna: doesn't

doon: down

downie: an eiderdown quilt, a duvet

drewie lines: a type of seaweed made of long strands

duke: duck

dukey-hole: pond for ducks

du kens: you know

dyck, dyke: a wall, generally drystone, i.e. built without cement

eart: direction, *the eart o wind*

ee now: right now

eela: fishing, generally these days a competition

everywye: everywhere

from, frae: from

faersome: frightening

faither, usually *faider*: father

fanted: hungry, often *black fanted*, absolutely starving

folk: people

gansey: a knitted jumper

gant: to yawn

geen: gone

gluff: fright

greff: the area in front of a peat bank

gret: cried

guid: good

guid kens: God knows

hae: have

hadna: hadn't

harled: exterior plaster using small stones

heid: head

hoosie: little house, usually for bairns

howk: to search among: I *howked* ida box o auld claes.

isna: isn't

ken, kent: know, knew

keek: peep at

kirk: church

kirkyard: graveyard

kishie: wicker basket carried on the back, supported by a *kishie baand* around the forehead

kleber: soapstone

knowe: hillock

Lerook: Lerwick

lem: china

likit: liked

lintie: skylark

lipper: a cheeky or harum-scarum child, generally affectionate

mad: annoyed

mair: more

makkin belt: a knitting belt with a padded oval, perforated for holding the 'wires' or knitting needles.

mam: mum

mareel: sea phosphorescence, caused by plankton, which makes every wave break in a curl of gold sparks

meids: shore features to line up against each other to pinpoint a spot on the water

midder: mother

mind: remember

moorit: coloured brown or black, usually used of sheep

mooritoog: earwig

muckle: big – as in Muckle Roe, the big red island. Vikings were very literal in their names, and almost all Shetland names come from the Norse

muckle biscuit: large water biscuit, for putting cheese on

myrd: a good number and variety – a *myrd* o peerie things

na: no, or more emphatically, *nall*

needna: needn't

Norroway: the old Shetland pronunciation of Norway

o: of

oot: out

ower: over

park: fenced field

peat: brick-like lump of dried peat earth, used as fuel

peelie-wally: pale-faced, looking unwell

peerie: small

peerie biscuit: small sweet biscuit

Peeriebreeks: affectionate name for a small thing, person or animal

piltick: a sea fish common in Shetland waters

pinnie: apron

postie: postman

quen: when

redding up: tidying

redd up kin: get in touch with family – for example, a five-generations New Zealander might come to meet Shetland cousins still staying in the house his or her forebears had left

reestit mutton: wind-dried shanks of mutton

riggit: dressed, sometimes with the sense dressed up

roadymen: men working on the roads

roog: a pile of peats

rummle: untidy scattering

Santy: Santa Claus

scaddy man's heids: sea urchins

scattald: common grazing land

scuppered: put paid to, done for

selkie: seal, or seal person who came ashore at night, cast his/her skin and became human

Setturday: Saturday

shalder: oystercatcher

sheeksing: chatting

sho: she

shoulda: should have

shouldna: shouldn't have

SIBC: Shetland Islands Broadcasting Company, the independent radio station

skafe: squint

skerry: a rock in the sea

smoorikins: kisses

snicked: move a switch that makes a clicking noise

snyirked: made a squeaking or rattling noise

solan: gannet

somewye: somewhere

sooking up: sucking up

soothified: behaving like someone from outwith Shetland

spew: be sick

spewings: piles of sick

splatched: walked in a splashy way with wet feet, or in water

steekit mist: thick mist

sun-gaits: with the sun – it's bad luck to go against the sun, particularly walking around a church

swack: smart, fine

swee: to sting (of injury)

tak: take

tatties: potatoes

tay: tea, or meal eaten in the evening

tink: think

tirricks: Arctic terns

toorie, toorie-cap: a round, knitted hat

trows: trolls

tushker: L-shaped spade for cutting peat

twa: two

twartree: a small number, several

tulley: pocket knife

unken: unknown

vexed: sorry or sympathetic: 'I was that *vexed* to hear that'

vee-lined: lined with wood planking

voe: sea inlet

voehead: the landwards end of a sea inlet

waander: wander

waar: seaweed

whatna: what

wasna: wasn't

wha's: who is

whit: what

whitteret: weasel

wi: with

wir: we've – in Shetlan grammar, 'we are' is sometimes 'we have'

wir: our

wife: woman, not necessarily married

wouldna: would not

wupple: to twist or turn a bit of rope around something, to tangle

yaird: enclosed area around or near the croft house

yoal: a traditional clinker-built six-oared rowing boat

ACKNOWLEDGEMENTS

To Captain Sture and all the real crew of the sail-training ship *Sørlandet*: thank you for a wonderful voyage from Kristiansand to Belfast. My highlights include Freida taking me up to the first platform, and Lydia taking me out on the yard, the dolphins in the North Sea, the joy of just being out at sea, with no land in sight, and, proudest moment of all, being at the helm as we came into Belfast, with Captain Sture giving me orders just as if I was one of her crew. I apologise, sir, for giving your ship such a crew as would never be tolerated aboard the real *Sørlandet*. Thank you, Jenn, for letting me use your 'moments of awesome'; thank you, Simon, for the shanties; thank you, Jill, for showing me how to use a sextant, and Tom, for teaching me to end-splice; thank you, Chief Steward Carsten and the *hjalleygirls*, for keeping us fed. Thank you, Kjell Sigurd, for the cups of tea, and Lena, for your enthusiasm and beautiful smile. Thank you, Marko, back at the office, for encouraging me to bring murder and mayhem on board – I wish I could have used all the ideas for ingenious and gory deaths that I was offered!

Particularly, hello and thank you to all the members of the blue watch: Tom, the third mate and navigator; Drew, our watch leader; ABs Lydia and Freida; and my fellow trainees: Aage, Anna, Ben, Dimitris, Ellen, Gabriel, Ismail, Jan-Ole, Johan, Ludwig, Maria, Naseem, Nine, Nora, Samir and Sindre. Thank you, fellow trainees, for letting me use you as Cass's watch in this book. To the young people on board, it was a great pleasure meeting you all. I hope that by the time you read this book your lives have gone upwards and upwards, and that you are moving towards fulfilling the potential you showed aboard.

On the publishing side, thank you, as always, to my wonderful agent, Teresa Chris, for her advice, encouragement and support. Thank you, all the members of my new publishing family at Allison & Busby, for your welcome. It's lovely being with you!

MARSALI TAYLOR grew up near Edinburgh, and moved to Shetland as a newly qualified teacher. She is a tourist guide who is fascinated by history, as well as a keen sailor who enjoys exploring in her own yacht. She currently lives on Shetland's scenic west side.

marsalitaylor.co.uk
@MarsaliTaylor